2

A HOUSE DIVIDED

A LIGHT IN THE DARKNESS, A LOCK IN THE DOOR

HAIKO HÖRNIG • MARIUS PAWLITZA

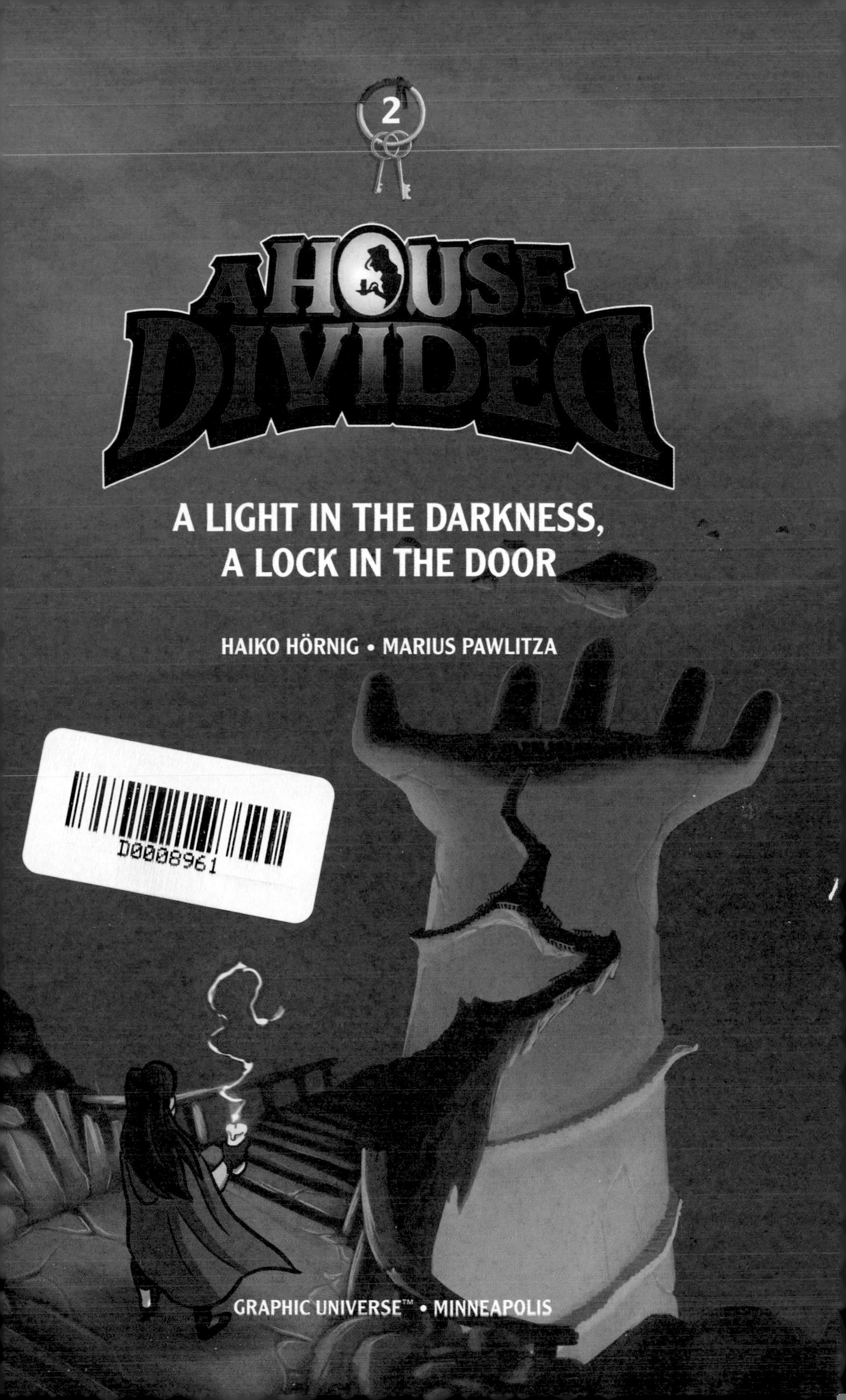

GRAPHIC UNIVERSE™ • MINNEAPOLIS

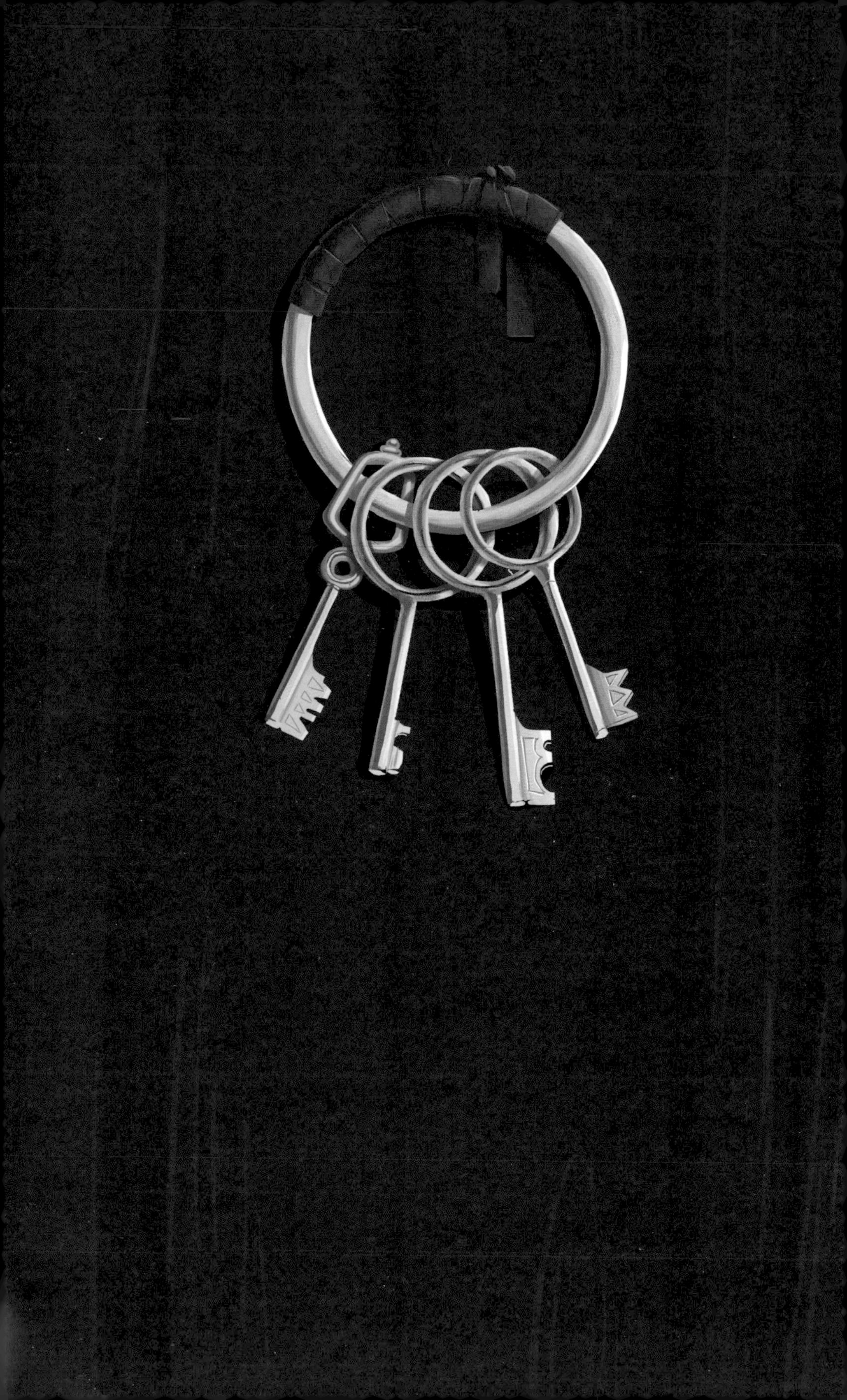

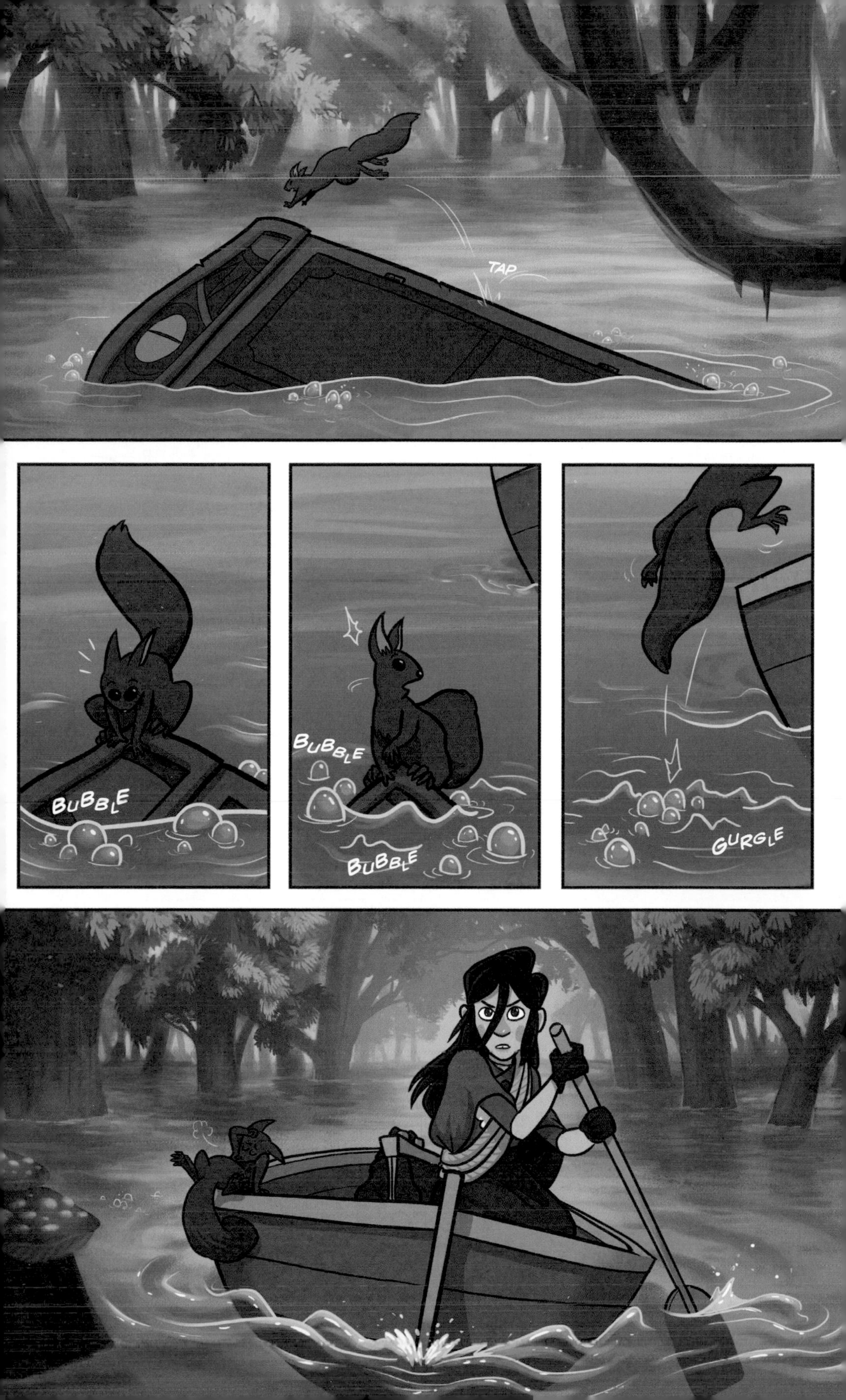
TAP
BUBBLE
BUBBLE
BUBBLE
GURGLE

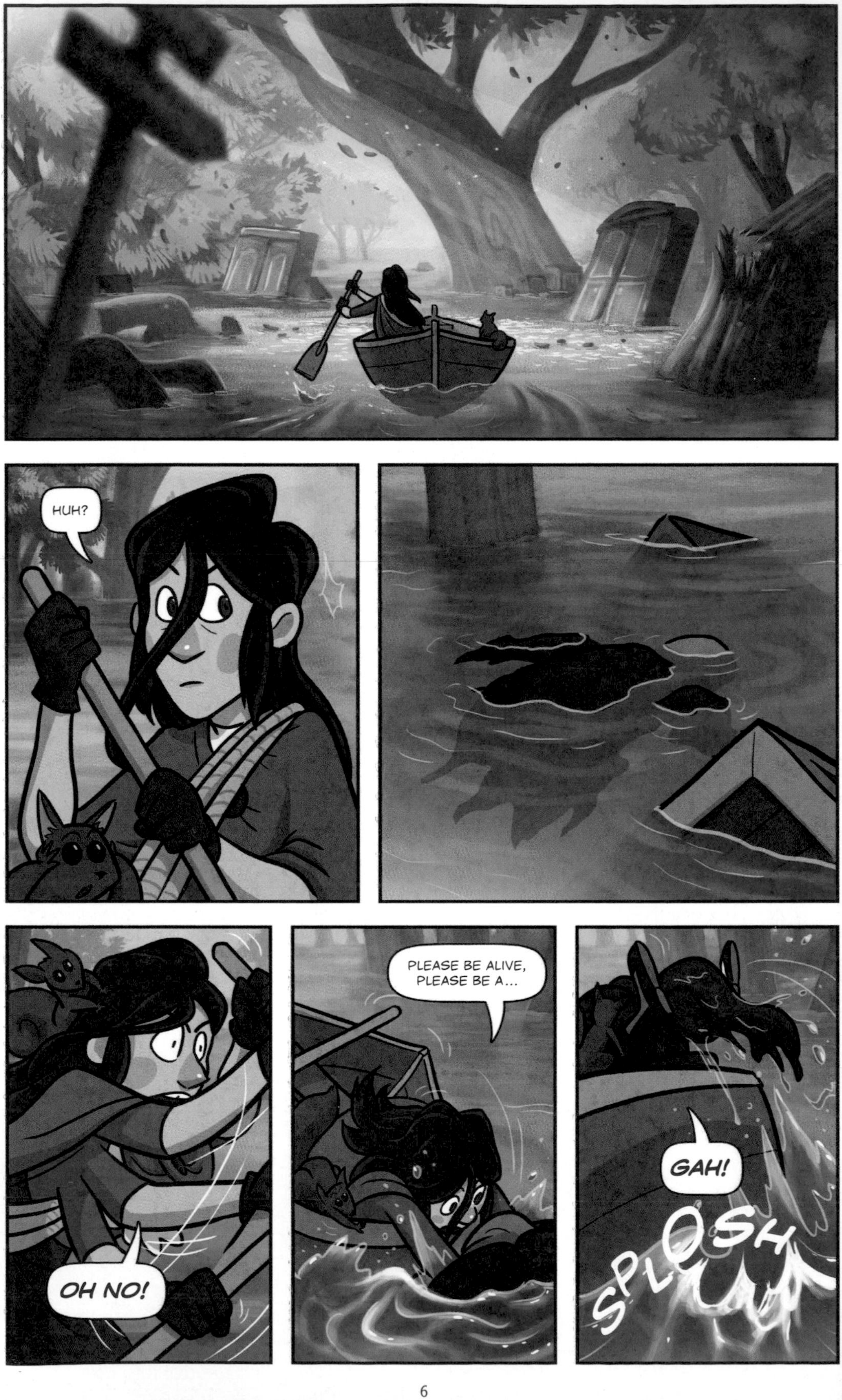

HUH?
PLEASE BE ALIVE, PLEASE BE A...
OH NO!
GAH!
SPLOSH

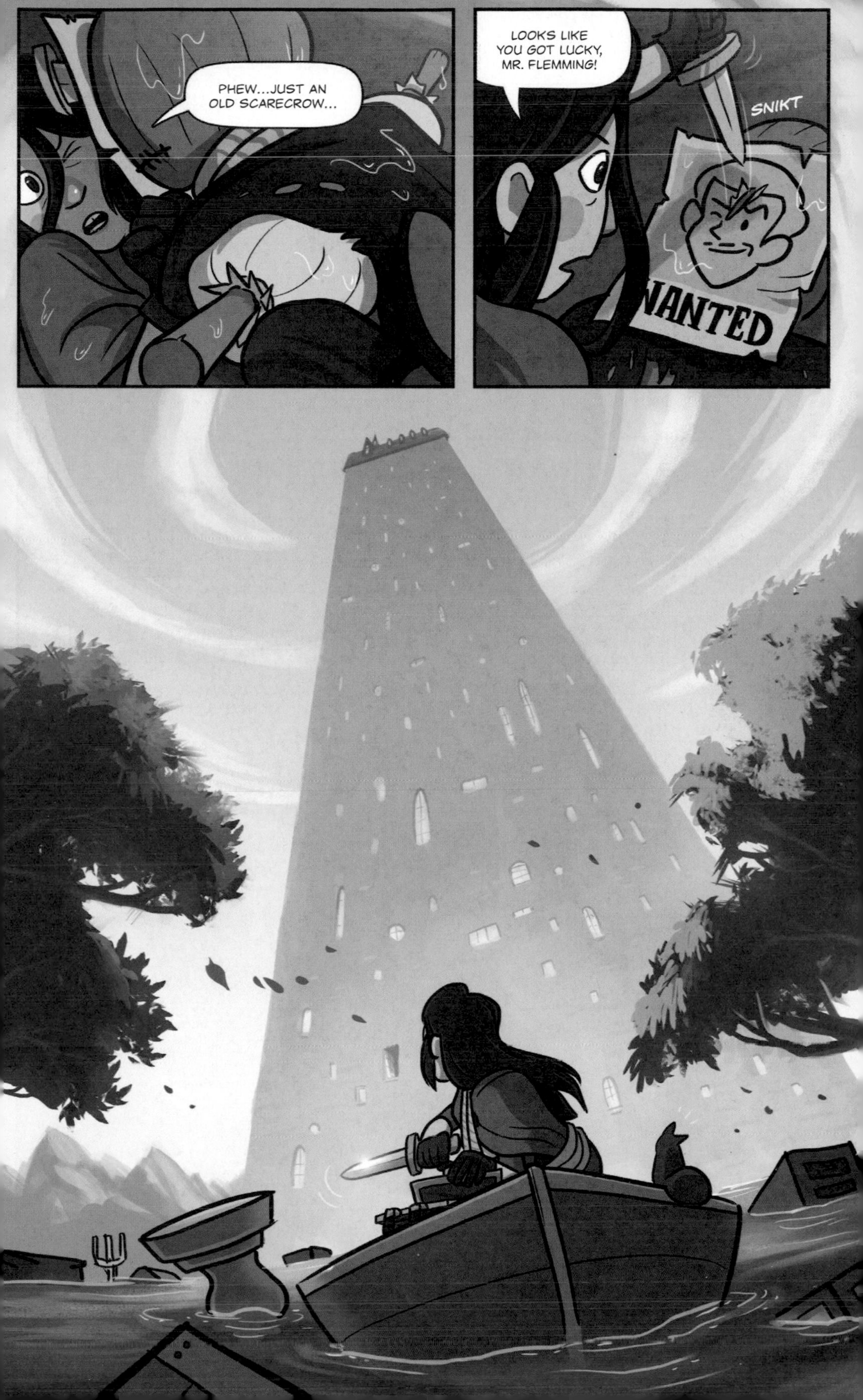
PHEW...JUST AN OLD SCARECROW...
LOOKS LIKE YOU GOT LUCKY, MR. FLEMMING!
SNIKT
WANTED

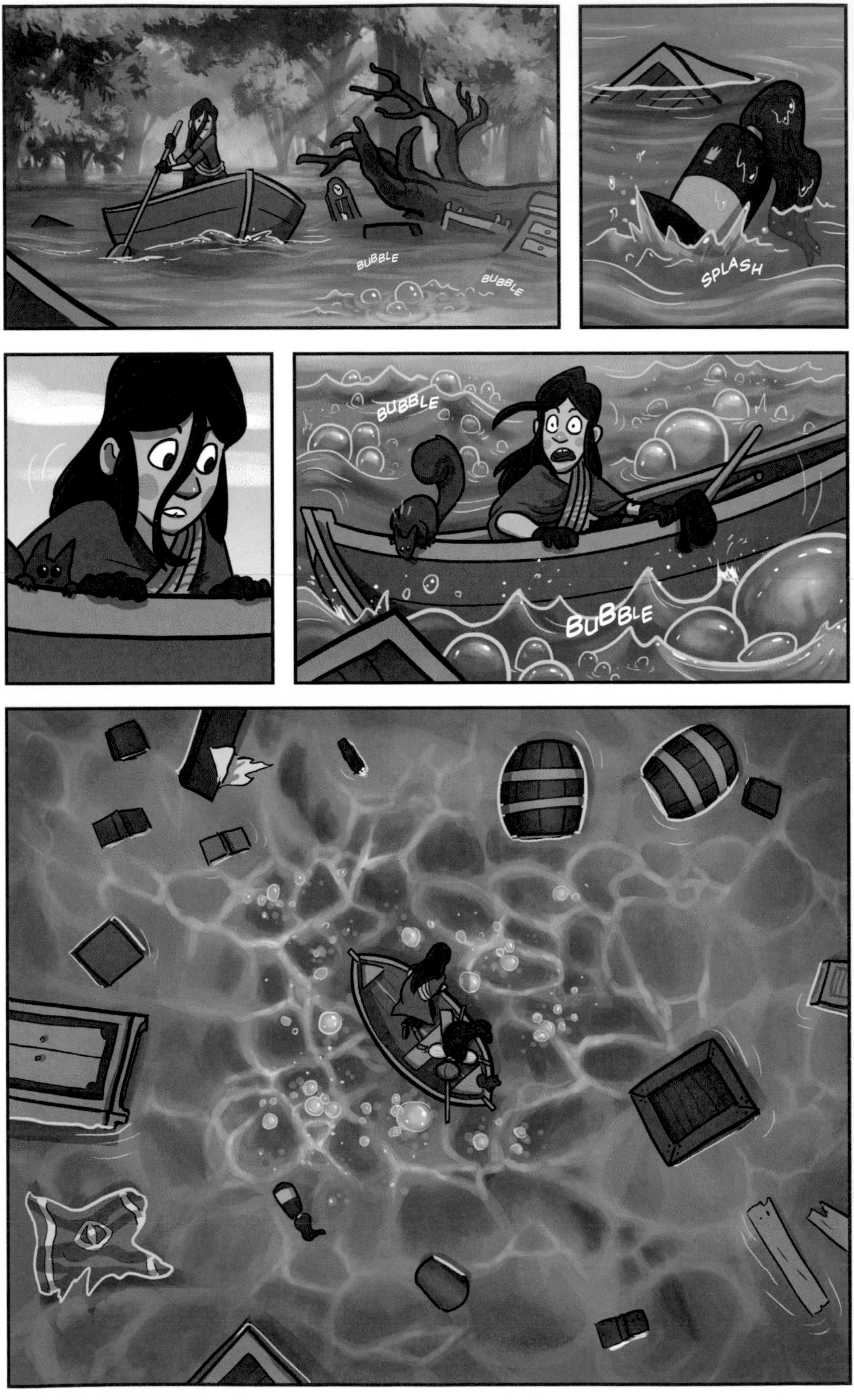
BUBBLE
BUBBLE
SPLASH
BUBBLE
BUBBLE

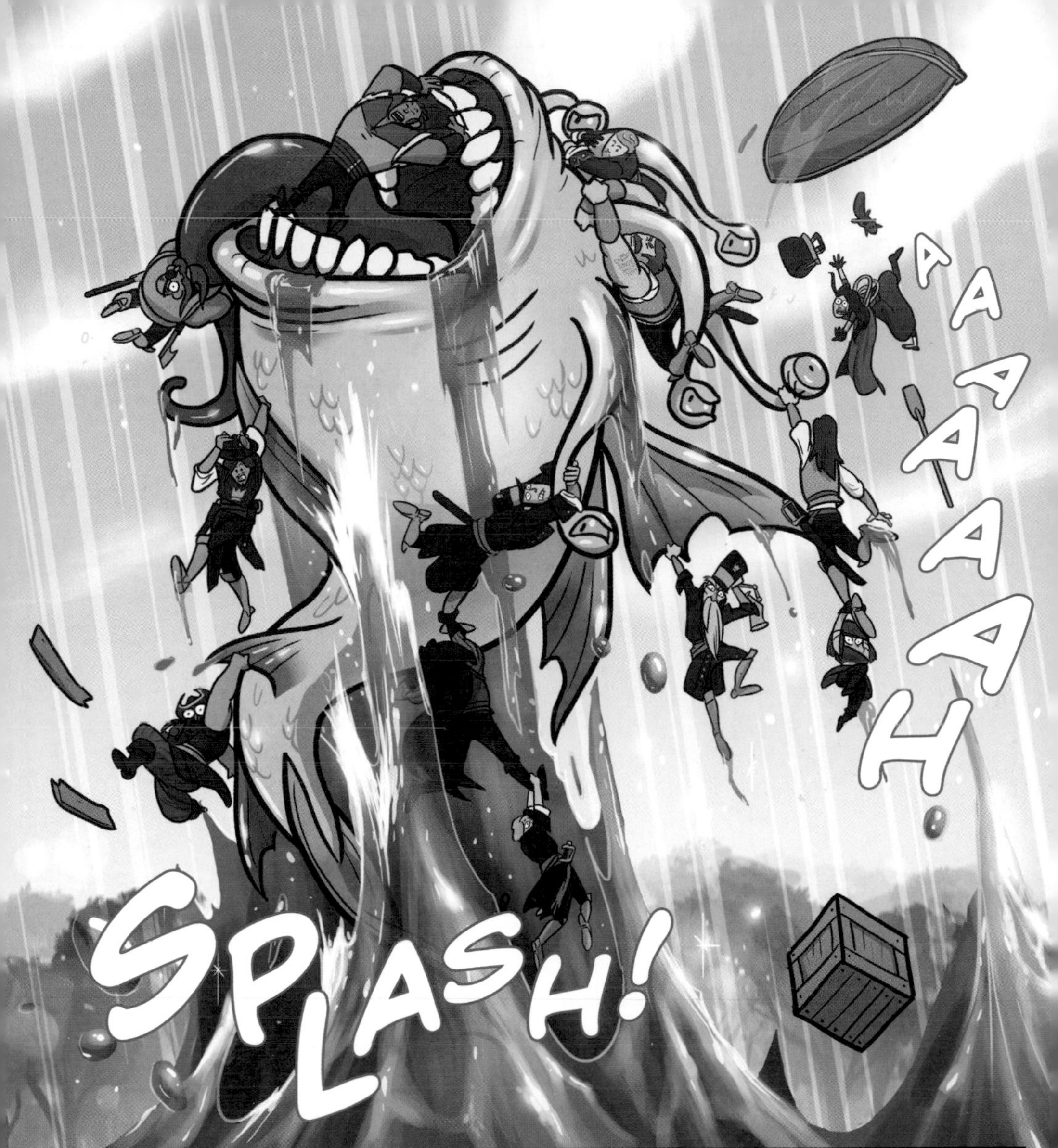
AAAAAAH
SPLASH!

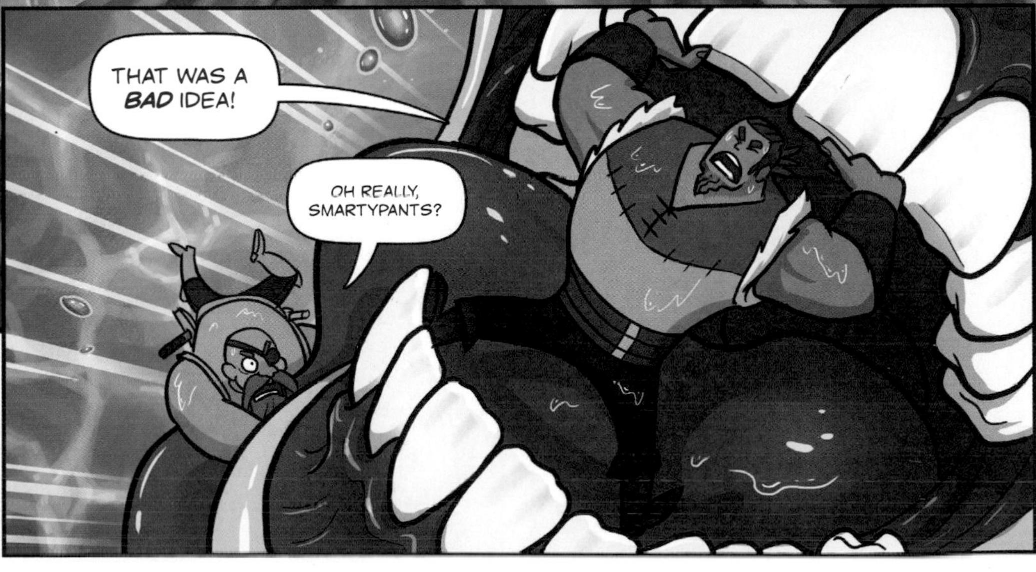
THAT WAS A *BAD* IDEA!
OH REALLY, SMARTYPANTS?

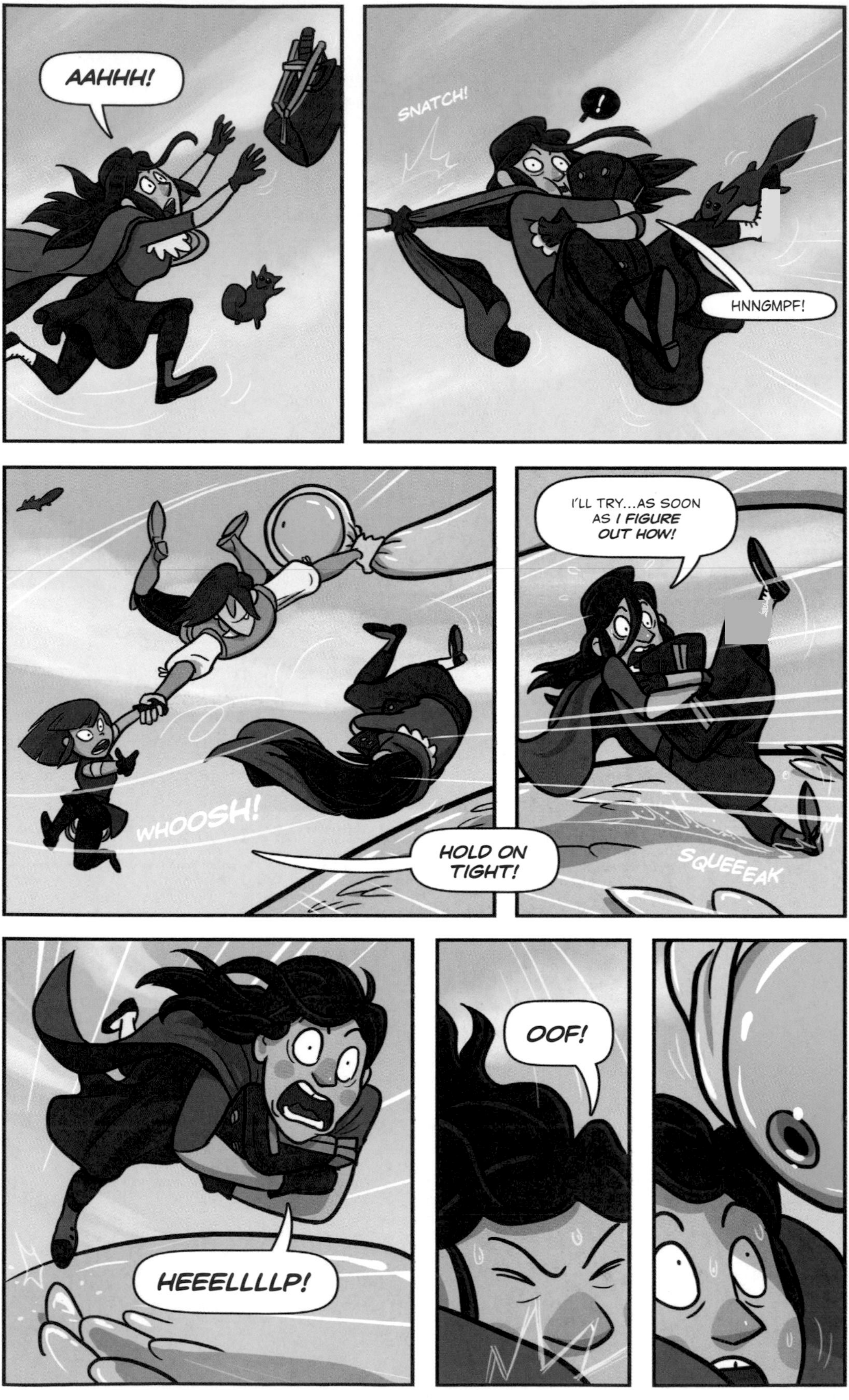
AAHHH!
SNATCH!
!
HNNGMPF!
WHOOSH!
HOLD ON TIGHT!
I'LL TRY...AS SOON AS *I FIGURE OUT HOW!*
SQUEEEAK
HEEELLLLP!
OOF!

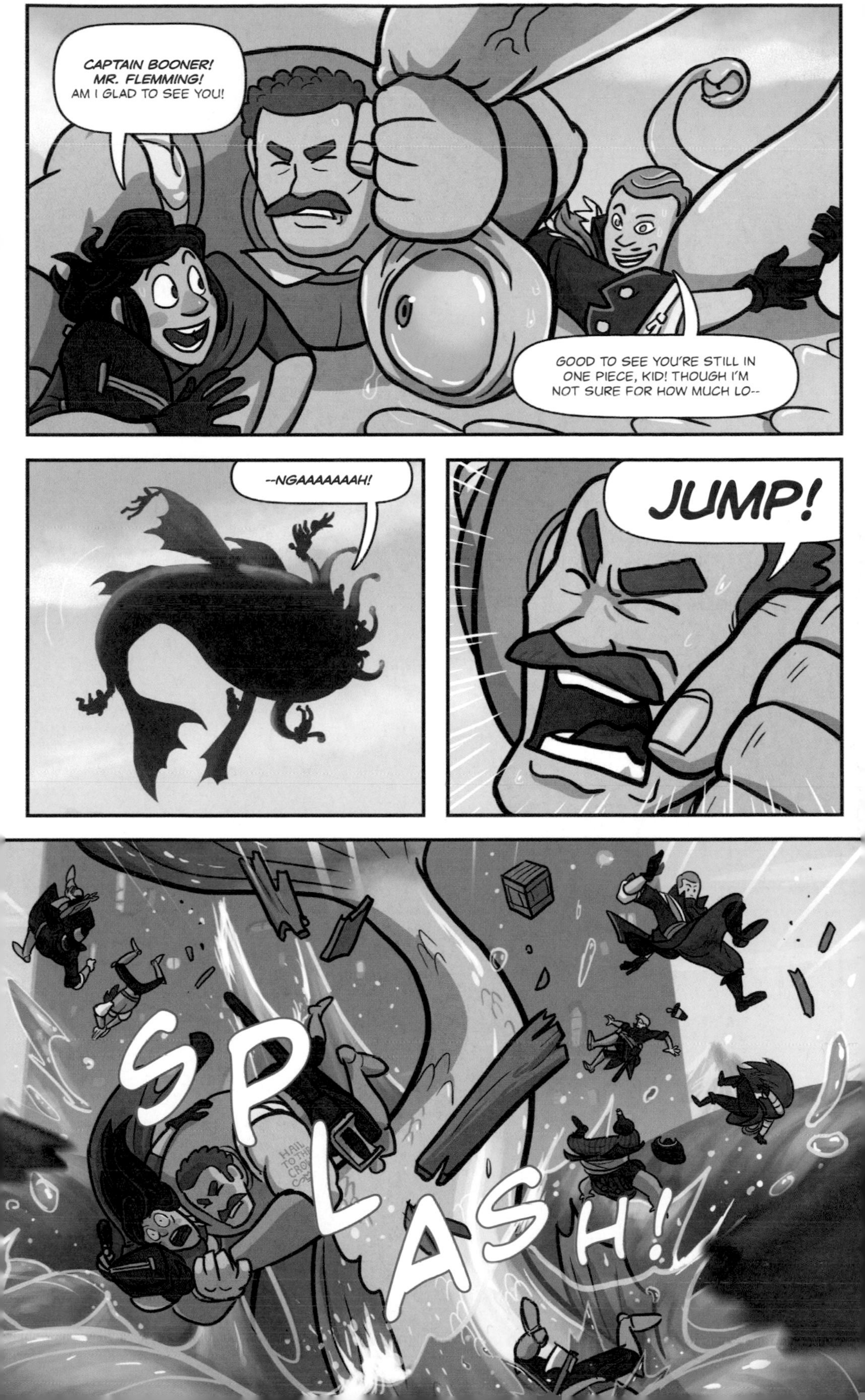
CAPTAIN BOONER! MR. FLEMMING! AM I GLAD TO SEE YOU!
GOOD TO SEE YOU'RE STILL IN ONE PIECE, KID! THOUGH I'M NOT SURE FOR HOW MUCH LO--
--NGAAAAAAAH!
JUMP!
SPLASH!

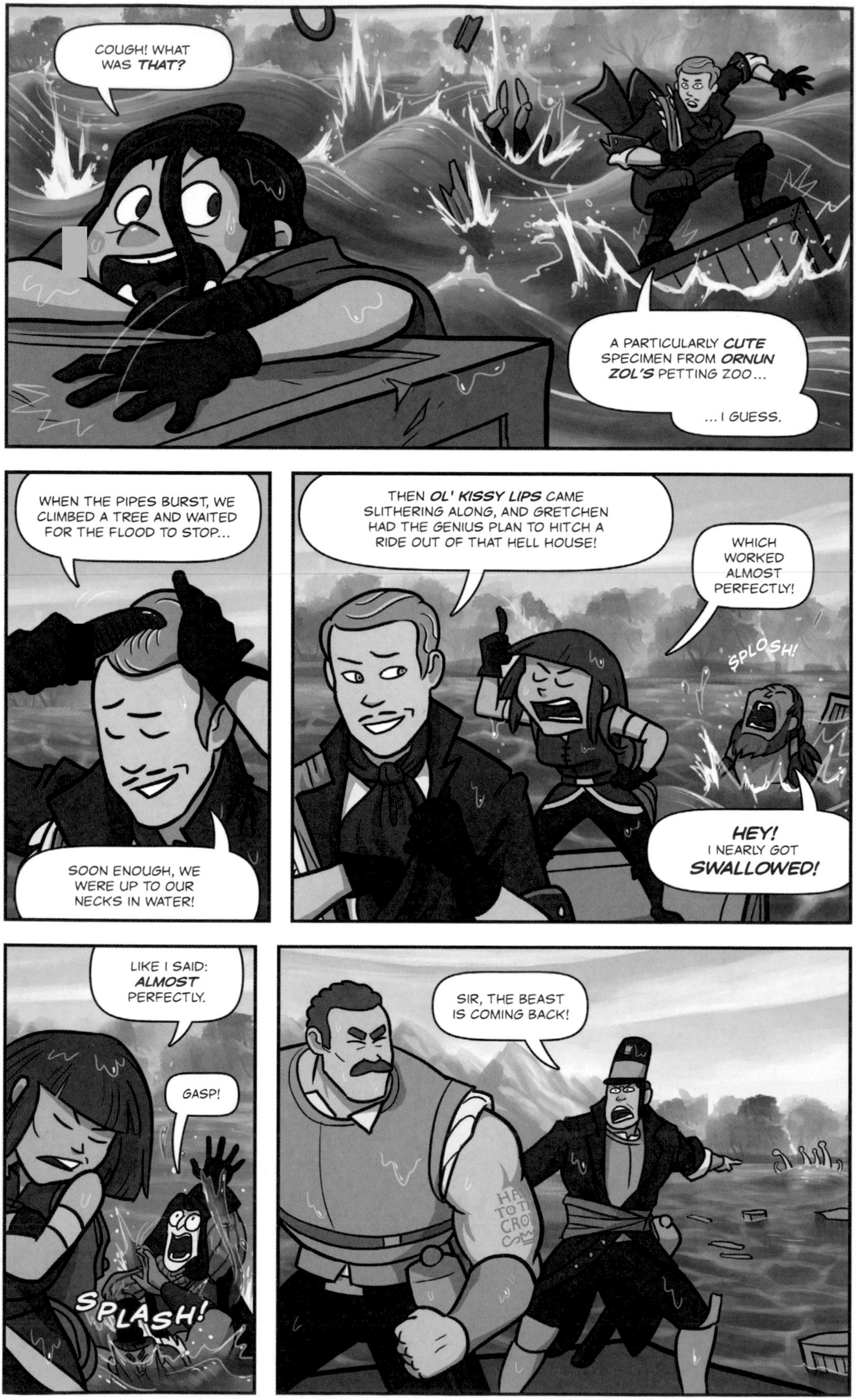
COUGH! WHAT WAS *THAT?*
A PARTICULARLY *CUTE* SPECIMEN FROM *ORNUN ZOL'S* PETTING ZOO...
...I GUESS.
WHEN THE PIPES BURST, WE CLIMBED A TREE AND WAITED FOR THE FLOOD TO STOP...
SOON ENOUGH, WE WERE UP TO OUR NECKS IN WATER!
THEN *OL' KISSY LIPS* CAME SLITHERING ALONG, AND GRETCHEN HAD THE GENIUS PLAN TO HITCH A RIDE OUT OF THAT HELL HOUSE!
WHICH WORKED ALMOST PERFECTLY!
SPLOSH!
HEY! I NEARLY GOT **SWALLOWED!**
LIKE I SAID: *ALMOST* PERFECTLY.
GASP!
SPLASH!
SIR, THE BEAST IS COMING BACK!

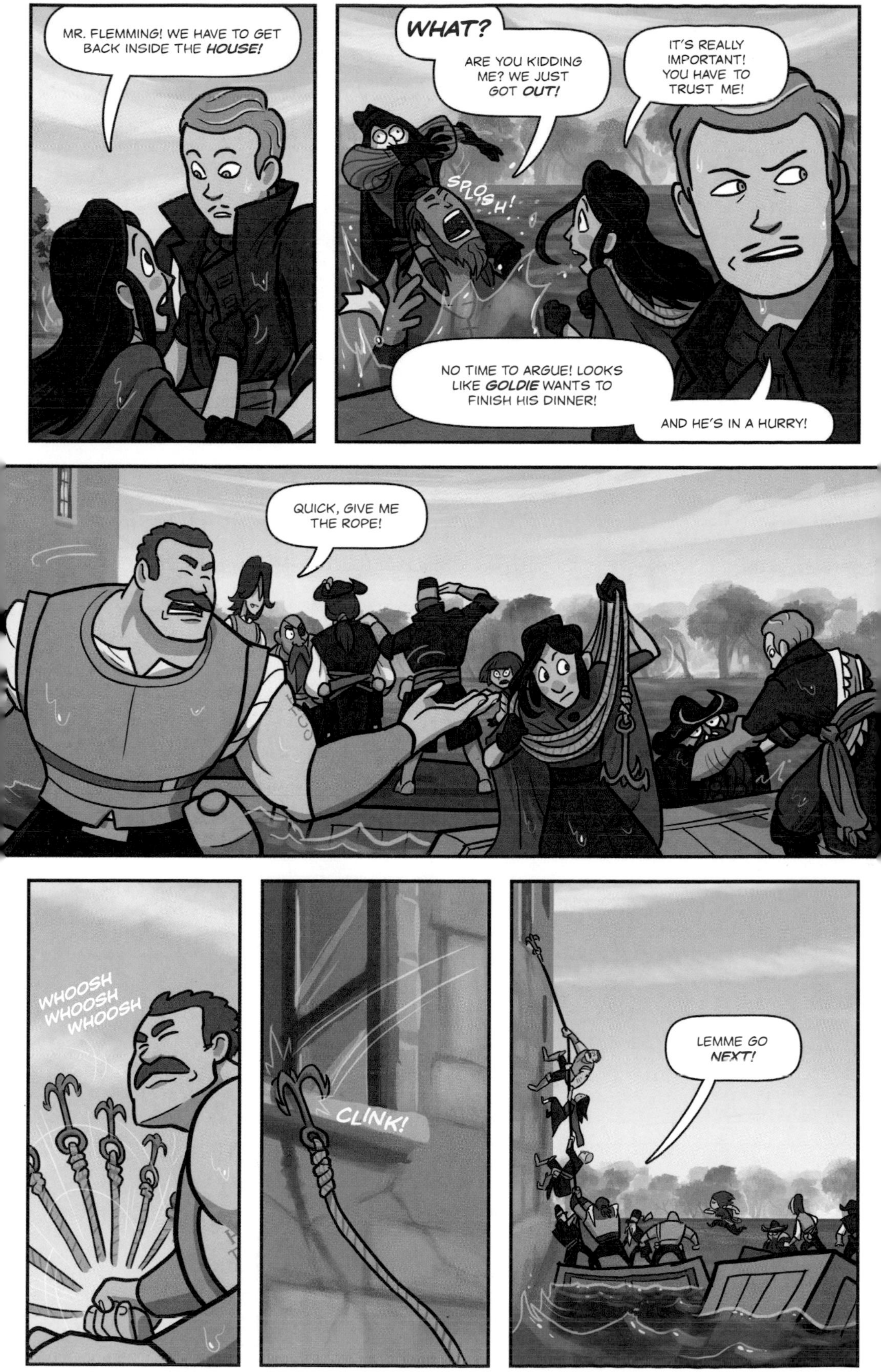
MR. FLEMMING! WE HAVE TO GET BACK INSIDE THE HOUSE!
WHAT?
ARE YOU KIDDING ME? WE JUST GOT OUT!
SPLOSH!
IT'S REALLY IMPORTANT! YOU HAVE TO TRUST ME!
NO TIME TO ARGUE! LOOKS LIKE GOLDIE WANTS TO FINISH HIS DINNER!
AND HE'S IN A HURRY!
QUICK, GIVE ME THE ROPE!
WHOOSH WHOOSH WHOOSH
CLINK!
LEMME GO NEXT!

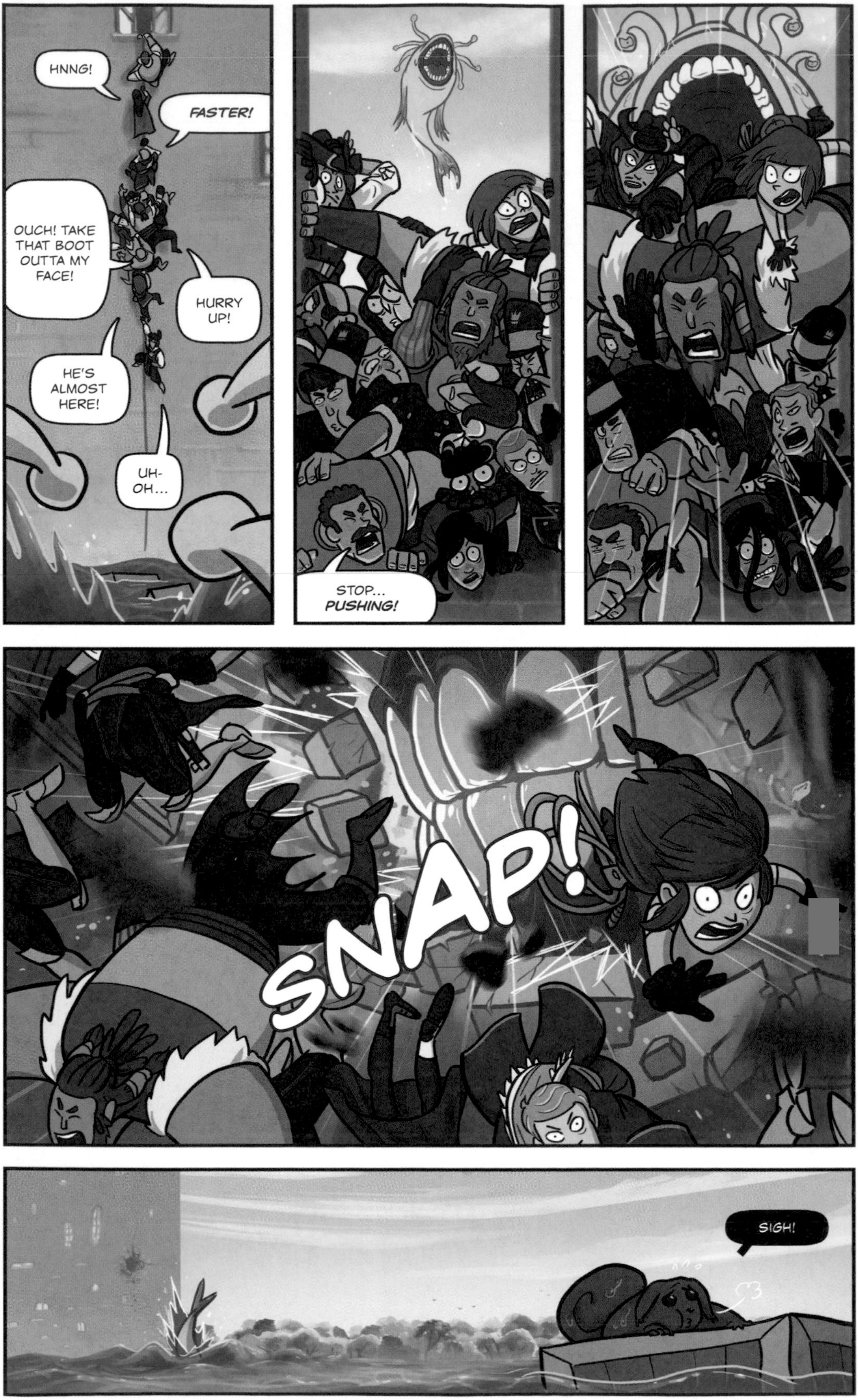
HNNG!
FASTER!
OUCH! TAKE THAT BOOT OUTTA MY FACE!
HURRY UP!
HE'S ALMOST HERE!
UH-OH...
STOP... PUSHING!
SNAP!
SIGH!

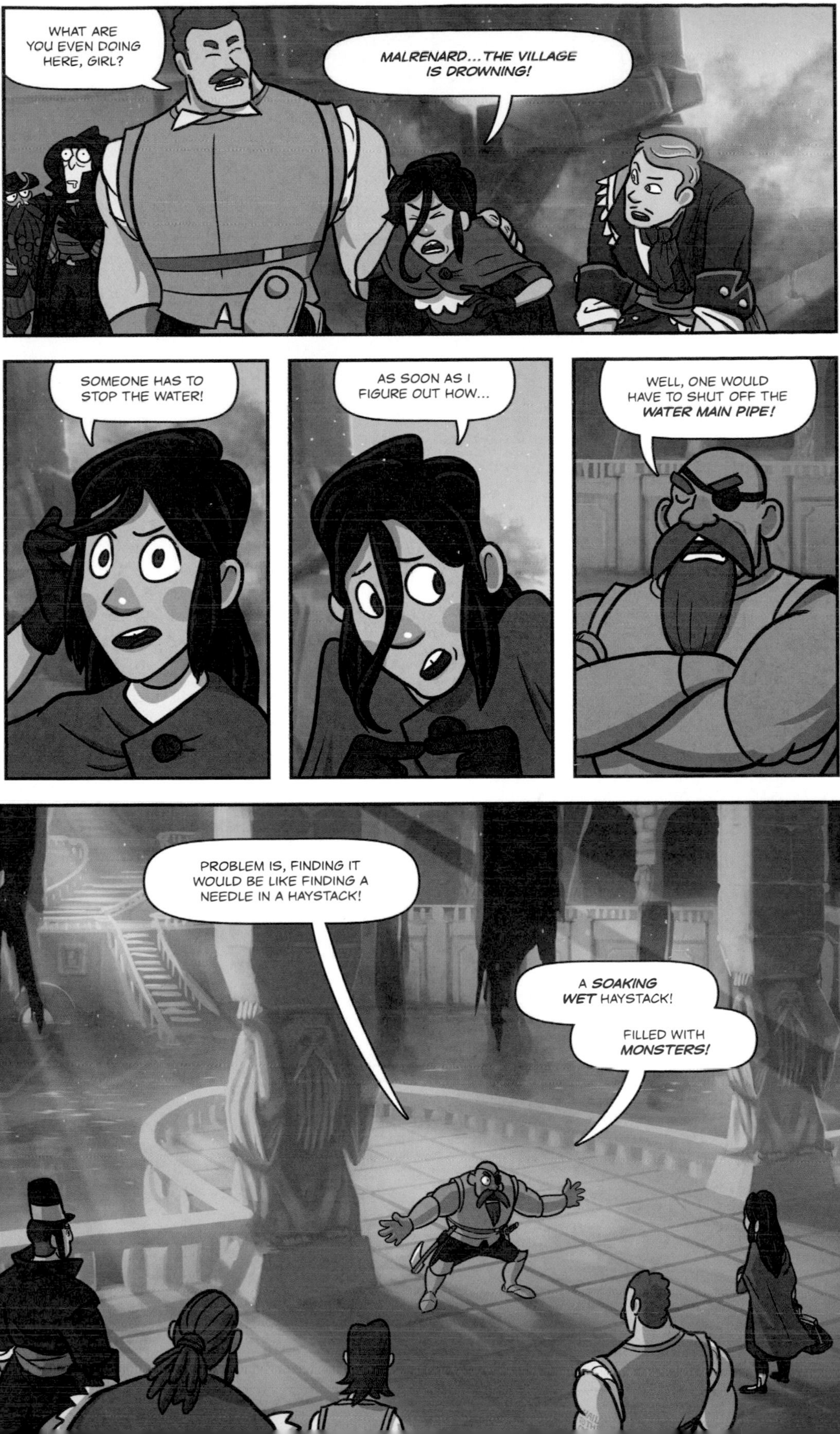
WHAT ARE YOU EVEN DOING HERE, GIRL?
MALRENARD... THE VILLAGE IS DROWNING!
SOMEONE HAS TO STOP THE WATER!
AS SOON AS I FIGURE OUT HOW...
WELL, ONE WOULD HAVE TO SHUT OFF THE WATER MAIN PIPE!
PROBLEM IS, FINDING IT WOULD BE LIKE FINDING A NEEDLE IN A HAYSTACK!
A SOAKING WET HAYSTACK!
FILLED WITH MONSTERS!

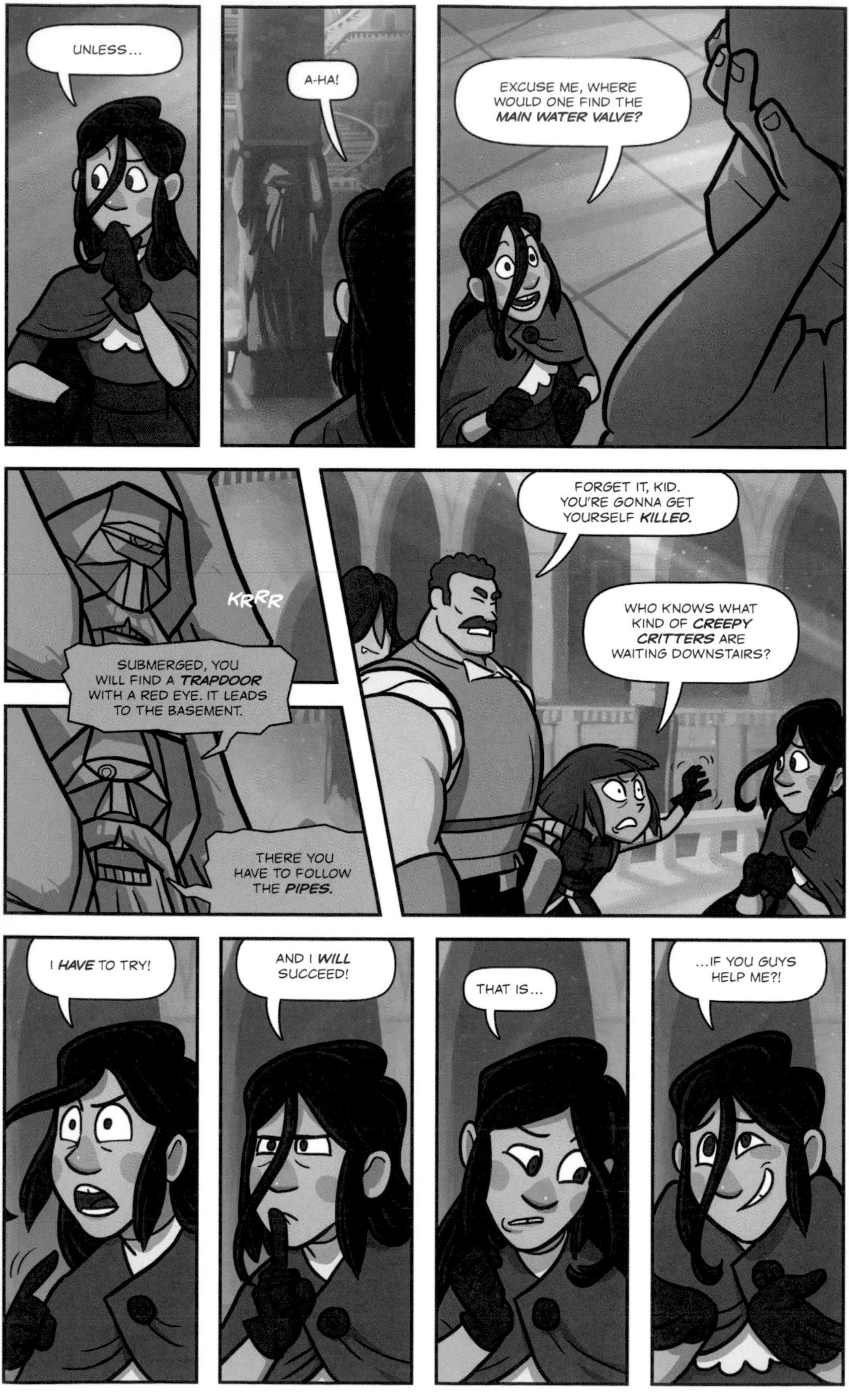
UNLESS...
A-HA!
EXCUSE ME, WHERE WOULD ONE FIND THE **MAIN WATER VALVE?**
KRRR
SUBMERGED, YOU WILL FIND A **TRAPDOOR** WITH A RED EYE. IT LEADS TO THE BASEMENT.
THERE YOU HAVE TO FOLLOW THE **PIPES.**
FORGET IT, KID. YOU'RE GONNA GET YOURSELF **KILLED.**
WHO KNOWS WHAT KIND OF **CREEPY CRITTERS** ARE WAITING DOWNSTAIRS?
I **HAVE** TO TRY!
AND I **WILL** SUCCEED!
THAT IS...
...IF YOU GUYS HELP ME?!

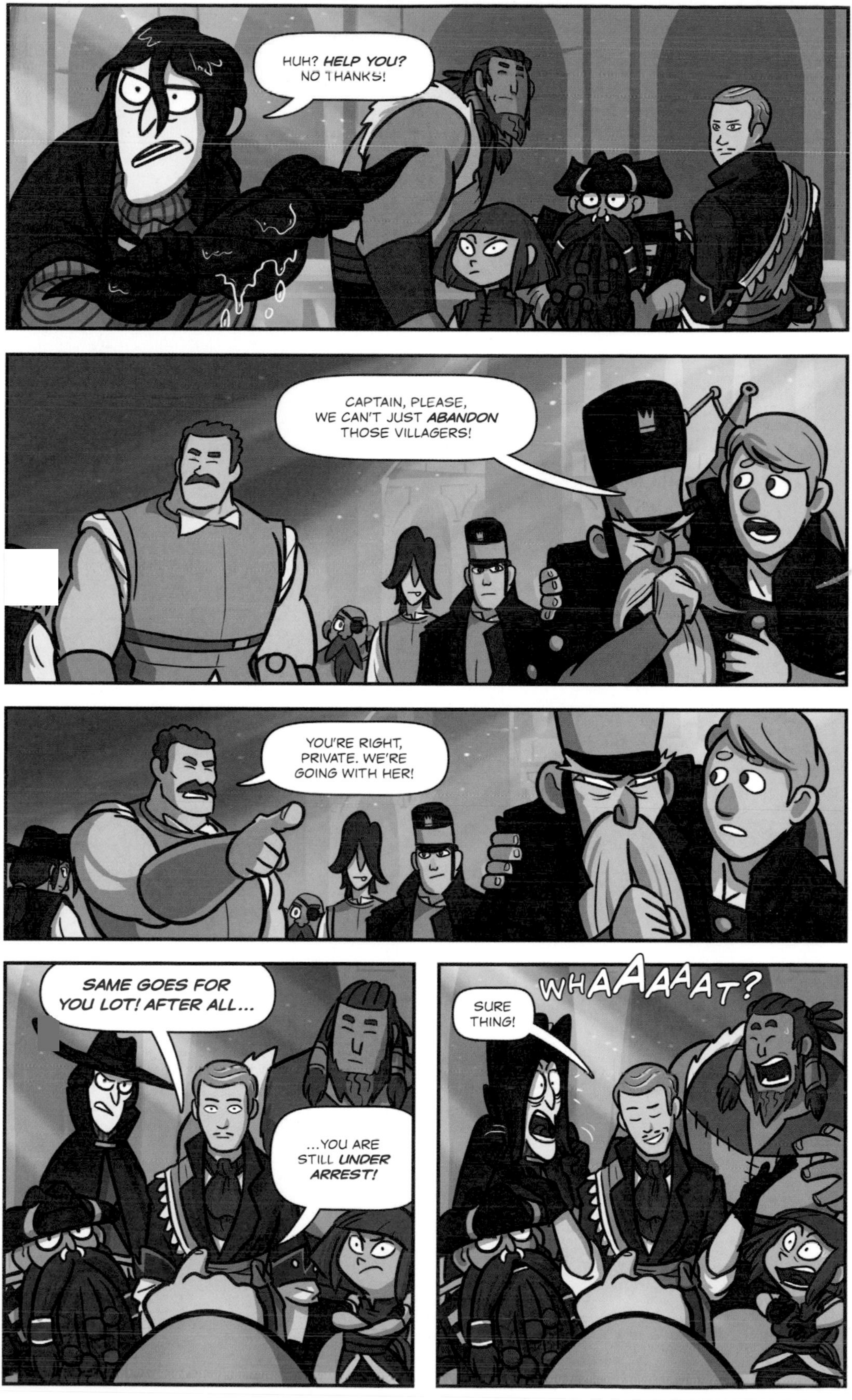

HUH? HELP YOU? NO THANKS!
CAPTAIN, PLEASE, WE CAN'T JUST ABANDON THOSE VILLAGERS!
YOU'RE RIGHT, PRIVATE. WE'RE GOING WITH HER!
SAME GOES FOR YOU LOT! AFTER ALL...
...YOU ARE STILL UNDER ARREST!
WHAAAAAT?
SURE THING!

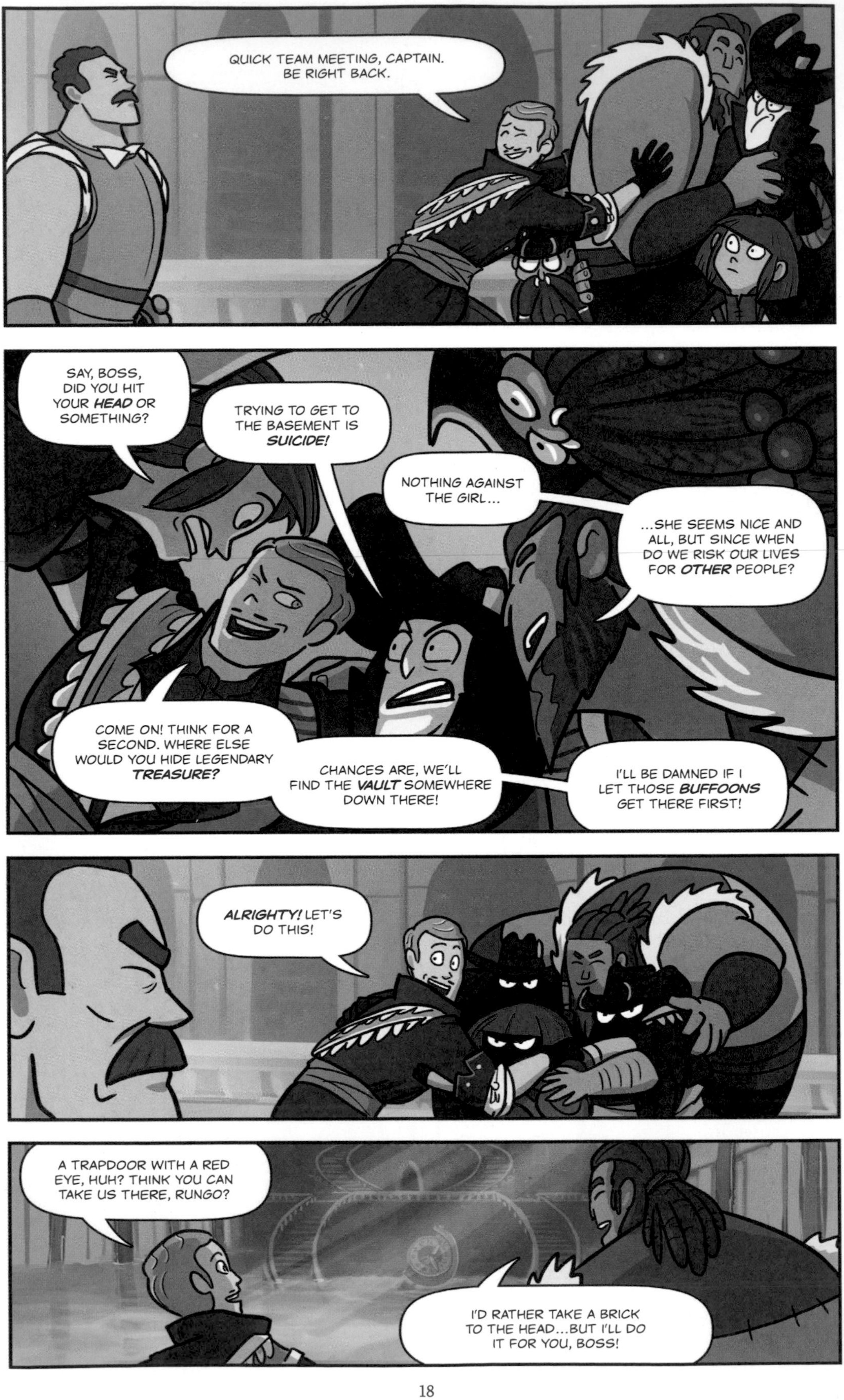
QUICK TEAM MEETING, CAPTAIN. BE RIGHT BACK.
SAY, BOSS, DID YOU HIT YOUR *HEAD* OR SOMETHING?
TRYING TO GET TO THE BASEMENT IS *SUICIDE!*
NOTHING AGAINST THE GIRL...
...SHE SEEMS NICE AND ALL, BUT SINCE WHEN DO WE RISK OUR LIVES FOR *OTHER* PEOPLE?
COME ON! THINK FOR A SECOND. WHERE ELSE WOULD YOU HIDE LEGENDARY *TREASURE?*
CHANCES ARE, WE'LL FIND THE *VAULT* SOMEWHERE DOWN THERE!
I'LL BE DAMNED IF I LET THOSE *BUFFOONS* GET THERE FIRST!
ALRIGHTY! LET'S DO THIS!
A TRAPDOOR WITH A RED EYE, HUH? THINK YOU CAN TAKE US THERE, RUNGO?
I'D RATHER TAKE A BRICK TO THE HEAD...BUT I'LL DO IT FOR YOU, BOSS!

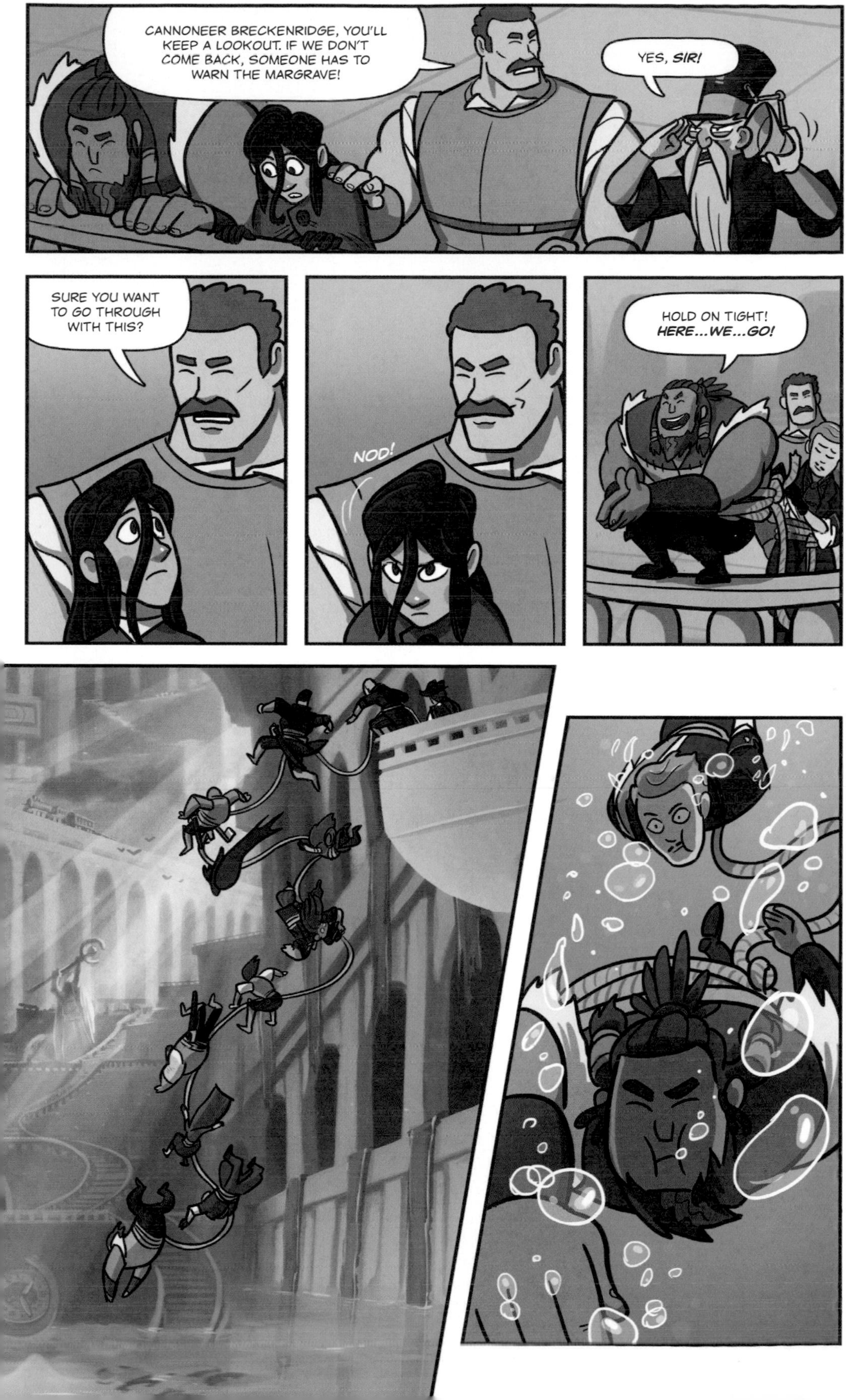
CANNONEER BRECKENRIDGE, YOU'LL KEEP A LOOKOUT. IF WE DON'T COME BACK, SOMEONE HAS TO WARN THE MARGRAVE!
YES, *SIR!*
SURE YOU WANT TO GO THROUGH WITH THIS?
NOD!
HOLD ON TIGHT! *HERE...WE...GO!*

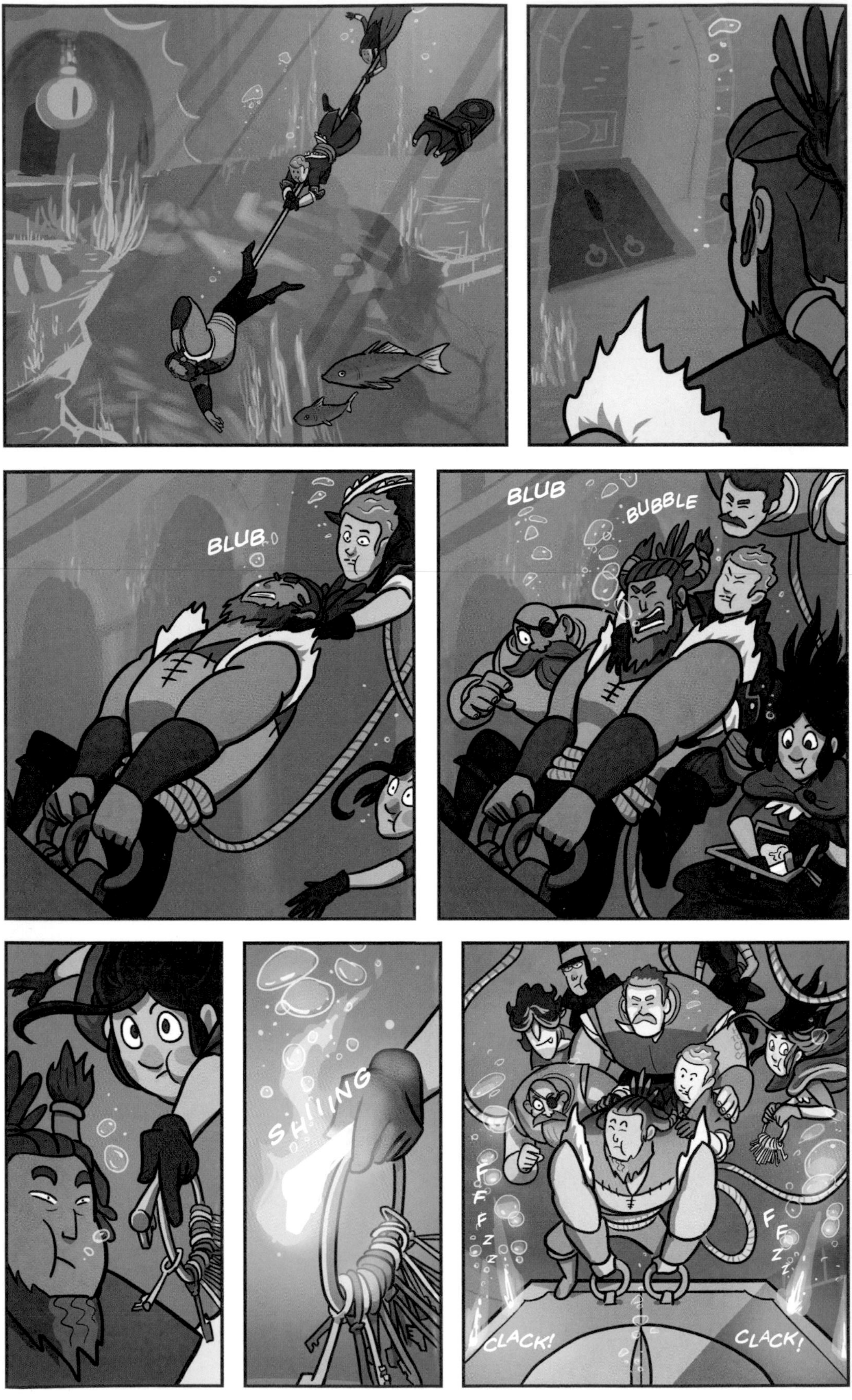
BLUB
BLUB
BUBBLE
SHIIING
FFFZZZ
FFZZ
CLACK!
CLACK!

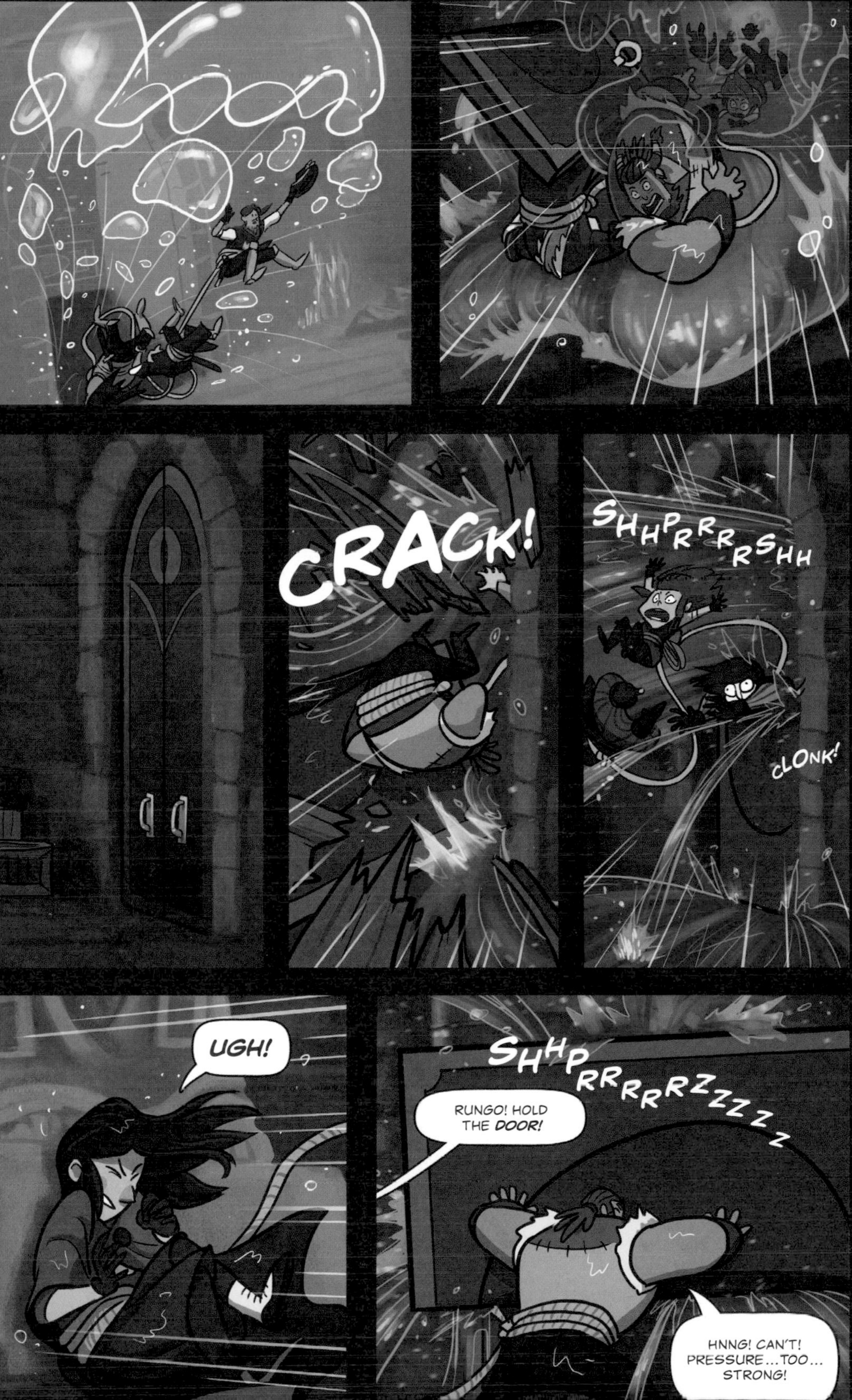
CRACK!
SHHPRRRRSHH
CLONK!
UGH!
SHHPRRRRRZZZZZ
RUNGO! HOLD THE DOOR!
HNNG! CAN'T! PRESSURE...TOO... STRONG!

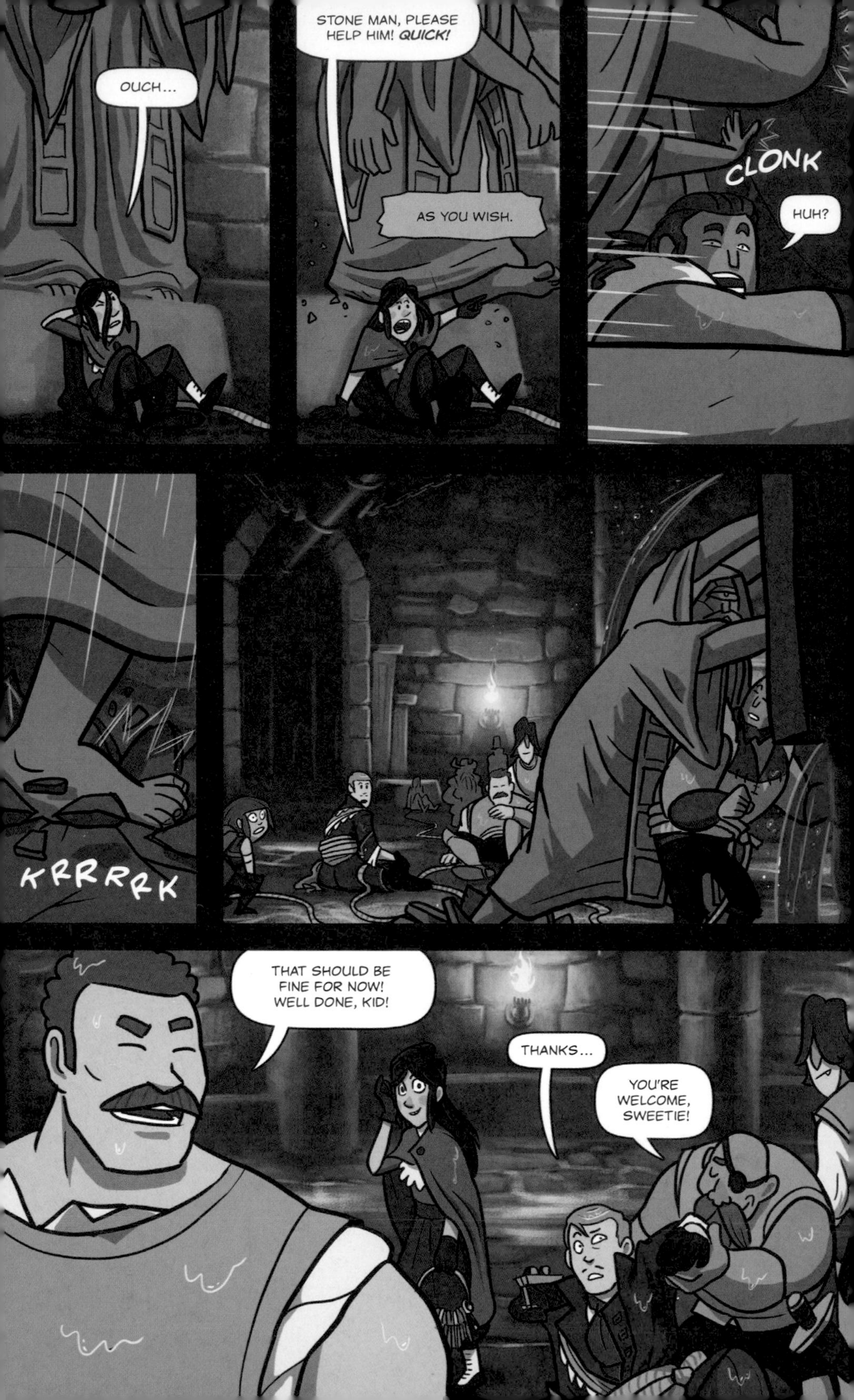
OUCH...
STONE MAN, PLEASE HELP HIM! QUICK!
AS YOU WISH.
CLONK
HUH?
KRRRRRK
THAT SHOULD BE FINE FOR NOW! WELL DONE, KID!
THANKS...
YOU'RE WELCOME, SWEETIE!

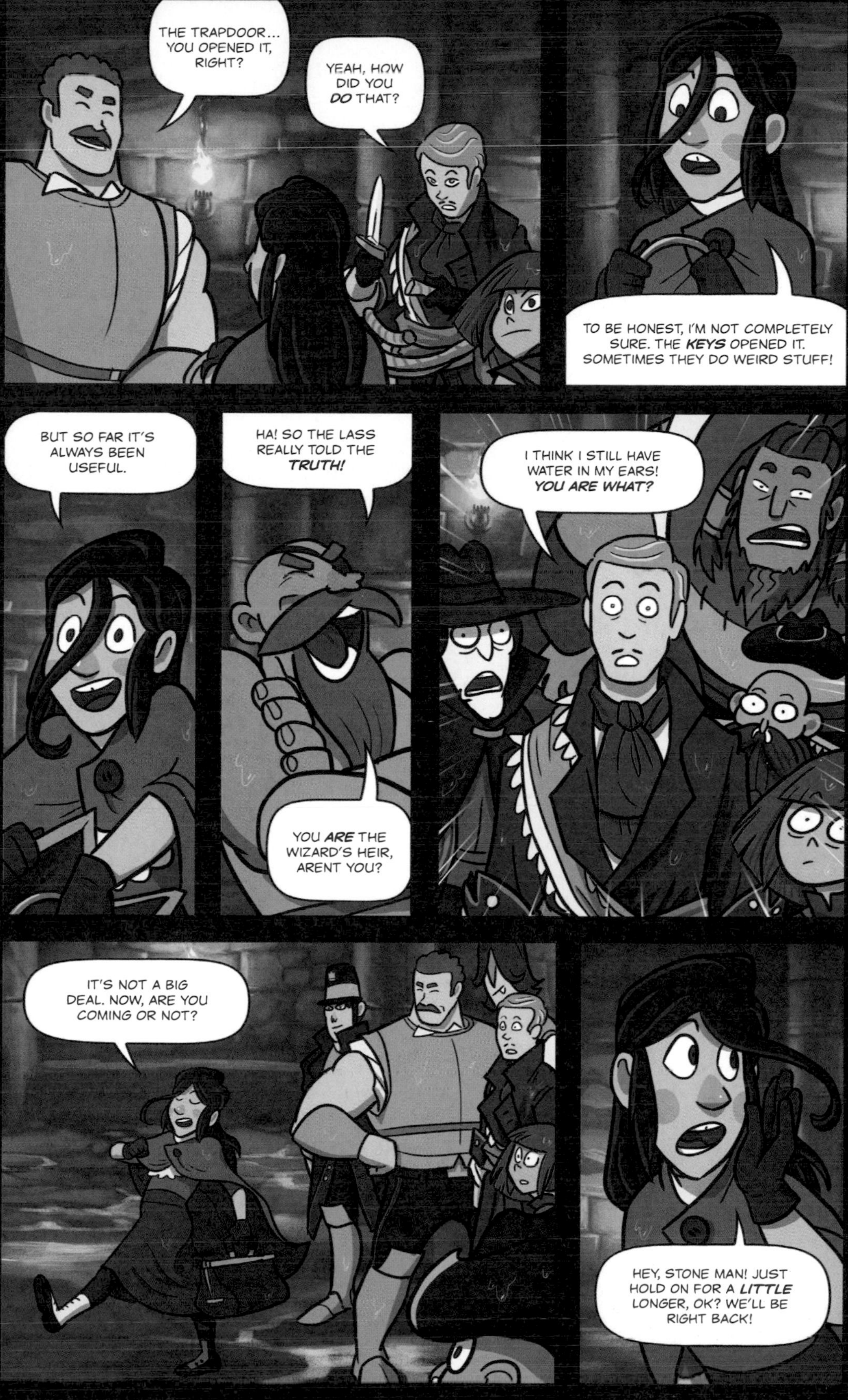
THE TRAPDOOR... YOU OPENED IT, RIGHT?
YEAH, HOW DID YOU *DO* THAT?
TO BE HONEST, I'M NOT COMPLETELY SURE. THE ***KEYS*** OPENED IT. SOMETIMES THEY DO WEIRD STUFF!
BUT SO FAR IT'S ALWAYS BEEN USEFUL.
HA! SO THE LASS REALLY TOLD THE ***TRUTH!***
YOU ***ARE*** THE WIZARD'S HEIR, ARENT YOU?
I THINK I STILL HAVE WATER IN MY EARS! ***YOU ARE WHAT?***
IT'S NOT A BIG DEAL. NOW, ARE YOU COMING OR NOT?
HEY, STONE MAN! JUST HOLD ON FOR A ***LITTLE*** LONGER, OK? WE'LL BE RIGHT BACK!

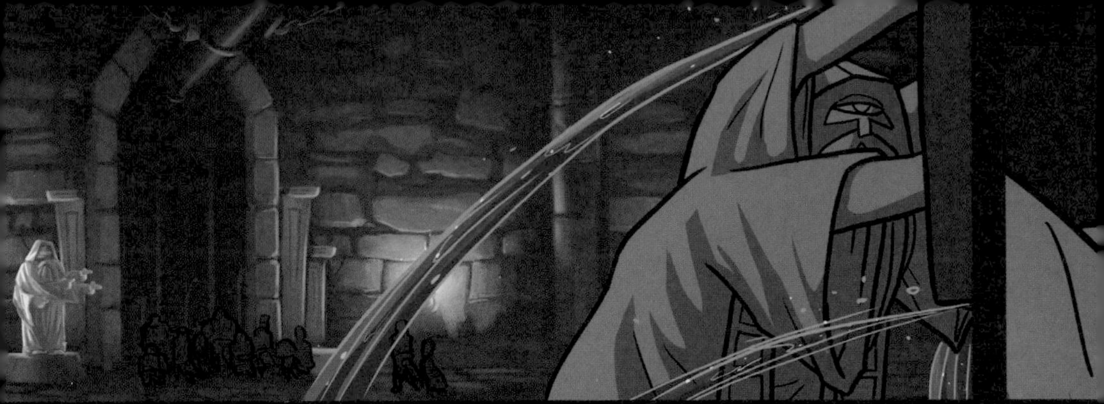

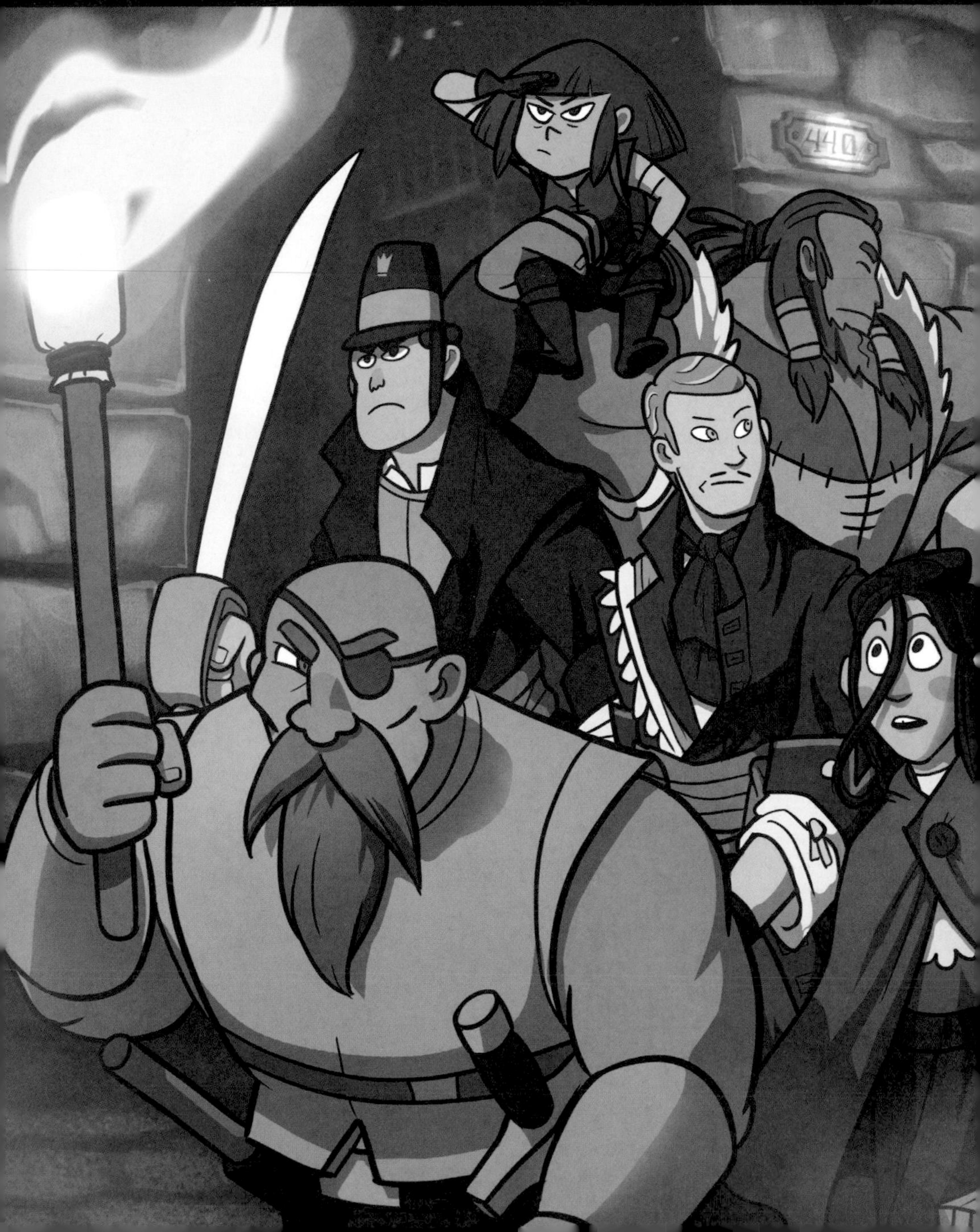
440

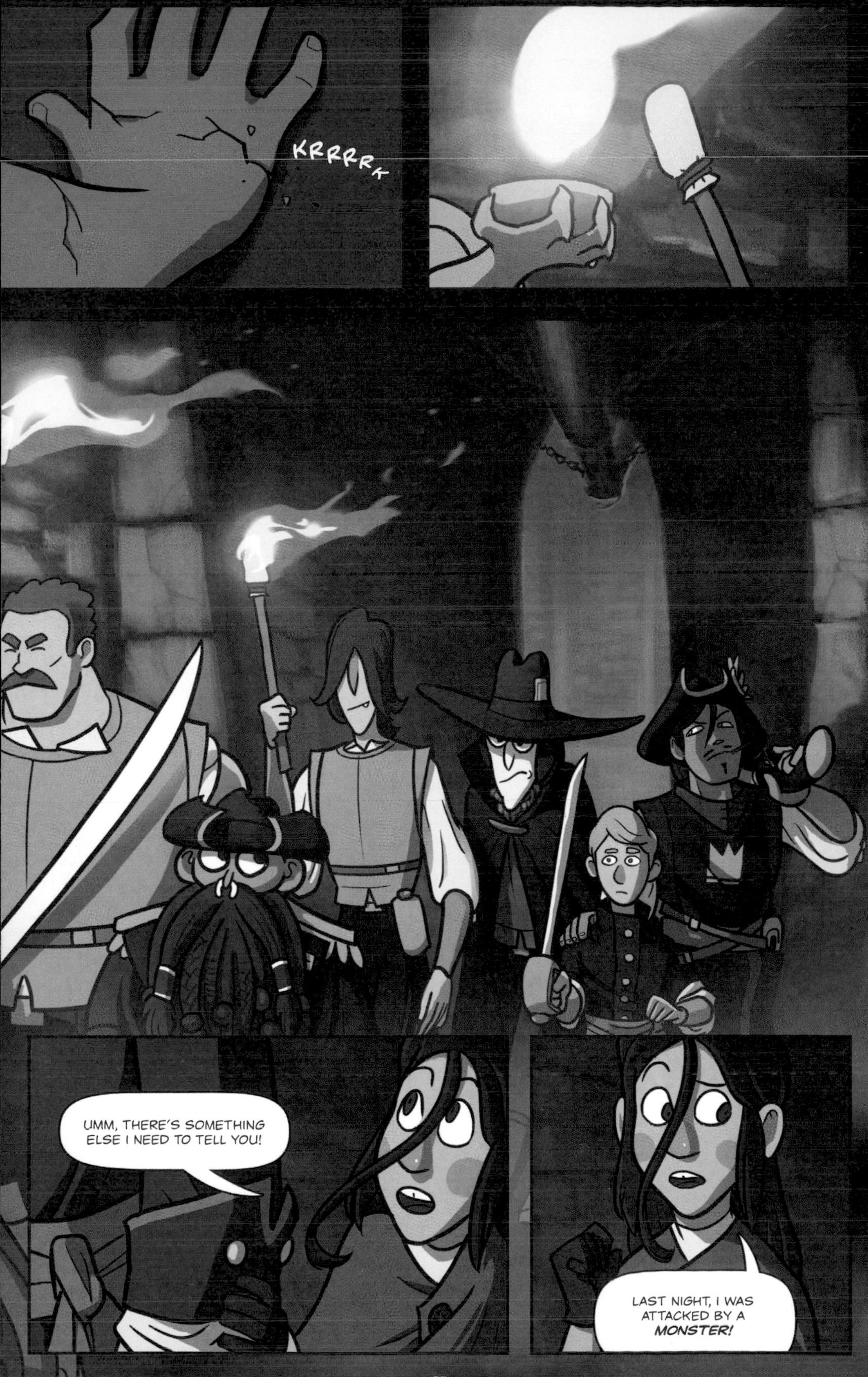
KRRRRK
UMM, THERE'S SOMETHING ELSE I NEED TO TELL YOU!
LAST NIGHT, I WAS ATTACKED BY A ***MONSTER!***

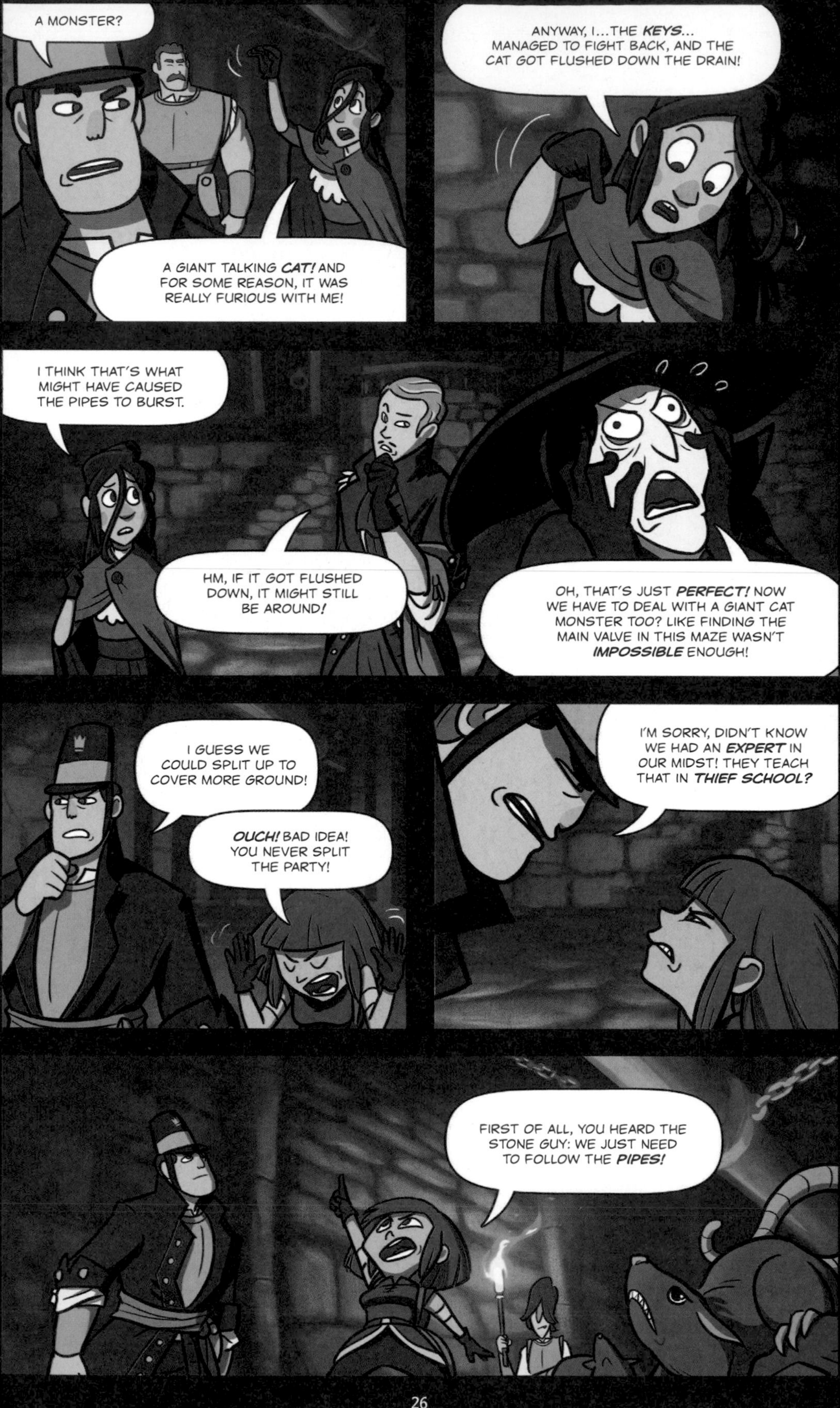

A MONSTER?
A GIANT TALKING CAT! AND FOR SOME REASON, IT WAS REALLY FURIOUS WITH ME!
ANYWAY, I...THE KEYS... MANAGED TO FIGHT BACK, AND THE CAT GOT FLUSHED DOWN THE DRAIN!
I THINK THAT'S WHAT MIGHT HAVE CAUSED THE PIPES TO BURST.
HM, IF IT GOT FLUSHED DOWN, IT MIGHT STILL BE AROUND!
OH, THAT'S JUST PERFECT! NOW WE HAVE TO DEAL WITH A GIANT CAT MONSTER TOO? LIKE FINDING THE MAIN VALVE IN THIS MAZE WASN'T IMPOSSIBLE ENOUGH!
I GUESS WE COULD SPLIT UP TO COVER MORE GROUND!
OUCH! BAD IDEA! YOU NEVER SPLIT THE PARTY!
I'M SORRY, DIDN'T KNOW WE HAD AN EXPERT IN OUR MIDST! THEY TEACH THAT IN THIEF SCHOOL?
FIRST OF ALL, YOU HEARD THE STONE GUY: WE JUST NEED TO FOLLOW THE PIPES!

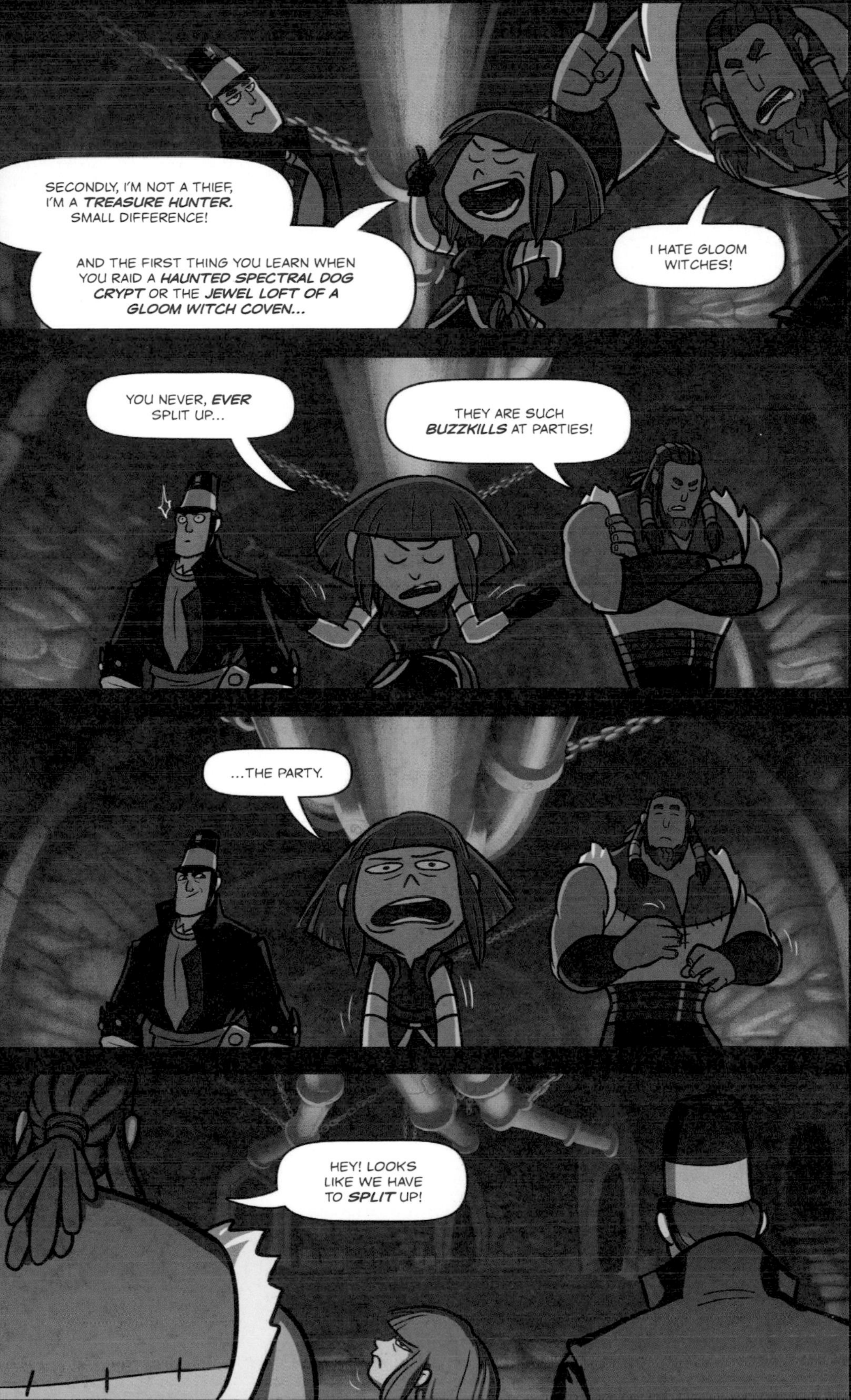
SECONDLY, I'M NOT A THIEF, I'M A **TREASURE HUNTER.** SMALL DIFFERENCE!
AND THE FIRST THING YOU LEARN WHEN YOU RAID A **HAUNTED SPECTRAL DOG CRYPT** OR THE **JEWEL LOFT OF A GLOOM WITCH COVEN...**
I HATE GLOOM WITCHES!
YOU NEVER, **EVER** SPLIT UP...
THEY ARE SUCH **BUZZKILLS** AT PARTIES!
...THE PARTY.
HEY! LOOKS LIKE WE HAVE TO **SPLIT** UP!

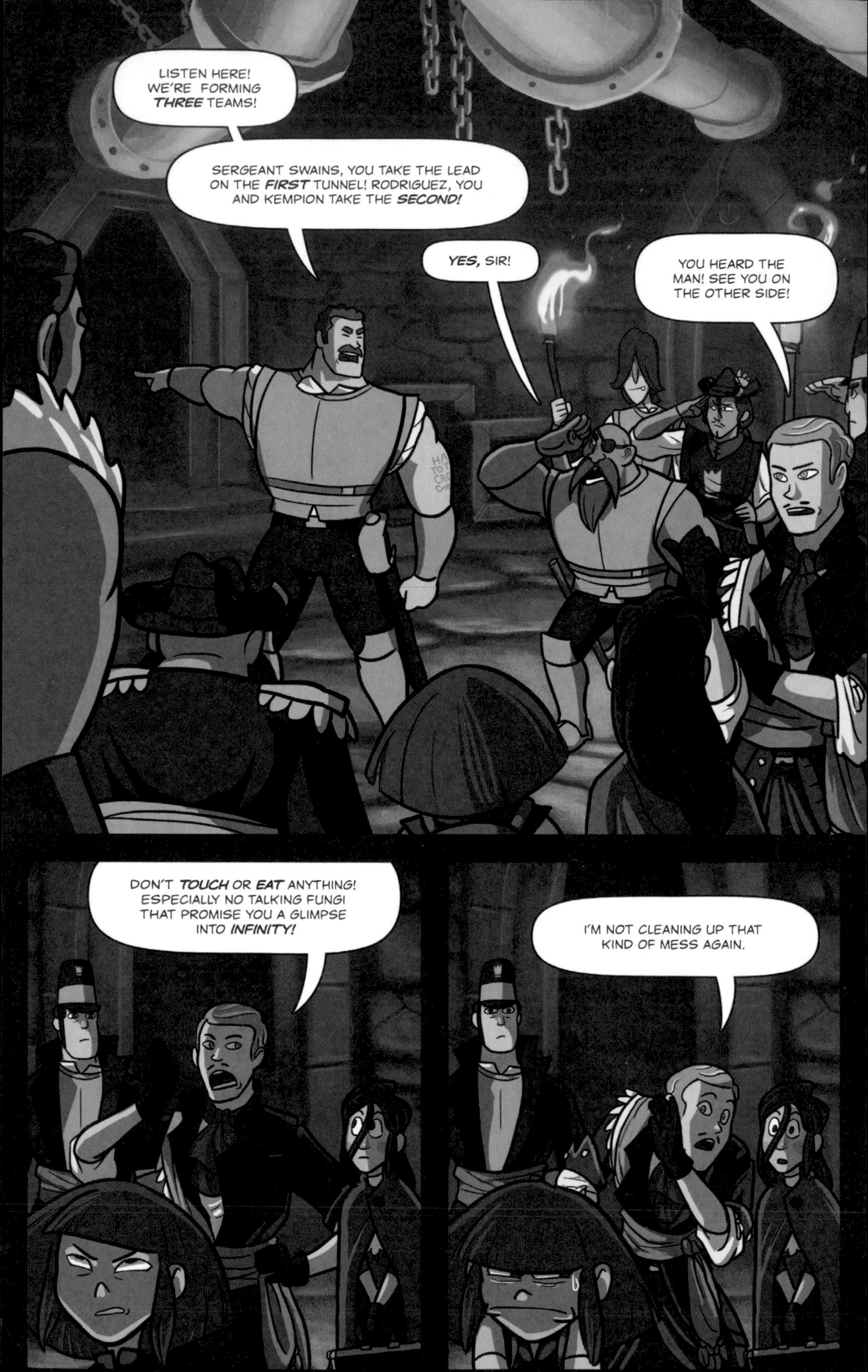
LISTEN HERE! WE'RE FORMING THREE TEAMS!
SERGEANT SWAINS, YOU TAKE THE LEAD ON THE FIRST TUNNEL! RODRIGUEZ, YOU AND KEMPION TAKE THE SECOND!
YES, SIR!
YOU HEARD THE MAN! SEE YOU ON THE OTHER SIDE!
DON'T TOUCH OR EAT ANYTHING! ESPECIALLY NO TALKING FUNGI THAT PROMISE YOU A GLIMPSE INTO INFINITY!
I'M NOT CLEANING UP THAT KIND OF MESS AGAIN.

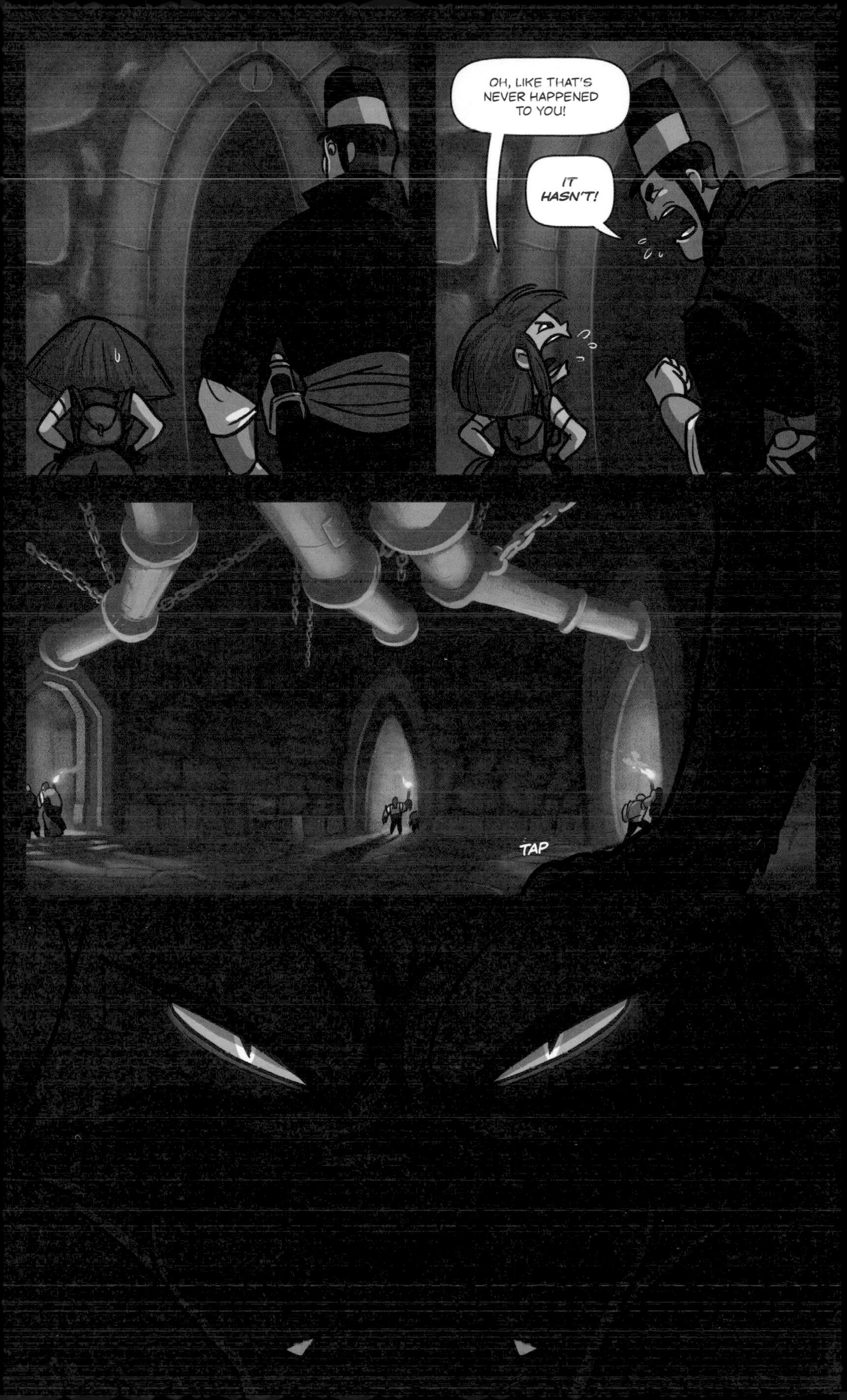
OH, LIKE THAT'S NEVER HAPPENED TO YOU!
IT HASN'T!
TAP

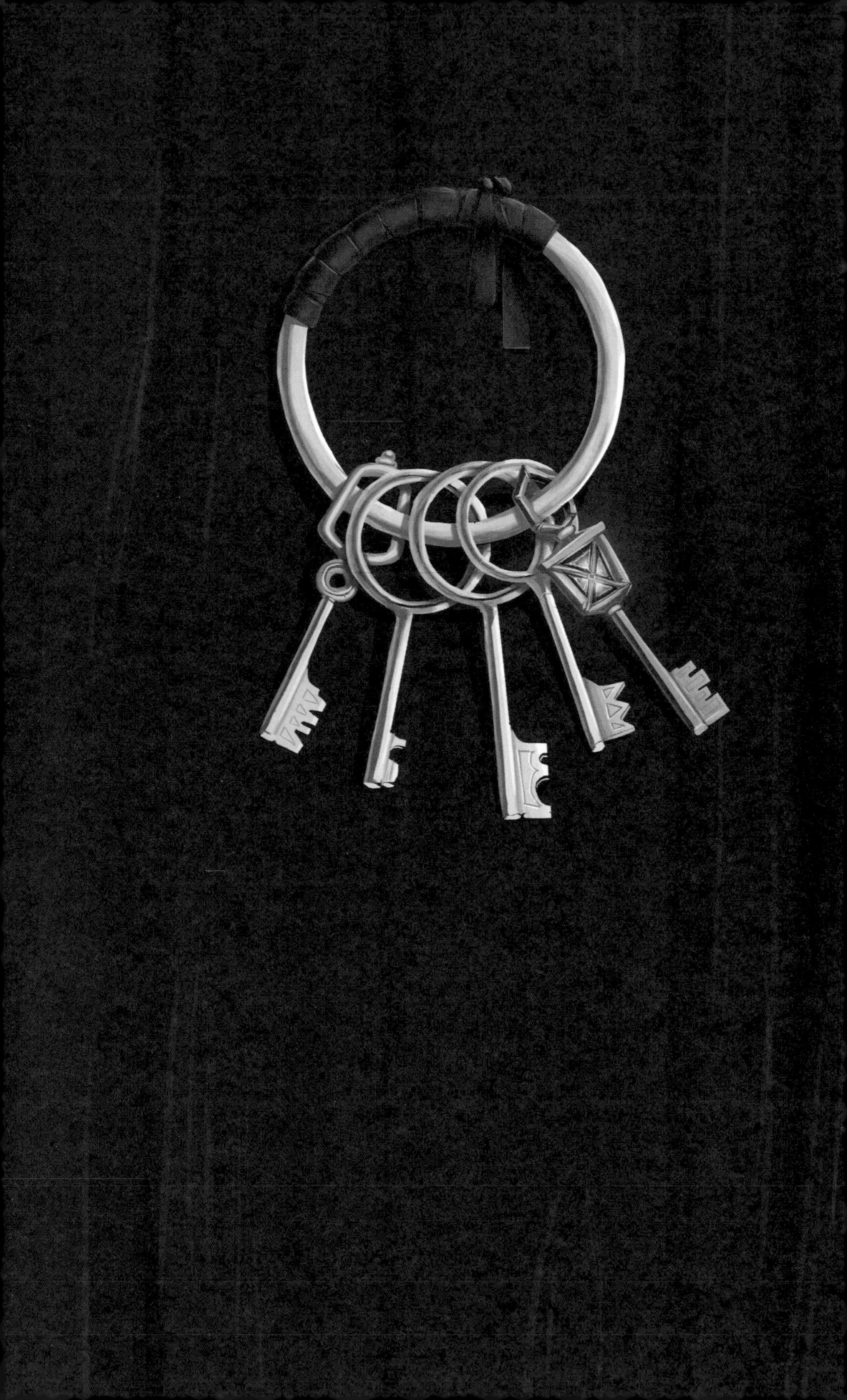

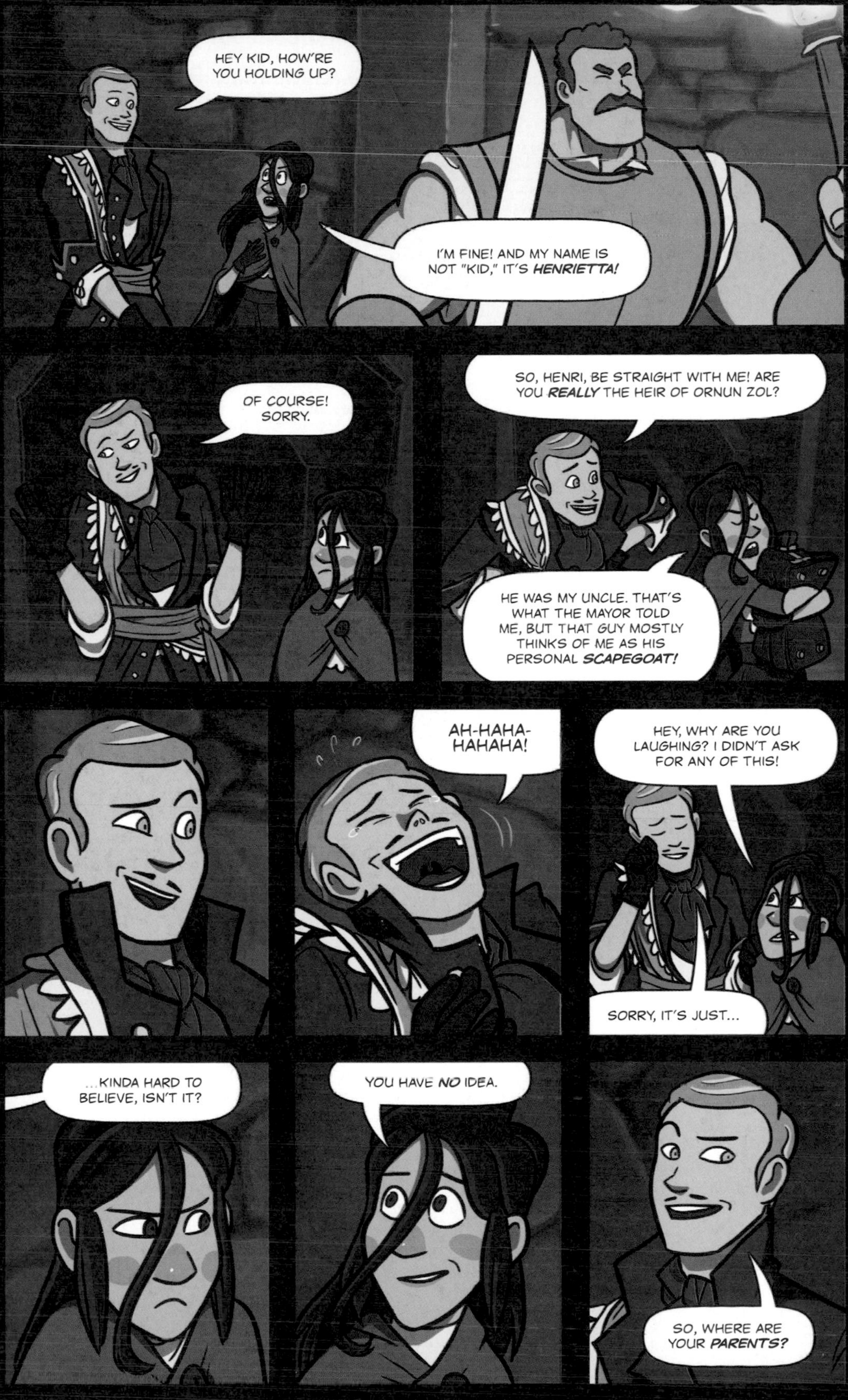

HEY KID, HOW'RE YOU HOLDING UP?
I'M FINE! AND MY NAME IS NOT "KID," IT'S **HENRIETTA!**
OF COURSE! SORRY.
SO, HENRI, BE STRAIGHT WITH ME! ARE YOU **REALLY** THE HEIR OF ORNUN ZOL?
HE WAS MY UNCLE. THAT'S WHAT THE MAYOR TOLD ME, BUT THAT GUY MOSTLY THINKS OF ME AS HIS PERSONAL **SCAPEGOAT!**
AH-HAHA-HAHAHA!
HEY, WHY ARE YOU LAUGHING? I DIDN'T ASK FOR ANY OF THIS!
SORRY, IT'S JUST...
...KINDA HARD TO BELIEVE, ISN'T IT?
YOU HAVE **NO** IDEA.
SO, WHERE ARE YOUR **PARENTS?**

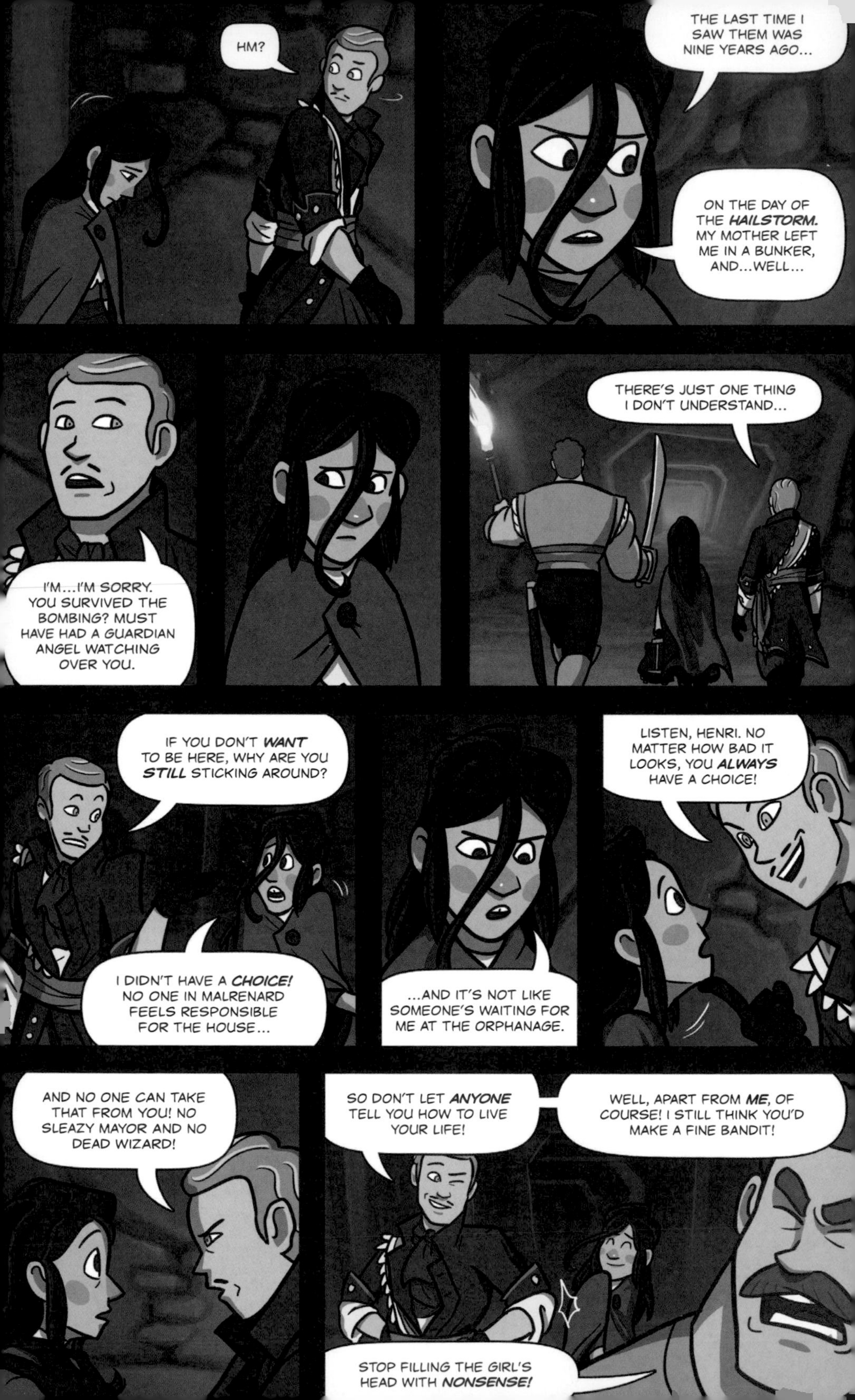
HM?
THE LAST TIME I SAW THEM WAS NINE YEARS AGO...
ON THE DAY OF THE ***HAILSTORM.*** MY MOTHER LEFT ME IN A BUNKER, AND...WELL...
I'M...I'M SORRY. YOU SURVIVED THE BOMBING? MUST HAVE HAD A GUARDIAN ANGEL WATCHING OVER YOU.
THERE'S JUST ONE THING I DON'T UNDERSTAND...
IF YOU DON'T ***WANT*** TO BE HERE, WHY ARE YOU ***STILL*** STICKING AROUND?
I DIDN'T HAVE A ***CHOICE!*** NO ONE IN MALRENARD FEELS RESPONSIBLE FOR THE HOUSE...
...AND IT'S NOT LIKE SOMEONE'S WAITING FOR ME AT THE ORPHANAGE.
LISTEN, HENRI. NO MATTER HOW BAD IT LOOKS, YOU ***ALWAYS*** HAVE A CHOICE!
AND NO ONE CAN TAKE THAT FROM YOU! NO SLEAZY MAYOR AND NO DEAD WIZARD!
SO DON'T LET ***ANYONE*** TELL YOU HOW TO LIVE YOUR LIFE!
WELL, APART FROM ***ME***, OF COURSE! I STILL THINK YOU'D MAKE A FINE BANDIT!
STOP FILLING THE GIRL'S HEAD WITH ***NONSENSE!***

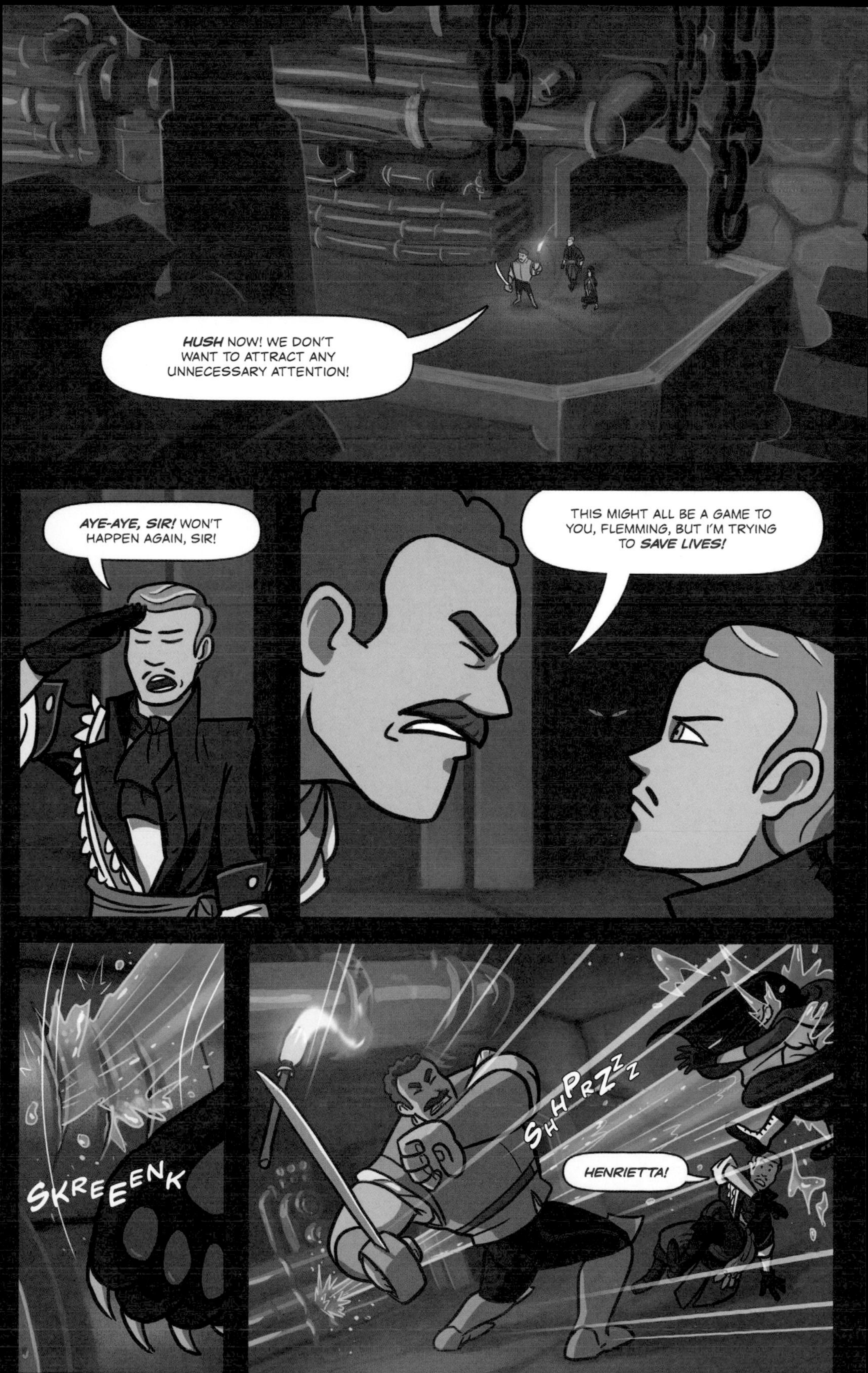
HUSH NOW! WE DON'T WANT TO ATTRACT ANY UNNECESSARY ATTENTION!
AYE-AYE, SIR! WON'T HAPPEN AGAIN, SIR!
THIS MIGHT ALL BE A GAME TO YOU, FLEMMING, BUT I'M TRYING TO SAVE LIVES!
SKREEENK
SHHPRZZZ
HENRIETTA!

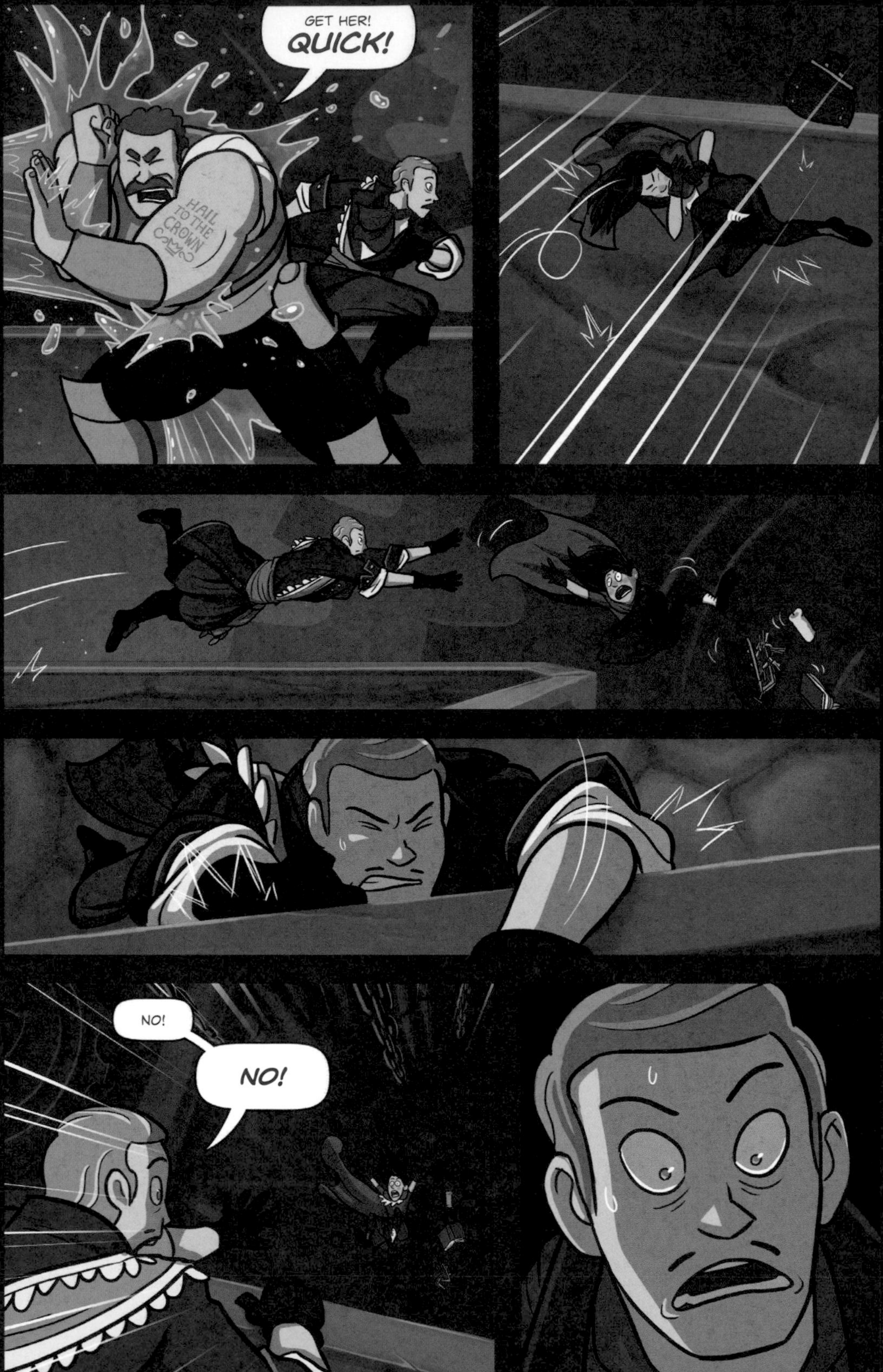
GET HER!
QUICK!
HAIL TO THE CROWN
NO!
NO!

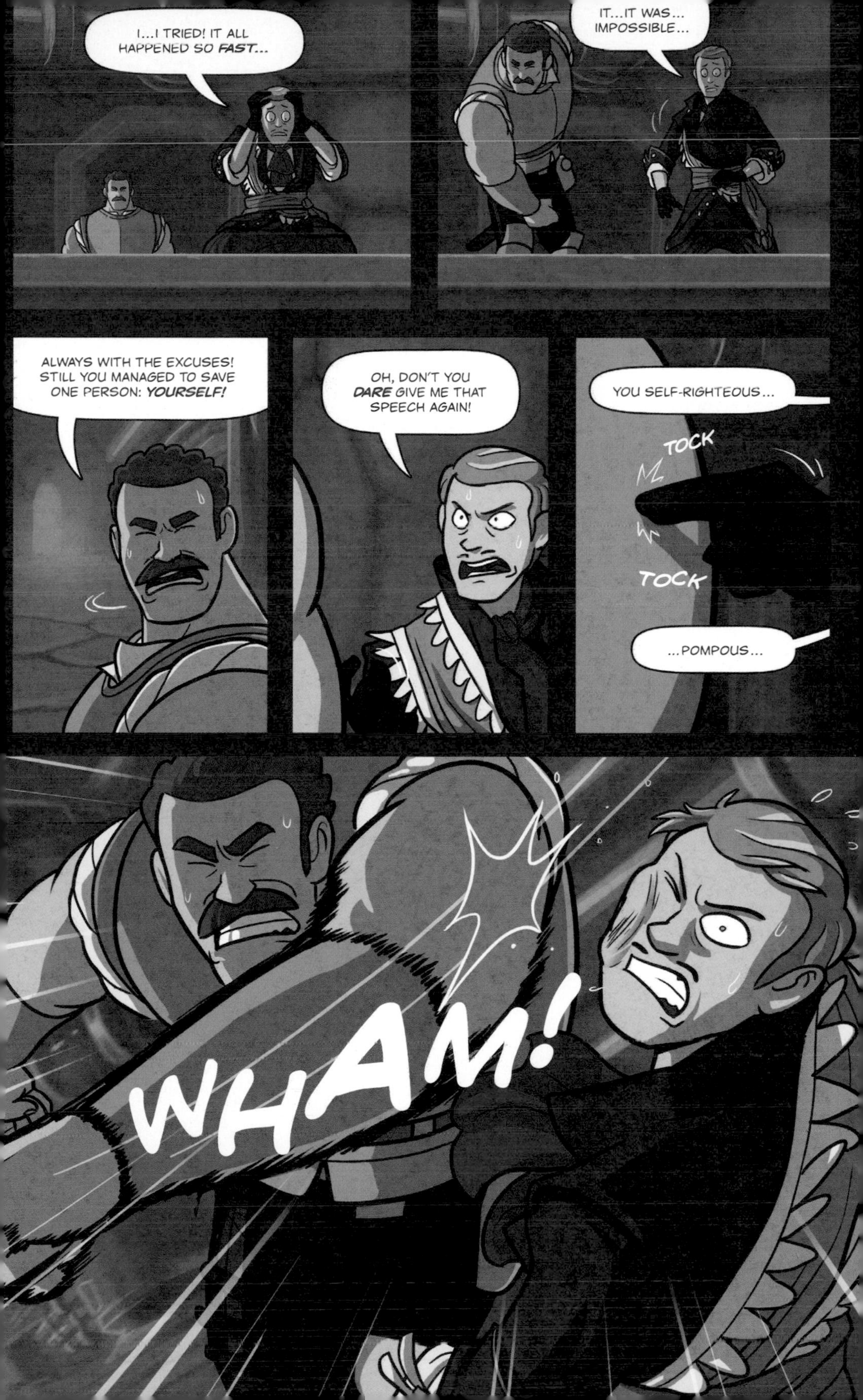
I...I TRIED! IT ALL HAPPENED SO FAST...
IT...IT WAS... IMPOSSIBLE...
ALWAYS WITH THE EXCUSES! STILL YOU MANAGED TO SAVE ONE PERSON: YOURSELF!
OH, DON'T YOU DARE GIVE ME THAT SPEECH AGAIN!
YOU SELF-RIGHTEOUS...
TOCK
TOCK
...POMPOUS...
WHAM!

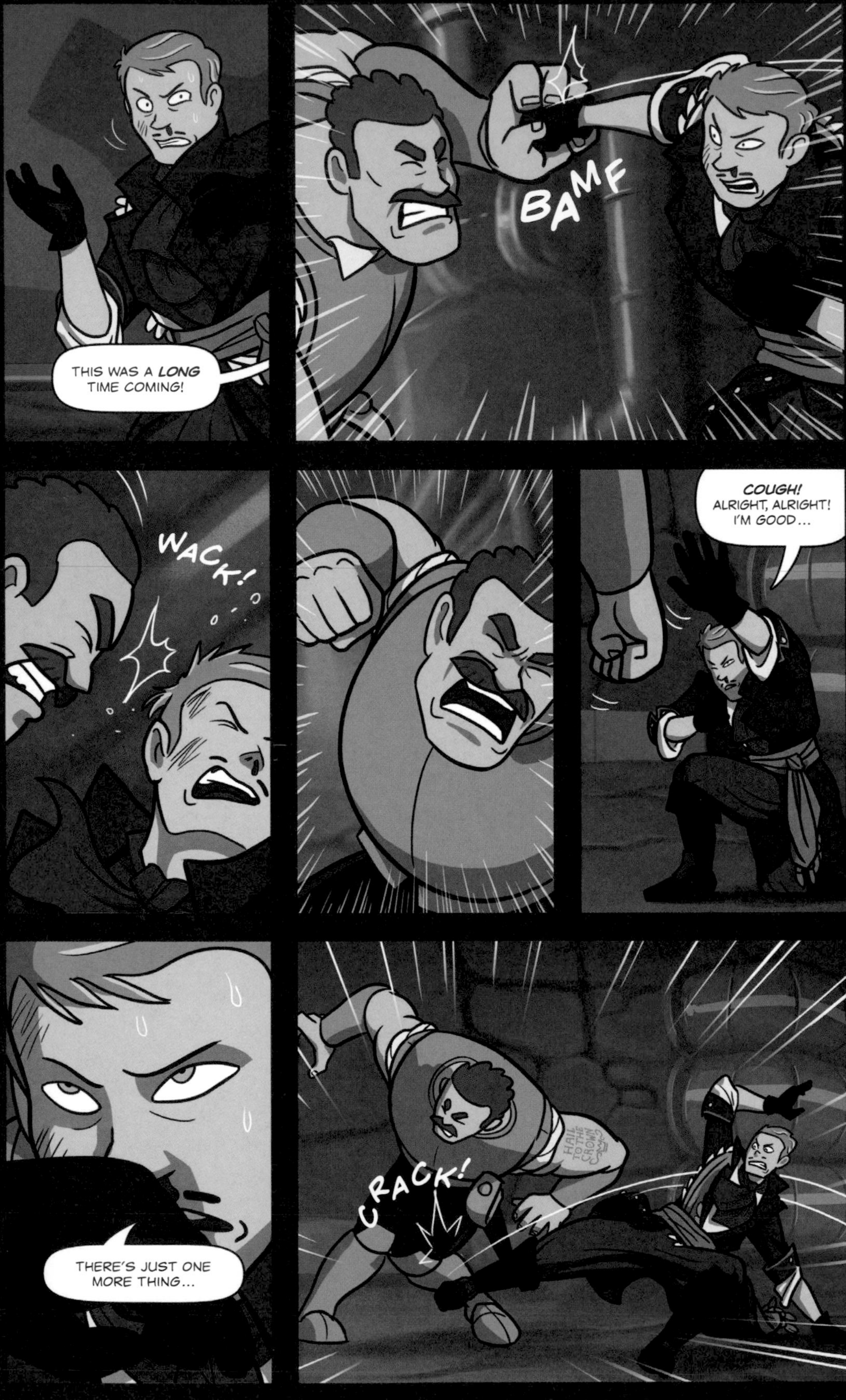
THIS WAS A LONG TIME COMING!
BAMF
WACK!
COUGH! ALRIGHT, ALRIGHT! I'M GOOD...
THERE'S JUST ONE MORE THING...
HAIL TO THE CROWN
CRACK!

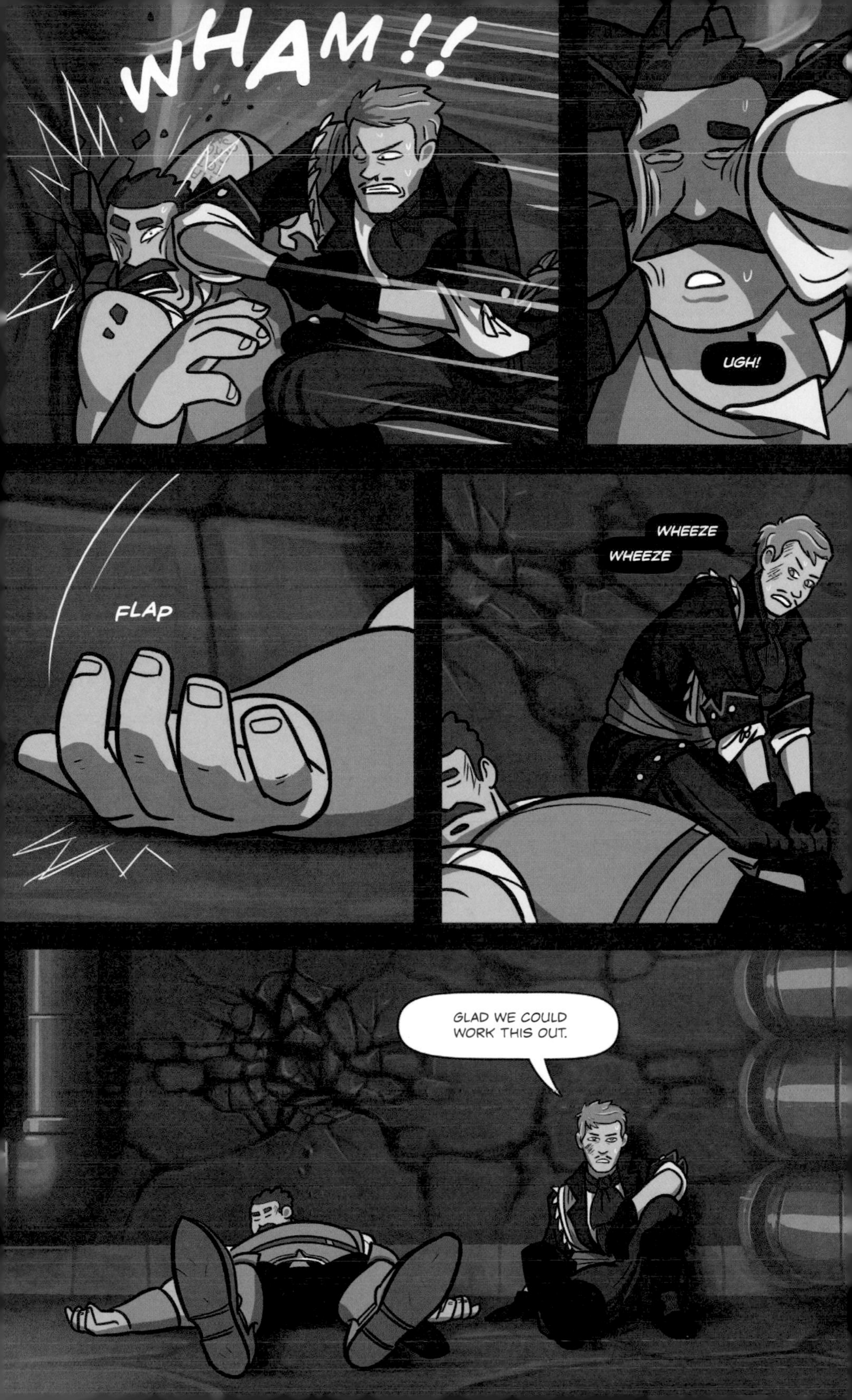
WHAM!!
UGH!
FLAP
WHEEZE
WHEEZE
GLAD WE COULD WORK THIS OUT.

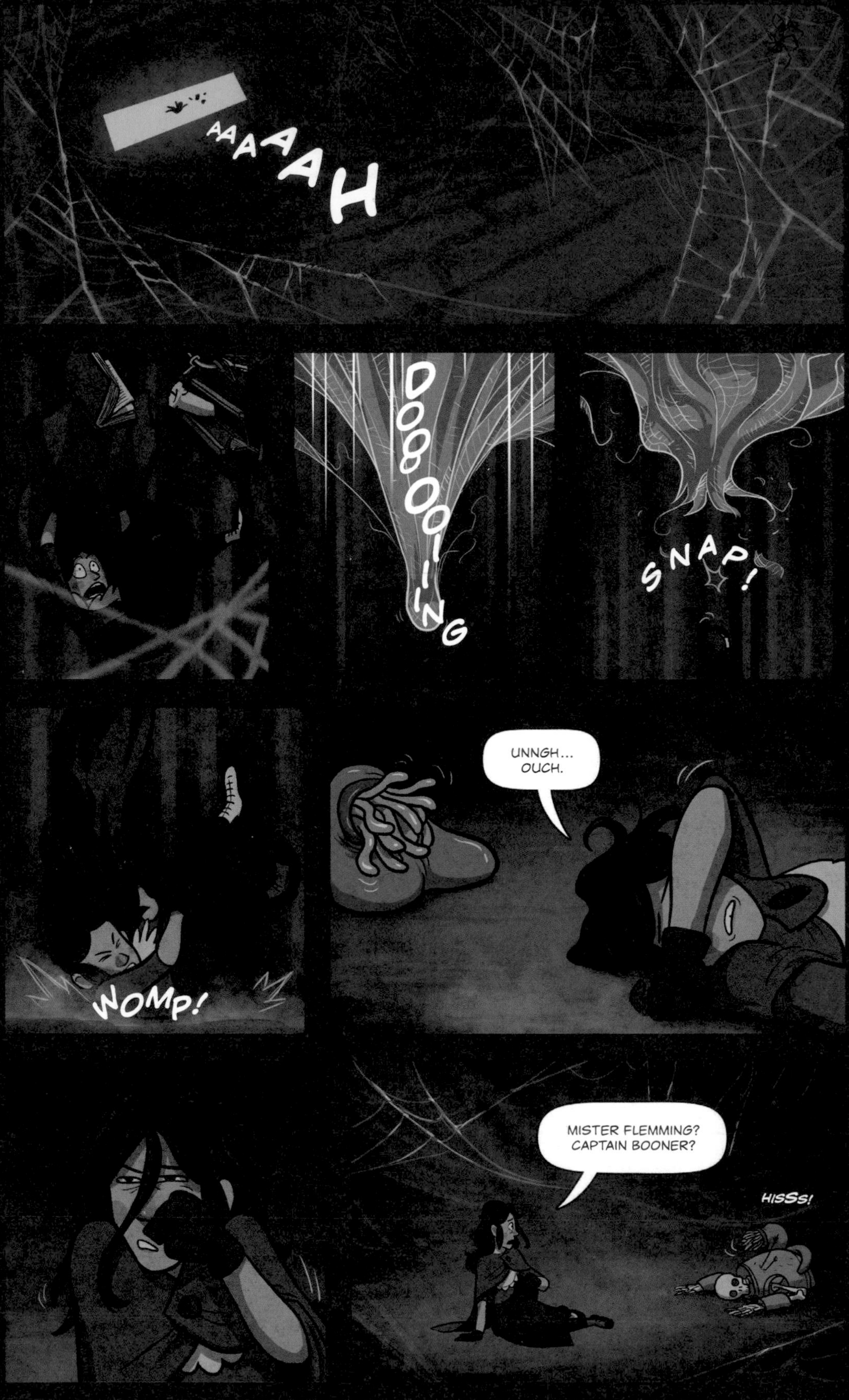
AAAAAH
DOOOOOOING
SNAP!
WOMP!
UNNGH... OUCH.
MISTER FLEMMING? CAPTAIN BOONER?
HISSS!

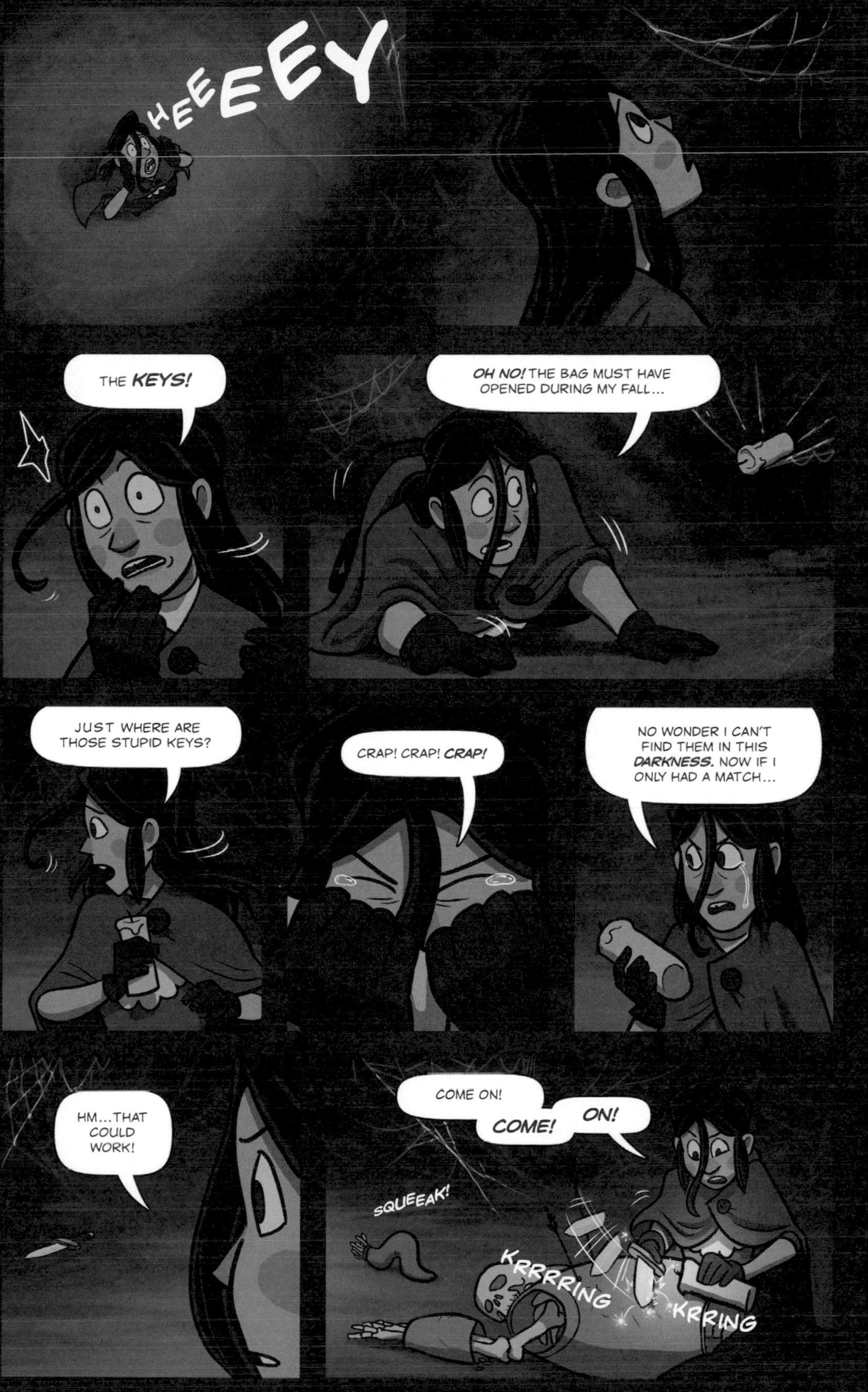
HEEEEY
THE KEYS!
OH NO! THE BAG MUST HAVE OPENED DURING MY FALL...
JUST WHERE ARE THOSE STUPID KEYS?
CRAP! CRAP! CRAP!
NO WONDER I CAN'T FIND THEM IN THIS DARKNESS. NOW IF I ONLY HAD A MATCH...
HM...THAT COULD WORK!
COME ON!
COME! ON!
SQUEEAK!
KRRRRING
KRRING

YESSS!

BUT NO WATER PIPES. HOW AM I GONNA CATCH UP WITH THE OTHERS NOW?

WHOOOOA!

WHAT THE...

GAAAAH!

HEY, WHERE ARE YOU GOING?

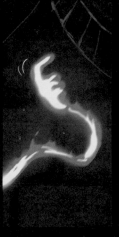

OKAY...SO I GUESS I'LL JUST FOLLOW THE LIVING FLAME, THEN. SURE. NOTHING WEIRD ABOUT THAT.

SIGH.

SCHLRRRP

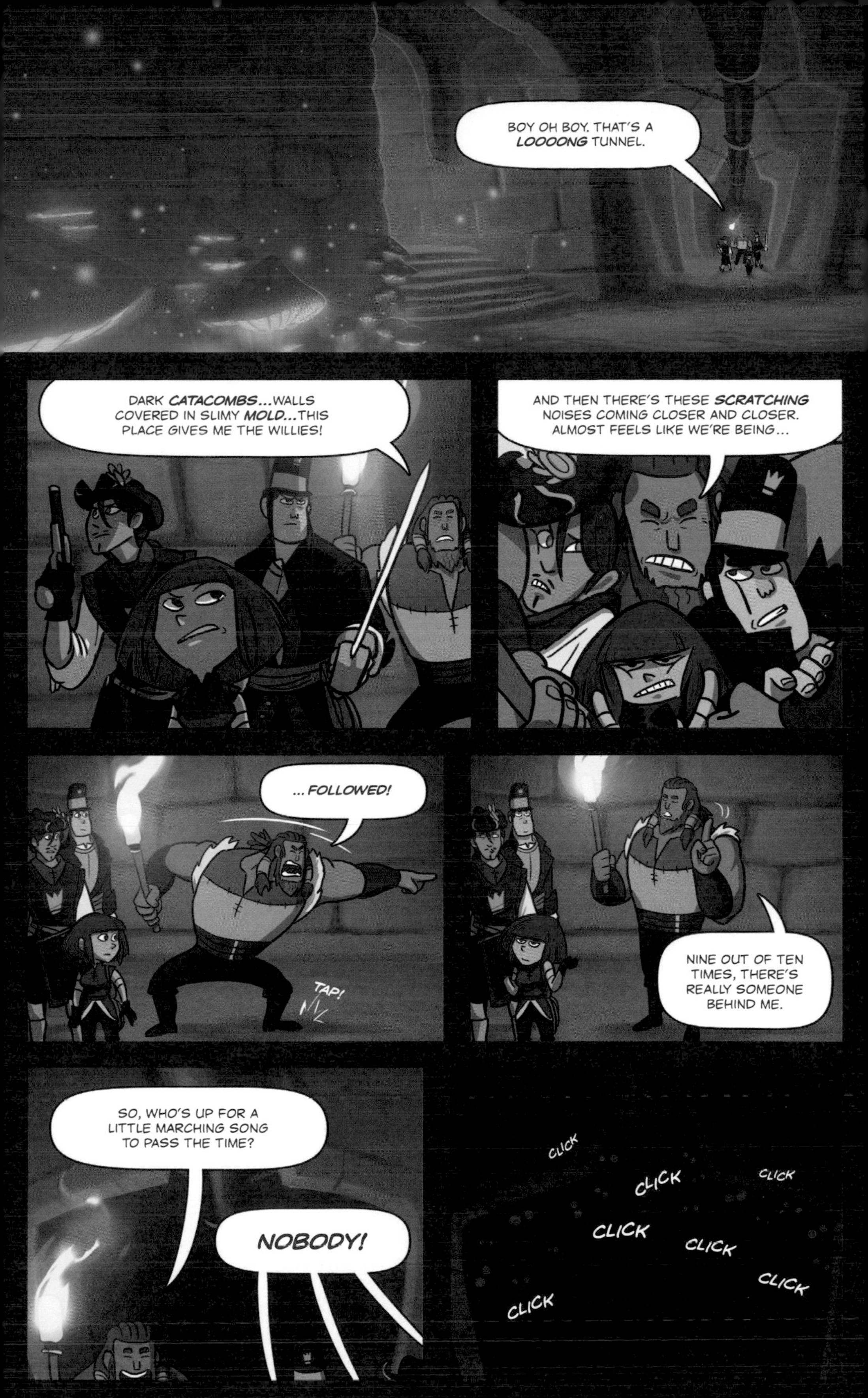
BOY OH BOY. THAT'S A LOOOONG TUNNEL.
DARK CATACOMBS...WALLS COVERED IN SLIMY MOLD...THIS PLACE GIVES ME THE WILLIES!
AND THEN THERE'S THESE SCRATCHING NOISES COMING CLOSER AND CLOSER. ALMOST FEELS LIKE WE'RE BEING...
...FOLLOWED!
TAP!
NINE OUT OF TEN TIMES, THERE'S REALLY SOMEONE BEHIND ME.
SO, WHO'S UP FOR A LITTLE MARCHING SONG TO PASS THE TIME?
NOBODY!
CLICK
CLICK
CLICK
CLICK
CLICK
CLICK
CLICK

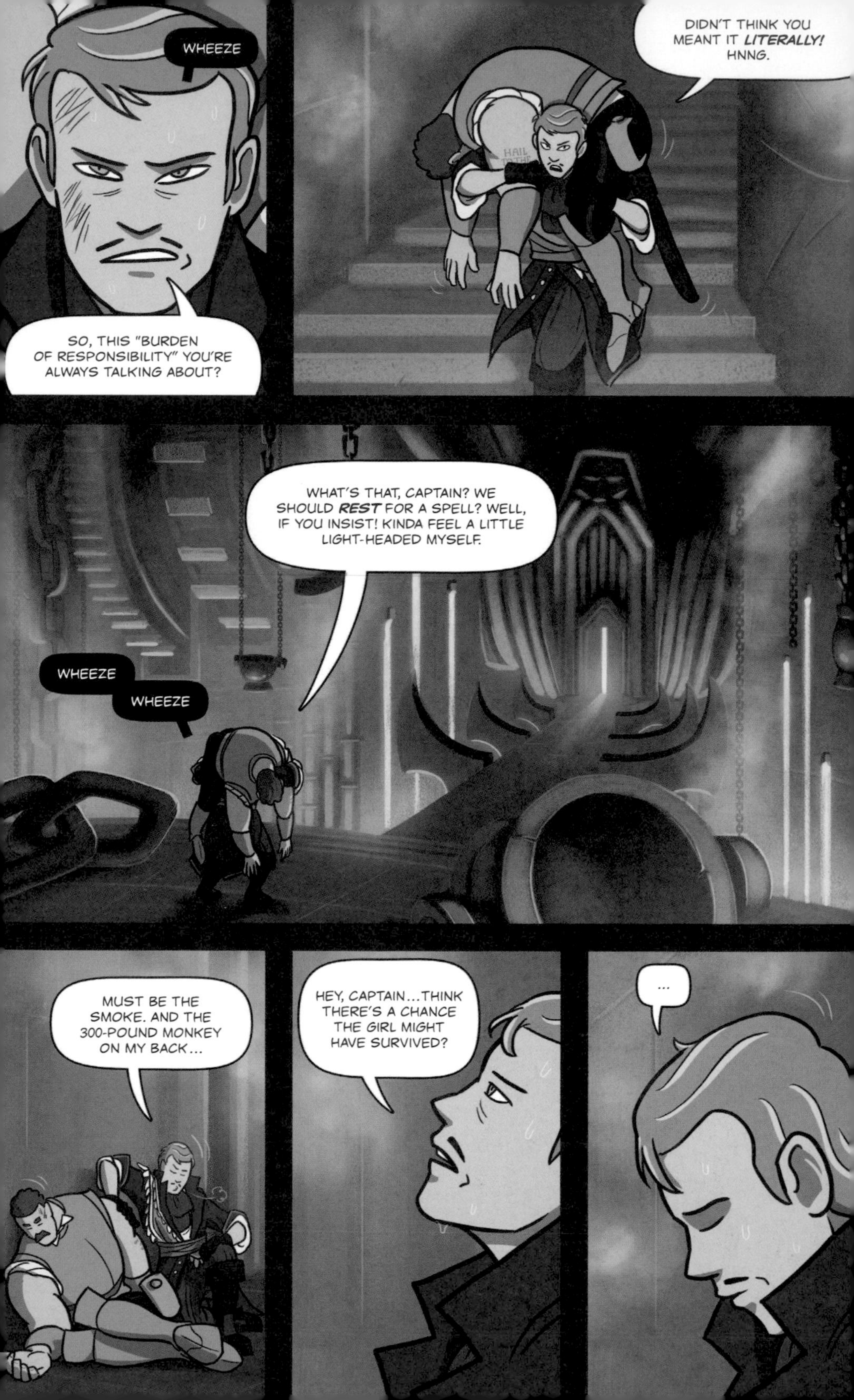
WHEEZE
SO, THIS "BURDEN OF RESPONSIBILITY" YOU'RE ALWAYS TALKING ABOUT?
DIDN'T THINK YOU MEANT IT ***LITERALLY!*** HNNG.
WHAT'S THAT, CAPTAIN? WE SHOULD ***REST*** FOR A SPELL? WELL, IF YOU INSIST! KINDA FEEL A LITTLE LIGHT-HEADED MYSELF.
WHEEZE
WHEEZE
MUST BE THE SMOKE. AND THE 300-POUND MONKEY ON MY BACK...
HEY, CAPTAIN...THINK THERE'S A CHANCE THE GIRL MIGHT HAVE SURVIVED?
...

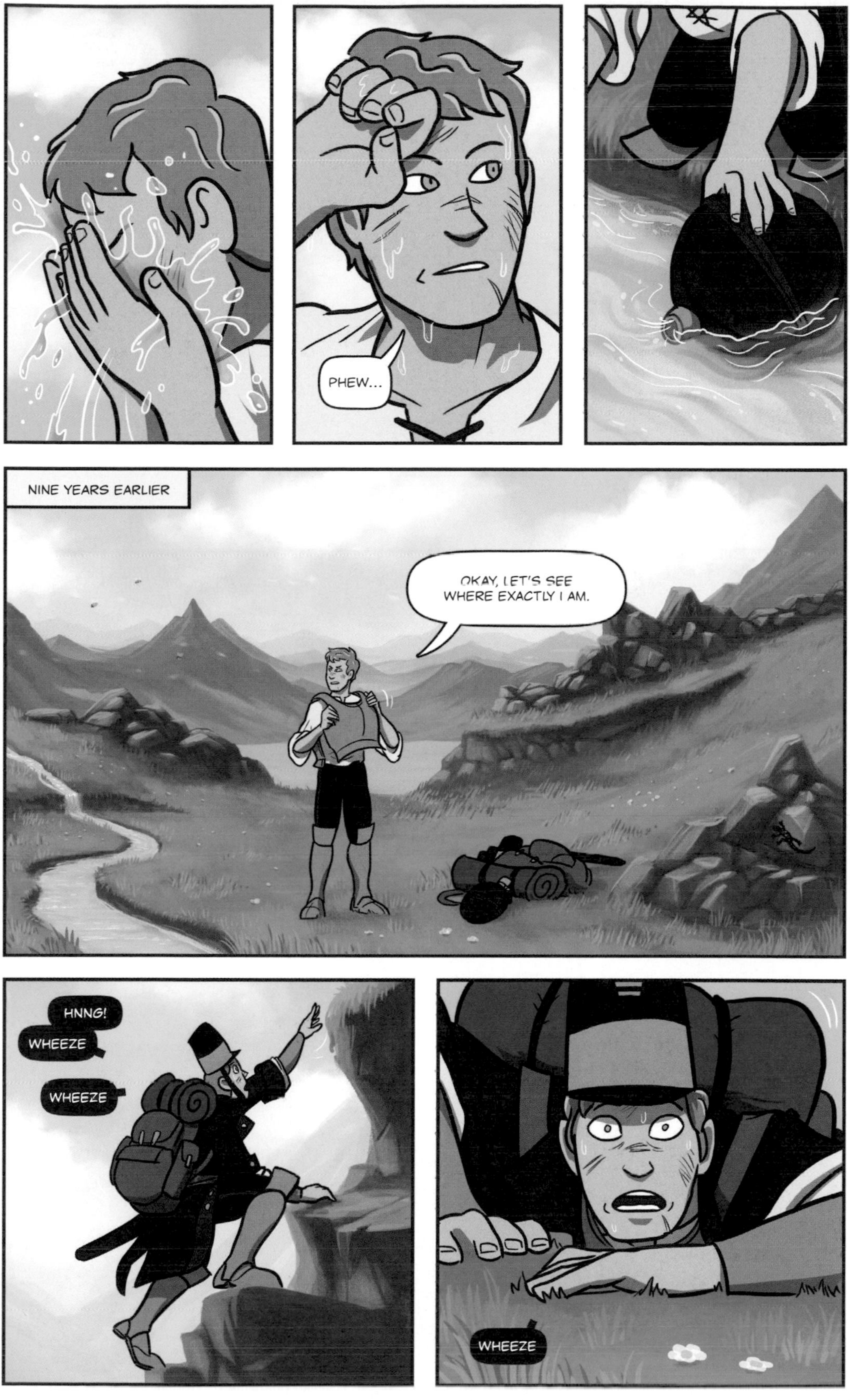
PHEW...
NINE YEARS EARLIER
OKAY, LET'S SEE WHERE EXACTLY I AM.
HNNG!
WHEEZE
WHEEZE
WHEEZE

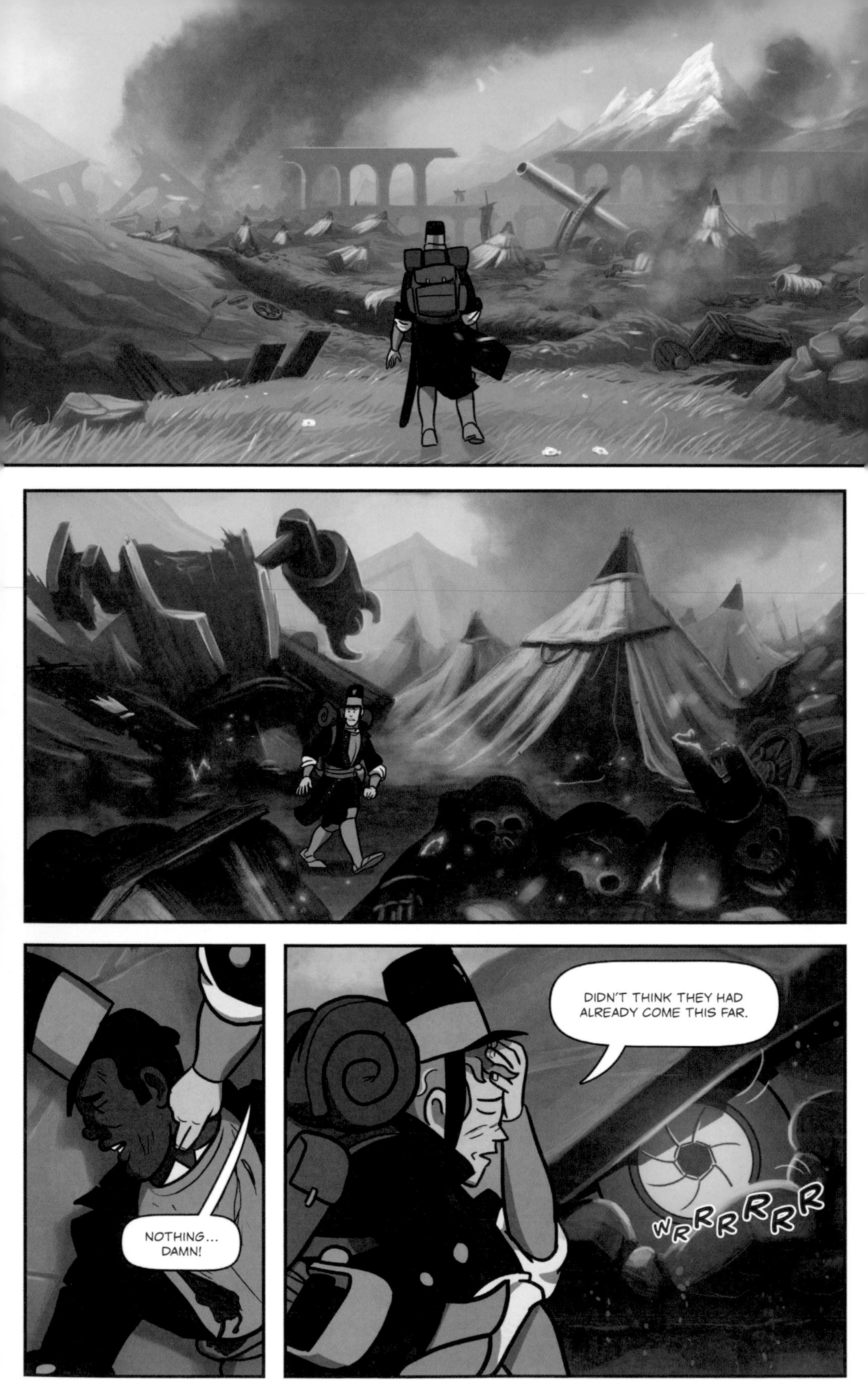
NOTHING... DAMN!
DIDN'T THINK THEY HAD ALREADY COME THIS FAR.
WRRRRRR

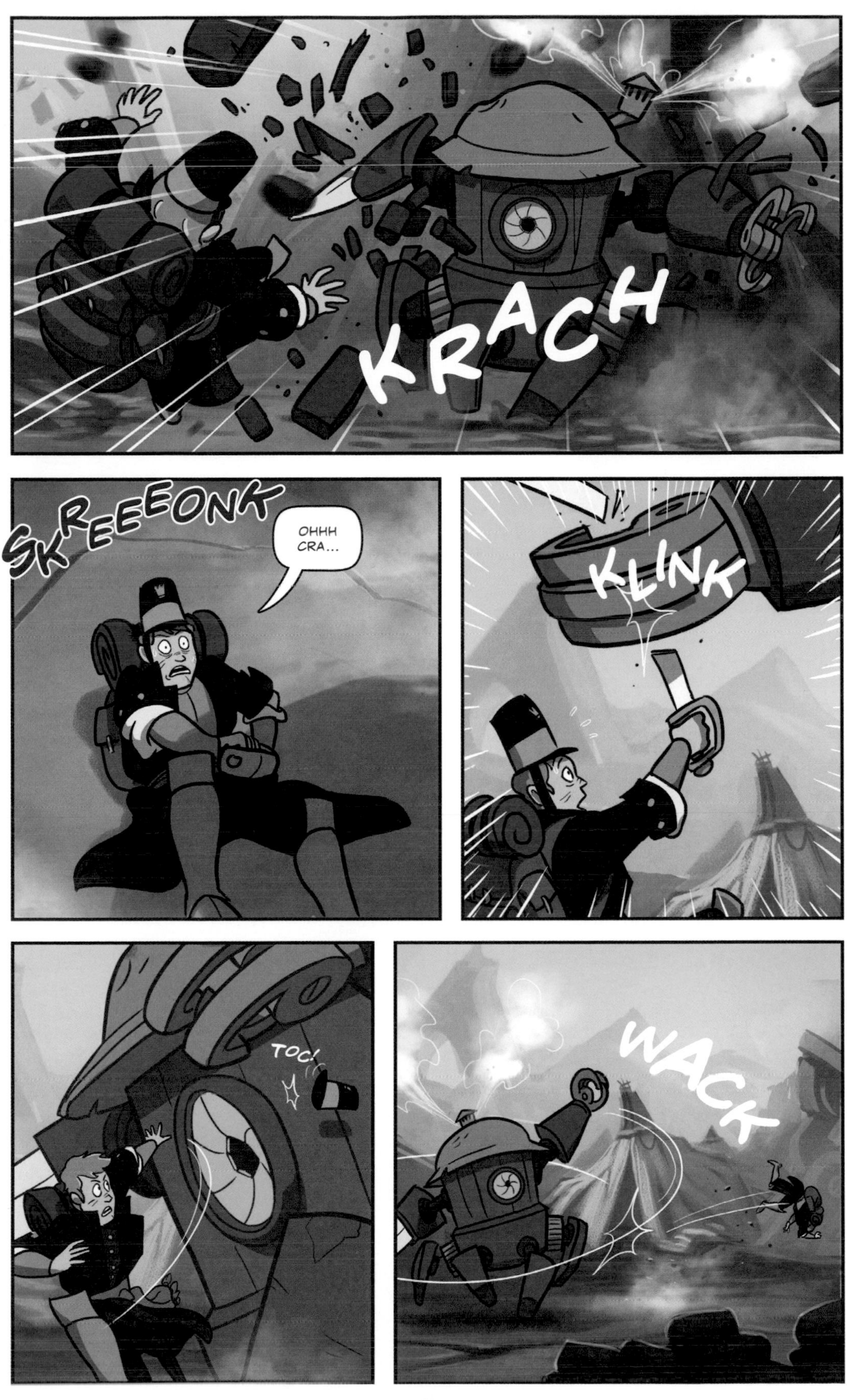
KRACH
SKREEEONK
OHHH CRA...
KLINK
TOC!
WACK

SLAM

UGH!

SKRRREEONK

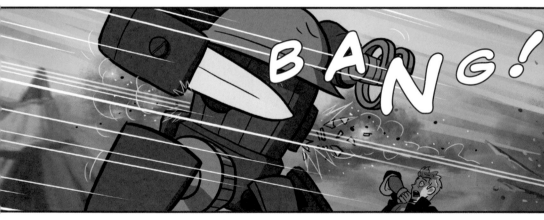

BANG!

CLONG

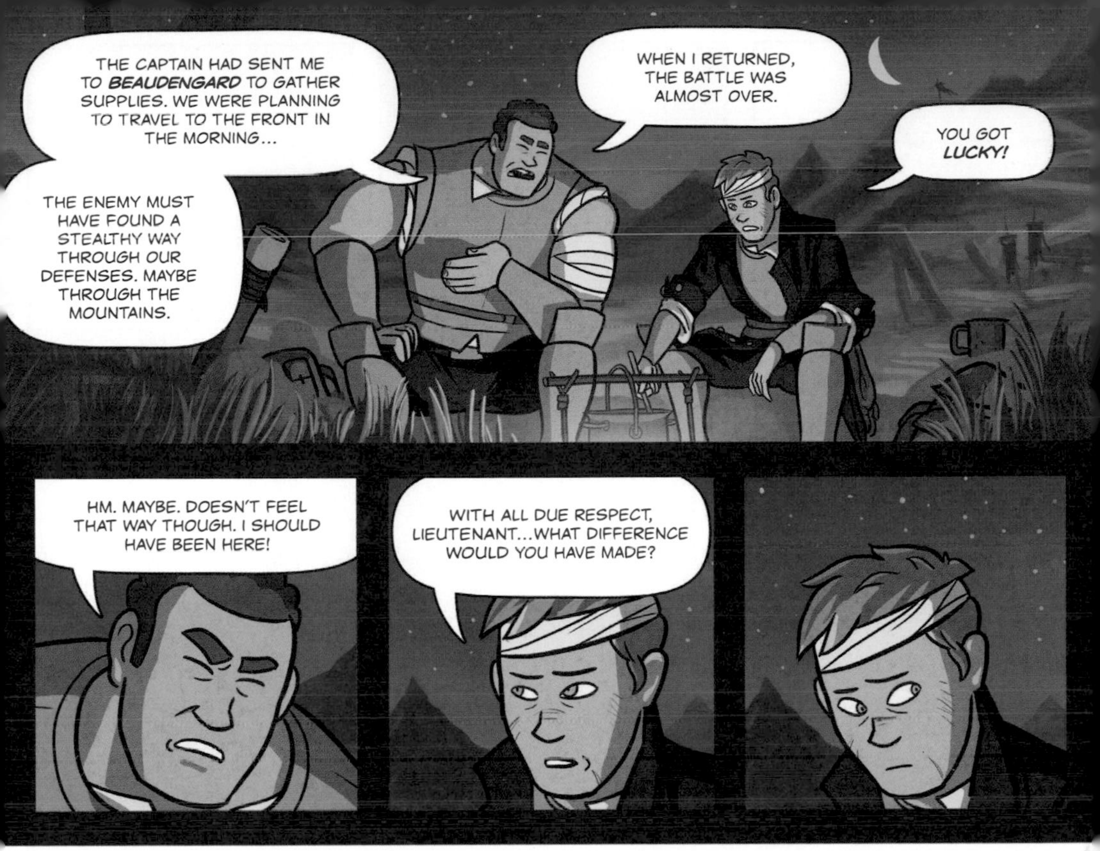
THE CAPTAIN HAD SENT ME TO BEAUDENGARD TO GATHER SUPPLIES. WE WERE PLANNING TO TRAVEL TO THE FRONT IN THE MORNING...
THE ENEMY MUST HAVE FOUND A STEALTHY WAY THROUGH OUR DEFENSES. MAYBE THROUGH THE MOUNTAINS.
WHEN I RETURNED, THE BATTLE WAS ALMOST OVER.
YOU GOT LUCKY!
HM. MAYBE. DOESN'T FEEL THAT WAY THOUGH. I SHOULD HAVE BEEN HERE!
WITH ALL DUE RESPECT, LIEUTENANT...WHAT DIFFERENCE WOULD YOU HAVE MADE?

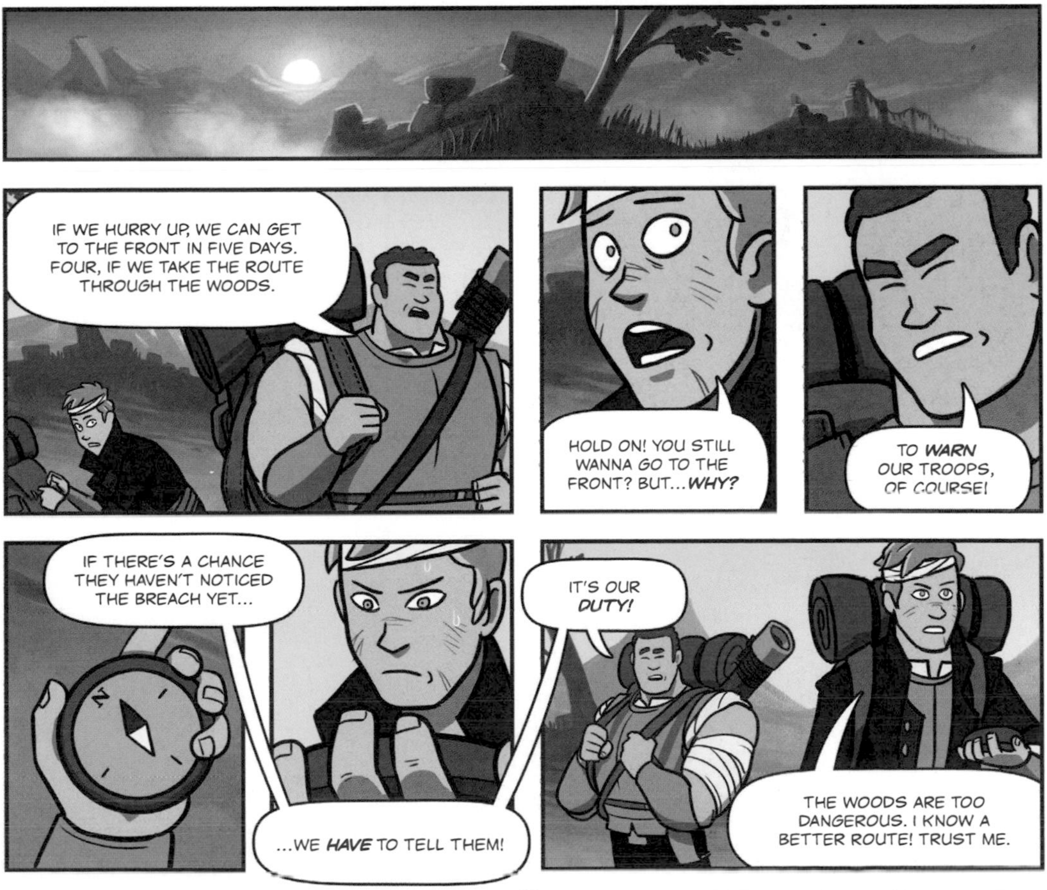
IF WE HURRY UP, WE CAN GET TO THE FRONT IN FIVE DAYS. FOUR, IF WE TAKE THE ROUTE THROUGH THE WOODS.
HOLD ON! YOU STILL WANNA GO TO THE FRONT? BUT...WHY?
TO WARN OUR TROOPS, OF COURSE!
IF THERE'S A CHANCE THEY HAVEN'T NOTICED THE BREACH YET...
...WE HAVE TO TELL THEM!
IT'S OUR DUTY!
THE WOODS ARE TOO DANGEROUS. I KNOW A BETTER ROUTE! TRUST ME.

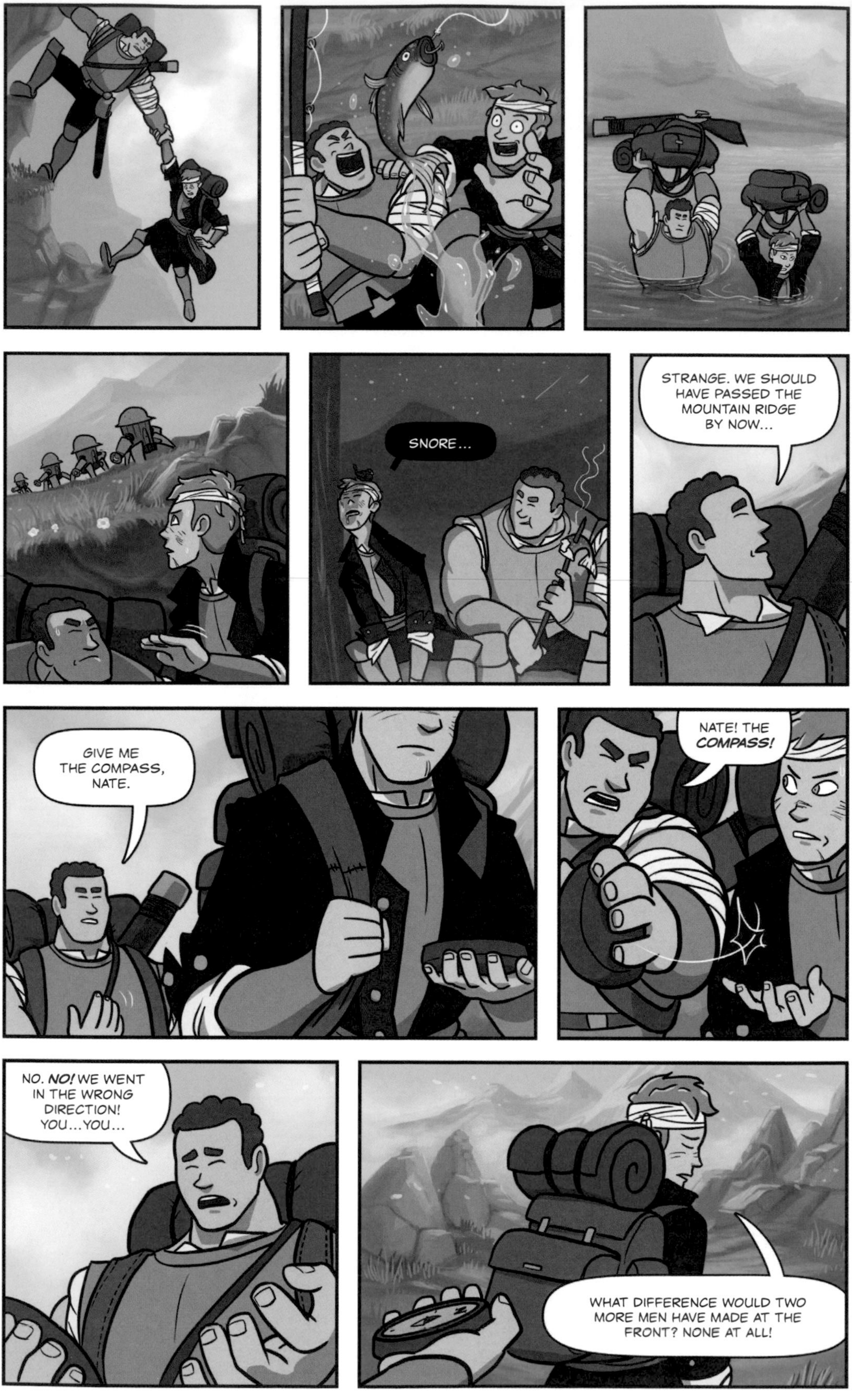
SNORE...
STRANGE. WE SHOULD HAVE PASSED THE MOUNTAIN RIDGE BY NOW...
GIVE ME THE COMPASS, NATE.
NATE! THE ***COMPASS!***
NO. ***NO!*** WE WENT IN THE WRONG DIRECTION! YOU...YOU...
WHAT DIFFERENCE WOULD TWO MORE MEN HAVE MADE AT THE FRONT? NONE AT ALL!

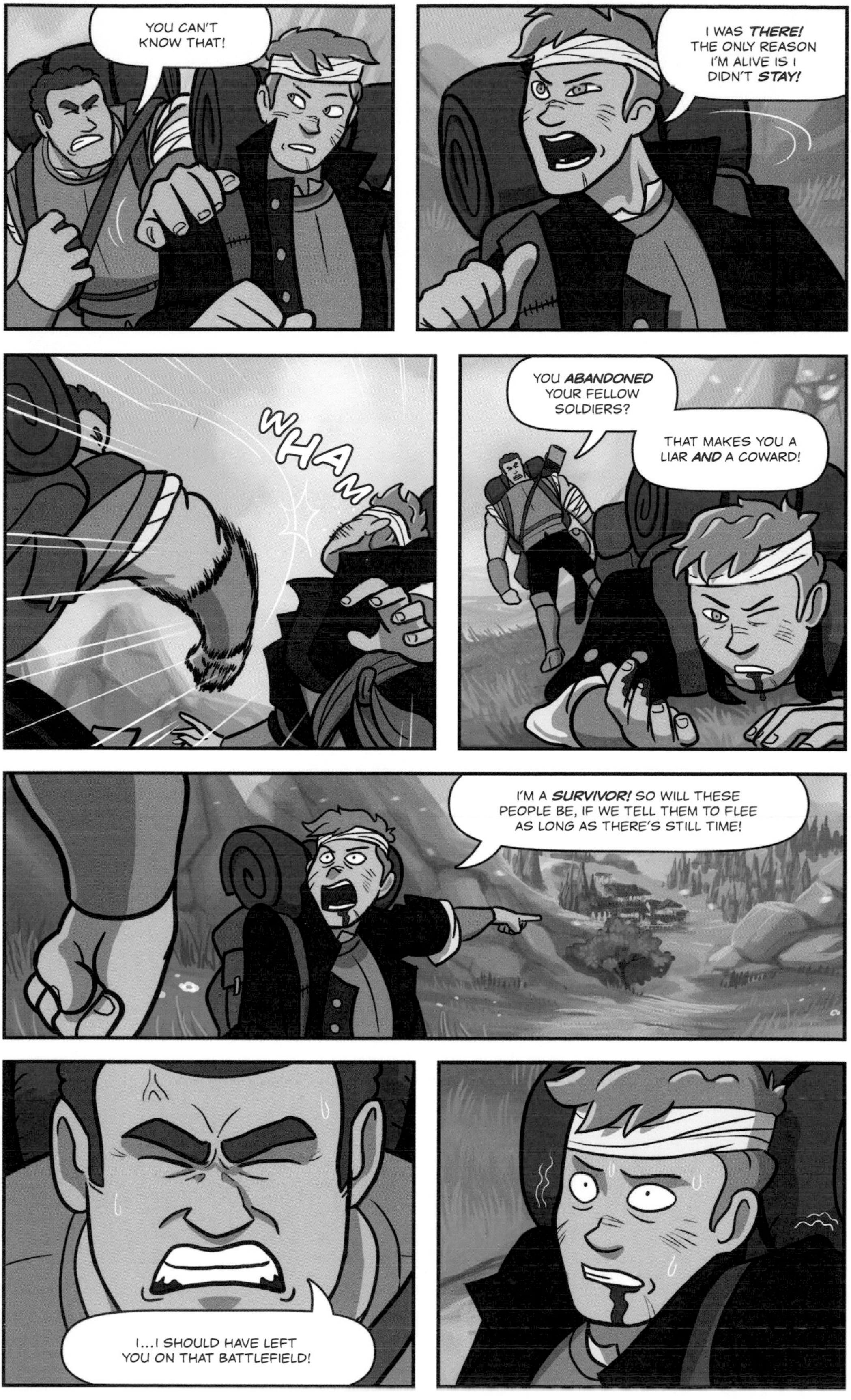
YOU CAN'T KNOW THAT!
I WAS THERE! THE ONLY REASON I'M ALIVE IS I DIDN'T STAY!
WHAM
YOU ABANDONED YOUR FELLOW SOLDIERS?
THAT MAKES YOU A LIAR AND A COWARD!
I'M A SURVIVOR! SO WILL THESE PEOPLE BE, IF WE TELL THEM TO FLEE AS LONG AS THERE'S STILL TIME!
I...I SHOULD HAVE LEFT YOU ON THAT BATTLEFIELD!

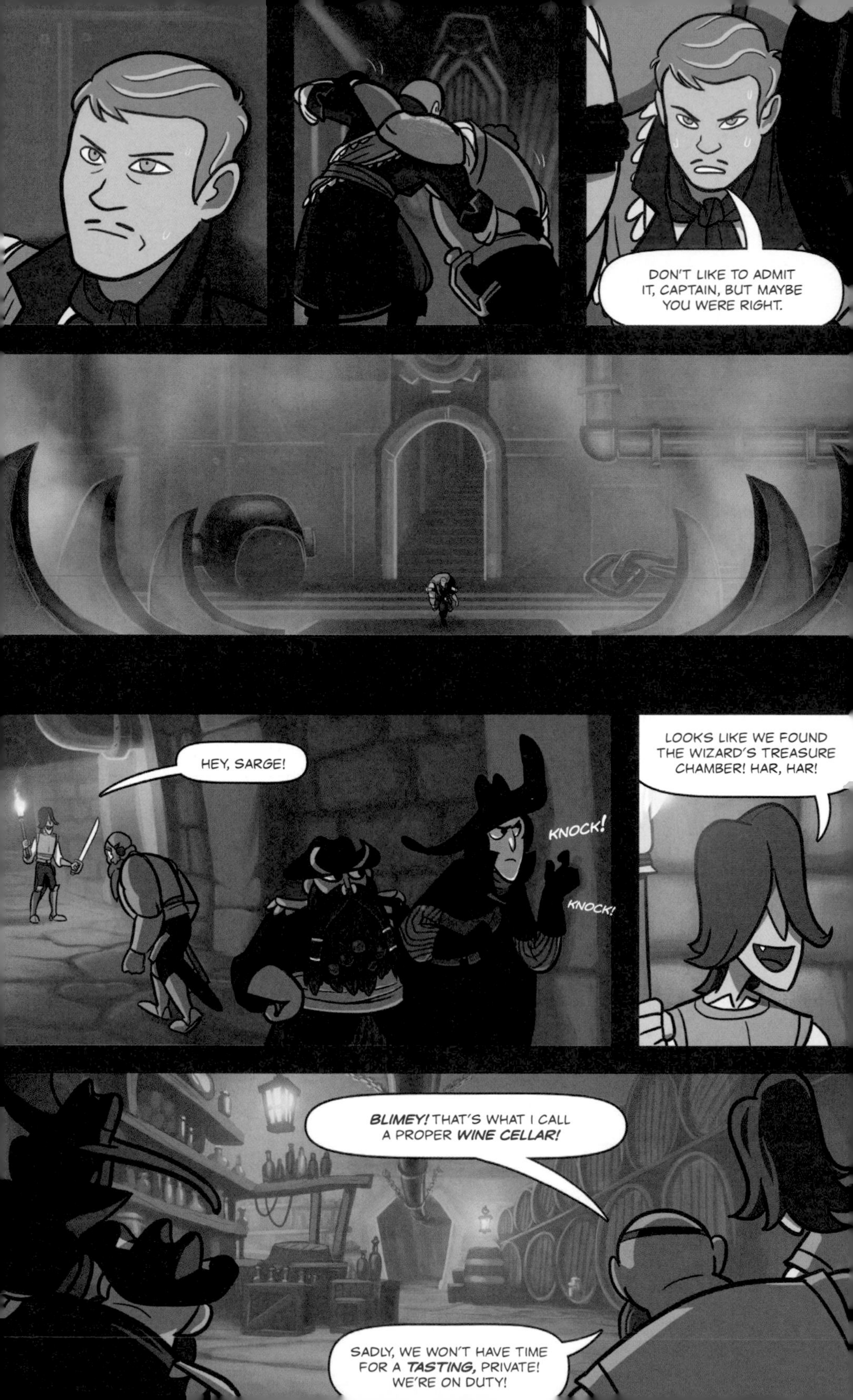
DON'T LIKE TO ADMIT IT, CAPTAIN, BUT MAYBE YOU WERE RIGHT.
HEY, SARGE!
KNOCK!
KNOCK!
LOOKS LIKE WE FOUND THE WIZARD'S TREASURE CHAMBER! HAR, HAR!
BLIMEY! THAT'S WHAT I CALL A PROPER WINE CELLAR!
SADLY, WE WON'T HAVE TIME FOR A TASTING, PRIVATE! WE'RE ON DUTY!

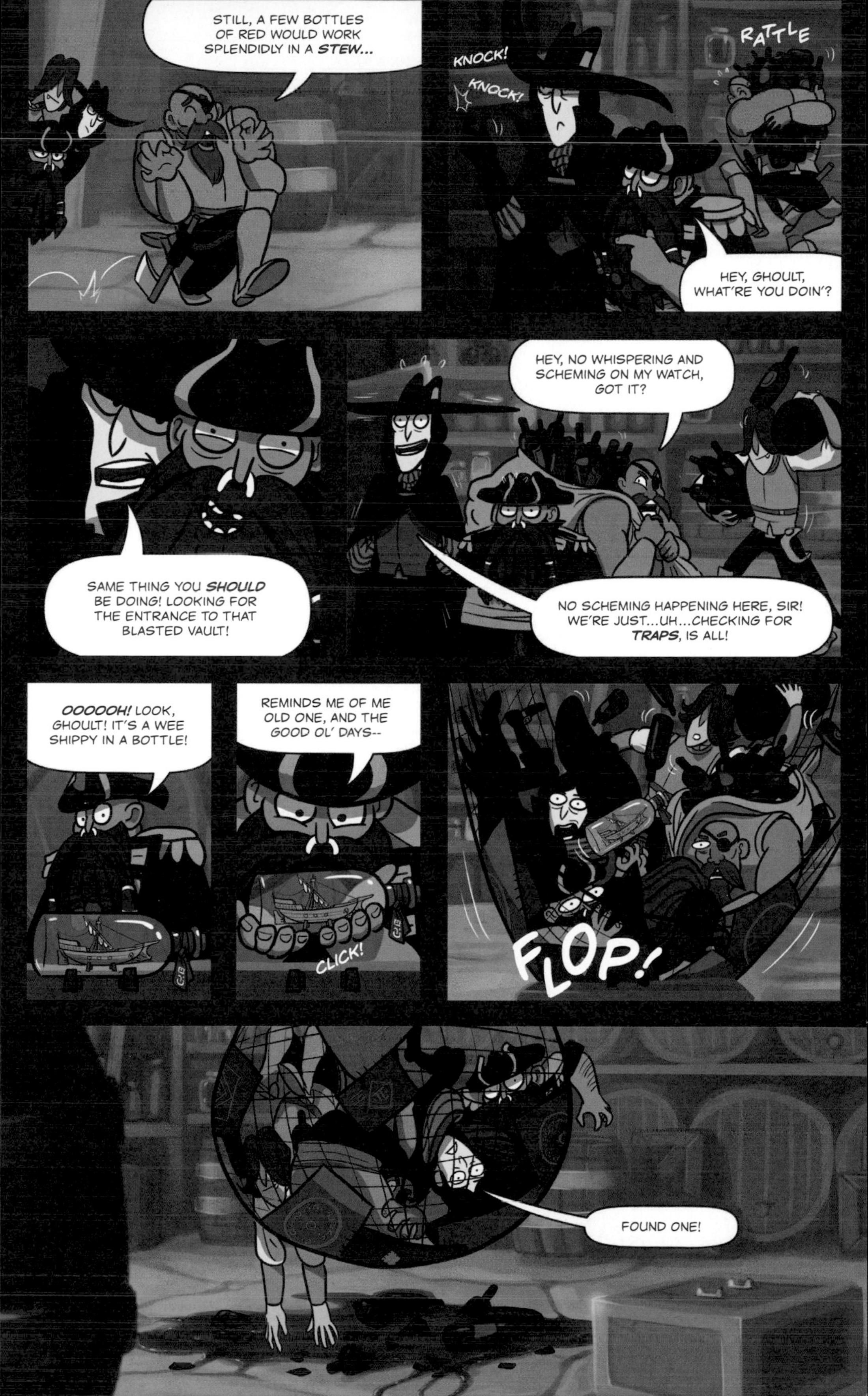
STILL, A FEW BOTTLES OF RED WOULD WORK SPLENDIDLY IN A *STEW...*
KNOCK!
KNOCK!
RATTLE
HEY, GHOULT, WHAT'RE YOU DOIN'?
SAME THING YOU *SHOULD* BE DOING! LOOKING FOR THE ENTRANCE TO THAT BLASTED VAULT!
HEY, NO WHISPERING AND SCHEMING ON MY WATCH, GOT IT?
NO SCHEMING HAPPENING HERE, SIR! WE'RE JUST...UH...CHECKING FOR *TRAPS*, IS ALL!
OOOOOH! LOOK, GHOULT! IT'S A WEE SHIPPY IN A BOTTLE!
REMINDS ME OF ME OLD ONE, AND THE GOOD OL' DAYS--
CLICK!
FLOP!
FOUND ONE!

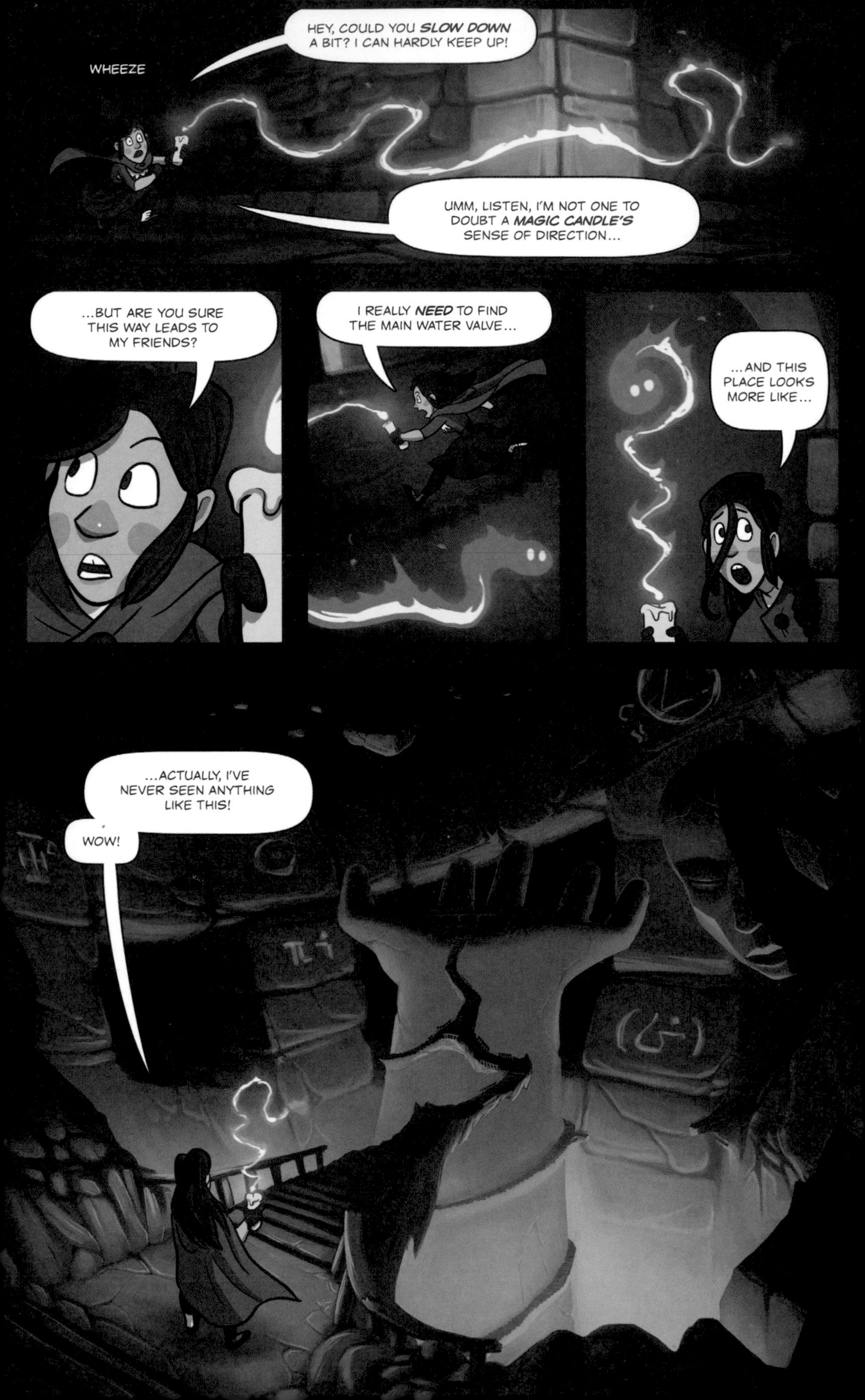
WHEEZE
HEY, COULD YOU SLOW DOWN A BIT? I CAN HARDLY KEEP UP!
UMM, LISTEN, I'M NOT ONE TO DOUBT A MAGIC CANDLE'S SENSE OF DIRECTION...
...BUT ARE YOU SURE THIS WAY LEADS TO MY FRIENDS?
I REALLY NEED TO FIND THE MAIN WATER VALVE...
...AND THIS PLACE LOOKS MORE LIKE...
...ACTUALLY, I'VE NEVER SEEN ANYTHING LIKE THIS!
WOW!

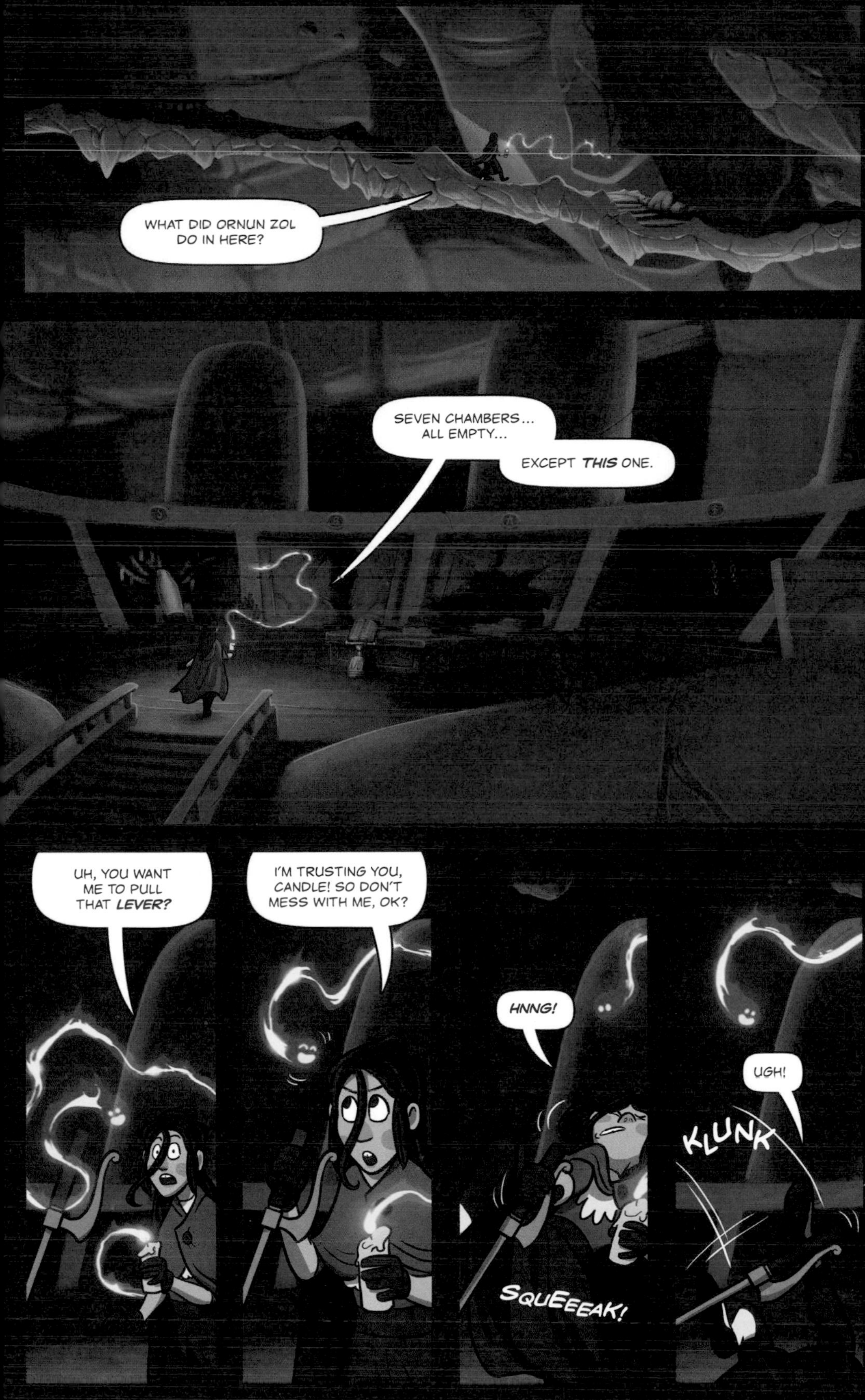
WHAT DID ORNUN ZOL DO IN HERE?
SEVEN CHAMBERS... ALL EMPTY...
EXCEPT *THIS* ONE.
UH, YOU WANT ME TO PULL THAT *LEVER?*
I'M TRUSTING YOU, CANDLE! SO DON'T MESS WITH ME, OK?
HNNG!
SQUEEEAK!
UGH!
KLUNK

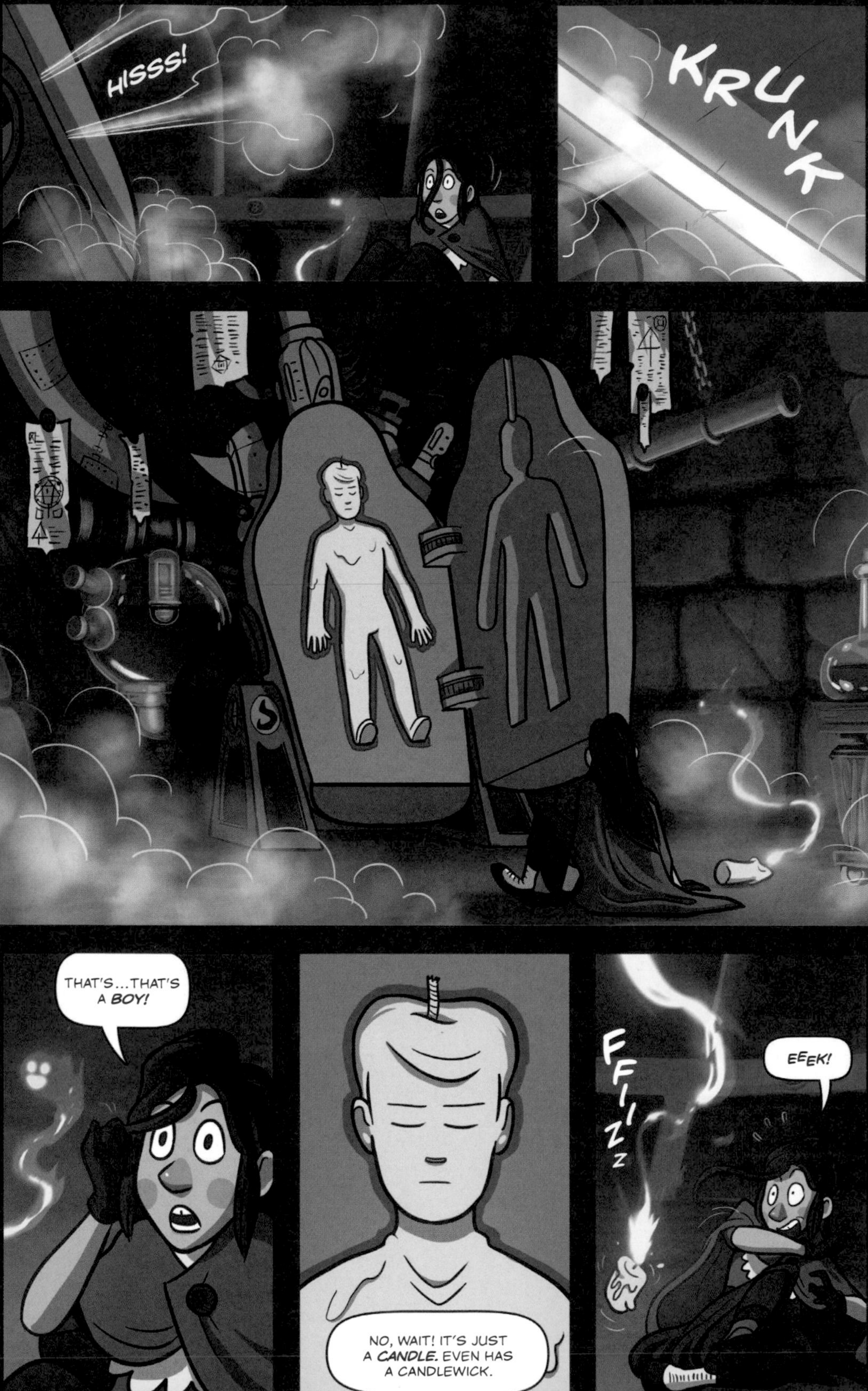
HISSS!
KRUNK
THAT'S...THAT'S A *BOY!*
NO, WAIT! IT'S JUST A *CANDLE.* EVEN HAS A CANDLEWICK.
FFIIZZZ
EEEK!

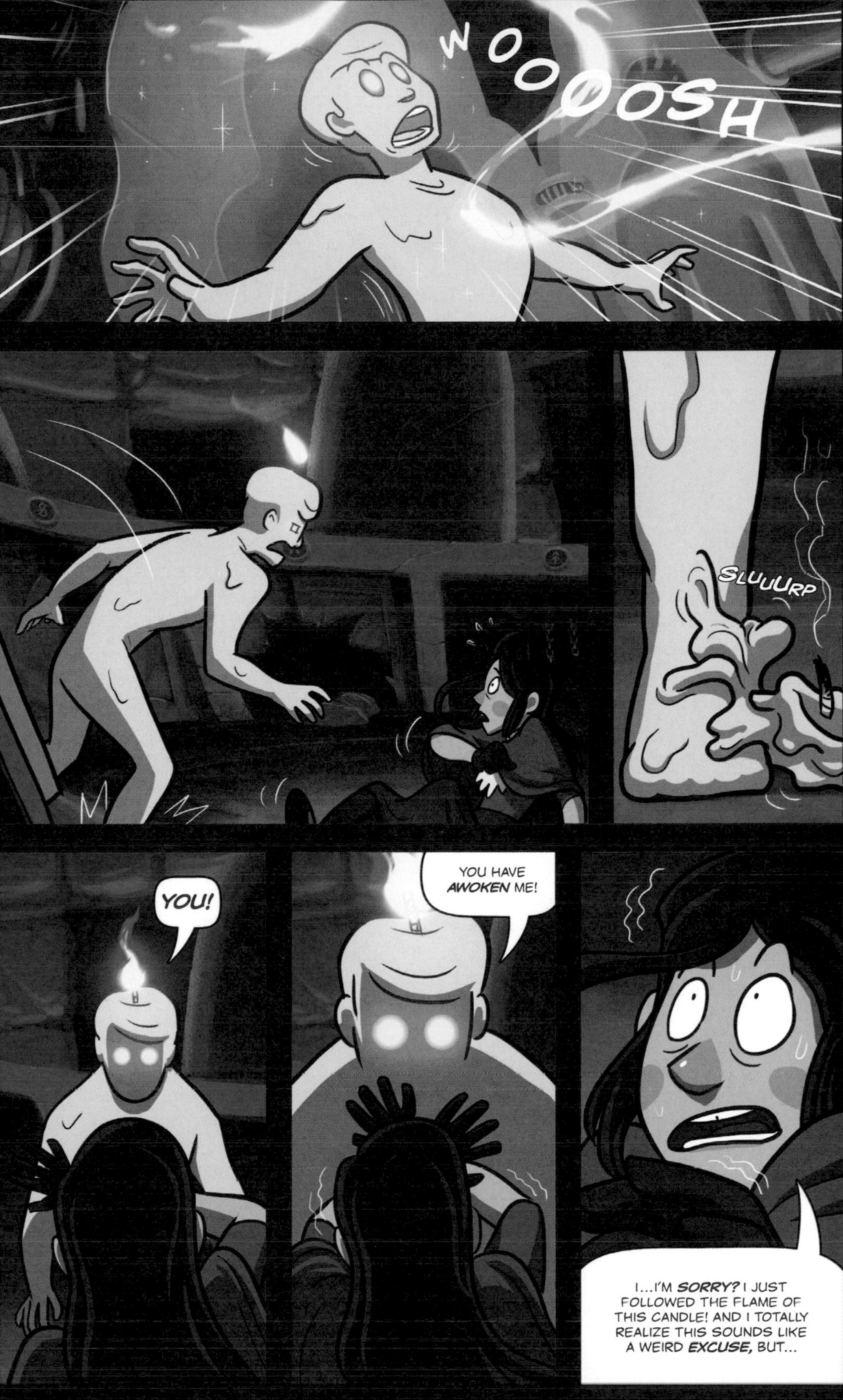
WOOOOOSH
SLUUURP
YOU!
YOU HAVE AWOKEN ME!
I...I'M SORRY? I JUST FOLLOWED THE FLAME OF THIS CANDLE! AND I TOTALLY REALIZE THIS SOUNDS LIKE A WEIRD EXCUSE, BUT...

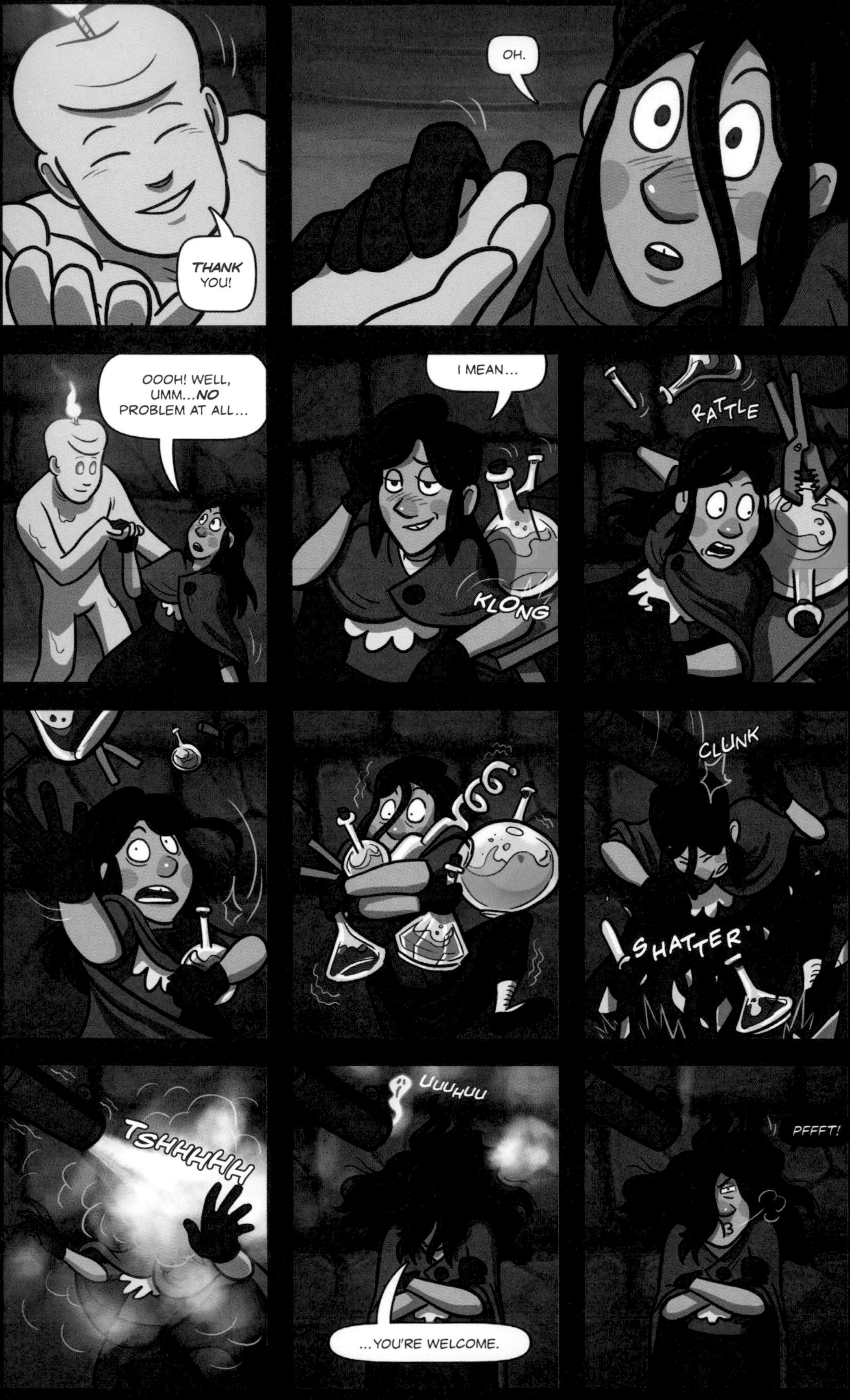
THANK YOU!
OH.
OOOH! WELL, UMM...NO PROBLEM AT ALL...
I MEAN...
KLONG
RATTLE
CLUNK
SHATTER
TSHHHHHH
UUUHUU
...YOU'RE WELCOME.
PFFFT!

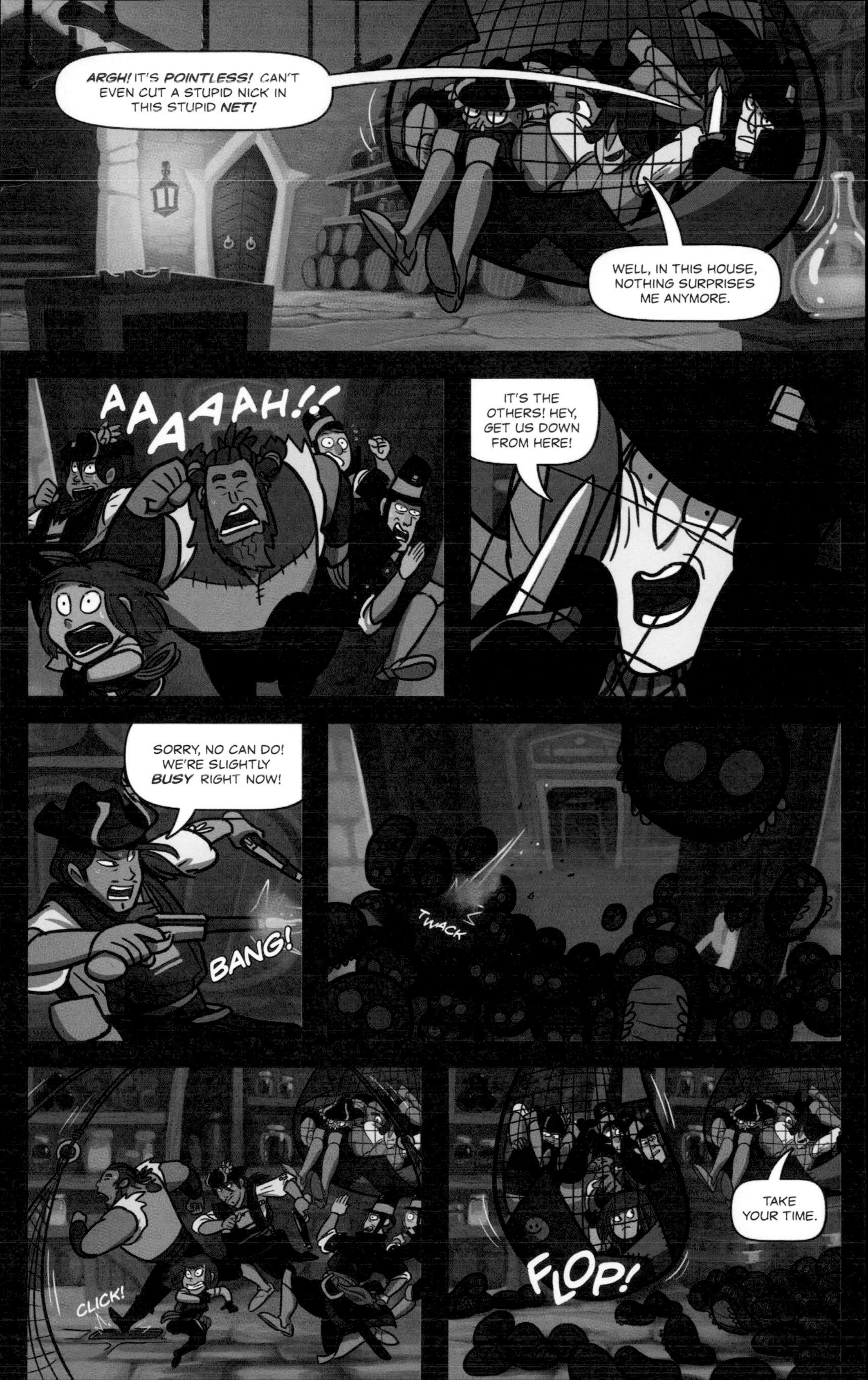
ARGH! IT'S POINTLESS! CAN'T EVEN CUT A STUPID NICK IN THIS STUPID NET!
WELL, IN THIS HOUSE, NOTHING SURPRISES ME ANYMORE.
AAAAAH!!!
IT'S THE OTHERS! HEY, GET US DOWN FROM HERE!
SORRY, NO CAN DO! WE'RE SLIGHTLY BUSY RIGHT NOW!
BANG!
TWACK
CLICK!
FLOP!
TAKE YOUR TIME.

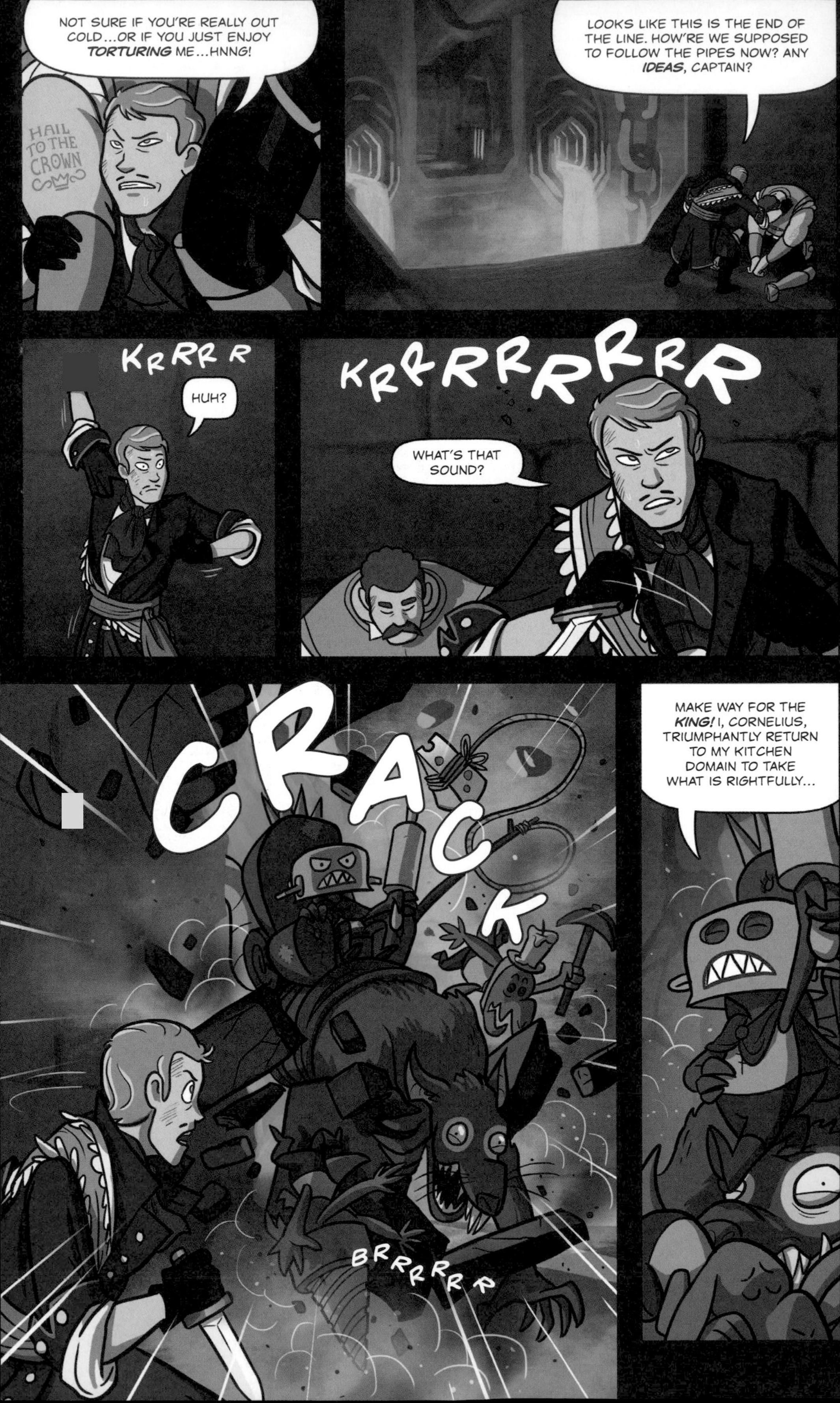
NOT SURE IF YOU'RE REALLY OUT COLD...OR IF YOU JUST ENJOY *TORTURING* ME...HNNG!
HAIL TO THE CROWN
LOOKS LIKE THIS IS THE END OF THE LINE. HOW'RE WE SUPPOSED TO FOLLOW THE PIPES NOW? ANY *IDEAS*, CAPTAIN?
KRRRR
HUH?
KRRRRRRRRRR
WHAT'S THAT SOUND?
CRACK
BRRRRRR
MAKE WAY FOR THE *KING!* I, CORNELIUS, TRIUMPHANTLY RETURN TO MY KITCHEN DOMAIN TO TAKE WHAT IS RIGHTFULLY...

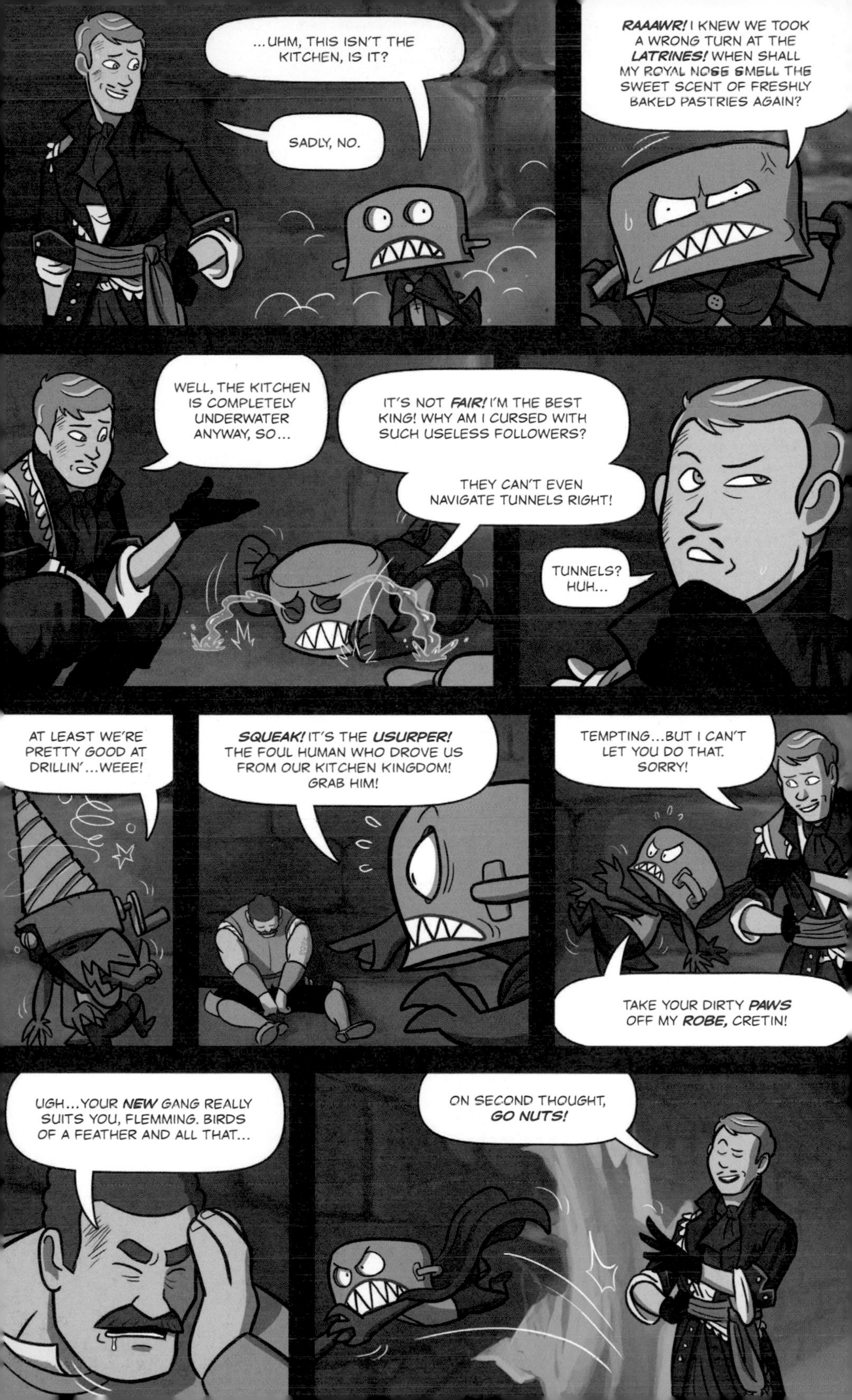
...UHM, THIS ISN'T THE KITCHEN, IS IT?
SADLY, NO.
RAAAWR! I KNEW WE TOOK A WRONG TURN AT THE LATRINES! WHEN SHALL MY ROYAL NOSE SMELL THE SWEET SCENT OF FRESHLY BAKED PASTRIES AGAIN?
WELL, THE KITCHEN IS COMPLETELY UNDERWATER ANYWAY, SO...
IT'S NOT FAIR! I'M THE BEST KING! WHY AM I CURSED WITH SUCH USELESS FOLLOWERS?
THEY CAN'T EVEN NAVIGATE TUNNELS RIGHT!
TUNNELS? HUH...
AT LEAST WE'RE PRETTY GOOD AT DRILLIN'...WEEE!
SQUEAK! IT'S THE USURPER! THE FOUL HUMAN WHO DROVE US FROM OUR KITCHEN KINGDOM! GRAB HIM!
TEMPTING...BUT I CAN'T LET YOU DO THAT. SORRY!
TAKE YOUR DIRTY PAWS OFF MY ROBE, CRETIN!
UGH...YOUR NEW GANG REALLY SUITS YOU, FLEMMING. BIRDS OF A FEATHER AND ALL THAT...
ON SECOND THOUGHT, GO NUTS!

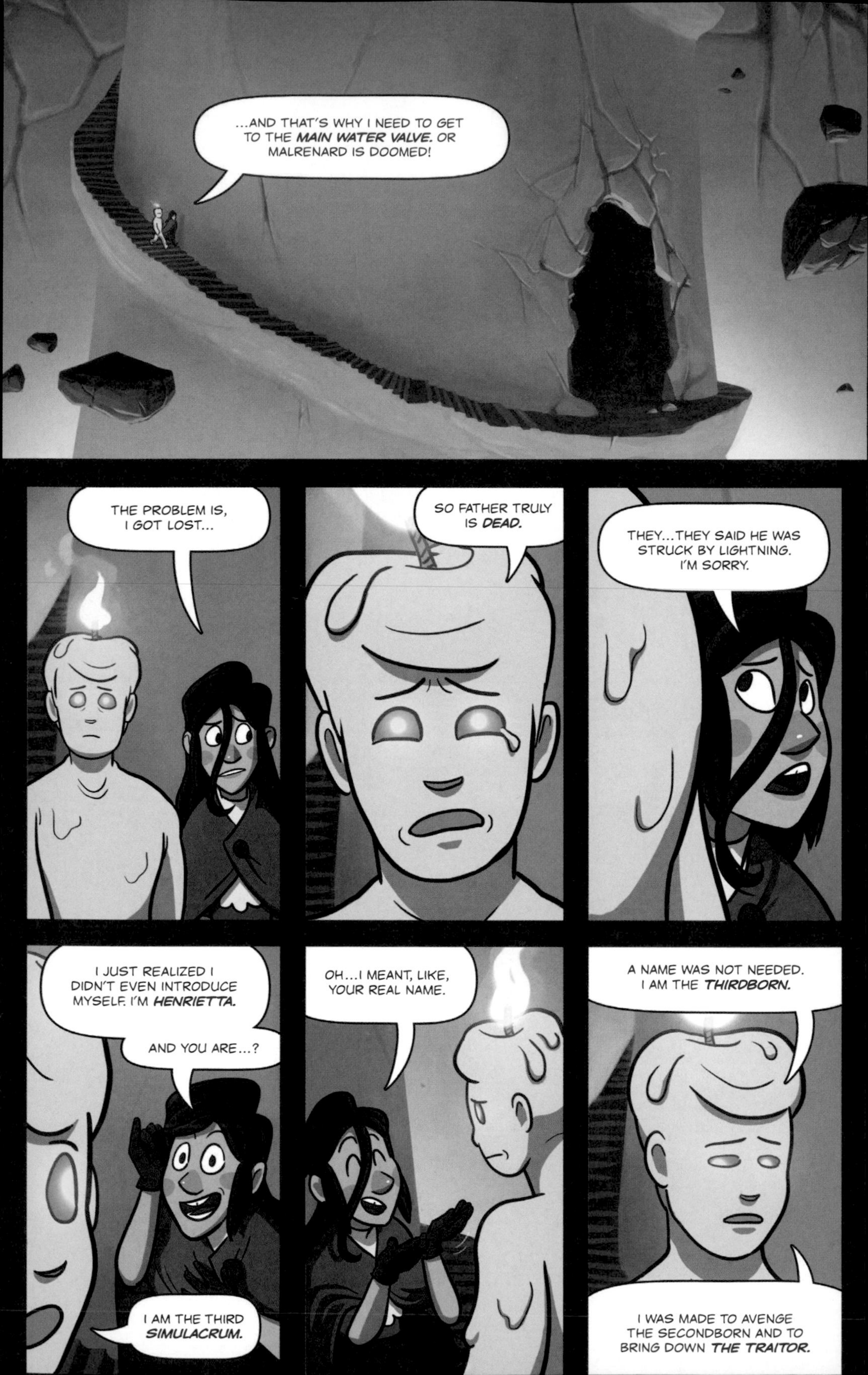

...AND THAT'S WHY I NEED TO GET TO THE ***MAIN WATER VALVE.*** OR MALRENARD IS DOOMED!
THE PROBLEM IS, I GOT LOST...
SO FATHER TRULY IS ***DEAD.***
THEY...THEY SAID HE WAS STRUCK BY LIGHTNING. I'M SORRY.
I JUST REALIZED I DIDN'T EVEN INTRODUCE MYSELF. I'M ***HENRIETTA.***
AND YOU ARE...?
I AM THE THIRD ***SIMULACRUM.***
OH...I MEANT, LIKE, YOUR REAL NAME.
A NAME WAS NOT NEEDED. I AM THE ***THIRDBORN.***
I WAS MADE TO AVENGE THE SECONDBORN AND TO BRING DOWN ***THE TRAITOR.***

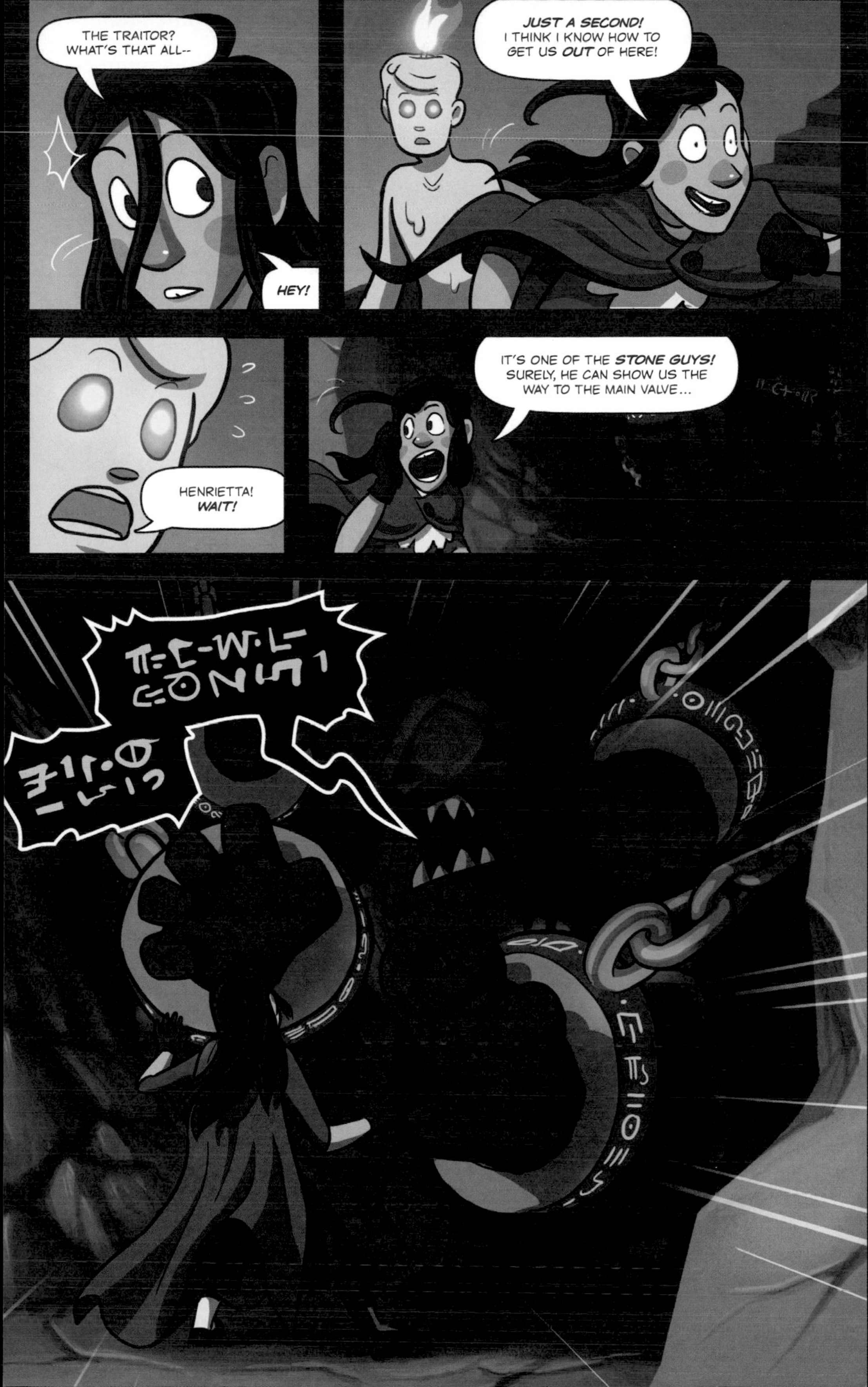
THE TRAITOR? WHAT'S THAT ALL--
HEY!
JUST A SECOND! I THINK I KNOW HOW TO GET US OUT OF HERE!
HENRIETTA! WAIT!
IT'S ONE OF THE STONE GUYS! SURELY, HE CAN SHOW US THE WAY TO THE MAIN VALVE...

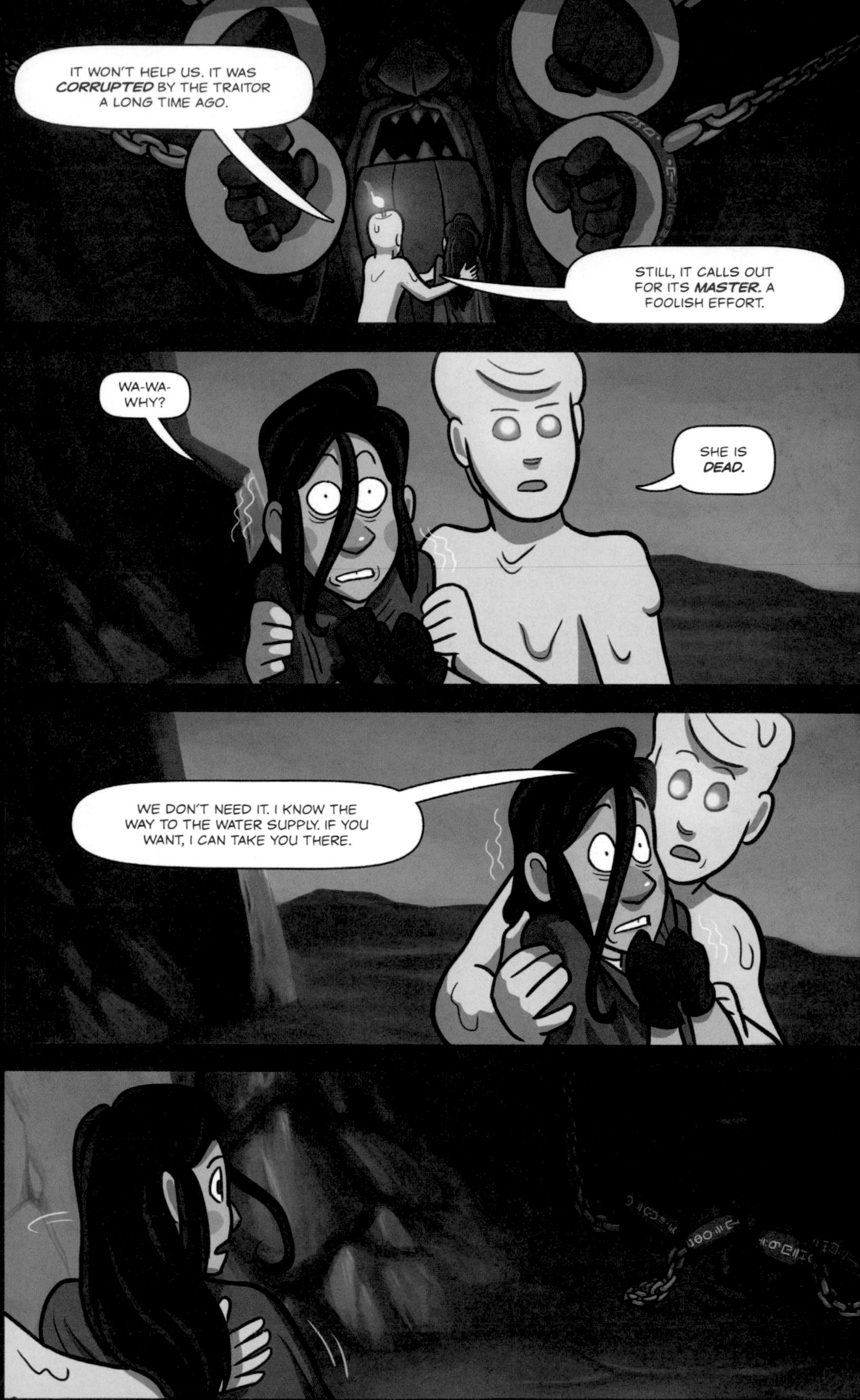
IT WON'T HELP US. IT WAS CORRUPTED BY THE TRAITOR A LONG TIME AGO.
STILL, IT CALLS OUT FOR ITS MASTER. A FOOLISH EFFORT.
WA-WA-WHY?
SHE IS DEAD.
WE DON'T NEED IT. I KNOW THE WAY TO THE WATER SUPPLY. IF YOU WANT, I CAN TAKE YOU THERE.

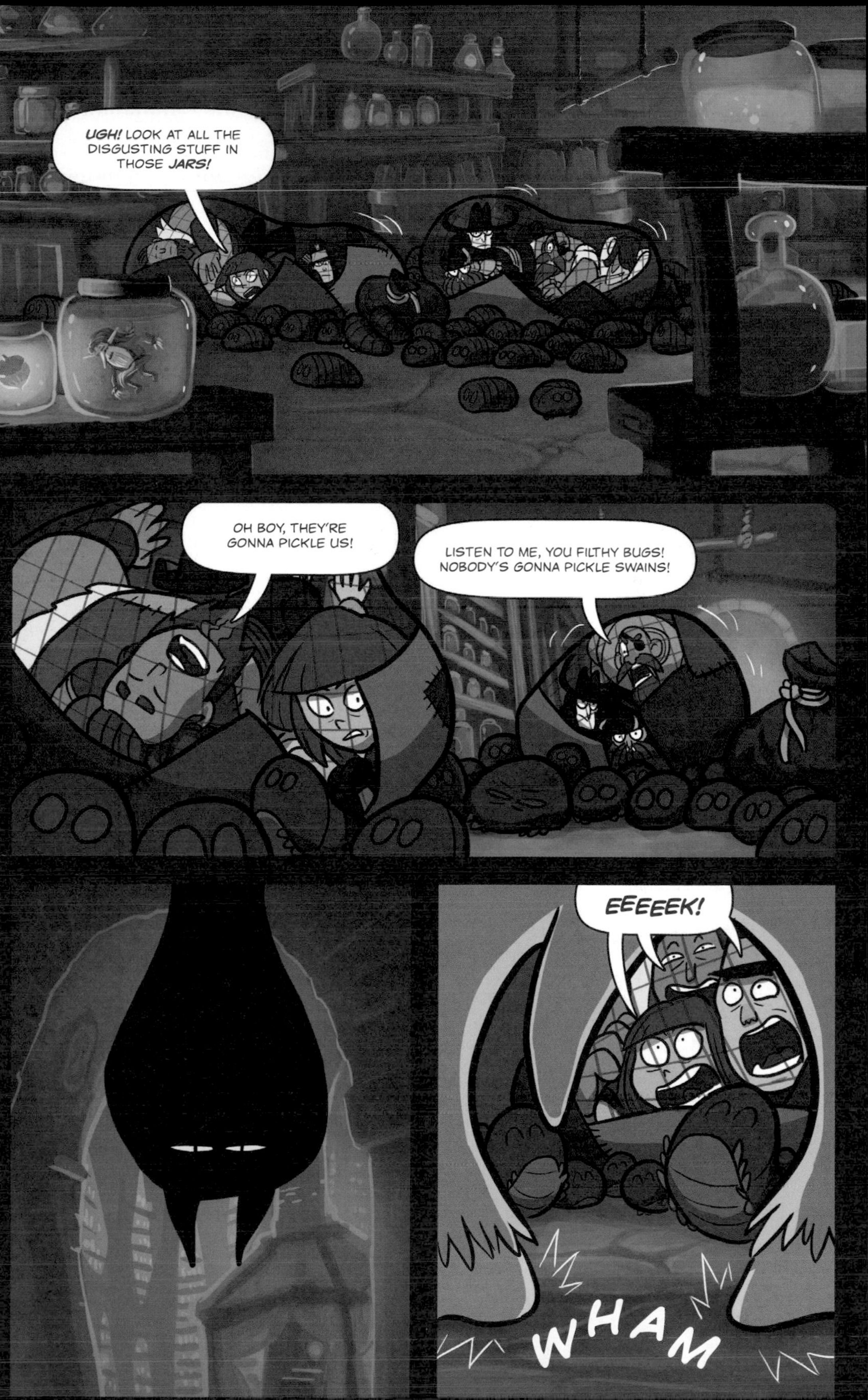
UGH! LOOK AT ALL THE DISGUSTING STUFF IN THOSE JARS!
OH BOY, THEY'RE GONNA PICKLE US!
LISTEN TO ME, YOU FILTHY BUGS! NOBODY'S GONNA PICKLE SWAINS!
EEEEEK!
WHAM

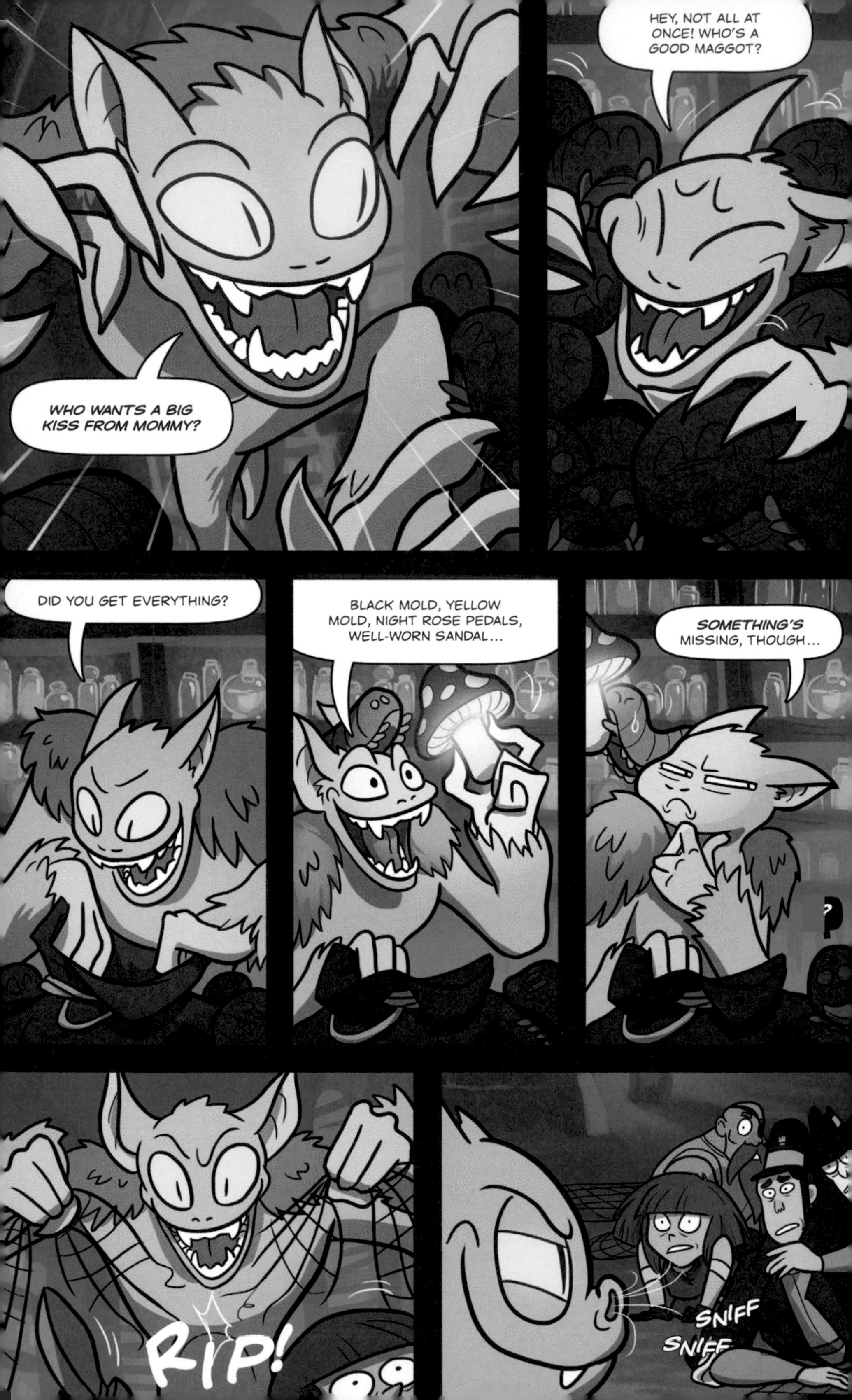

WHO WANTS A BIG KISS FROM MOMMY?
HEY, NOT ALL AT ONCE! WHO'S A GOOD MAGGOT?
DID YOU GET EVERYTHING?
BLACK MOLD, YELLOW MOLD, NIGHT ROSE PEDALS, WELL-WORN SANDAL...
SOMETHING'S MISSING, THOUGH...
RIP!
SNIFF
SNIFF

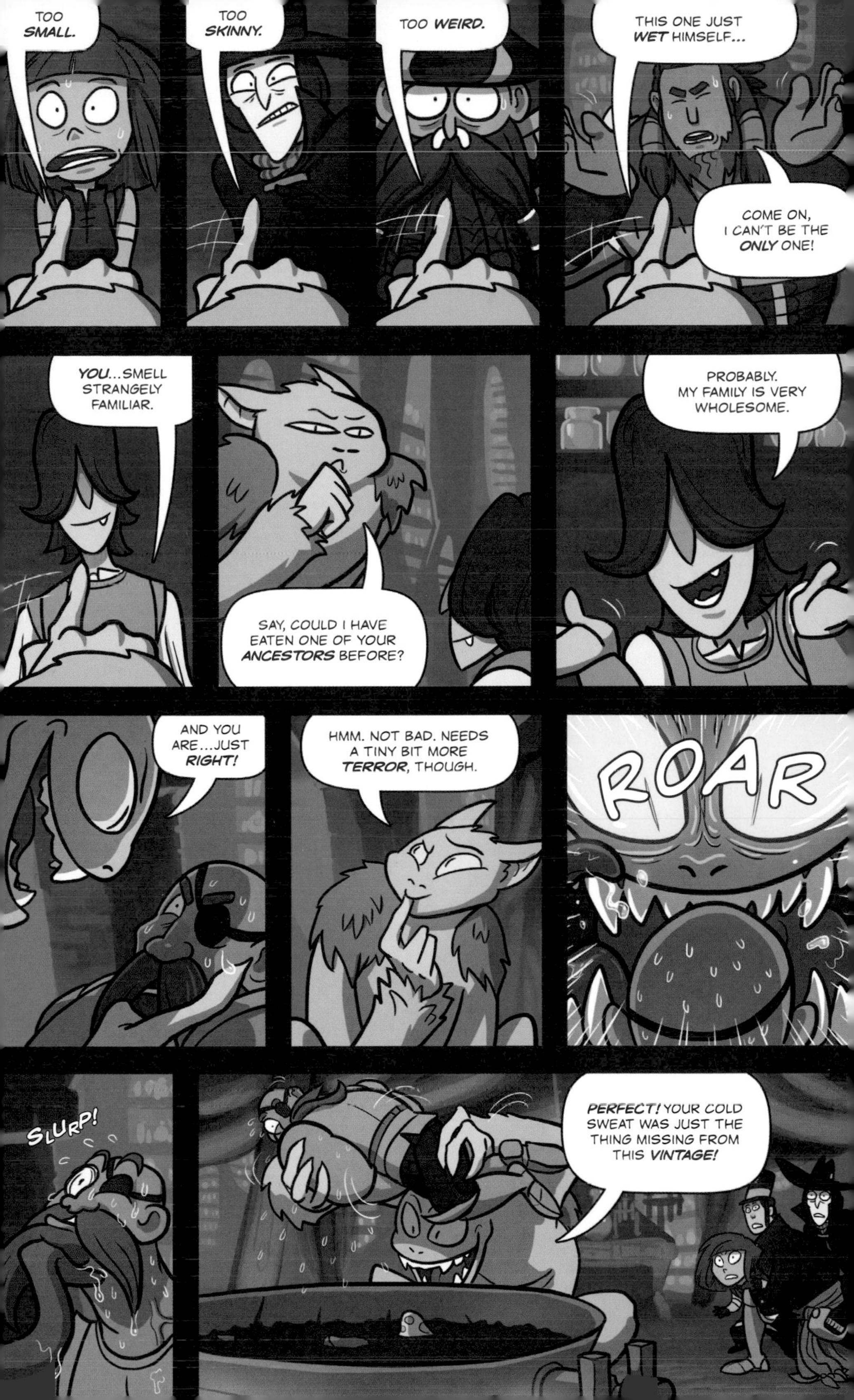
TOO SMALL.
TOO SKINNY.
TOO WEIRD.
THIS ONE JUST WET HIMSELF...
COME ON, I CAN'T BE THE ONLY ONE!
YOU...SMELL STRANGELY FAMILIAR.
SAY, COULD I HAVE EATEN ONE OF YOUR ANCESTORS BEFORE?
PROBABLY. MY FAMILY IS VERY WHOLESOME.
AND YOU ARE...JUST RIGHT!
HMM. NOT BAD. NEEDS A TINY BIT MORE TERROR, THOUGH.
ROAR
SLURP!
PERFECT! YOUR COLD SWEAT WAS JUST THE THING MISSING FROM THIS VINTAGE!

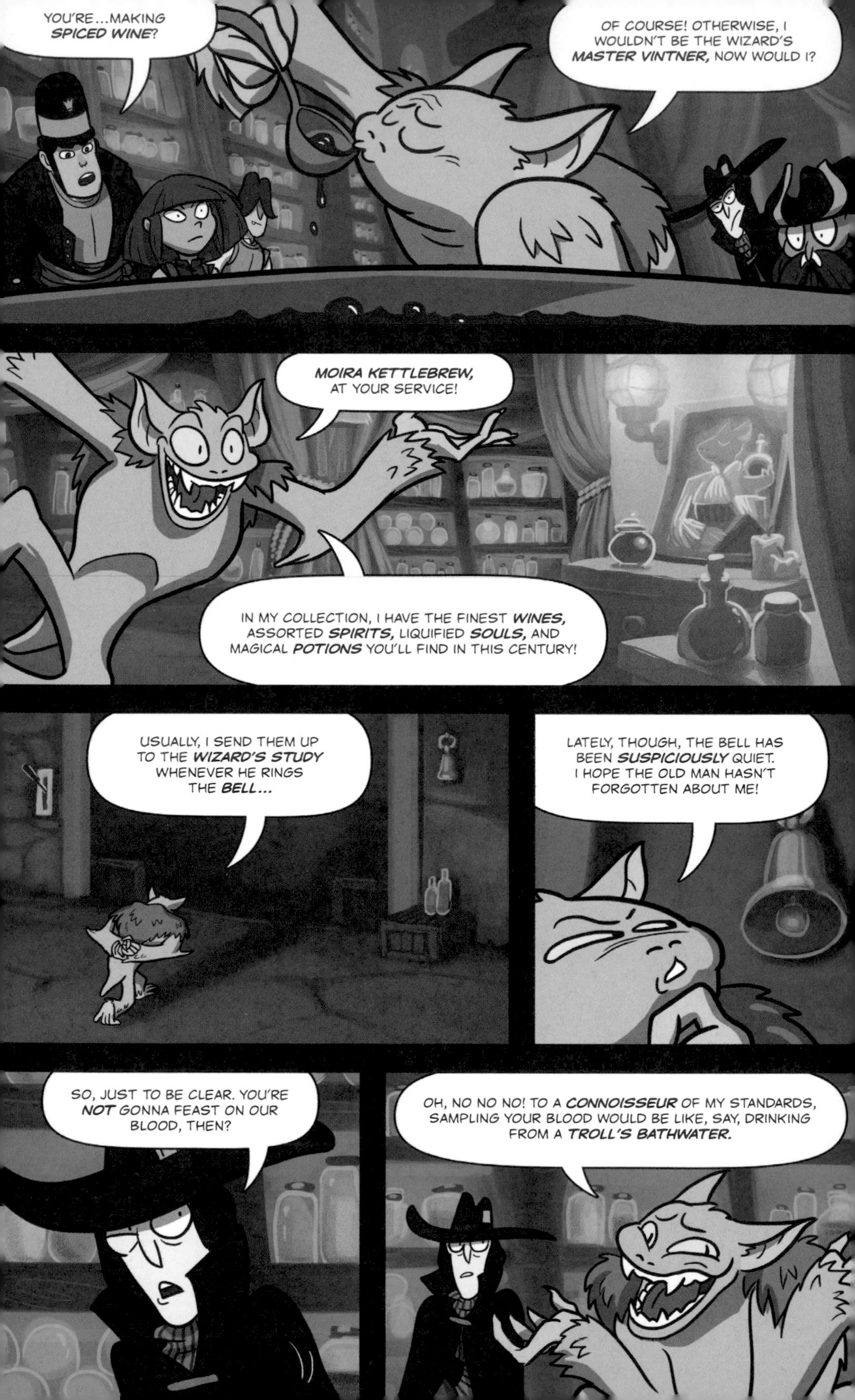
YOU'RE...MAKING SPICED WINE?
OF COURSE! OTHERWISE, I WOULDN'T BE THE WIZARD'S MASTER VINTNER, NOW WOULD I?
MOIRA KETTLEBREW, AT YOUR SERVICE!
IN MY COLLECTION, I HAVE THE FINEST WINES, ASSORTED SPIRITS, LIQUIFIED SOULS, AND MAGICAL POTIONS YOU'LL FIND IN THIS CENTURY!
USUALLY, I SEND THEM UP TO THE WIZARD'S STUDY WHENEVER HE RINGS THE BELL...
LATELY, THOUGH, THE BELL HAS BEEN SUSPICIOUSLY QUIET. I HOPE THE OLD MAN HASN'T FORGOTTEN ABOUT ME!
SO, JUST TO BE CLEAR. YOU'RE NOT GONNA FEAST ON OUR BLOOD, THEN?
OH, NO NO NO! TO A CONNOISSEUR OF MY STANDARDS, SAMPLING YOUR BLOOD WOULD BE LIKE, SAY, DRINKING FROM A TROLL'S BATHWATER.

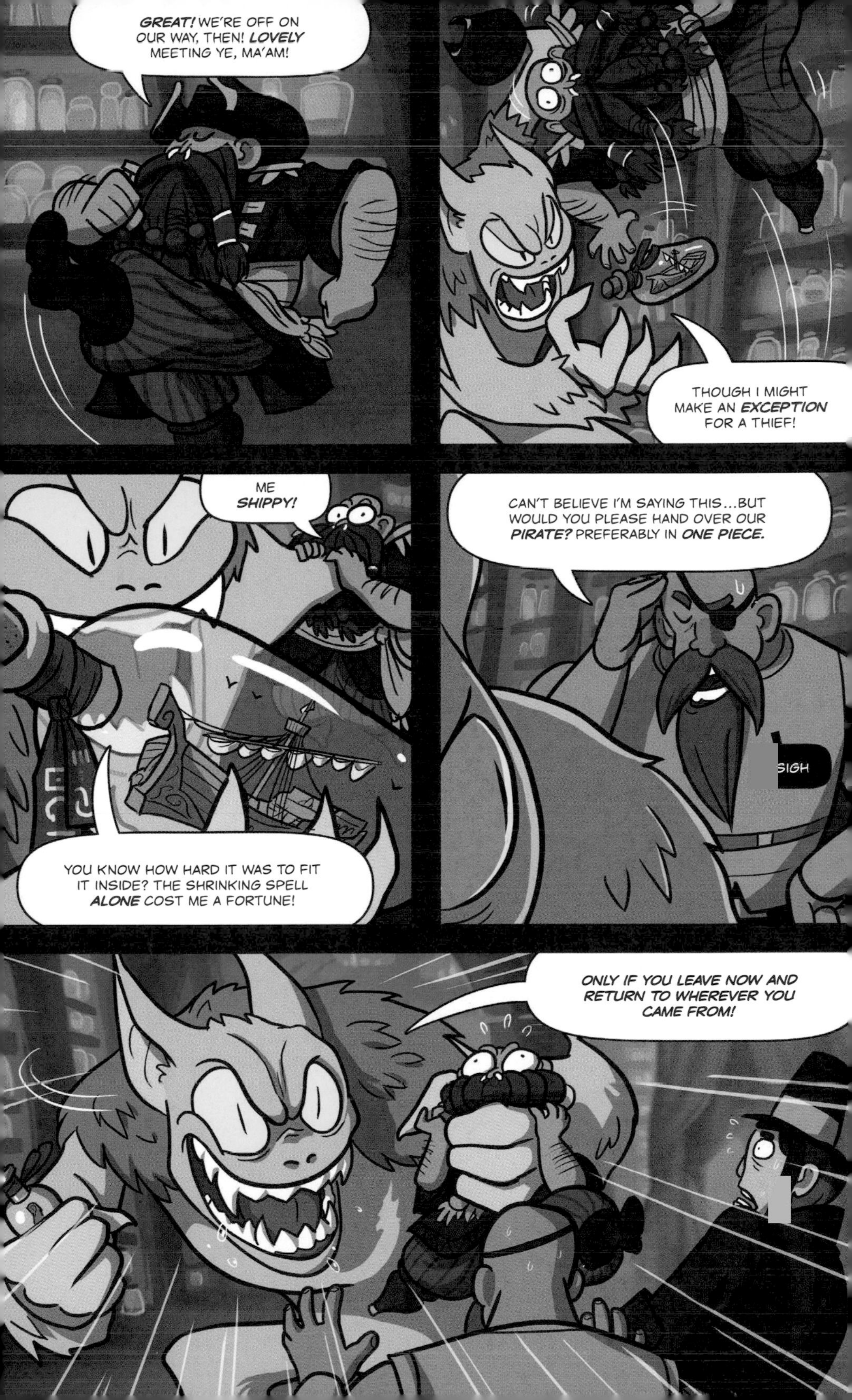
GREAT! WE'RE OFF ON OUR WAY, THEN! LOVELY MEETING YE, MA'AM!
THOUGH I MIGHT MAKE AN EXCEPTION FOR A THIEF!
ME SHIPPY!
YOU KNOW HOW HARD IT WAS TO FIT IT INSIDE? THE SHRINKING SPELL ALONE COST ME A FORTUNE!
CAN'T BELIEVE I'M SAYING THIS…BUT WOULD YOU PLEASE HAND OVER OUR PIRATE? PREFERABLY IN ONE PIECE.
SIGH
ONLY IF YOU LEAVE NOW AND RETURN TO WHEREVER YOU CAME FROM!

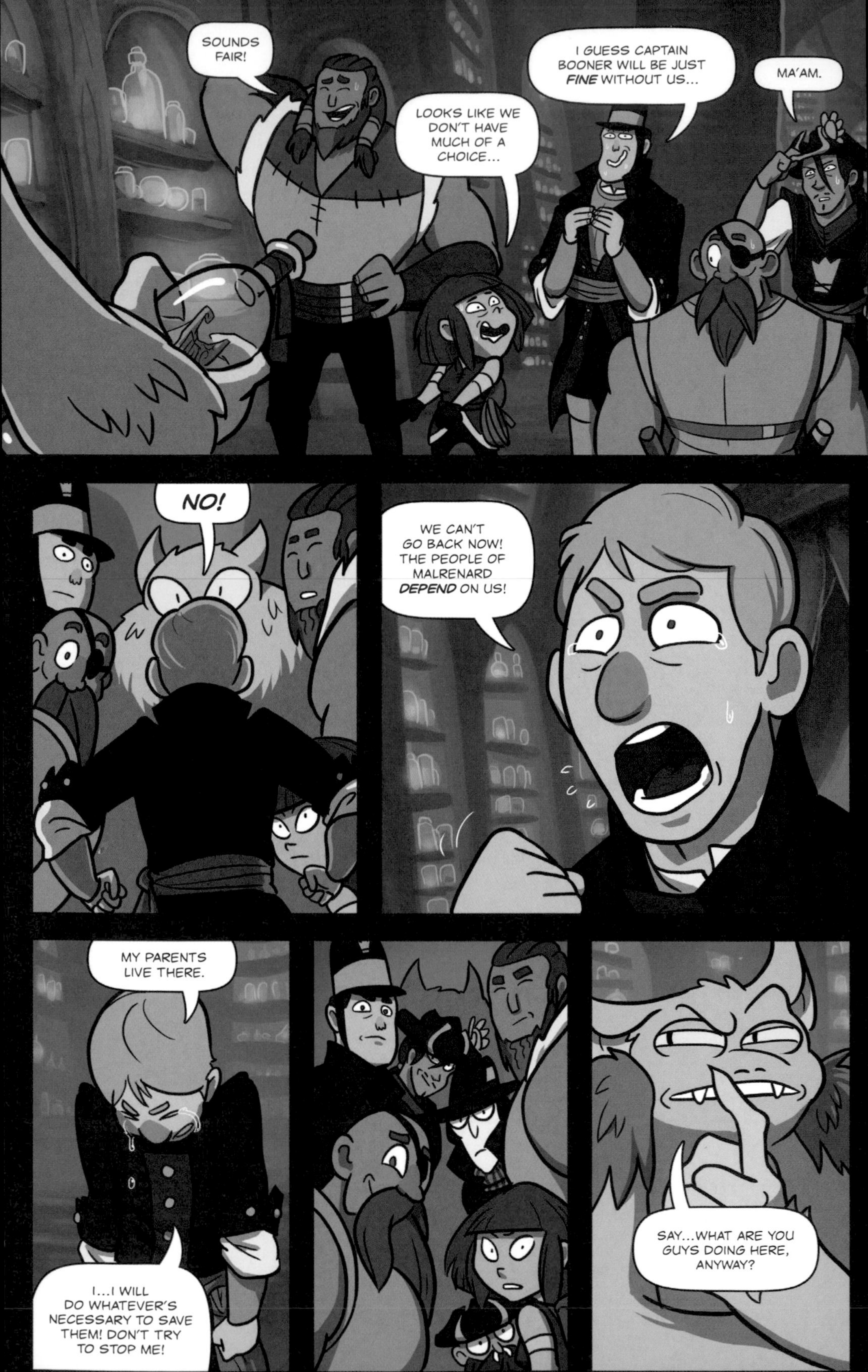
SOUNDS FAIR!
LOOKS LIKE WE DON'T HAVE MUCH OF A CHOICE...
I GUESS CAPTAIN BOONER WILL BE JUST *FINE* WITHOUT US...
MA'AM.
NO!
WE CAN'T GO BACK NOW! THE PEOPLE OF MALRENARD *DEPEND* ON US!
MY PARENTS LIVE THERE.
I...I WILL DO WHATEVER'S NECESSARY TO SAVE THEM! DON'T TRY TO STOP ME!
SAY...WHAT ARE YOU GUYS DOING HERE, ANYWAY?

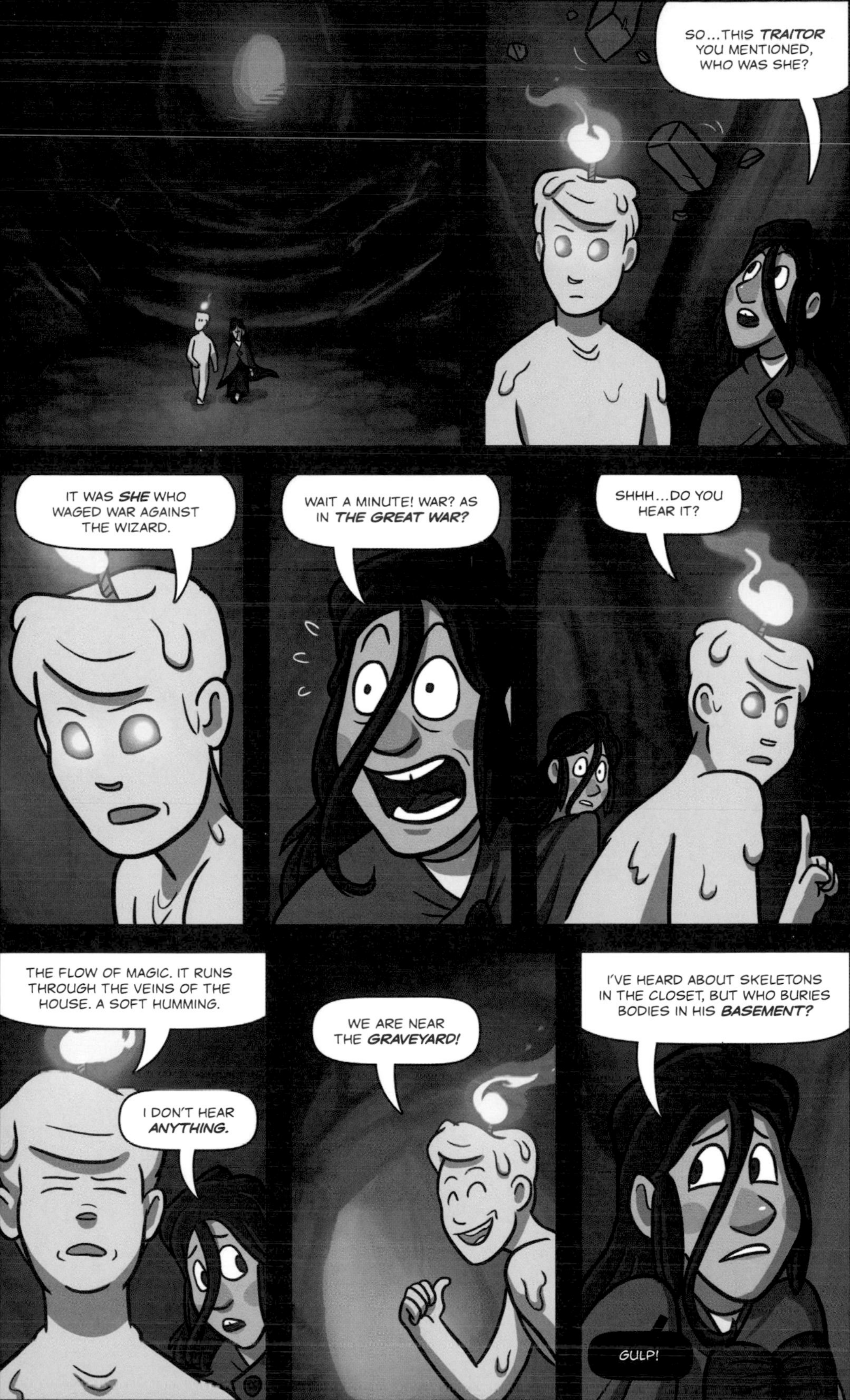

SO...THIS TRAITOR YOU MENTIONED, WHO WAS SHE?
IT WAS SHE WHO WAGED WAR AGAINST THE WIZARD.
WAIT A MINUTE! WAR? AS IN THE GREAT WAR?
SHHH...DO YOU HEAR IT?
THE FLOW OF MAGIC. IT RUNS THROUGH THE VEINS OF THE HOUSE. A SOFT HUMMING.
I DON'T HEAR ANYTHING.
WE ARE NEAR THE GRAVEYARD!
I'VE HEARD ABOUT SKELETONS IN THE CLOSET, BUT WHO BURIES BODIES IN HIS BASEMENT?
GULP!

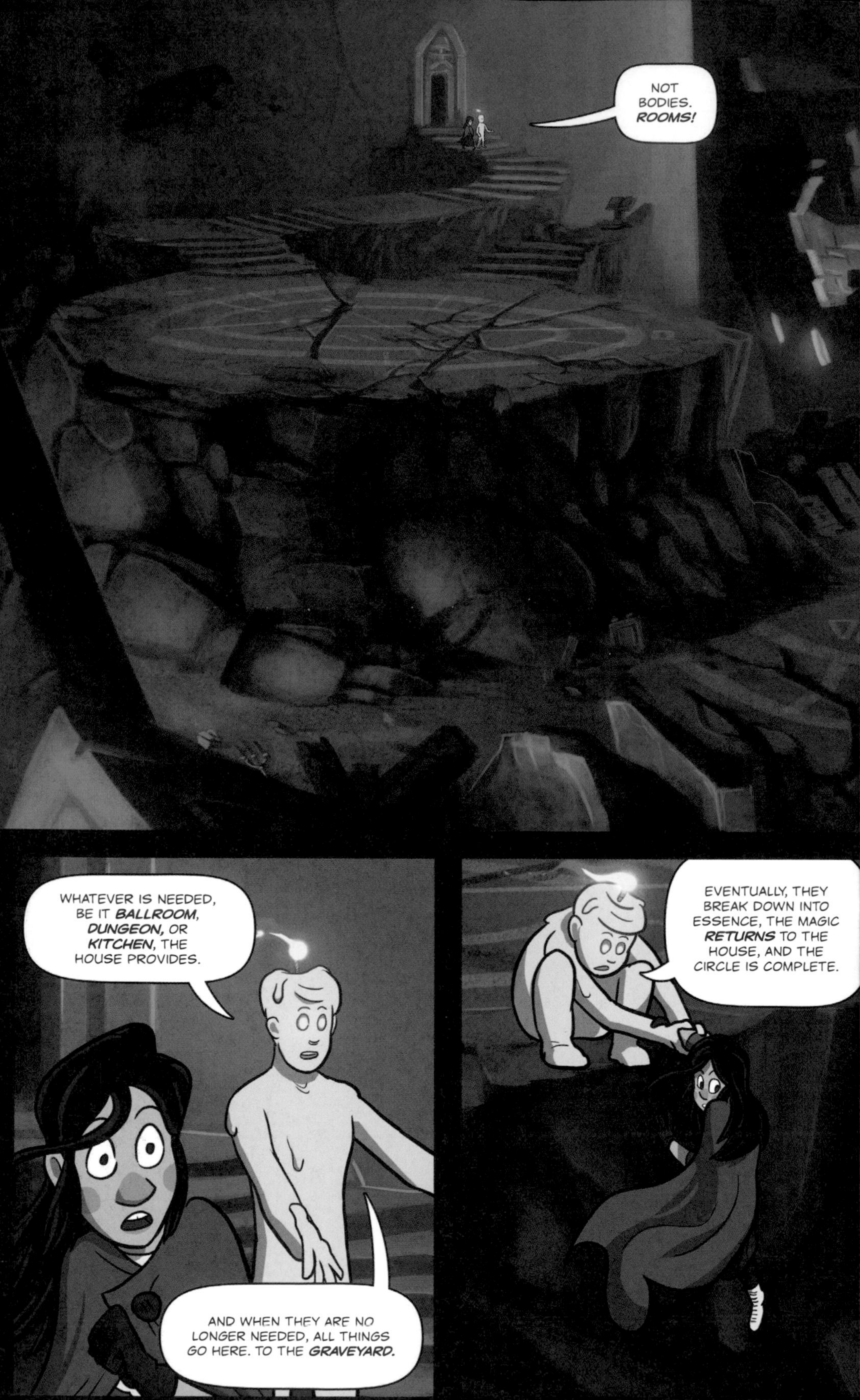
NOT BODIES. ROOMS!
WHATEVER IS NEEDED, BE IT BALLROOM, DUNGEON, OR KITCHEN, THE HOUSE PROVIDES.
AND WHEN THEY ARE NO LONGER NEEDED, ALL THINGS GO HERE. TO THE GRAVEYARD.
EVENTUALLY, THEY BREAK DOWN INTO ESSENCE, THE MAGIC RETURNS TO THE HOUSE, AND THE CIRCLE IS COMPLETE.

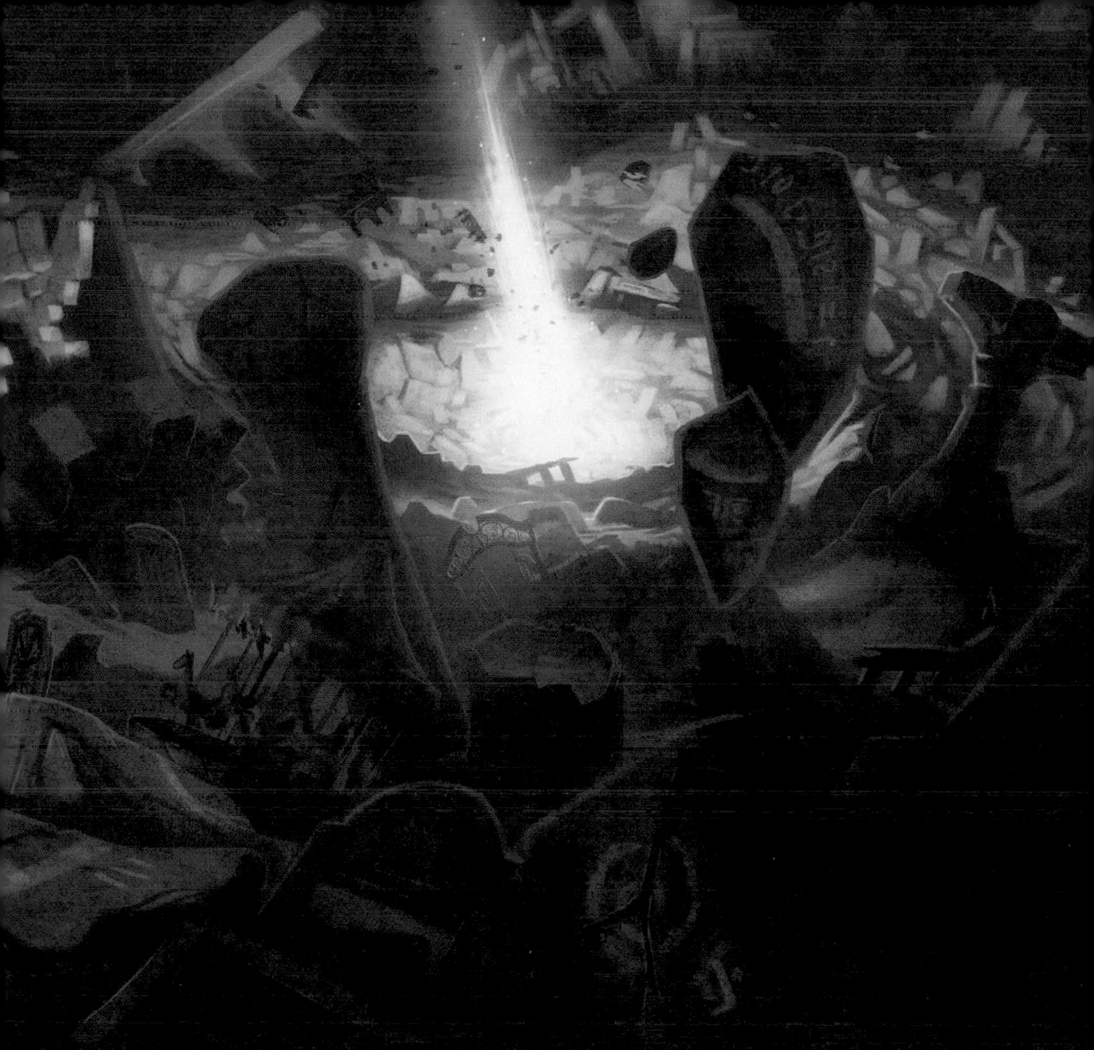

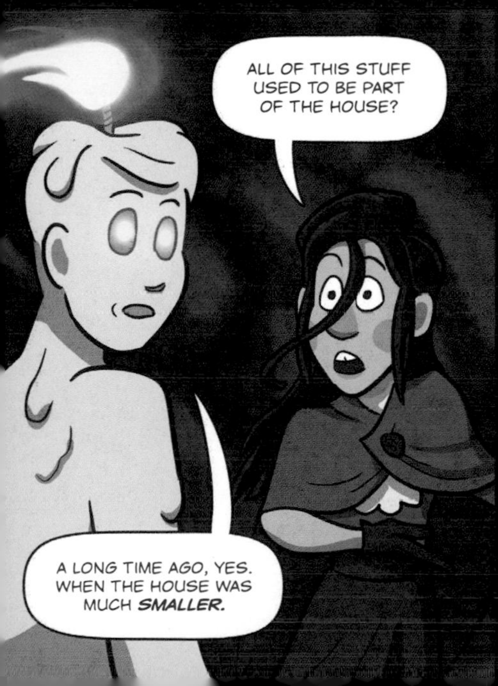
ALL OF THIS STUFF USED TO BE PART OF THE HOUSE?
A LONG TIME AGO, YES. WHEN THE HOUSE WAS MUCH **SMALLER.**

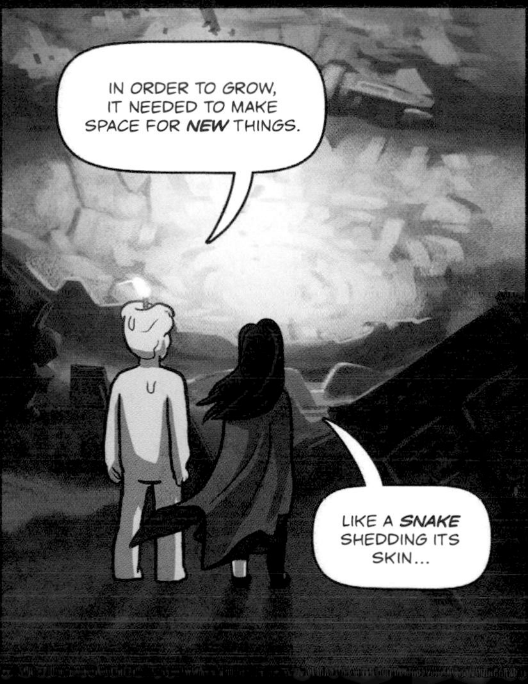
IN ORDER TO GROW, IT NEEDED TO MAKE SPACE FOR ***NEW*** THINGS.
LIKE A ***SNAKE*** SHEDDING ITS SKIN...

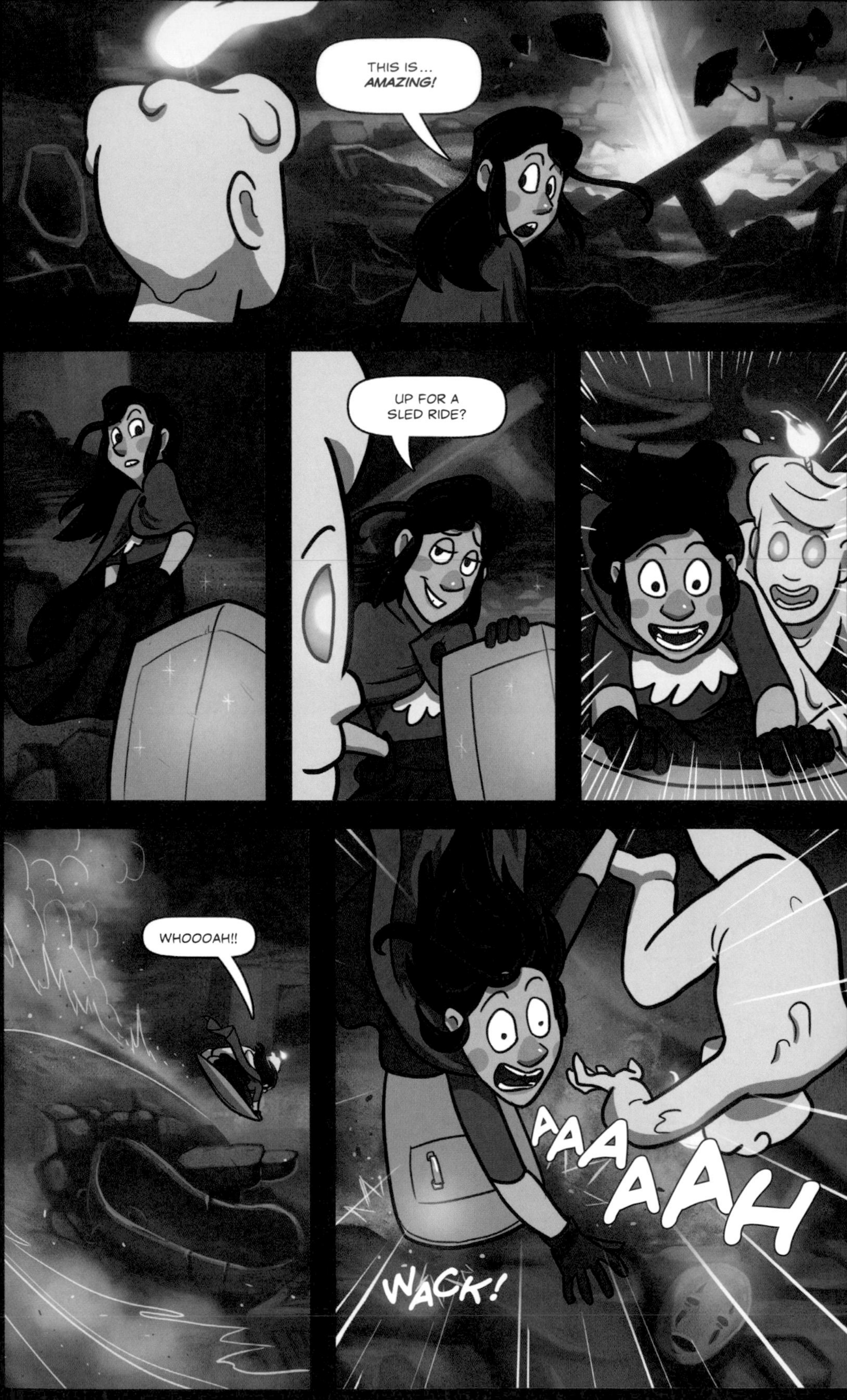
THIS IS... AMAZING!
UP FOR A SLED RIDE?
WHOOOAH!!
AAAAAAH
WACK!

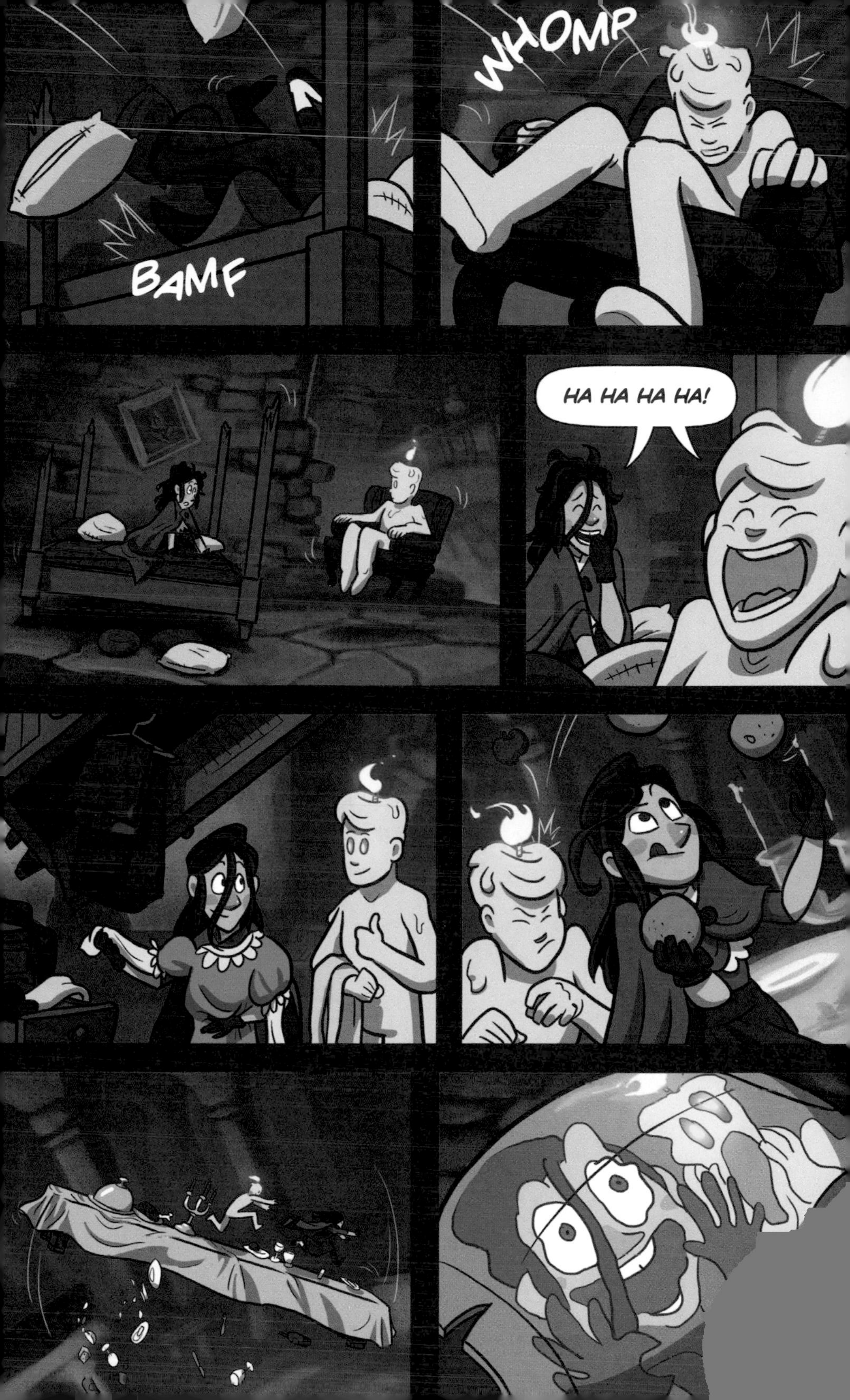
BAMF
WHOMP
HA HA HA HA!

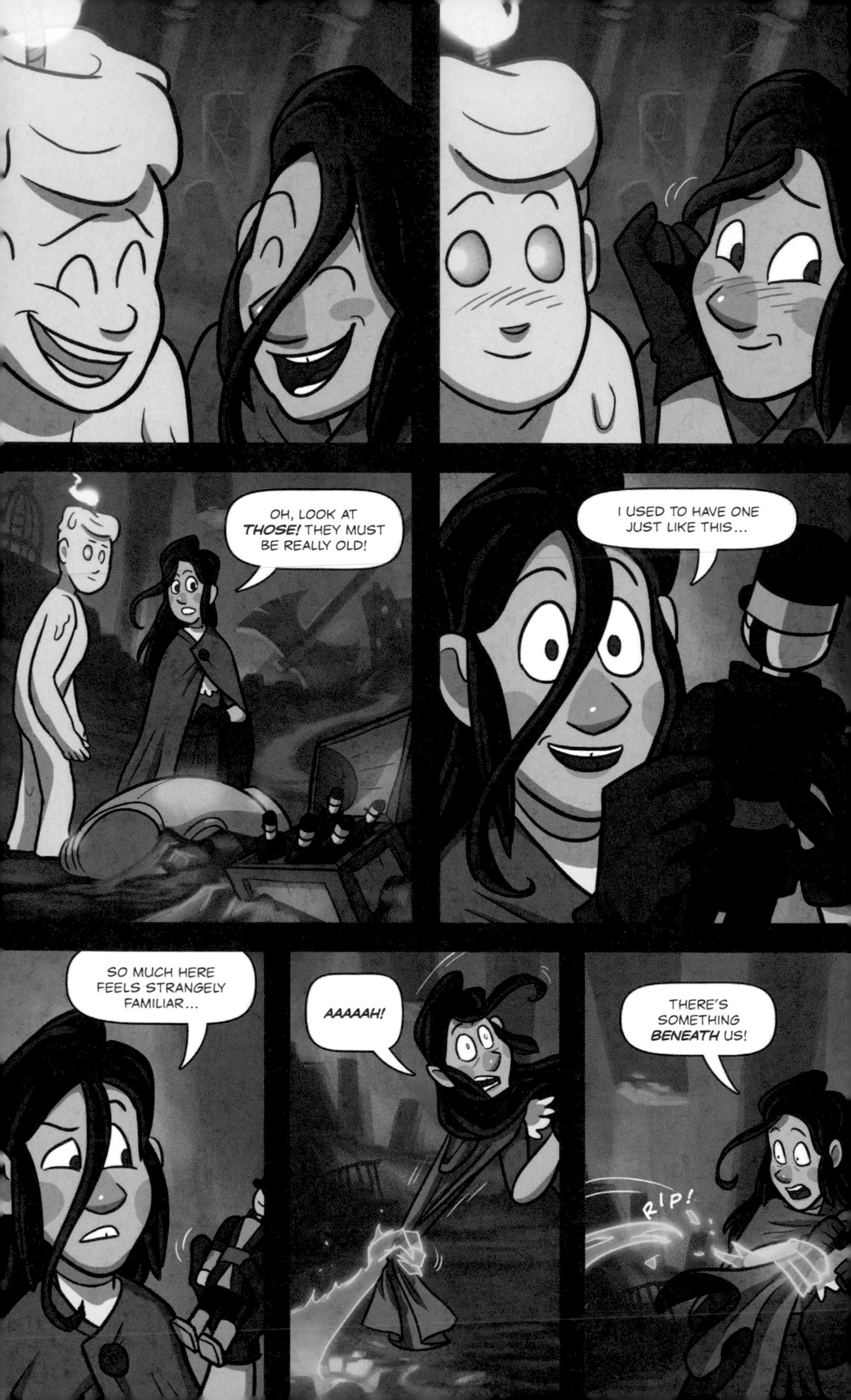
OH, LOOK AT *THOSE!* THEY MUST BE REALLY OLD!
I USED TO HAVE ONE JUST LIKE THIS...
SO MUCH HERE FEELS STRANGELY FAMILIAR...
AAAAAH!
THERE'S SOMETHING *BENEATH* US!
RIP!

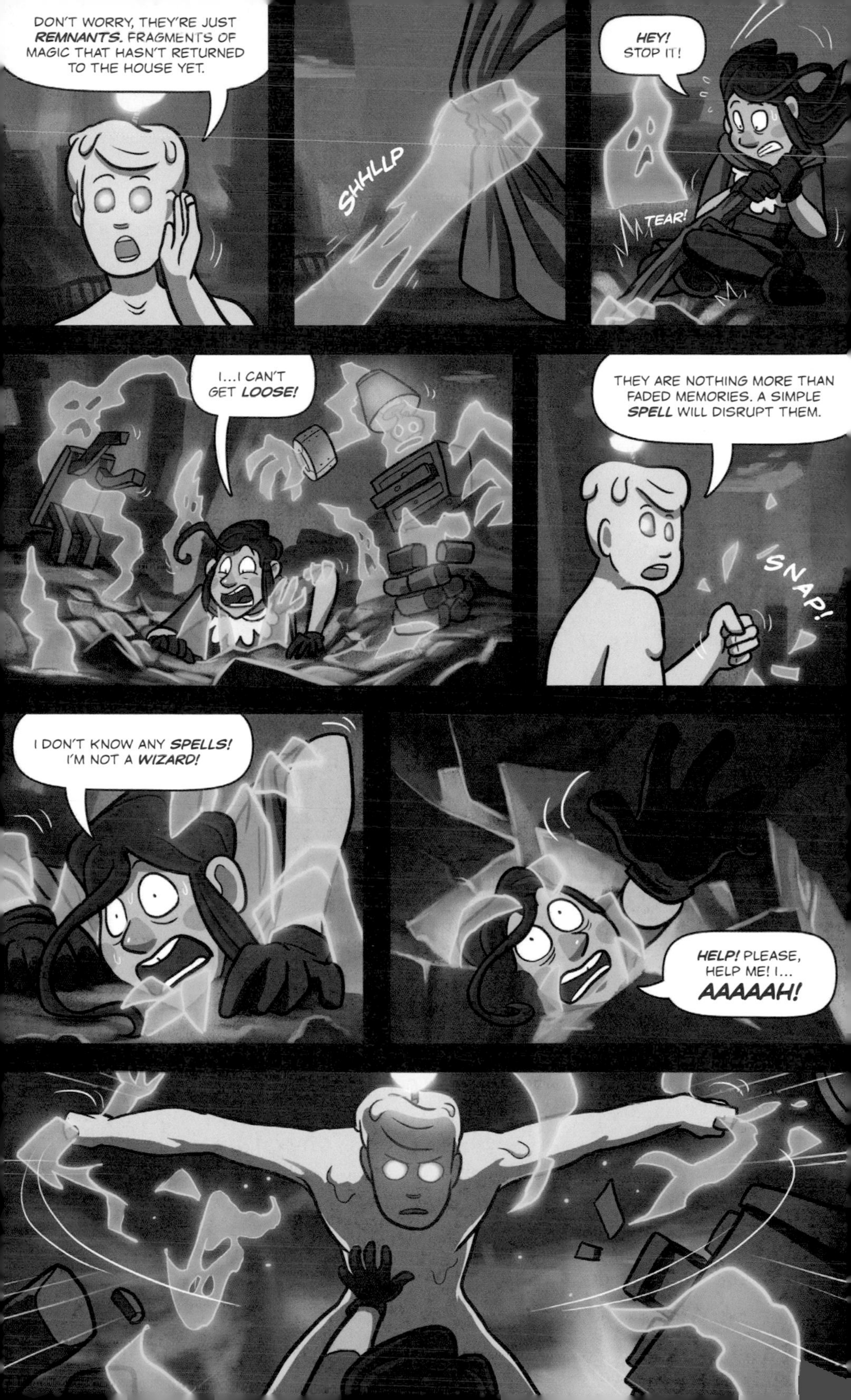

DON'T WORRY, THEY'RE JUST REMNANTS. FRAGMENTS OF MAGIC THAT HASN'T RETURNED TO THE HOUSE YET.
SHHLLP
HEY! STOP IT!
TEAR!
I...I CAN'T GET LOOSE!
THEY ARE NOTHING MORE THAN FADED MEMORIES. A SIMPLE SPELL WILL DISRUPT THEM.
SNAP!
I DON'T KNOW ANY SPELLS! I'M NOT A WIZARD!
HELP! PLEASE, HELP ME! I... AAAAAH!

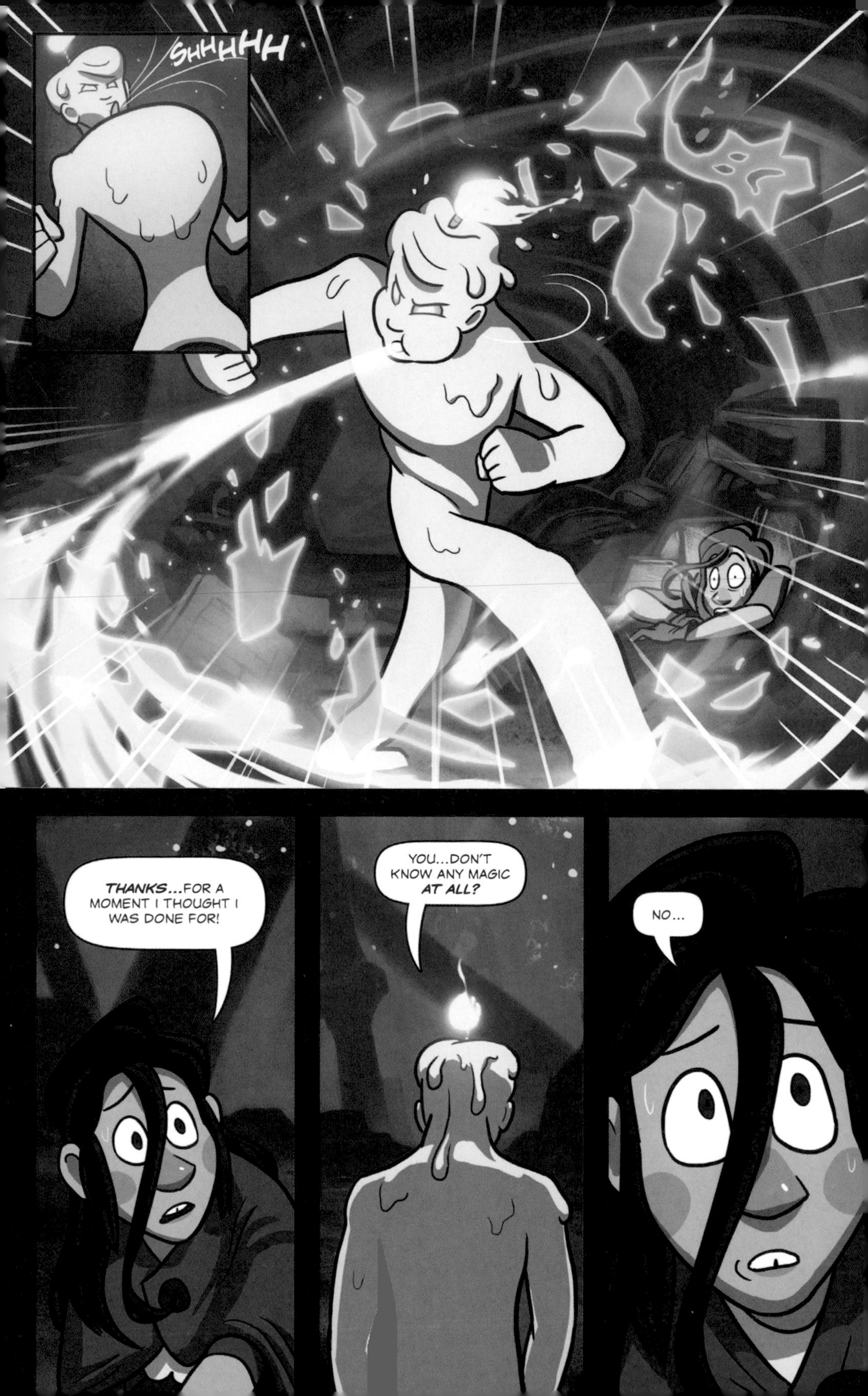
SHHHHH
THANKS...FOR A MOMENT I THOUGHT I WAS DONE FOR!
YOU...DON'T KNOW ANY MAGIC AT ALL?
NO...

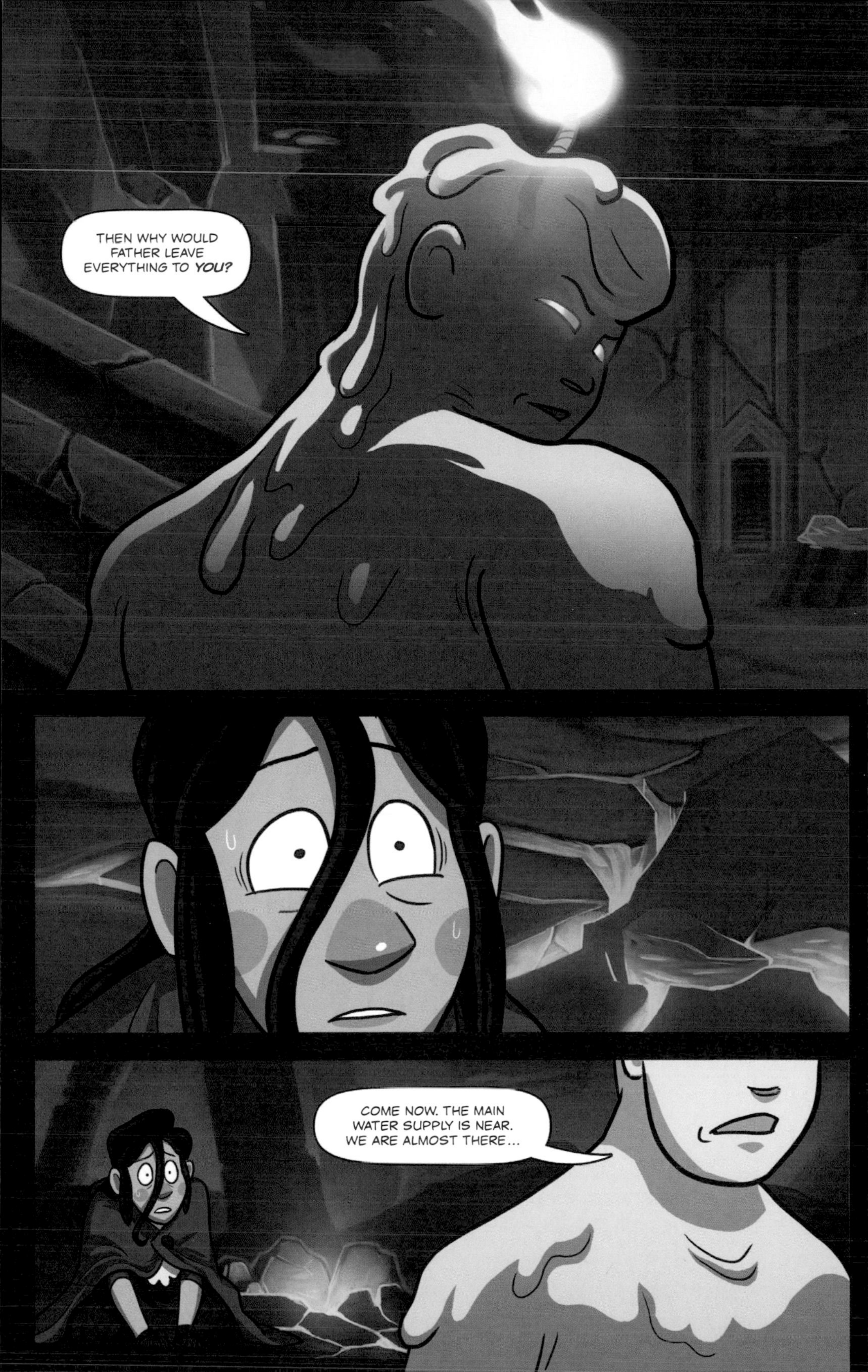
THEN WHY WOULD FATHER LEAVE EVERYTHING TO *YOU?*
COME NOW. THE MAIN WATER SUPPLY IS NEAR. WE ARE ALMOST THERE...

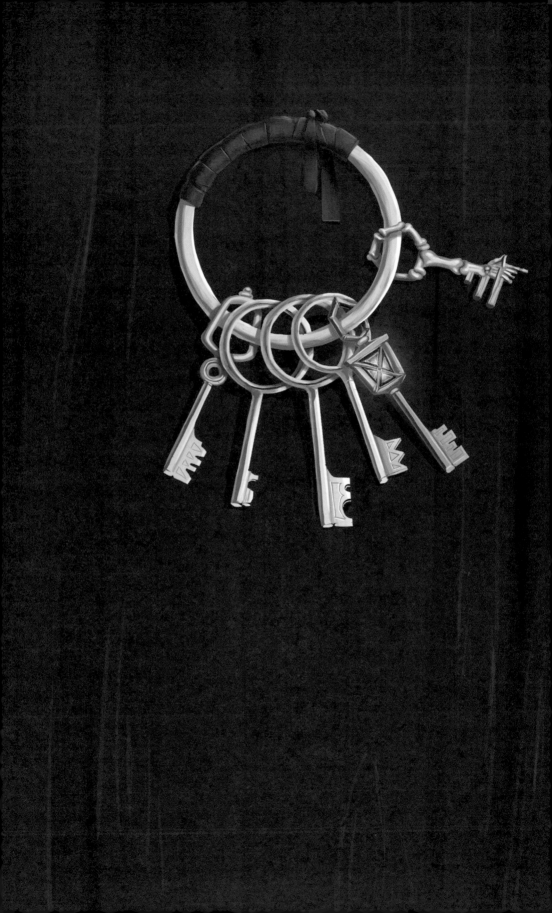

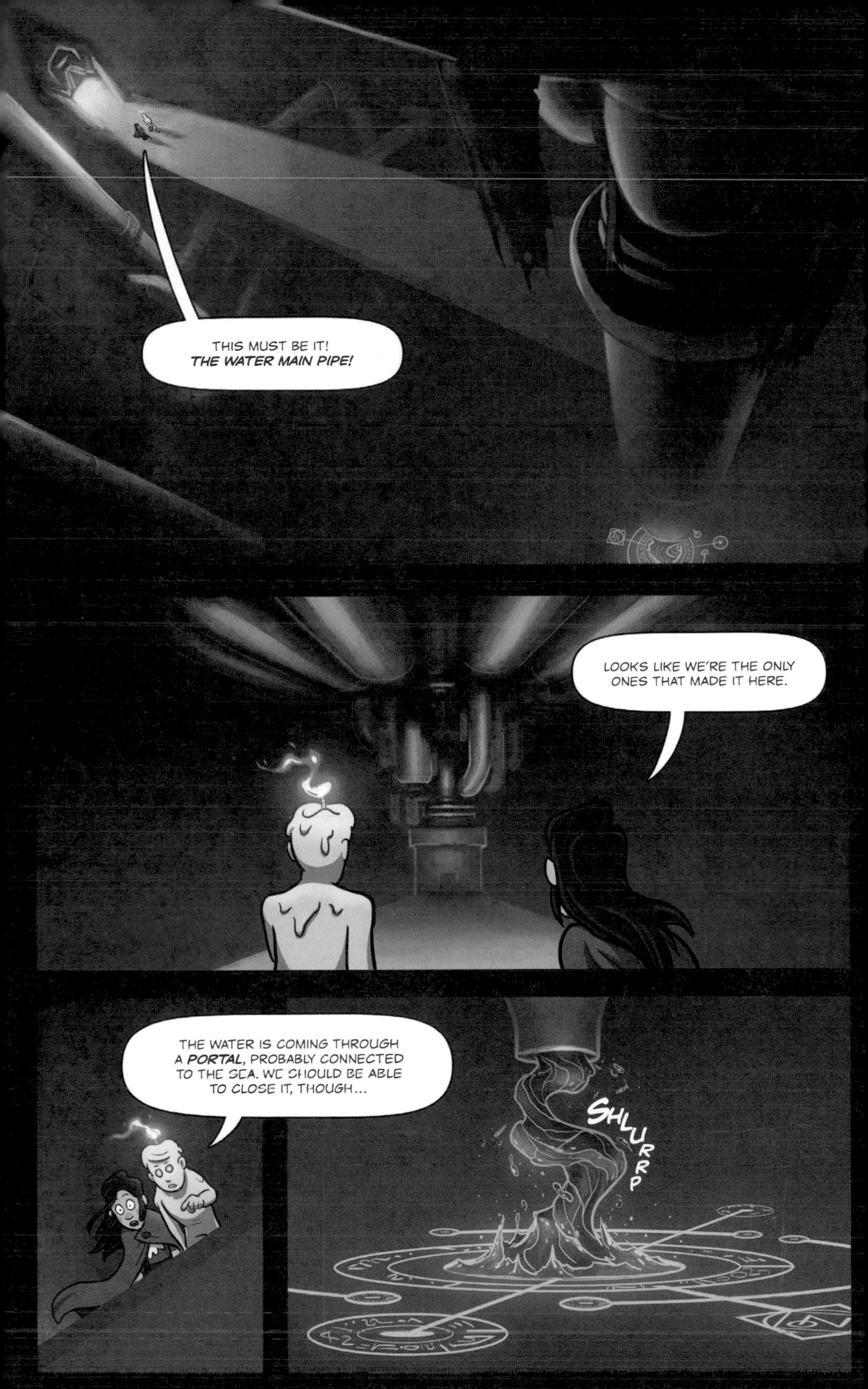
THIS MUST BE IT! THE WATER MAIN PIPE!
LOOKS LIKE WE'RE THE ONLY ONES THAT MADE IT HERE.
THE WATER IS COMING THROUGH A PORTAL, PROBABLY CONNECTED TO THE SEA. WE SHOULD BE ABLE TO CLOSE IT, THOUGH...
SHLURRP

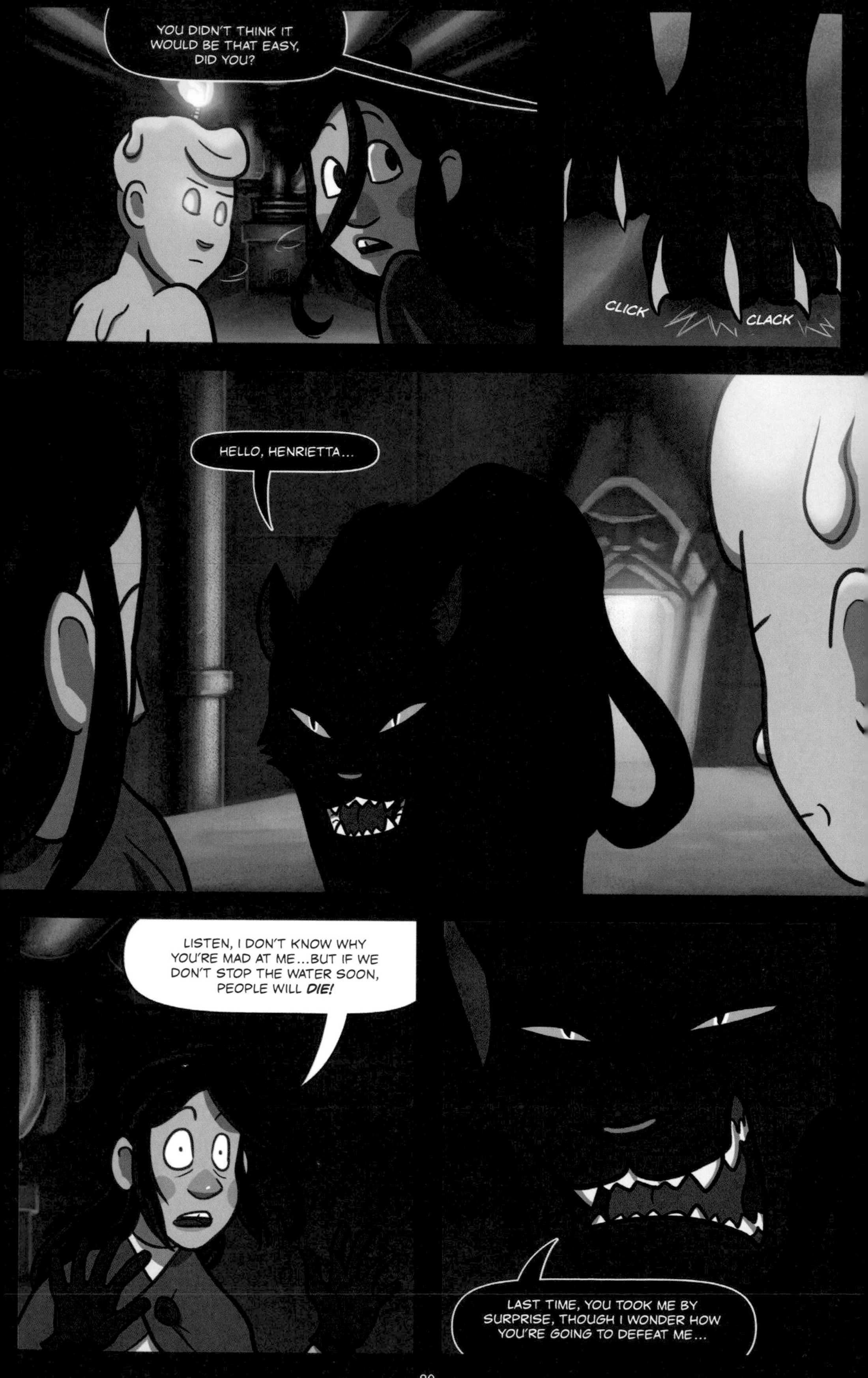
YOU DIDN'T THINK IT WOULD BE THAT EASY, DID YOU?
CLICK
CLACK
HELLO, HENRIETTA...
LISTEN, I DON'T KNOW WHY YOU'RE MAD AT ME...BUT IF WE DON'T STOP THE WATER SOON, PEOPLE WILL ***DIE!***
LAST TIME, YOU TOOK ME BY SURPRISE, THOUGH I WONDER HOW YOU'RE GOING TO DEFEAT ME...

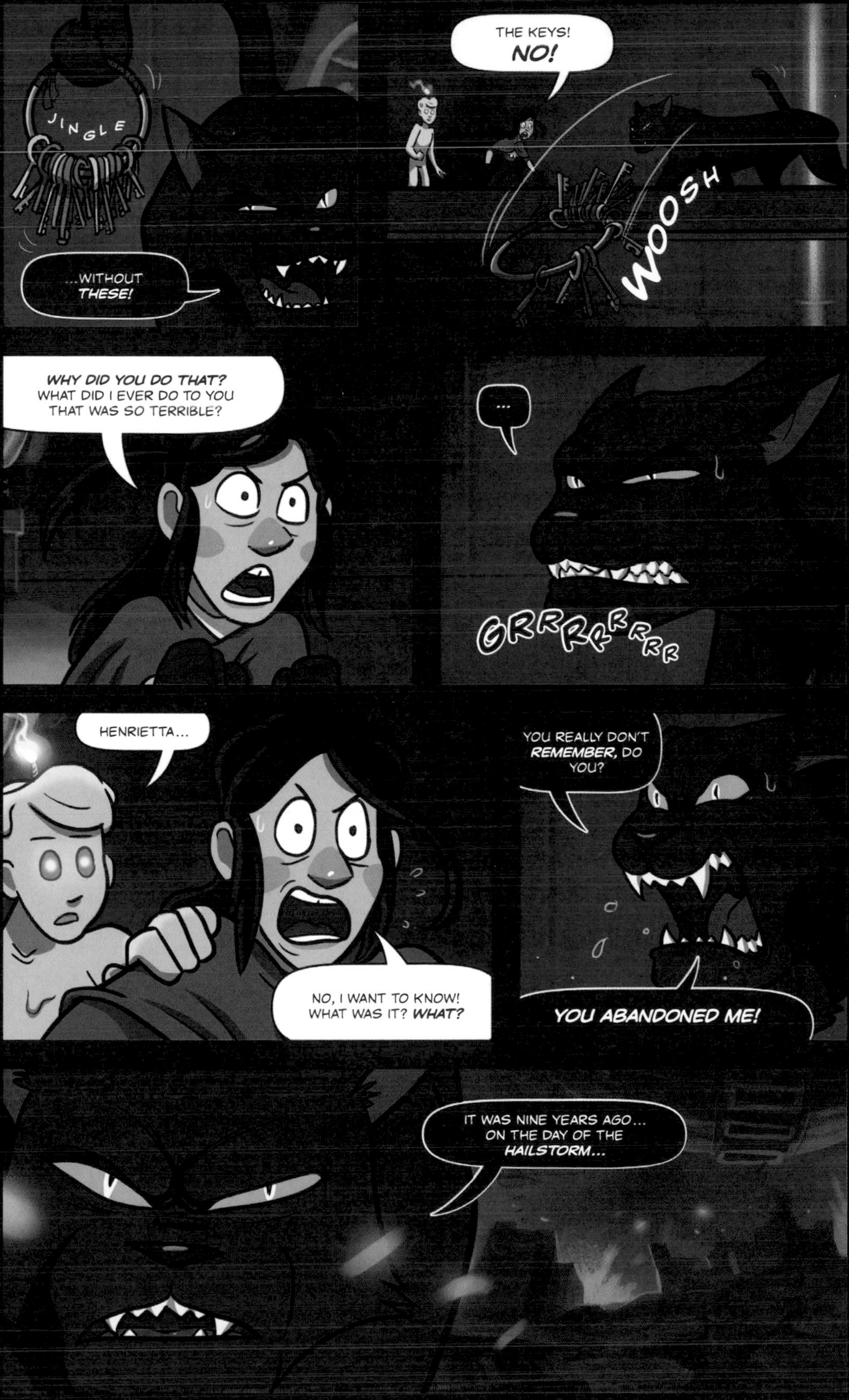
JINGLE
...WITHOUT THESE!
THE KEYS! NO!
WOOSH
WHY DID YOU DO THAT? WHAT DID I EVER DO TO YOU THAT WAS SO TERRIBLE?
...
GRRRRRRRRR
HENRIETTA...
NO, I WANT TO KNOW! WHAT WAS IT? WHAT?
YOU REALLY DON'T REMEMBER, DO YOU?
YOU ABANDONED ME!
IT WAS NINE YEARS AGO... ON THE DAY OF THE HAILSTORM...

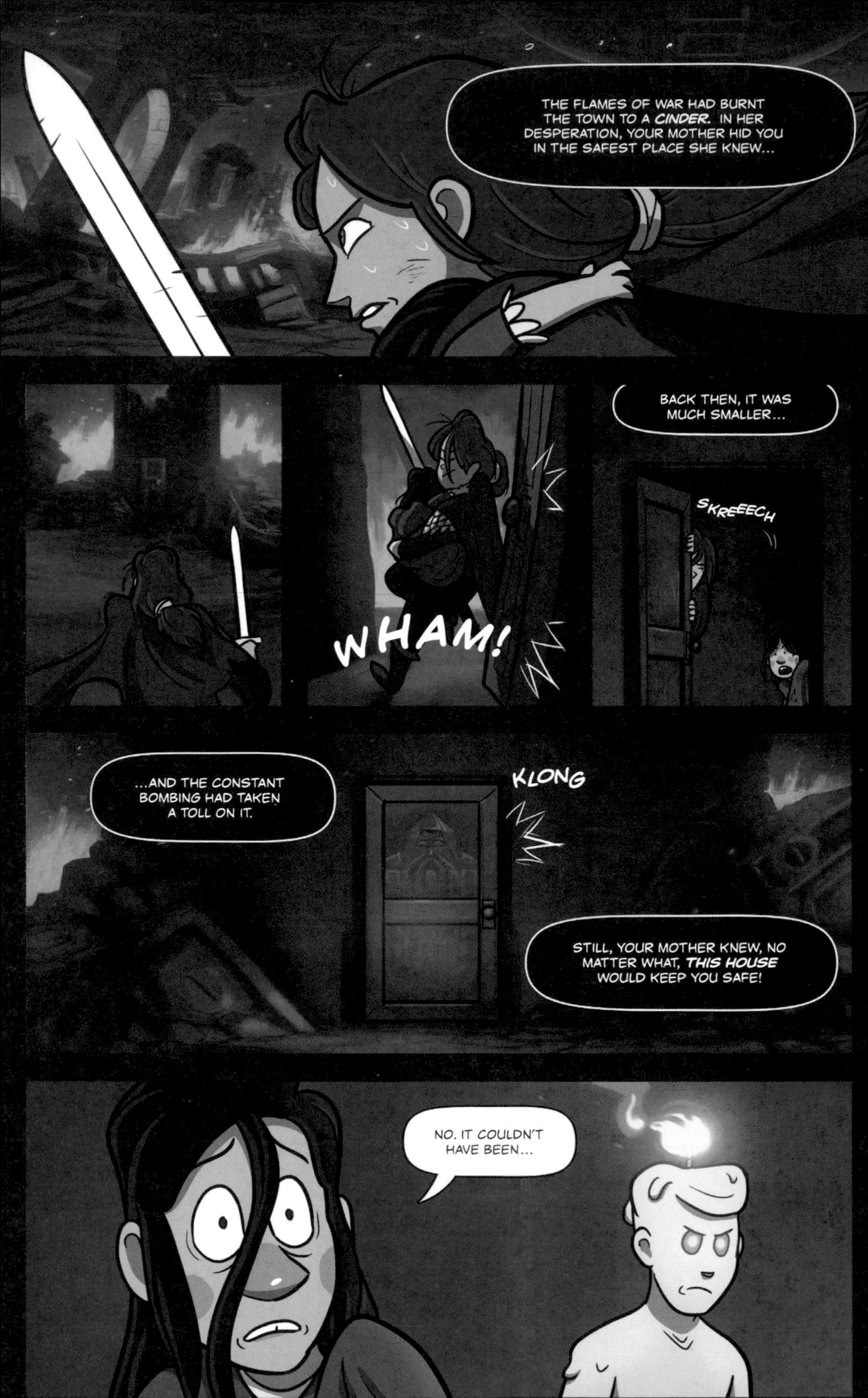
THE FLAMES OF WAR HAD BURNT THE TOWN TO A ***CINDER.*** IN HER DESPERATION, YOUR MOTHER HID YOU IN THE SAFEST PLACE SHE KNEW...
WHAM!
BACK THEN, IT WAS MUCH SMALLER...
SKREEECH
...AND THE CONSTANT BOMBING HAD TAKEN A TOLL ON IT.
KLONG
STILL, YOUR MOTHER KNEW, NO MATTER WHAT, ***THIS HOUSE*** WOULD KEEP YOU SAFE!
NO. IT COULDN'T HAVE BEEN...

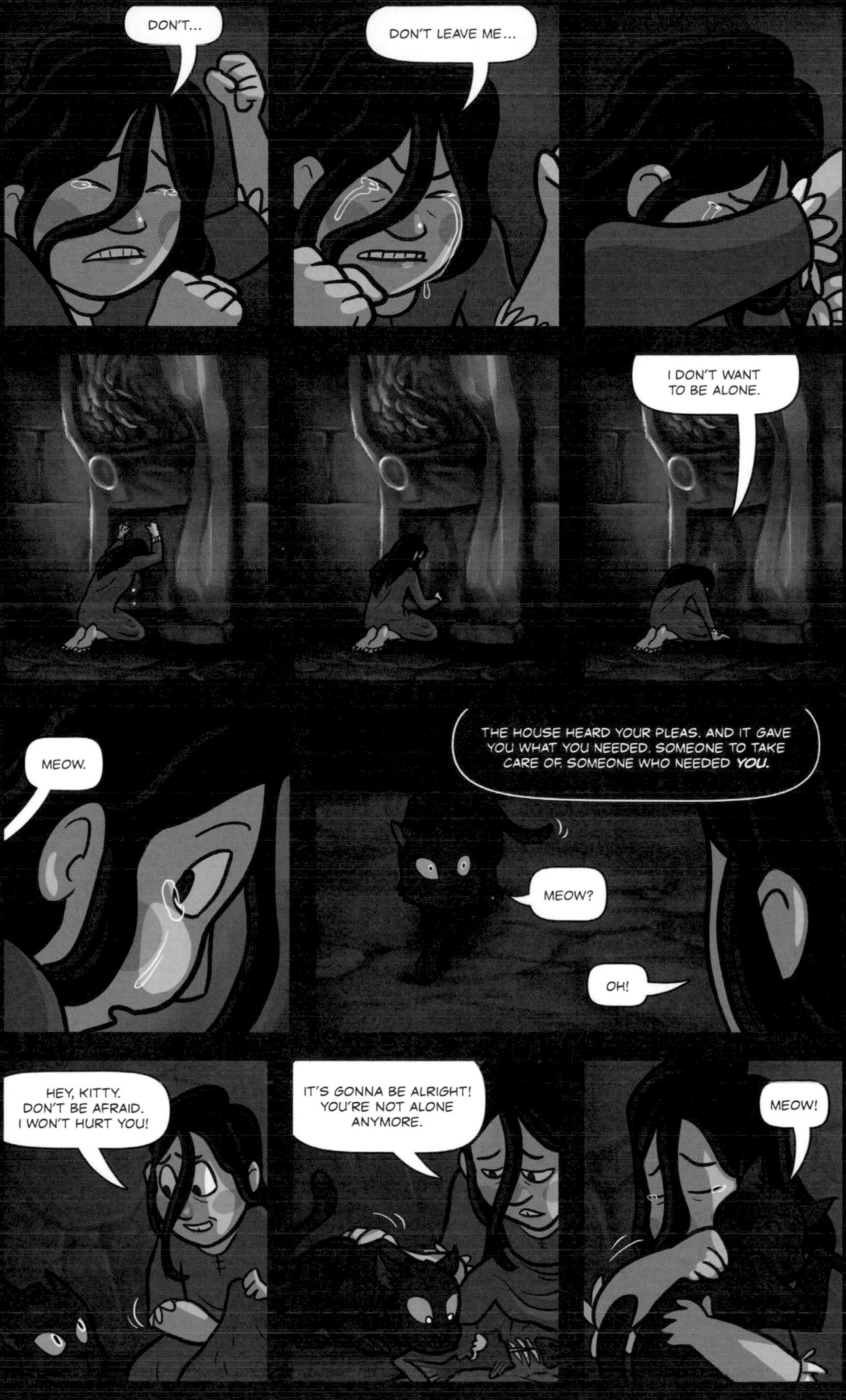
DON'T...
DON'T LEAVE ME...
I DON'T WANT TO BE ALONE.
MEOW.
THE HOUSE HEARD YOUR PLEAS. AND IT GAVE YOU WHAT YOU NEEDED. SOMEONE TO TAKE CARE OF. SOMEONE WHO NEEDED YOU.
MEOW?
OH!
HEY, KITTY. DON'T BE AFRAID. I WON'T HURT YOU!
IT'S GONNA BE ALRIGHT! YOU'RE NOT ALONE ANYMORE.
MEOW!

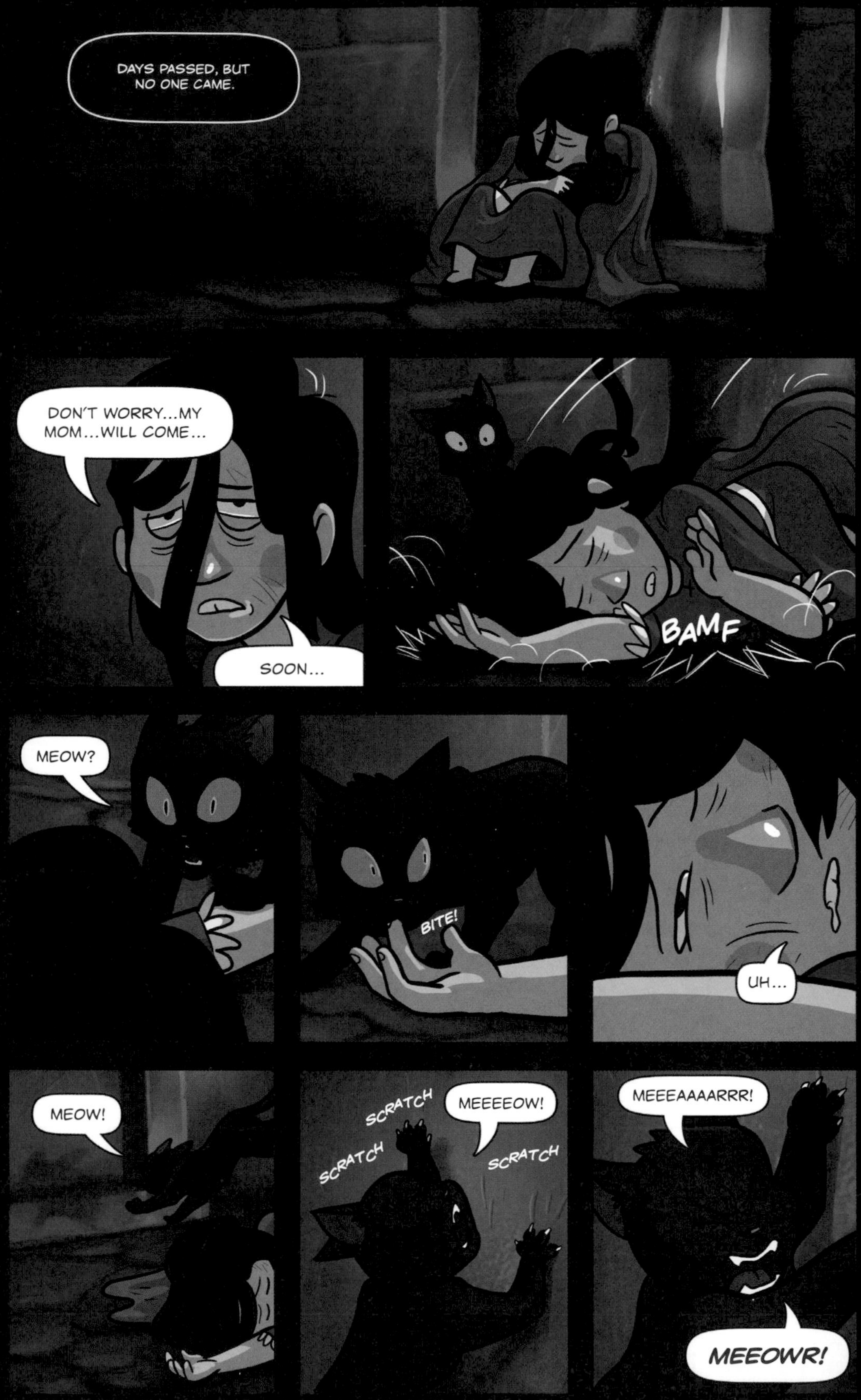
DAYS PASSED, BUT NO ONE CAME.
DON'T WORRY...MY MOM...WILL COME...
SOON...
BAMF
MEOW?
BITE!
UH...
MEOW!
SCRATCH
SCRATCH
MEEEEOW!
SCRATCH
MEEEAAAARRR!
MEEOWR!

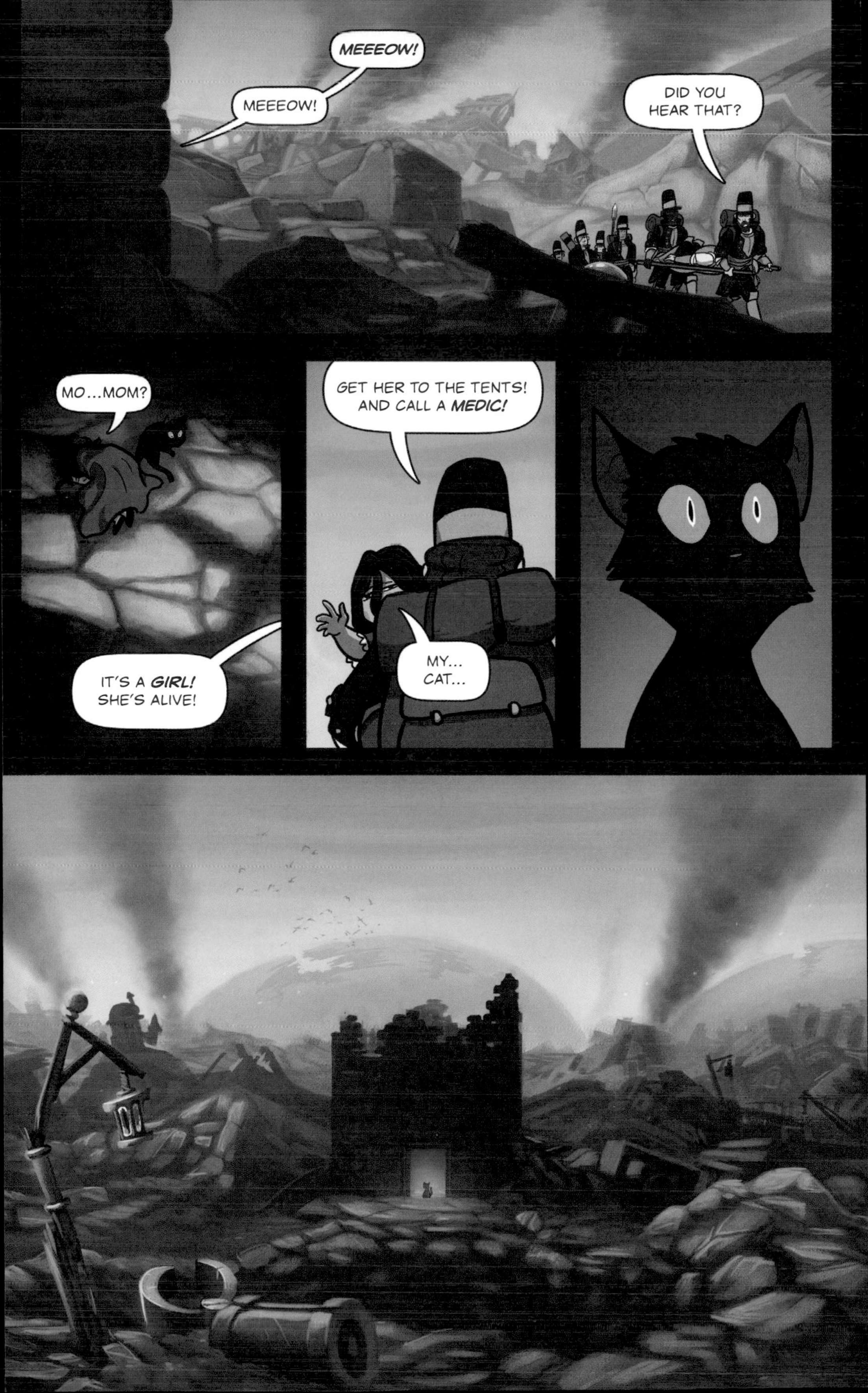
MEEEOW!
MEEEOW!
DID YOU HEAR THAT?
MO...MOM?
IT'S A GIRL! SHE'S ALIVE!
GET HER TO THE TENTS! AND CALL A MEDIC!
MY... CAT...

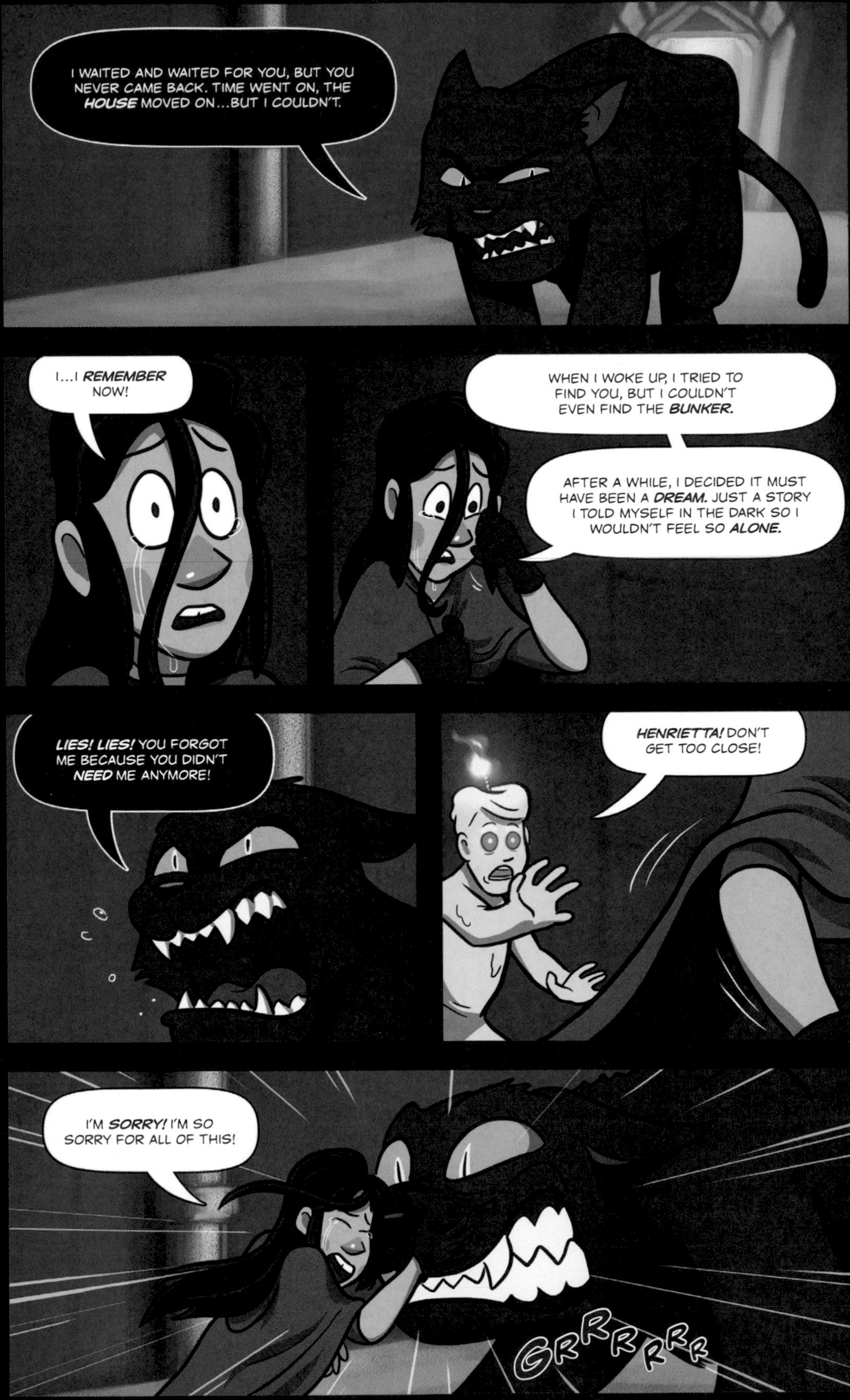
I WAITED AND WAITED FOR YOU, BUT YOU NEVER CAME BACK. TIME WENT ON, THE ***HOUSE*** MOVED ON…BUT I COULDN'T.
I…I ***REMEMBER*** NOW!
WHEN I WOKE UP, I TRIED TO FIND YOU, BUT I COULDN'T EVEN FIND THE ***BUNKER.***
AFTER A WHILE, I DECIDED IT MUST HAVE BEEN A ***DREAM.*** JUST A STORY I TOLD MYSELF IN THE DARK SO I WOULDN'T FEEL SO ***ALONE.***
LIES! LIES! YOU FORGOT ME BECAUSE YOU DIDN'T ***NEED*** ME ANYMORE!
HENRIETTA! DON'T GET TOO CLOSE!
I'M ***SORRY!*** I'M SO SORRY FOR ALL OF THIS!
GRRRRRRR

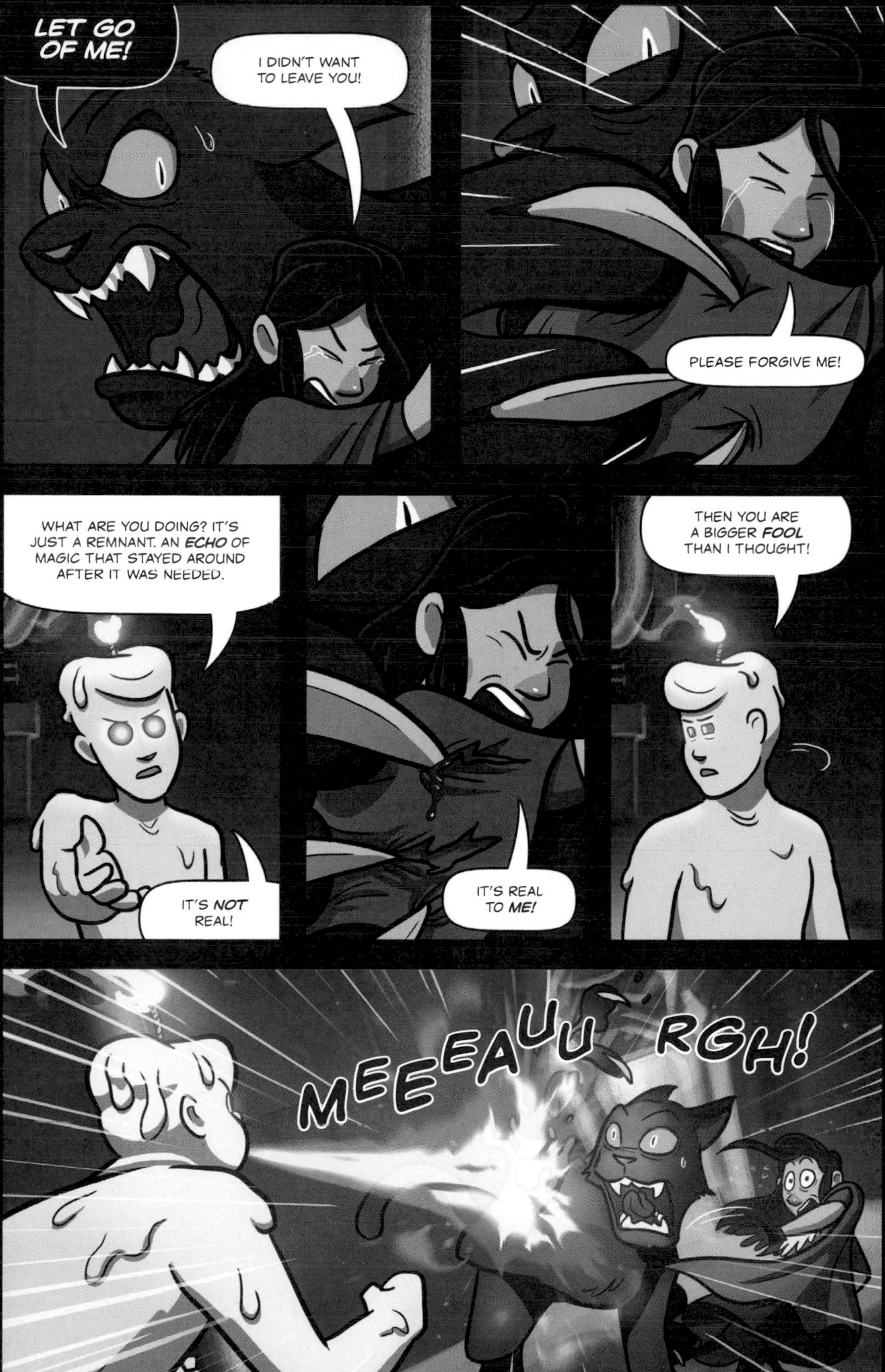

LET GO OF ME!
I DIDN'T WANT TO LEAVE YOU!
PLEASE FORGIVE ME!
WHAT ARE YOU DOING? IT'S JUST A REMNANT. AN *ECHO* OF MAGIC THAT STAYED AROUND AFTER IT WAS NEEDED.
IT'S *NOT* REAL!
IT'S REAL TO *ME!*
THEN YOU ARE A BIGGER *FOOL* THAN I THOUGHT!
MEEEAUU RGH!

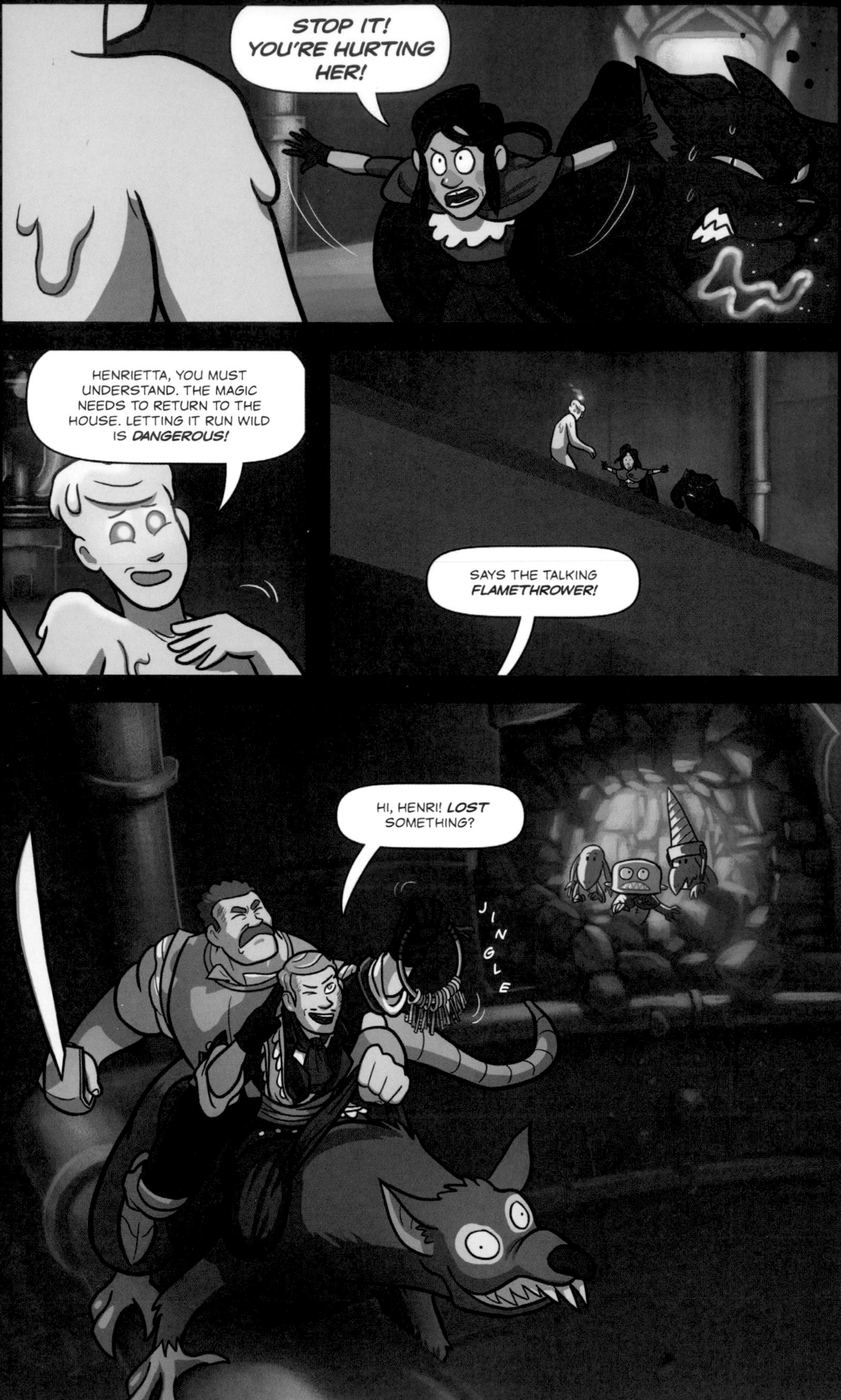
STOP IT! YOU'RE HURTING HER!
HENRIETTA, YOU MUST UNDERSTAND. THE MAGIC NEEDS TO RETURN TO THE HOUSE. LETTING IT RUN WILD IS DANGEROUS!
SAYS THE TALKING FLAMETHROWER!
HI, HENRI! LOST SOMETHING?
JINGLE

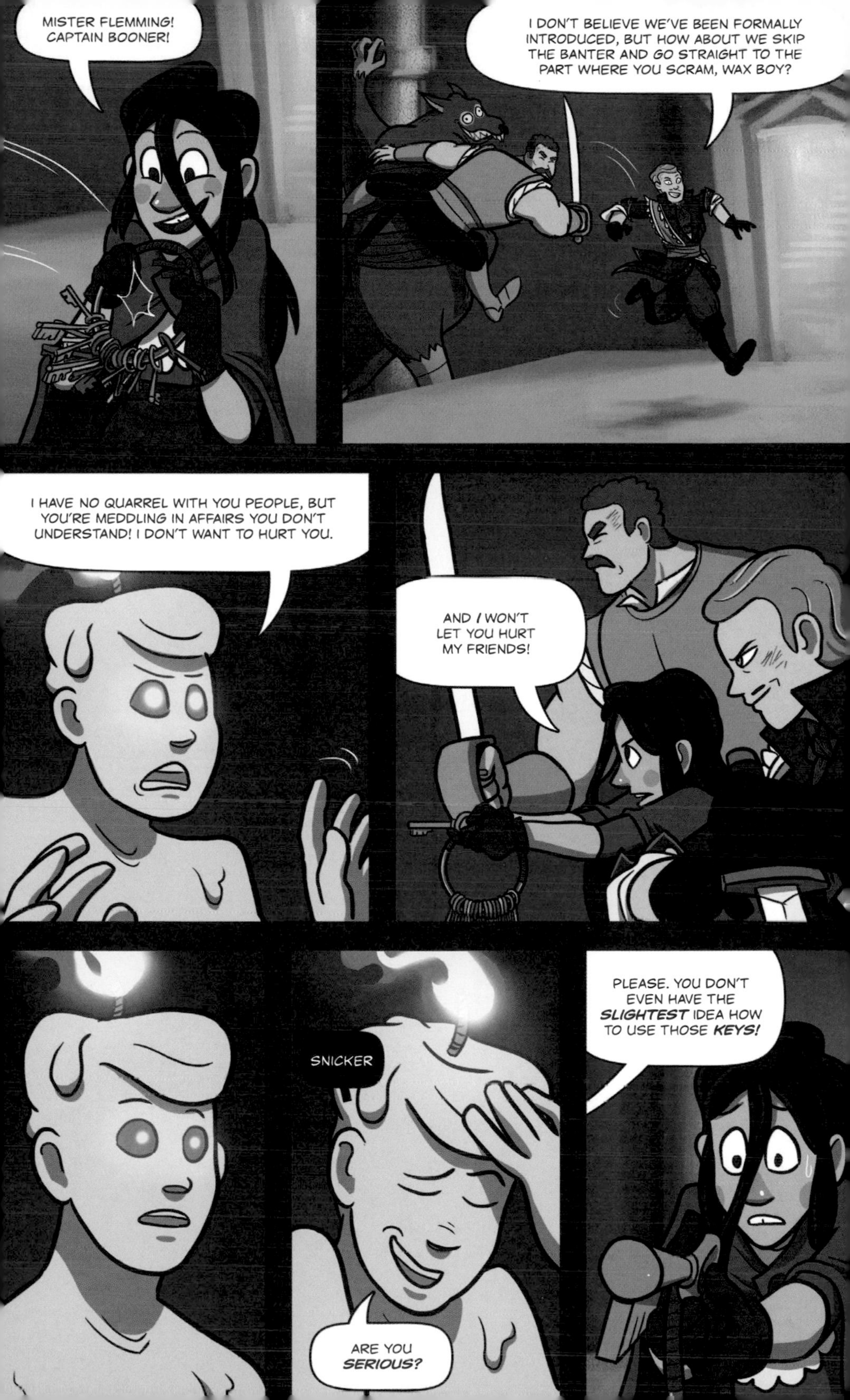
MISTER FLEMMING! CAPTAIN BOONER!
I DON'T BELIEVE WE'VE BEEN FORMALLY INTRODUCED, BUT HOW ABOUT WE SKIP THE BANTER AND GO STRAIGHT TO THE PART WHERE YOU SCRAM, WAX BOY?
I HAVE NO QUARREL WITH YOU PEOPLE, BUT YOU'RE MEDDLING IN AFFAIRS YOU DON'T UNDERSTAND! I DON'T WANT TO HURT YOU.
AND *I* WON'T LET YOU HURT MY FRIENDS!
SNICKER
ARE YOU ***SERIOUS?***
PLEASE. YOU DON'T EVEN HAVE THE ***SLIGHTEST*** IDEA HOW TO USE THOSE ***KEYS!***

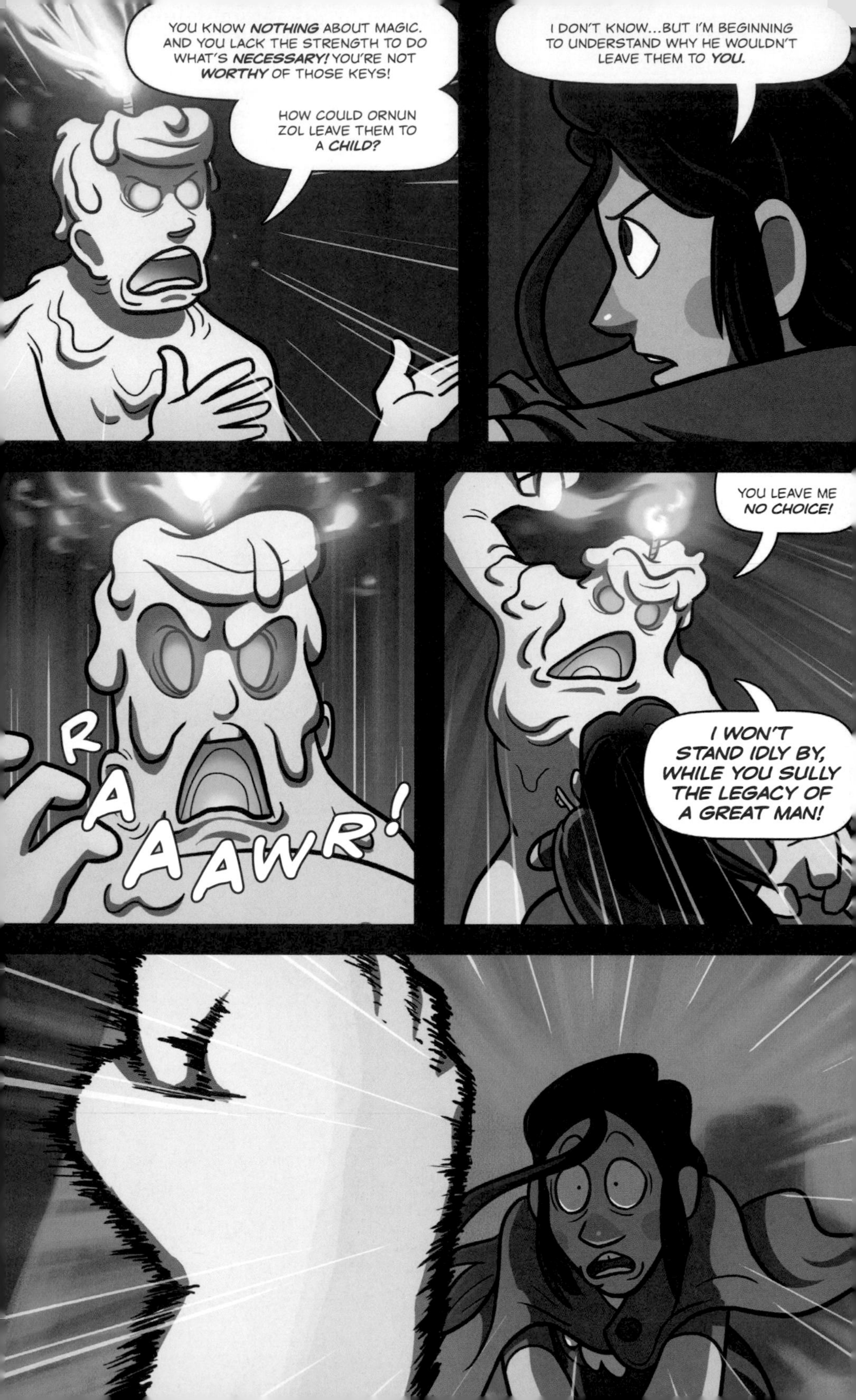
YOU KNOW NOTHING ABOUT MAGIC. AND YOU LACK THE STRENGTH TO DO WHAT'S NECESSARY! YOU'RE NOT WORTHY OF THOSE KEYS!
HOW COULD ORNUN ZOL LEAVE THEM TO A CHILD?
I DON'T KNOW...BUT I'M BEGINNING TO UNDERSTAND WHY HE WOULDN'T LEAVE THEM TO YOU.
RAAAWR!
YOU LEAVE ME NO CHOICE!
I WON'T STAND IDLY BY, WHILE YOU SULLY THE LEGACY OF A GREAT MAN!

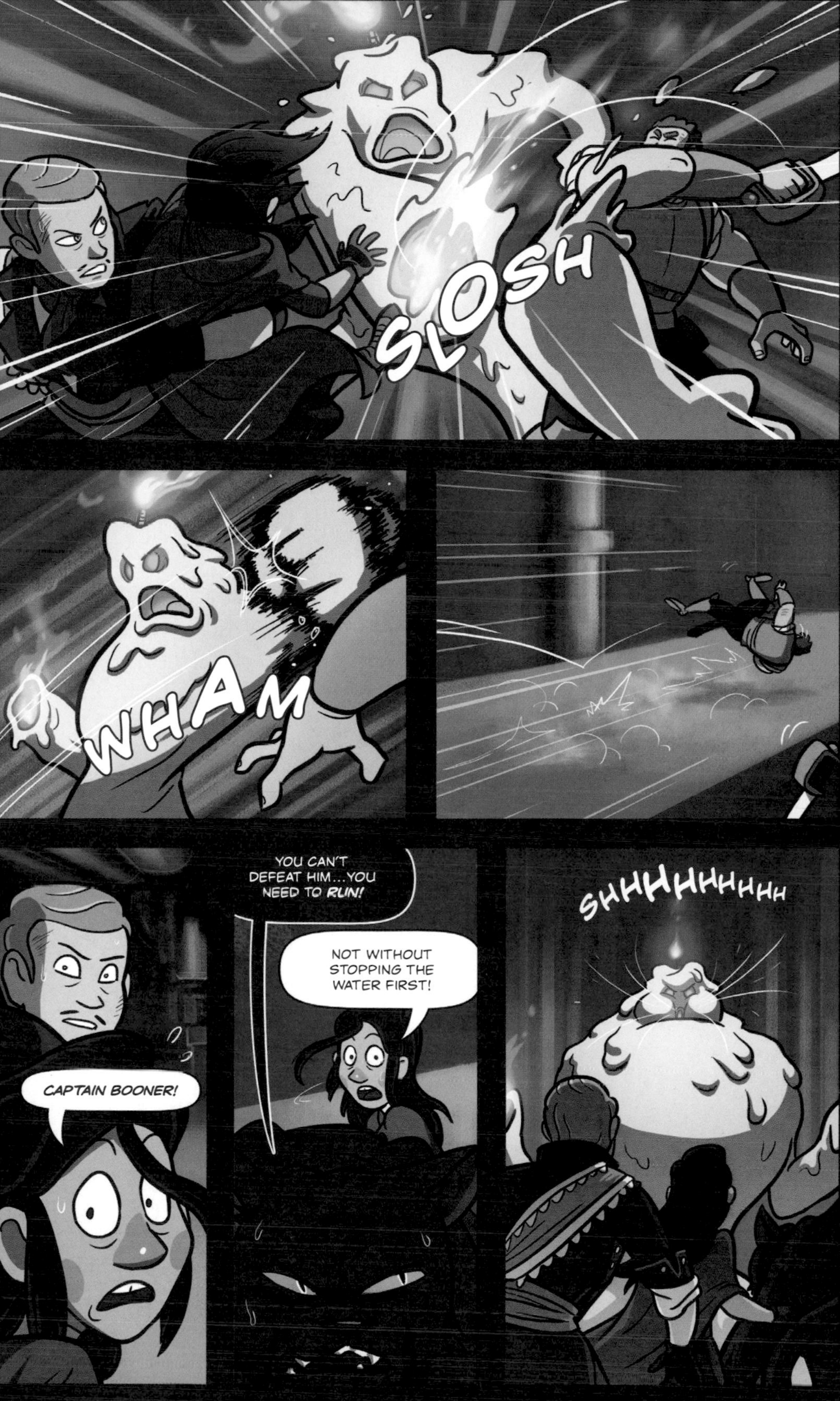
SLOSH
WHAM
CAPTAIN BOONER!
YOU CAN'T DEFEAT HIM...YOU NEED TO RUN!
NOT WITHOUT STOPPING THE WATER FIRST!
SHHHHHHHHH

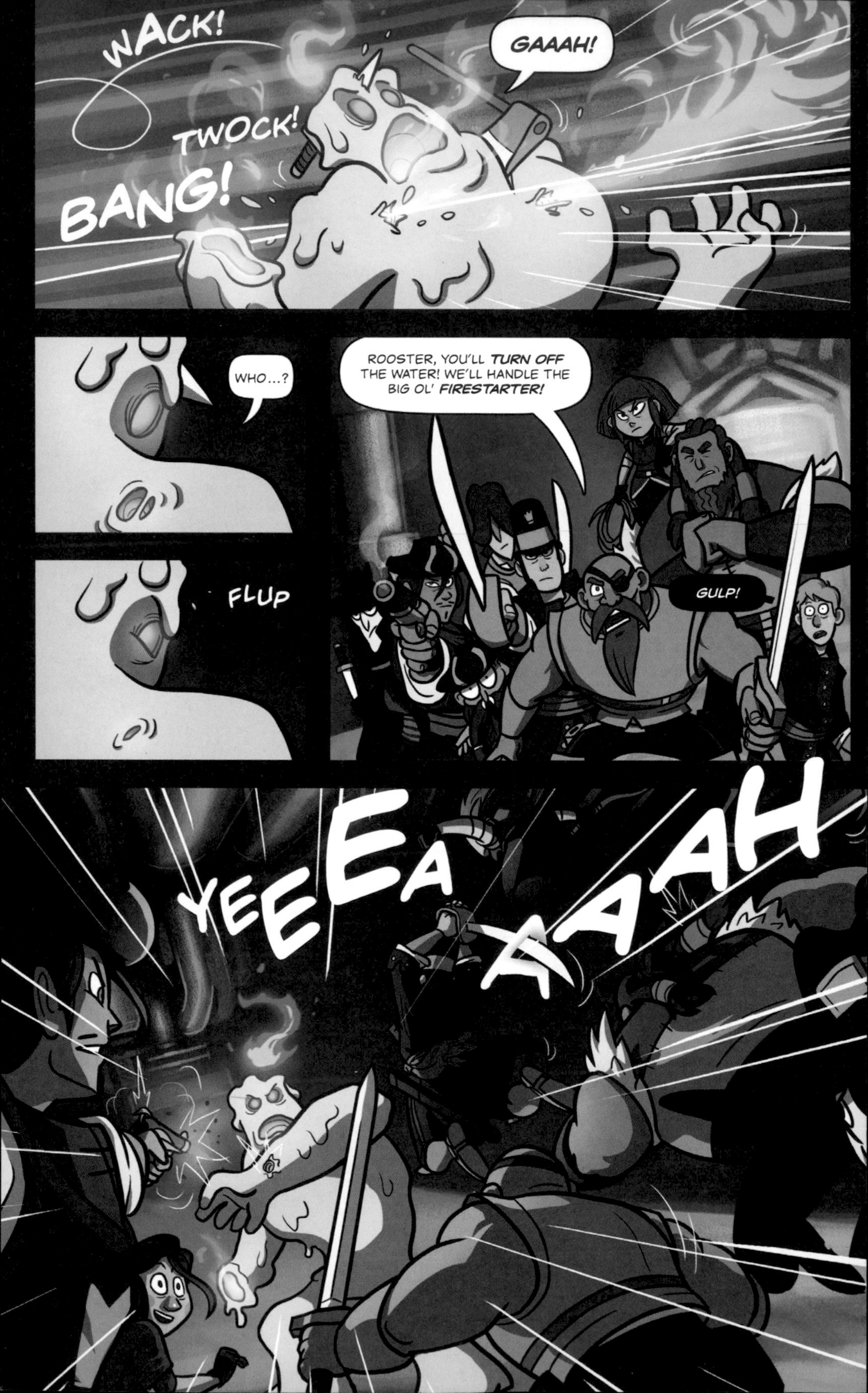
WACK!
TWOCK!
BANG!
GAAAH!
WHO...?
FLUP
ROOSTER, YOU'LL TURN OFF THE WATER! WE'LL HANDLE THE BIG OL' FIRESTARTER!
GULP!
YEEEAAAAH

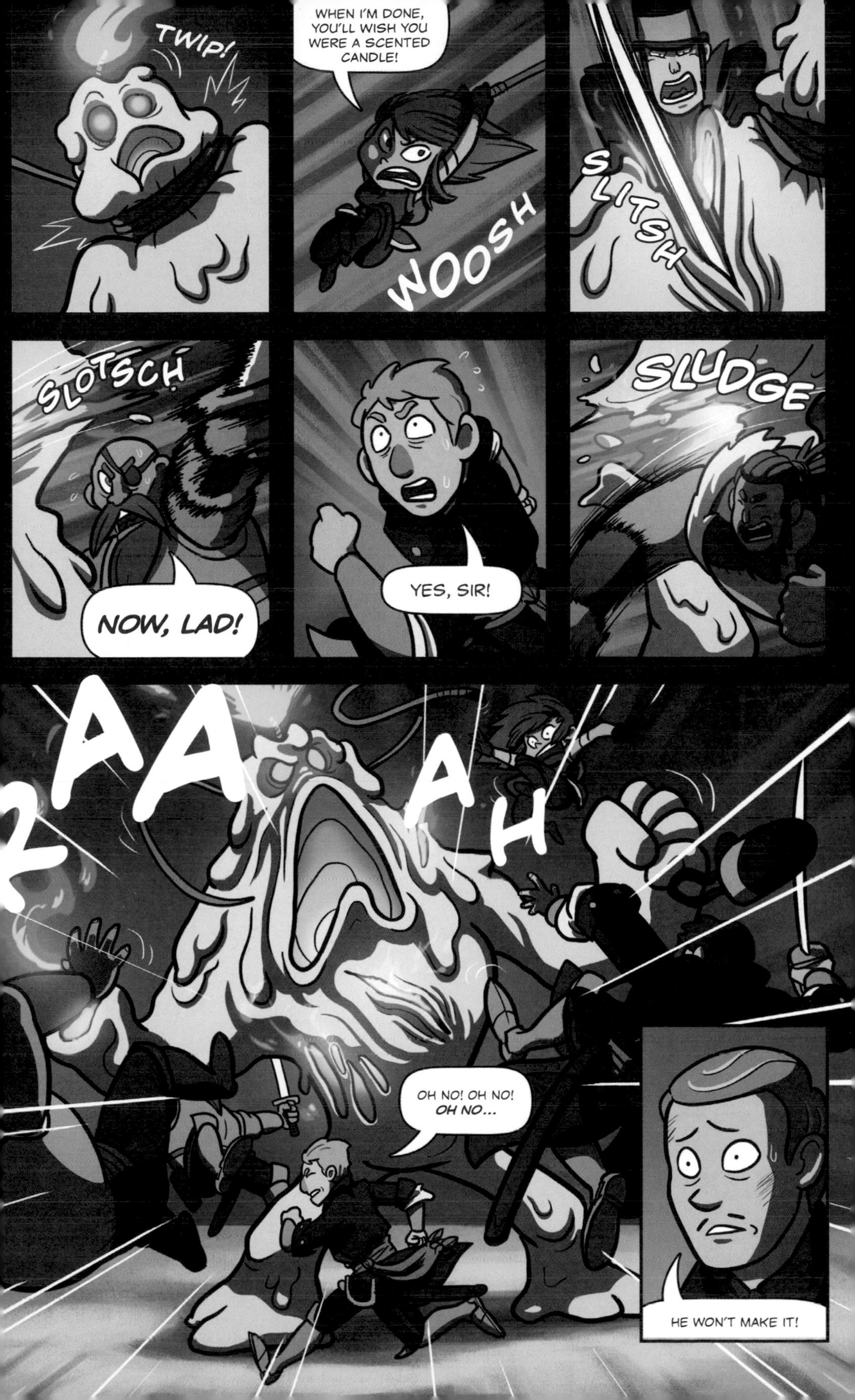
TWIP!
WHEN I'M DONE, YOU'LL WISH YOU WERE A SCENTED CANDLE!
WOOSH
SLITSH
SLOTSCH
NOW, LAD!
YES, SIR!
SLUDGE
RAAAAH
OH NO! OH NO! *OH NO...*
HE WON'T MAKE IT!

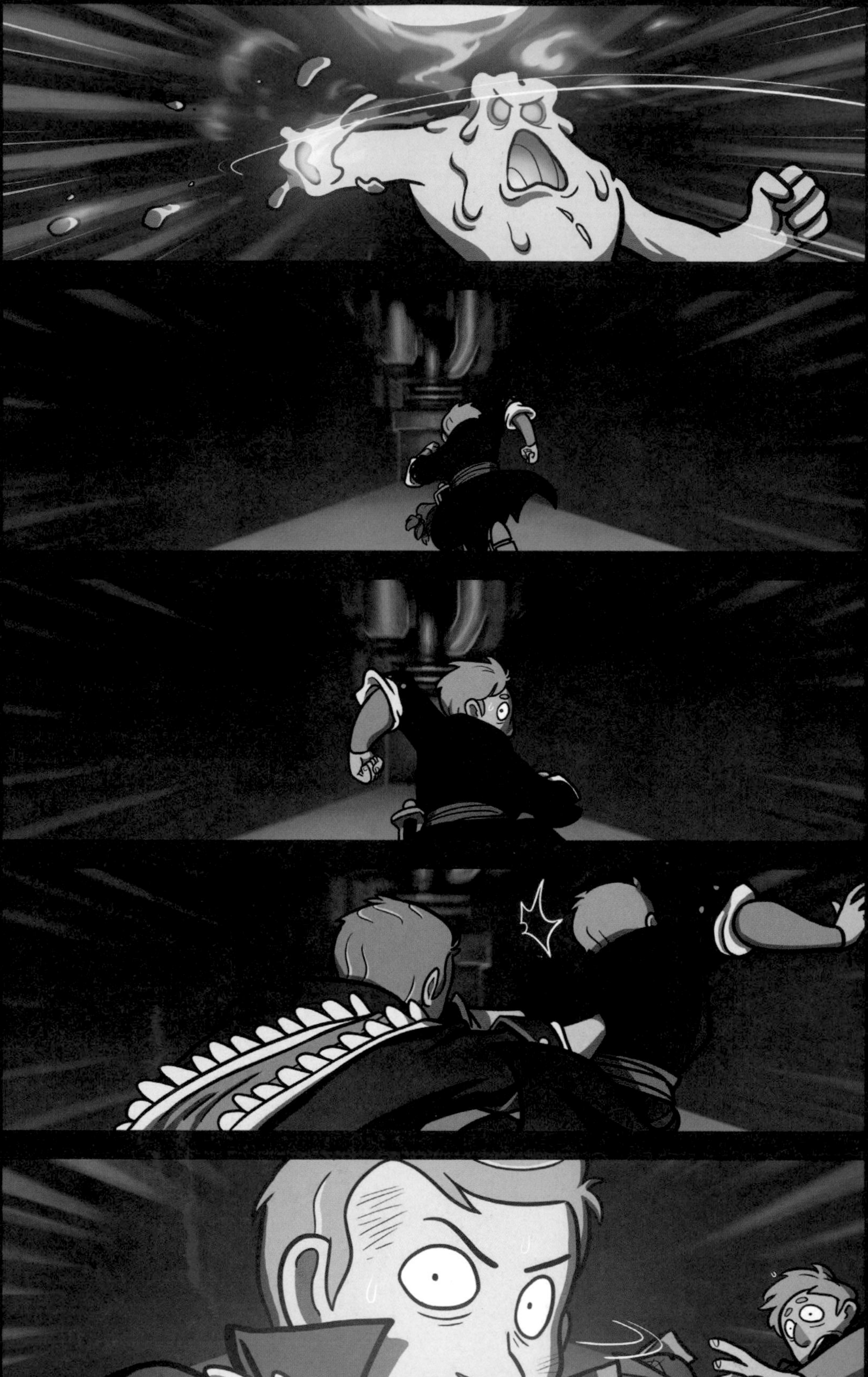

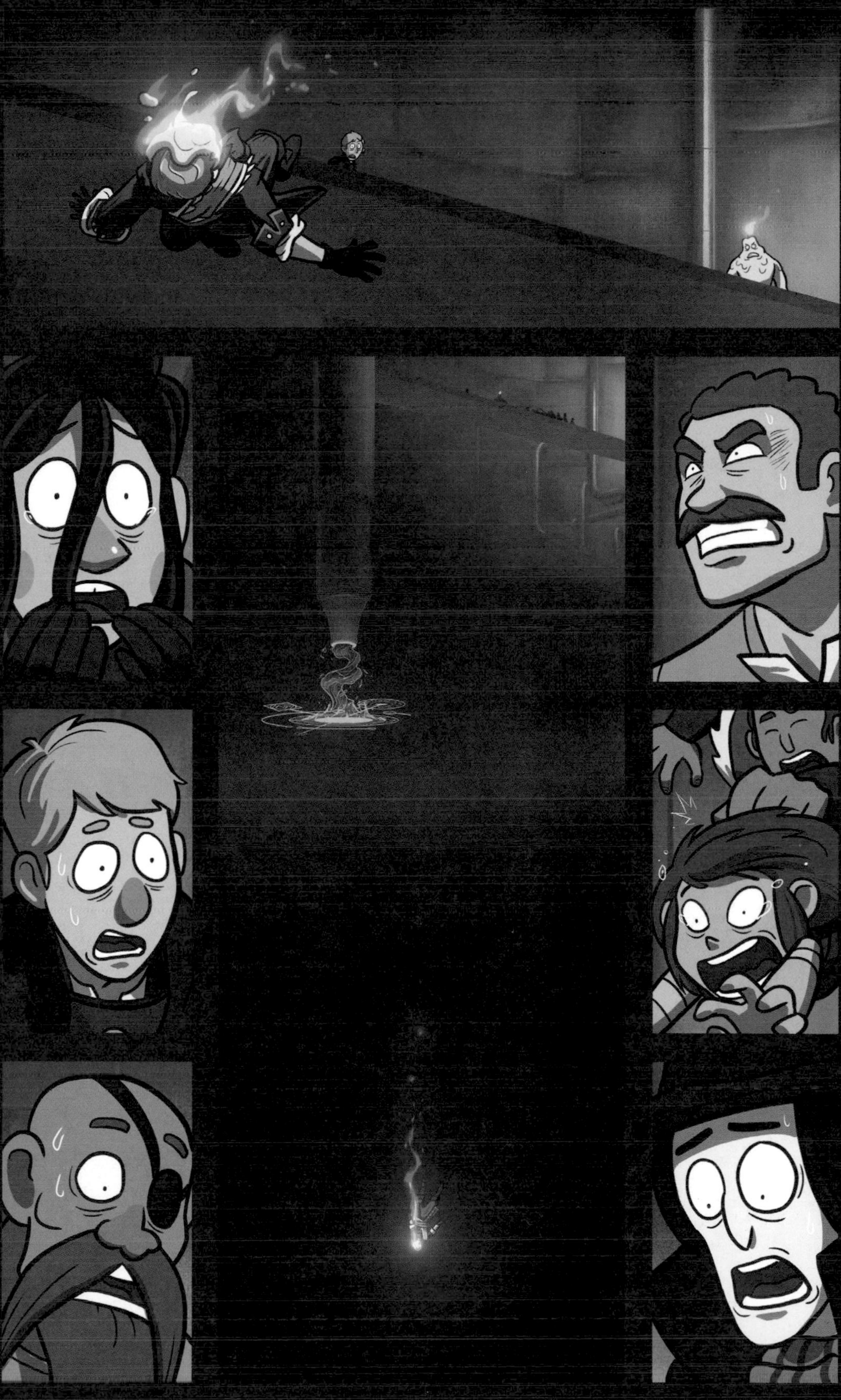

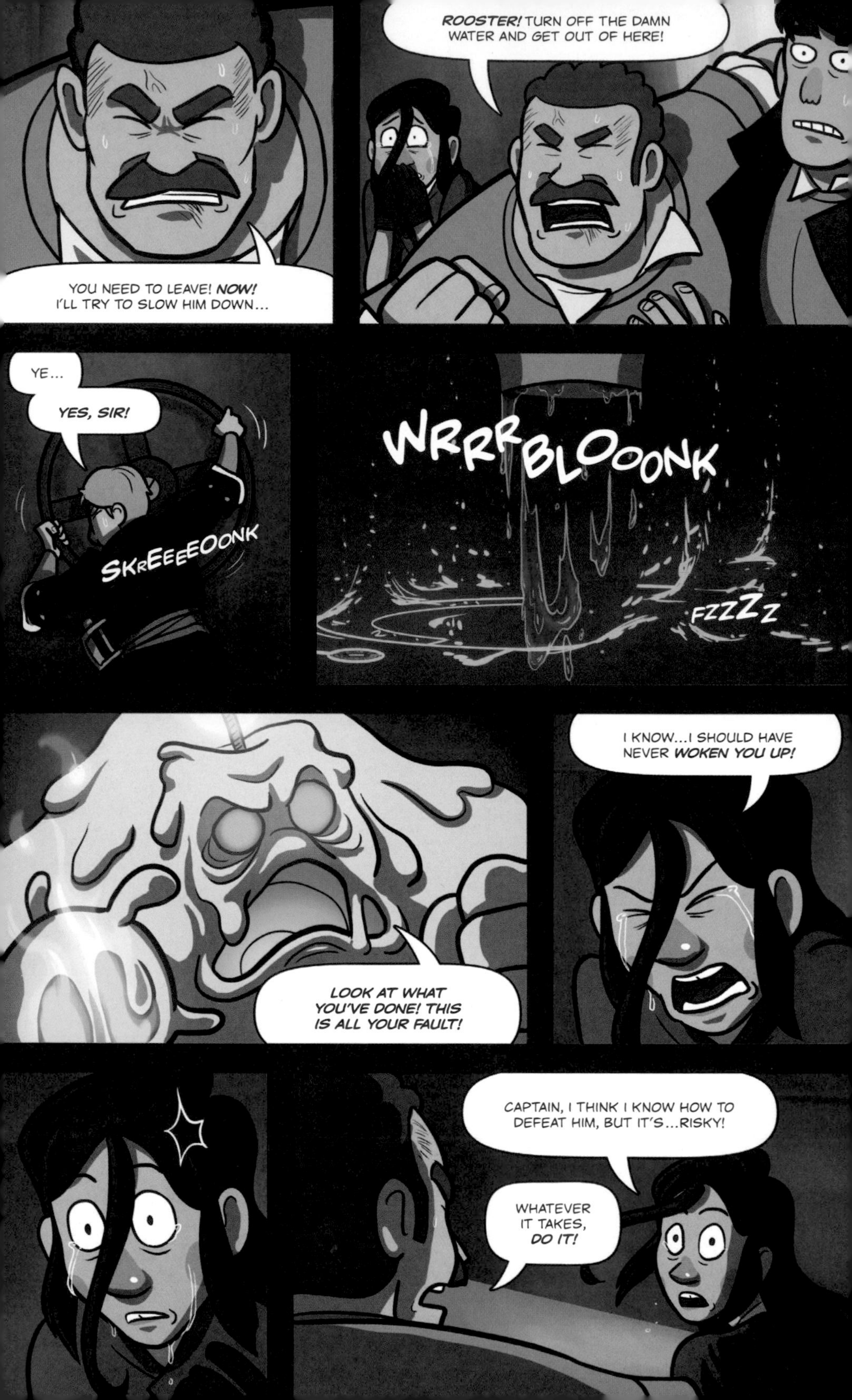
YOU NEED TO LEAVE! NOW! I'LL TRY TO SLOW HIM DOWN...
ROOSTER! TURN OFF THE DAMN WATER AND GET OUT OF HERE!
YE...
YES, SIR!
SKrEEEEEOONK
WRRR BLOOOONK
FZZZZ
LOOK AT WHAT YOU'VE DONE! THIS IS ALL YOUR FAULT!
I KNOW...I SHOULD HAVE NEVER WOKEN YOU UP!
CAPTAIN, I THINK I KNOW HOW TO DEFEAT HIM, BUT IT'S...RISKY!
WHATEVER IT TAKES, DO IT!

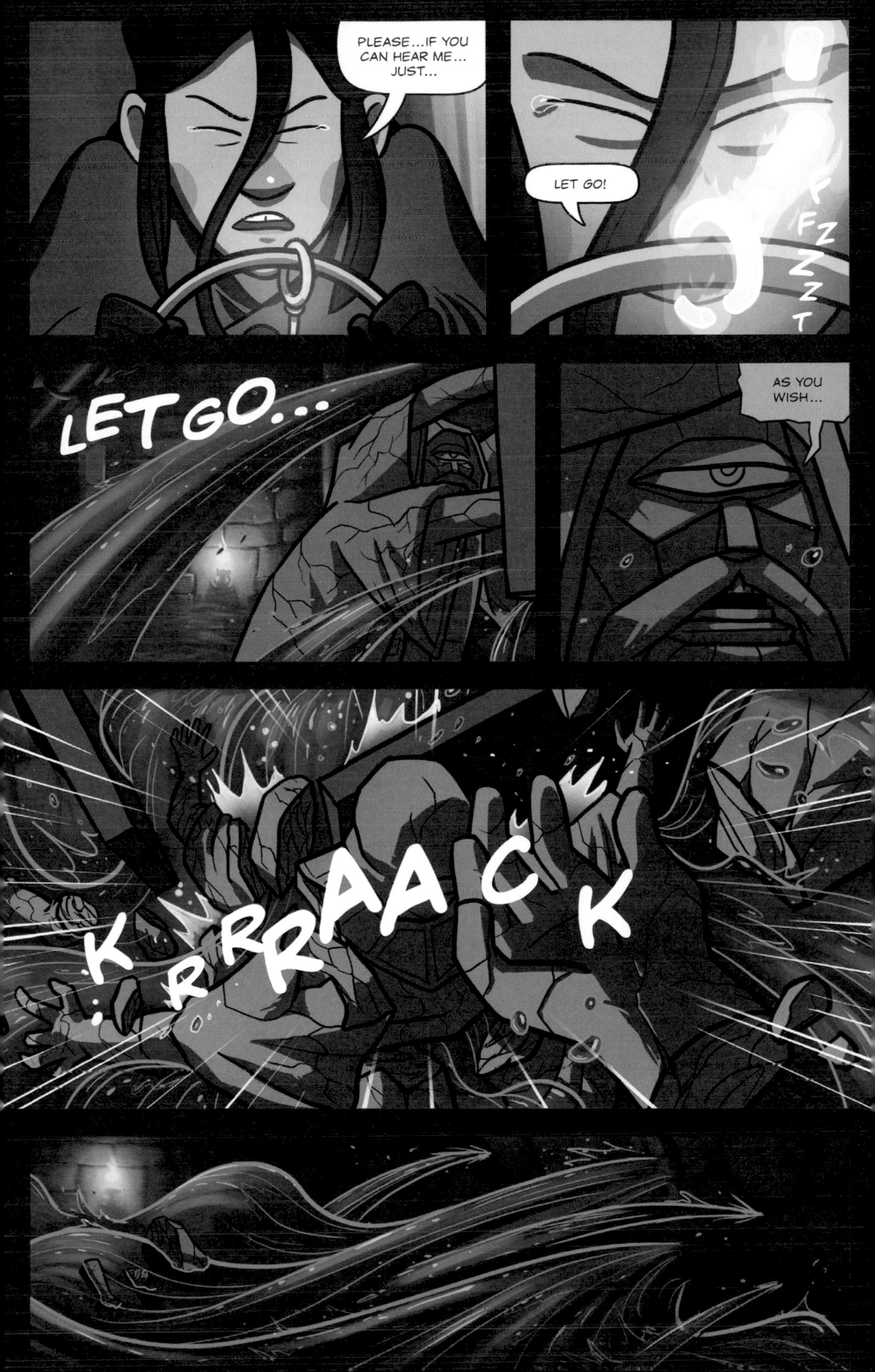
PLEASE...IF YOU CAN HEAR ME... JUST...
LET GO!
FFZZZZT
LET GO...
AS YOU WISH...
KRRRAACK

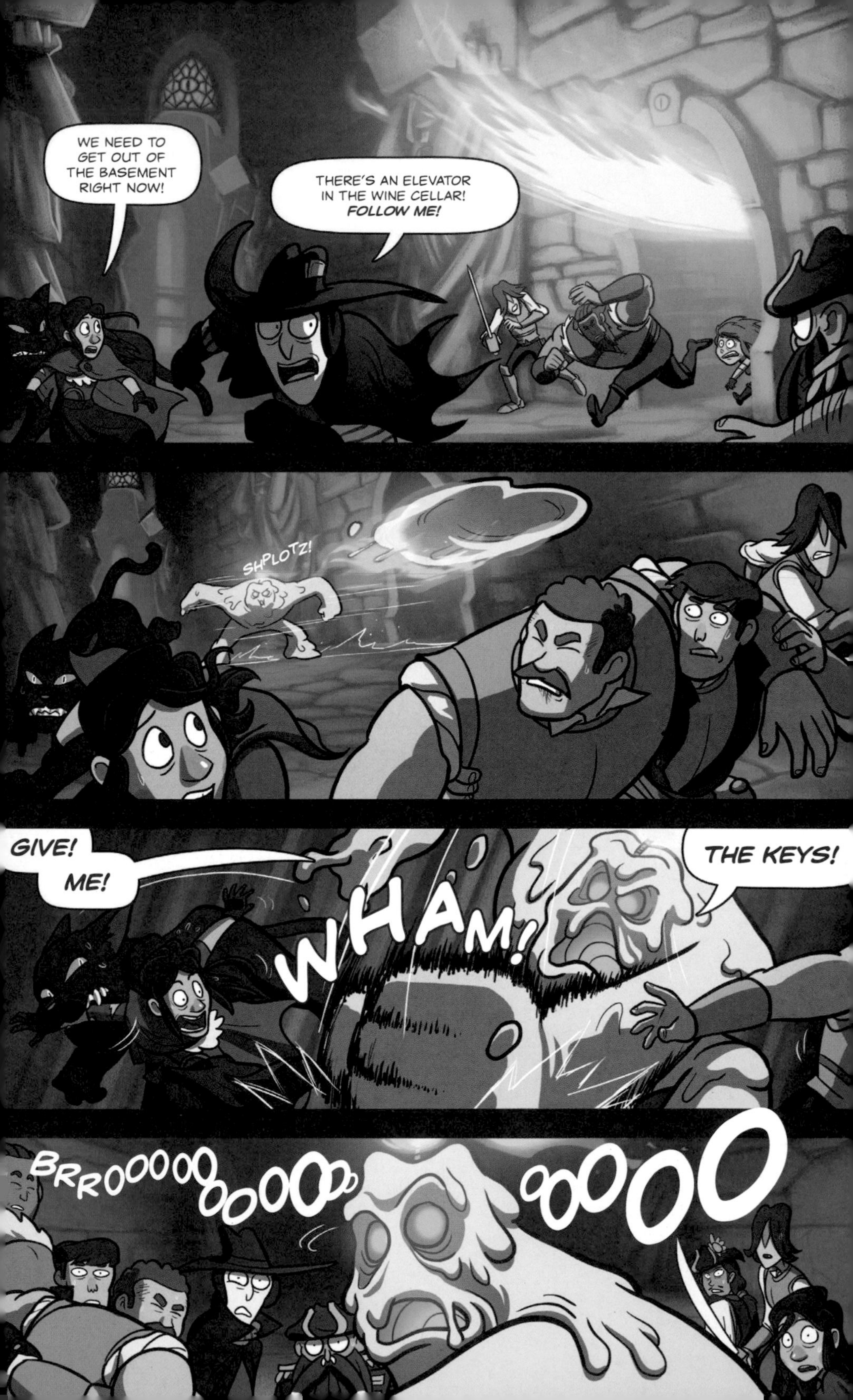
WE NEED TO GET OUT OF THE BASEMENT RIGHT NOW!
THERE'S AN ELEVATOR IN THE WINE CELLAR! *FOLLOW ME!*
SHPLOTZ!
GIVE! ME!
WHAM!
THE KEYS!
BRROOOOOOOOOOOOOOOO

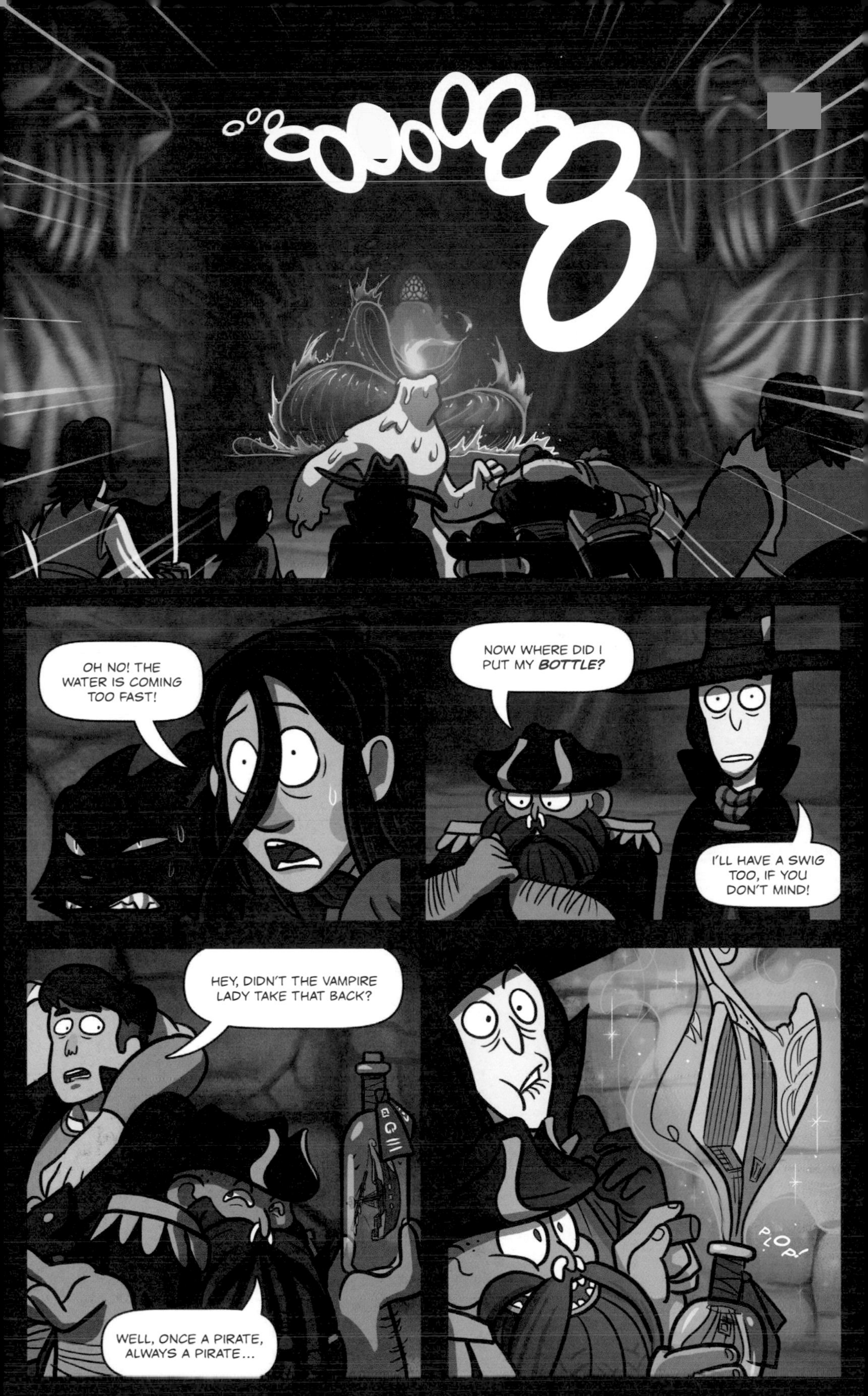
OH NO! THE WATER IS COMING TOO FAST!
NOW WHERE DID I PUT MY *BOTTLE?*
I'LL HAVE A SWIG TOO, IF YOU DON'T MIND!
HEY, DIDN'T THE VAMPIRE LADY TAKE THAT BACK?
WELL, ONCE A PIRATE, ALWAYS A PIRATE...
PLOP!

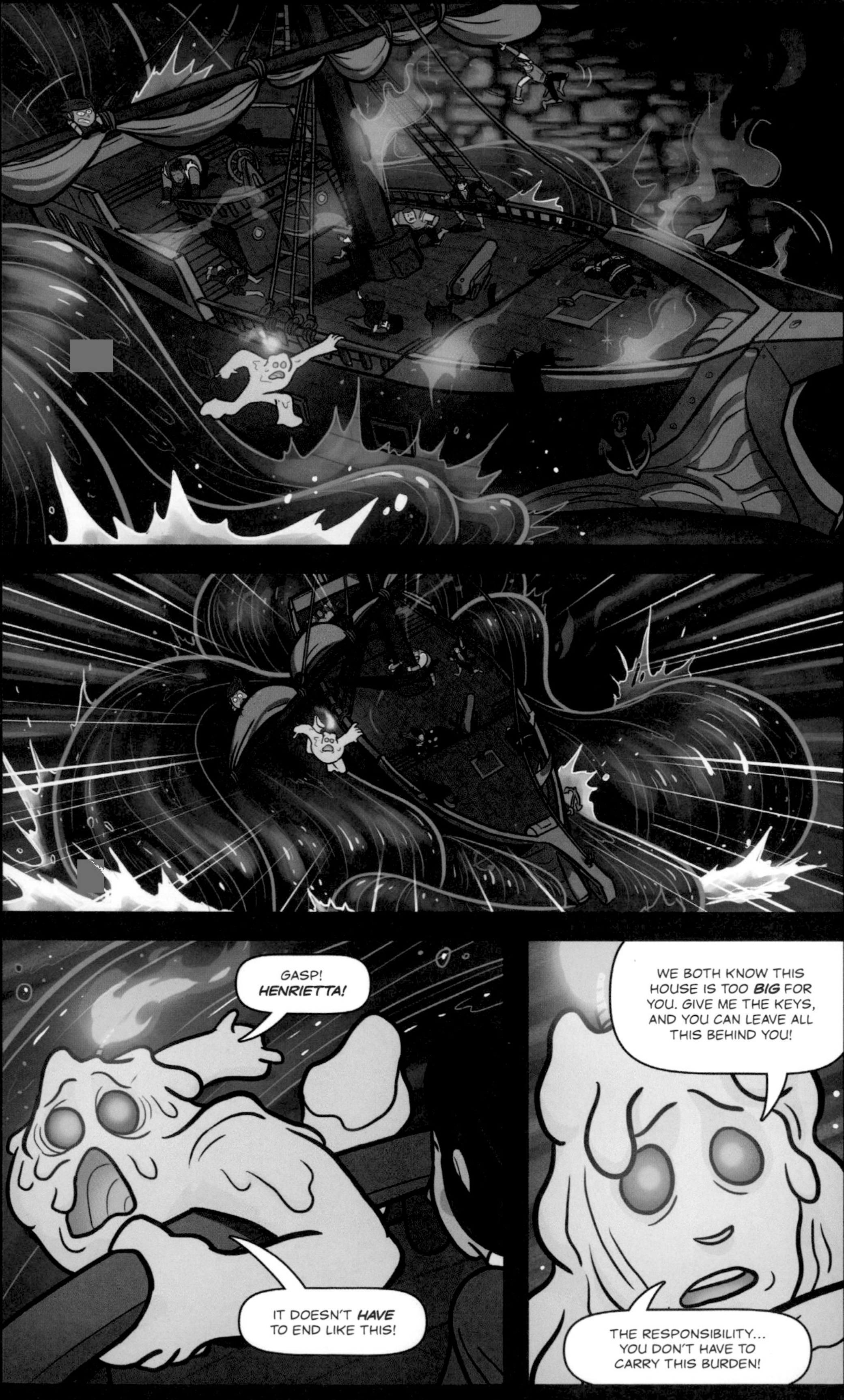
GASP! HENRIETTA!
IT DOESN'T HAVE TO END LIKE THIS!
WE BOTH KNOW THIS HOUSE IS TOO BIG FOR YOU. GIVE ME THE KEYS, AND YOU CAN LEAVE ALL THIS BEHIND YOU!
THE RESPONSIBILITY... YOU DON'T HAVE TO CARRY THIS BURDEN!

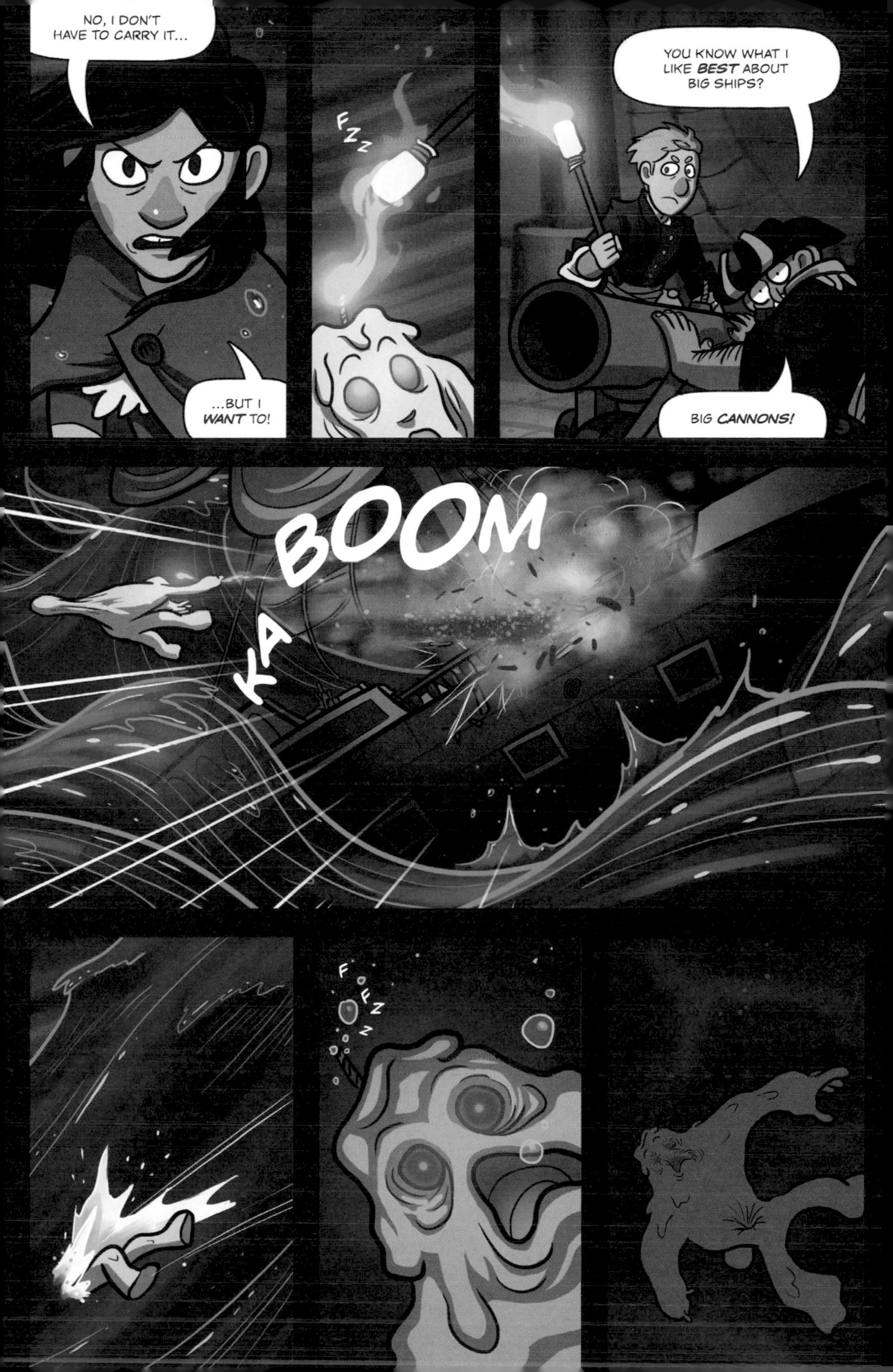

NO, I DON'T HAVE TO CARRY IT...
...BUT I *WANT* TO!
FZZ
YOU KNOW WHAT I LIKE *BEST* ABOUT BIG SHIPS?
BIG *CANNONS!*
KABOOM
FFZZ

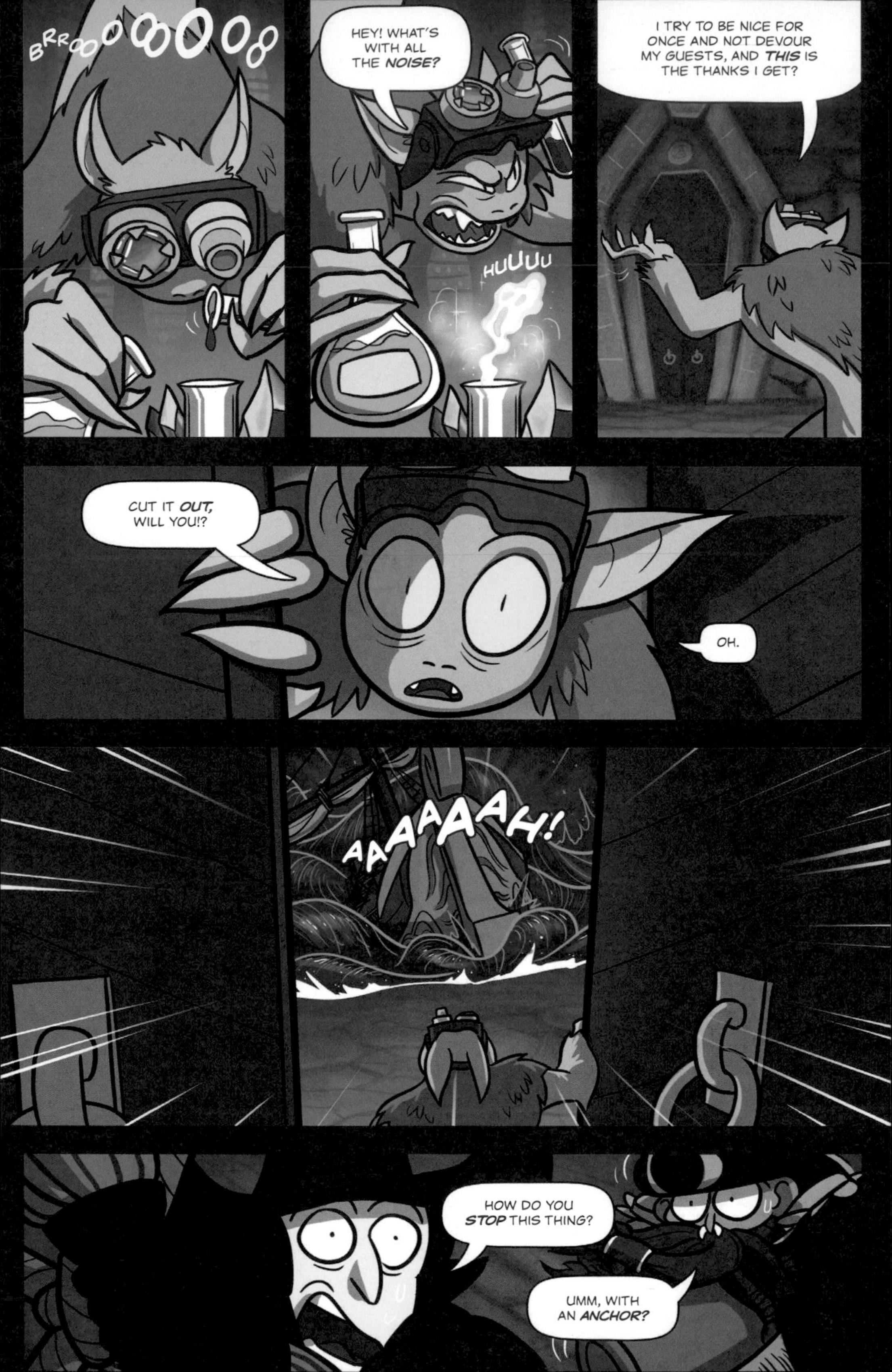
BRROOOOOOOO8
HEY! WHAT'S WITH ALL THE NOISE?
HUUUU
I TRY TO BE NICE FOR ONCE AND NOT DEVOUR MY GUESTS, AND THIS IS THE THANKS I GET?
CUT IT OUT, WILL YOU!?
OH.
AAAAAAH!
HOW DO YOU STOP THIS THING?
UMM, WITH AN ANCHOR?

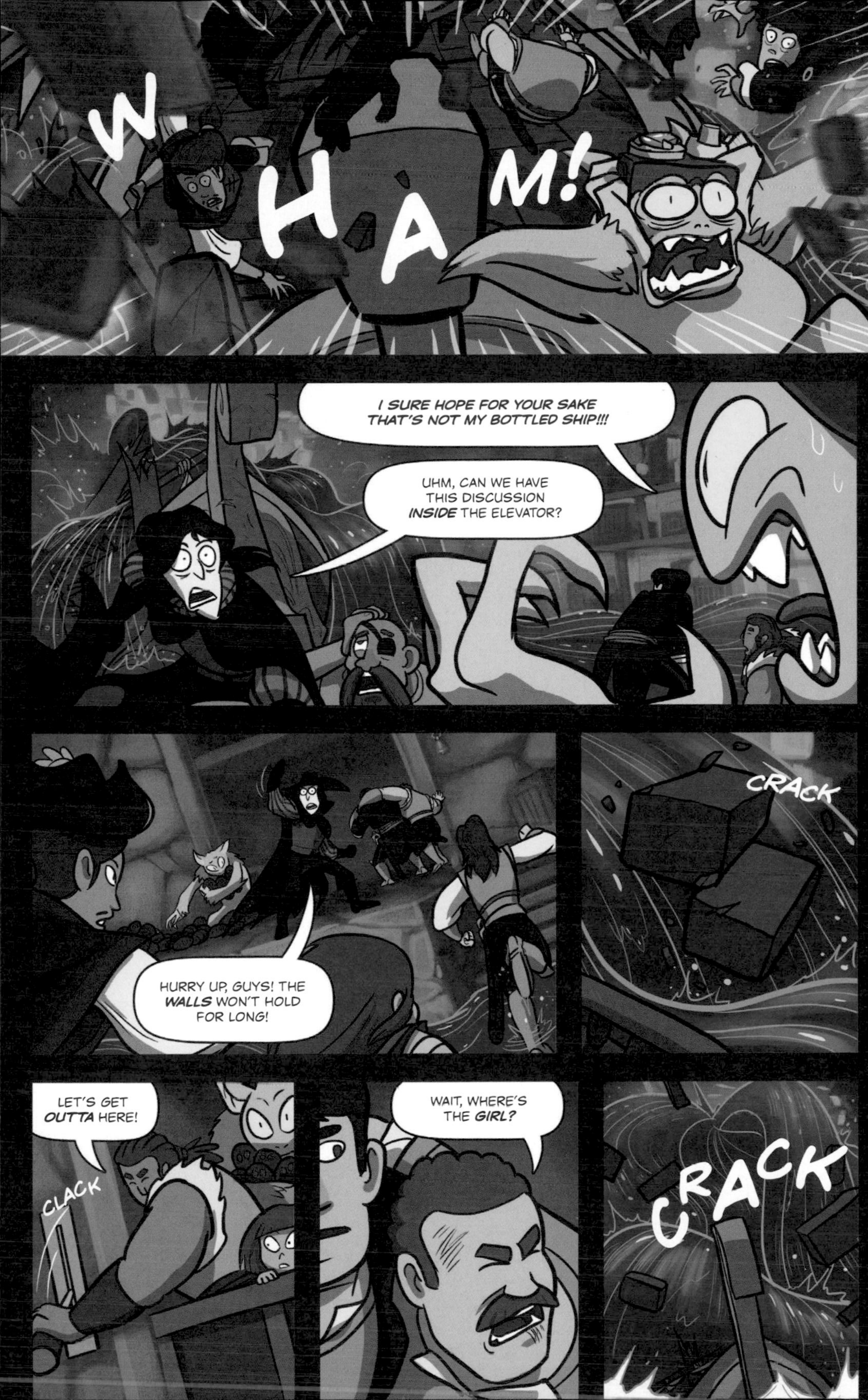
WHAM!
I SURE HOPE FOR YOUR SAKE THAT'S NOT MY BOTTLED SHIP!!!
UHM, CAN WE HAVE THIS DISCUSSION INSIDE THE ELEVATOR?
HURRY UP, GUYS! THE WALLS WON'T HOLD FOR LONG!
CRACK
LET'S GET OUTTA HERE!
CLACK
WAIT, WHERE'S THE GIRL?
CRACK

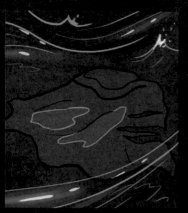

STOP THIS THING RIGHT NOW!

I...CAN'T REACH IT!

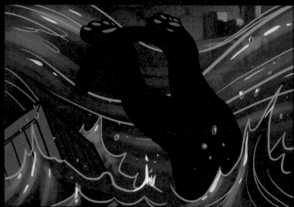

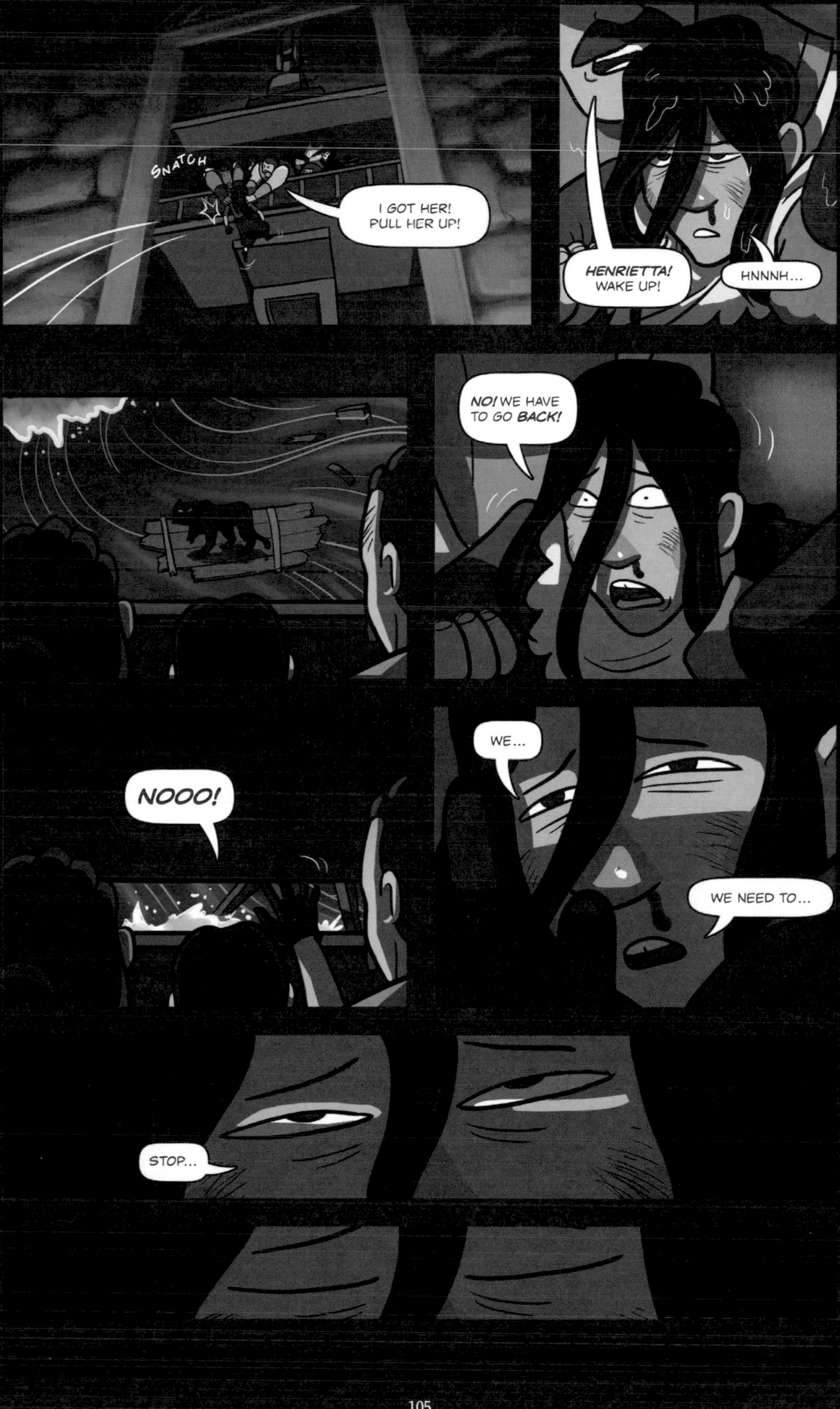
SNATCH
I GOT HER! PULL HER UP!
HENRIETTA! WAKE UP!
HNNNH...
NO! WE HAVE TO GO BACK!
NOOO!
WE...
WE NEED TO...
STOP...

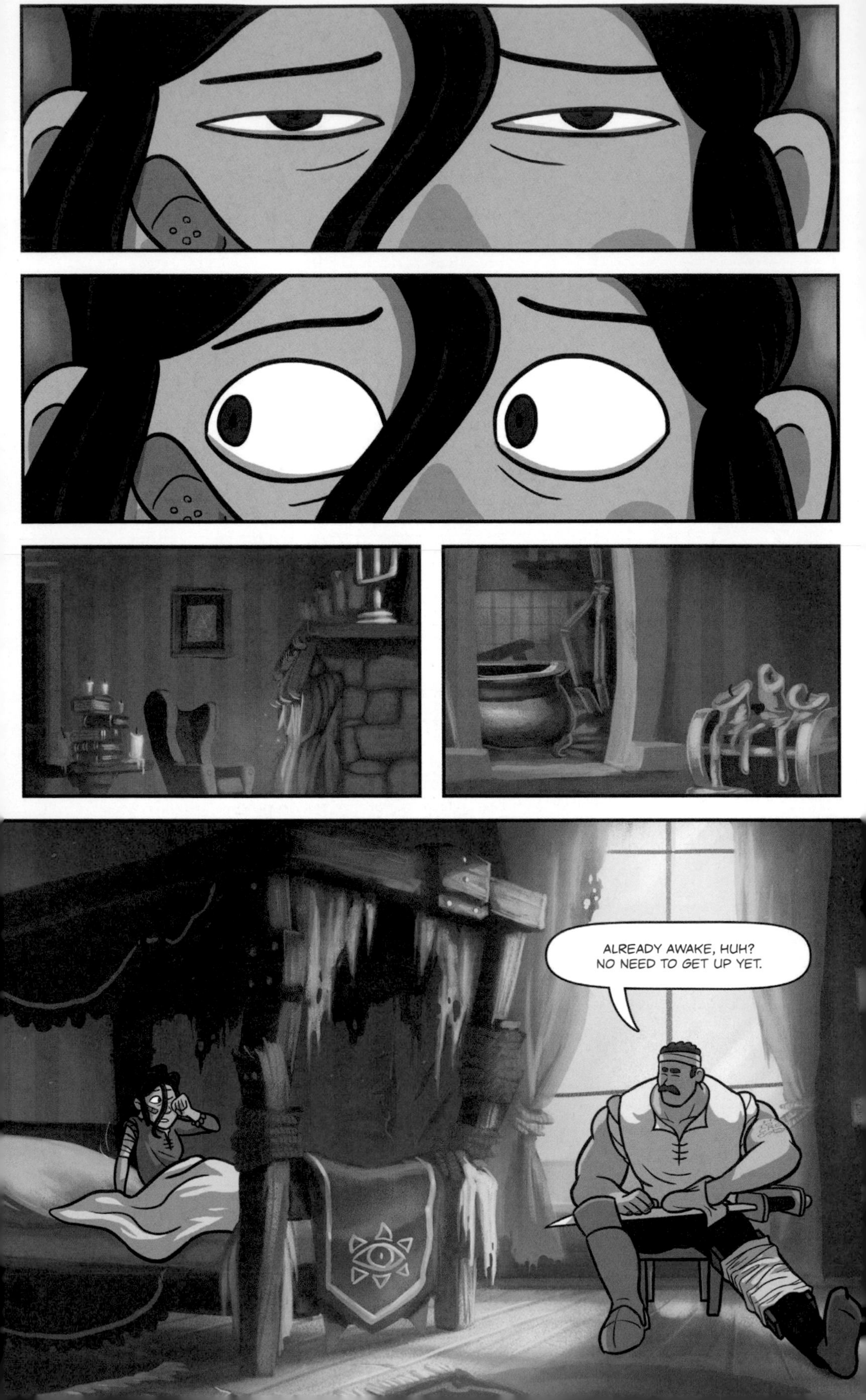
ALREADY AWAKE, HUH? NO NEED TO GET UP YET.

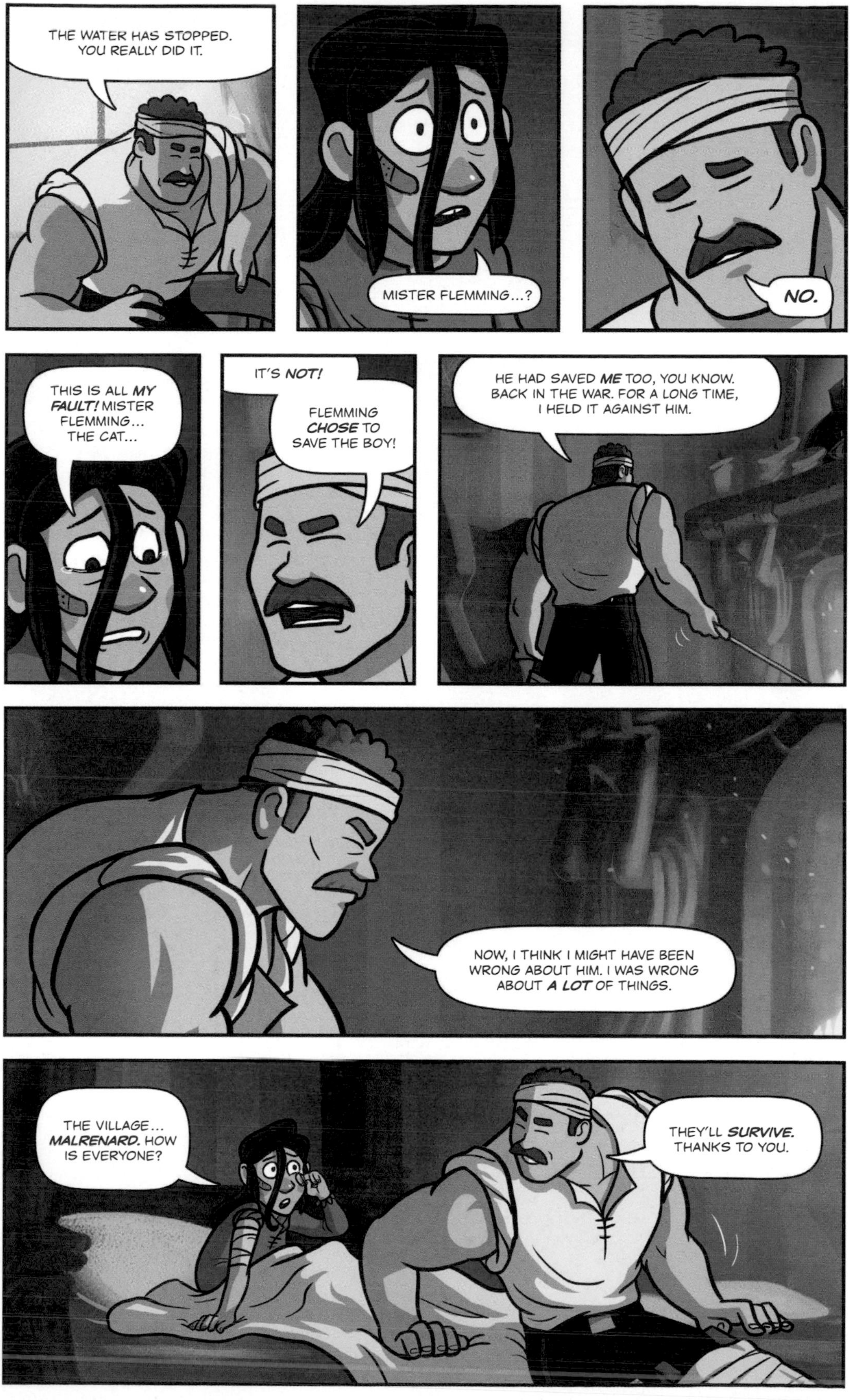
THE WATER HAS STOPPED. YOU REALLY DID IT.
MISTER FLEMMING...?
NO.
THIS IS ALL MY FAULT! MISTER FLEMMING... THE CAT...
IT'S NOT!
FLEMMING CHOSE TO SAVE THE BOY!
HE HAD SAVED ME TOO, YOU KNOW. BACK IN THE WAR. FOR A LONG TIME, I HELD IT AGAINST HIM.
NOW, I THINK I MIGHT HAVE BEEN WRONG ABOUT HIM. I WAS WRONG ABOUT A LOT OF THINGS.
THE VILLAGE... MALRENARD. HOW IS EVERYONE?
THEY'LL SURVIVE. THANKS TO YOU.

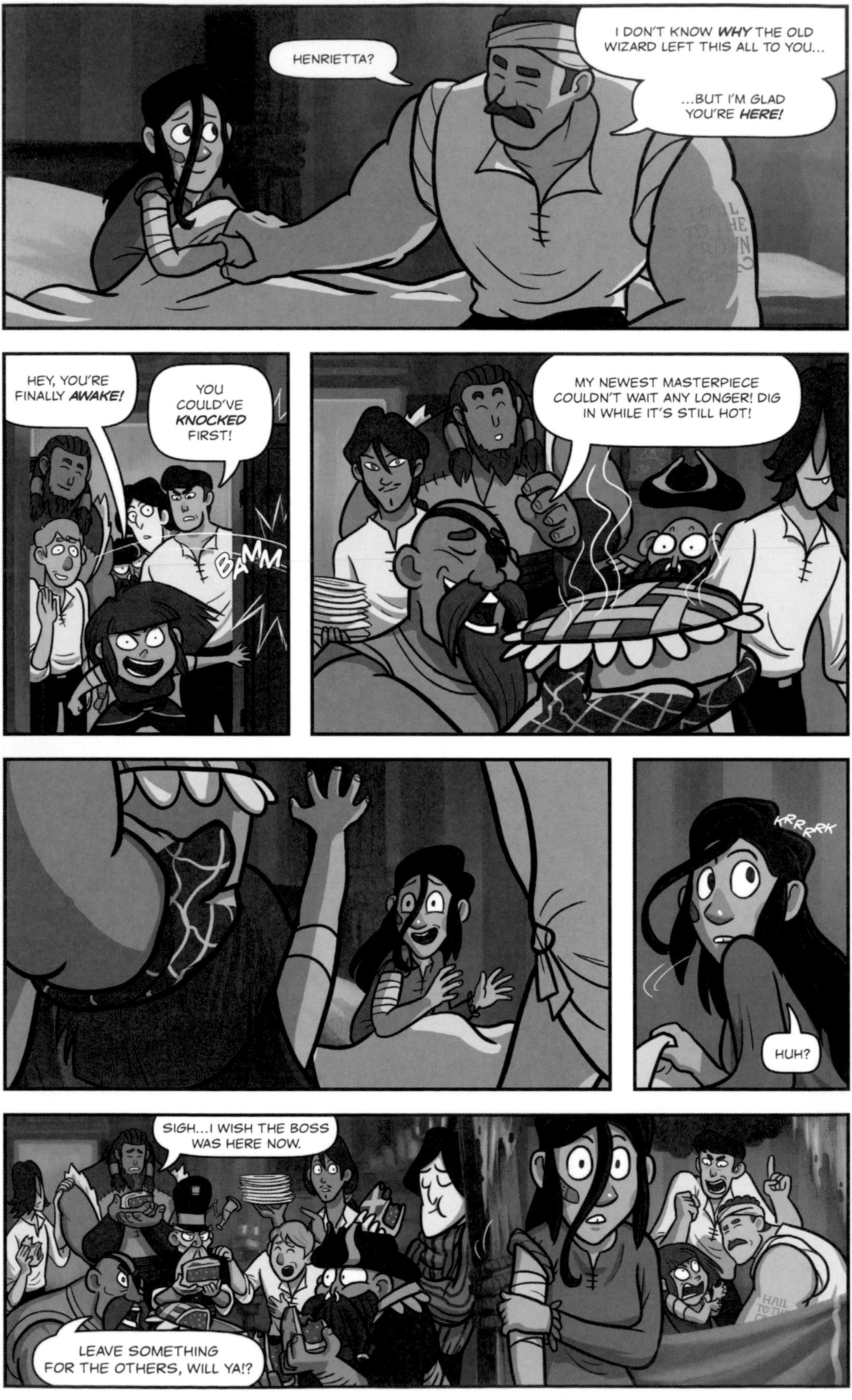
HENRIETTA?
I DON'T KNOW WHY THE OLD WIZARD LEFT THIS ALL TO YOU...
...BUT I'M GLAD YOU'RE HERE!
HAIL TO THE CROWN
HEY, YOU'RE FINALLY AWAKE!
YOU COULD'VE KNOCKED FIRST!
BAMM
MY NEWEST MASTERPIECE COULDN'T WAIT ANY LONGER! DIG IN WHILE IT'S STILL HOT!
KRRRRK
HUH?
SIGH...I WISH THE BOSS WAS HERE NOW.
LEAVE SOMETHING FOR THE OTHERS, WILL YA!?
HAIL TO THE CR

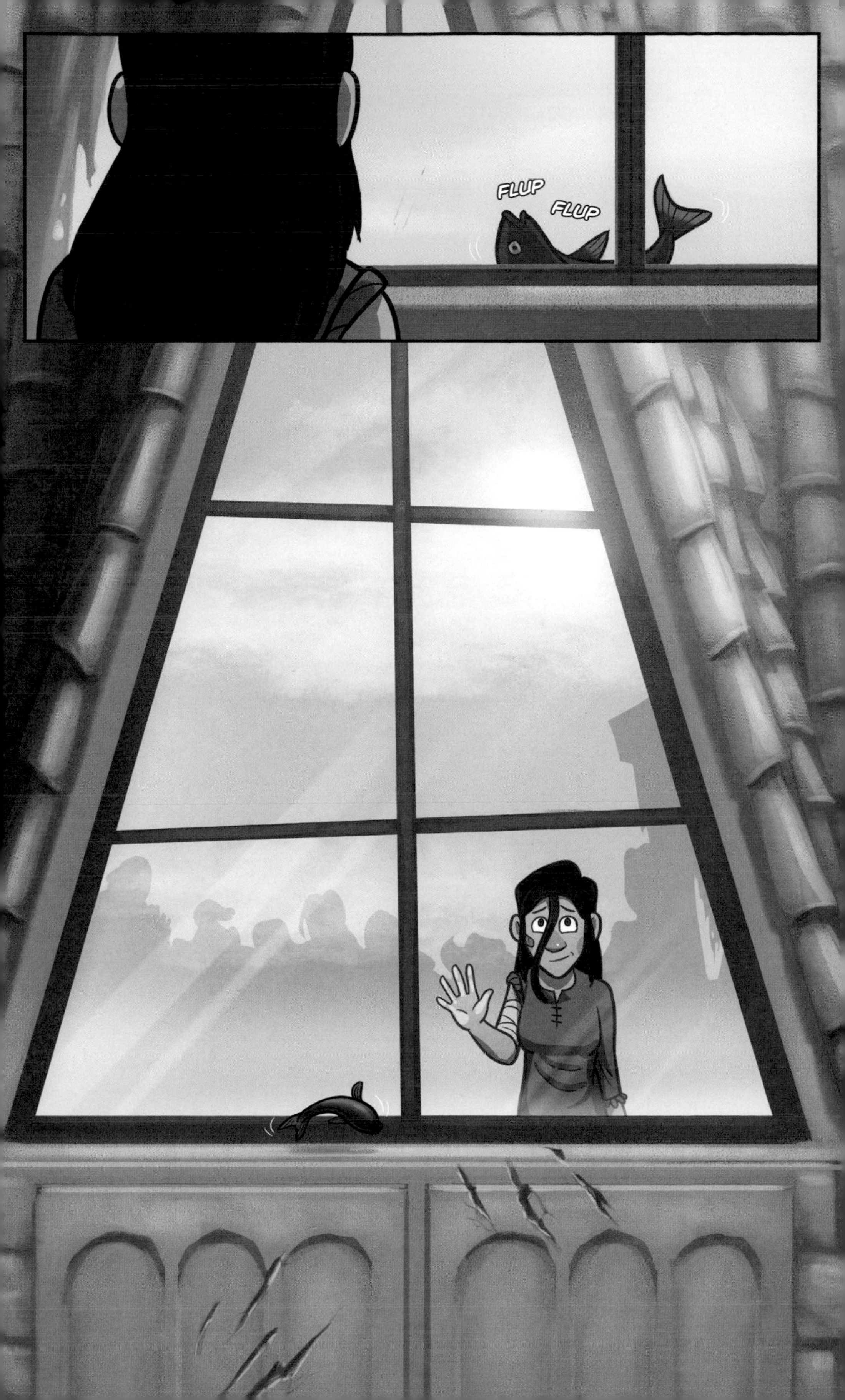
FLUP
FLUP

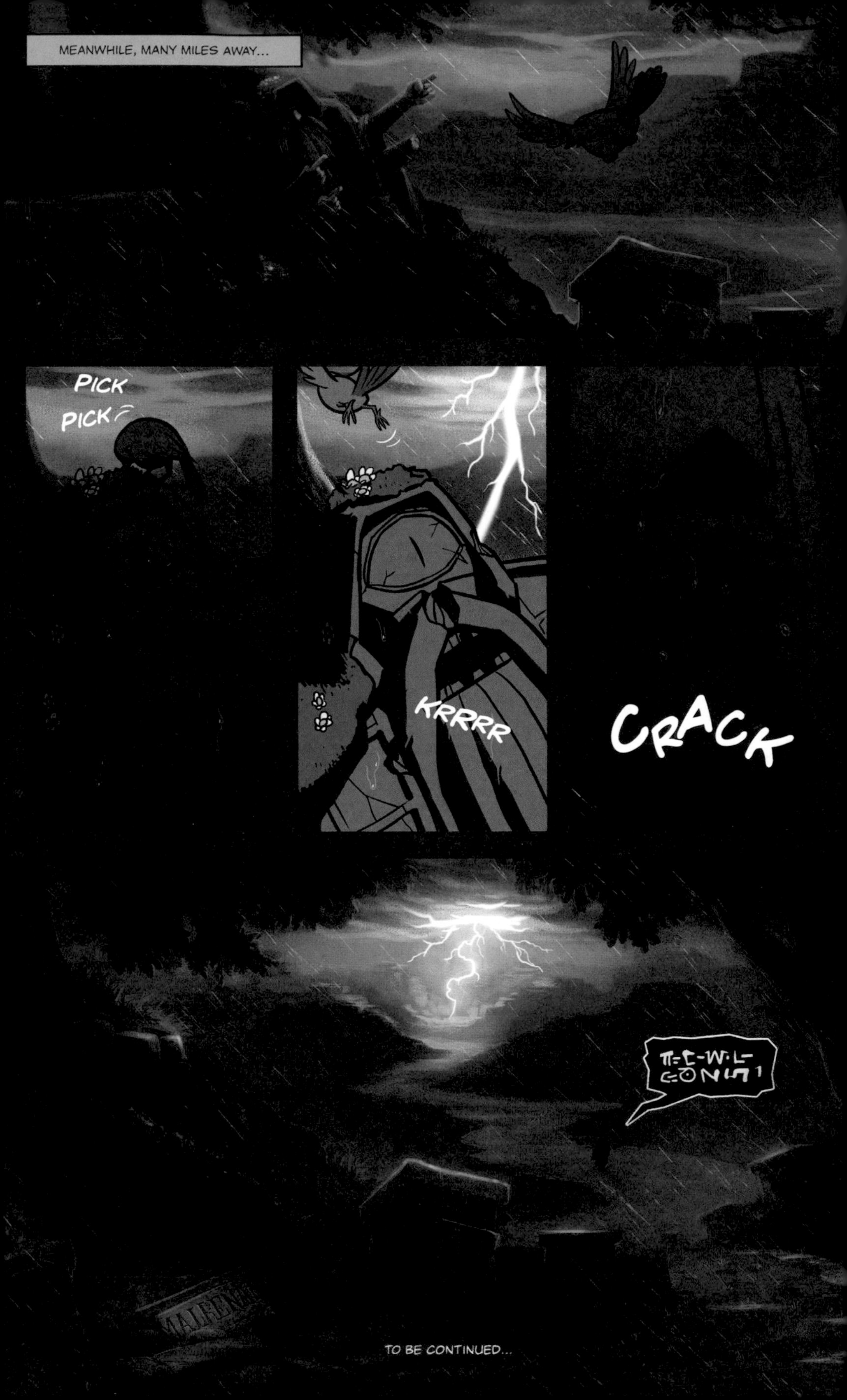
MEANWHILE, MANY MILES AWAY...
PICK
PICK
KRRRR
CRACK
TO BE CONTINUED...

Moira's Magical
Dragon Blood Punch

PREPARATION:

1. Pour black currant juice, cherry juice, cranberry juice, and apple juice into a medium-sized pot. Heat slowly under low heat.

2. After pouring the juices, add the cinnamon stick and vanilla sugar.

3. Let the mixture simmer for another 10 minutes on medium heat.

4. Using tongs, take out the cinnamon stick. Pour the potion into a hollow dragon skull. (If you can't find a dragon skull, a glass punch bowl is fine too.)

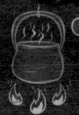

5. For the final step, just add fruit. And enjoy your dragon blood punch!

INGREDIENTS:

1 liter fresh dragon blood. (If there should be a shortage of juicy dragons, you can also use the following substitute ingredients.)

- 6-8 fluid ounces (200 mL) cranberry juice
- 6-8 fl oz (200 mL) cherry juice
- 6-8 fl oz (200 mL) black currant juice
- 6-8 fl oz (200 mL) apple juice
- 1 cinnamon stick
- 4 teaspoons vanilla sugar
- 1 nectarine, sliced
- 1 handful fresh raspberries
- 1 handful red grapes
- 1 handful cherries

Don't forget to share.
Yarr!

THE ART OF

A HOUSE DIVIDED

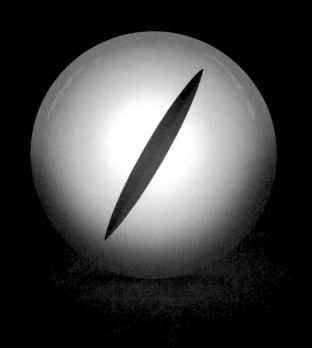

A LOOK INSIDE THE ATTIC

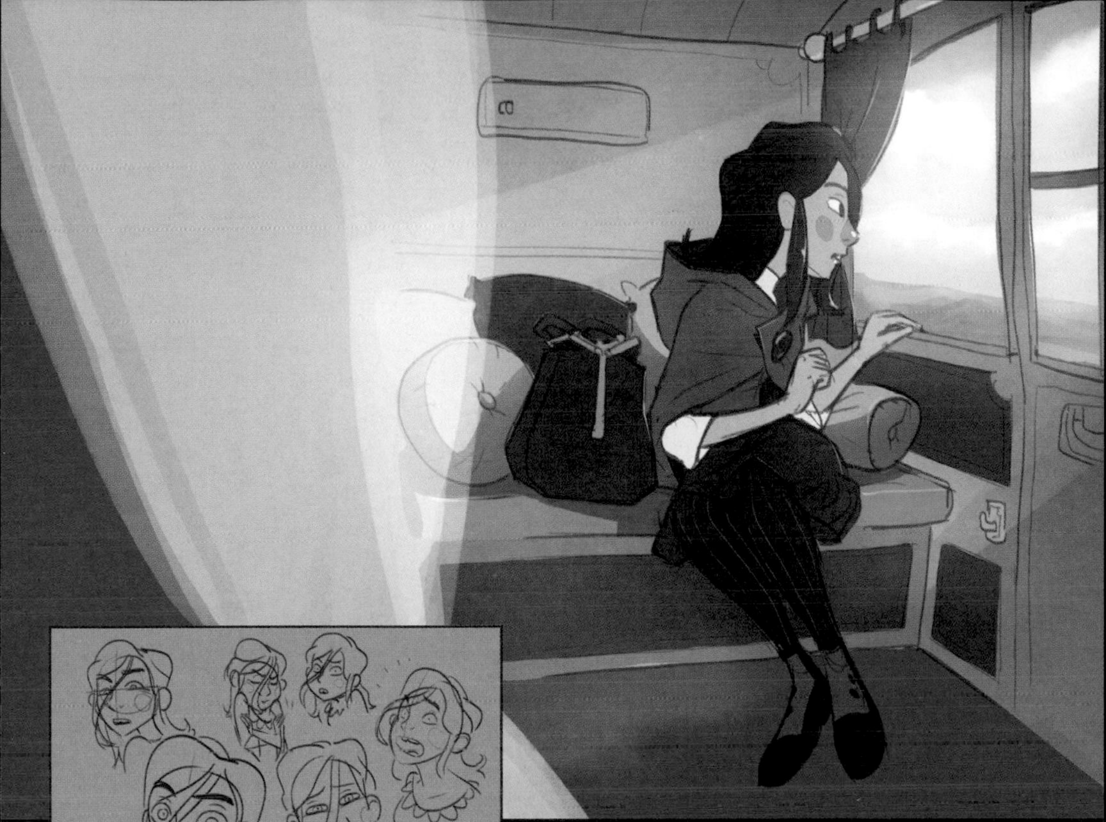

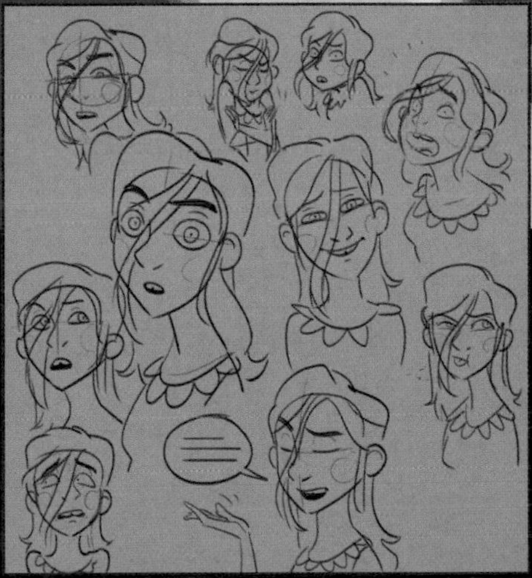

HENRIETTA

Getting Henrietta's design right was quite a challenge. We wanted her to feel real and relatable, and for that, she needed to have some human imperfections—like the tenacious strand of hair that always falls across her face and the little gap between her front teeth.

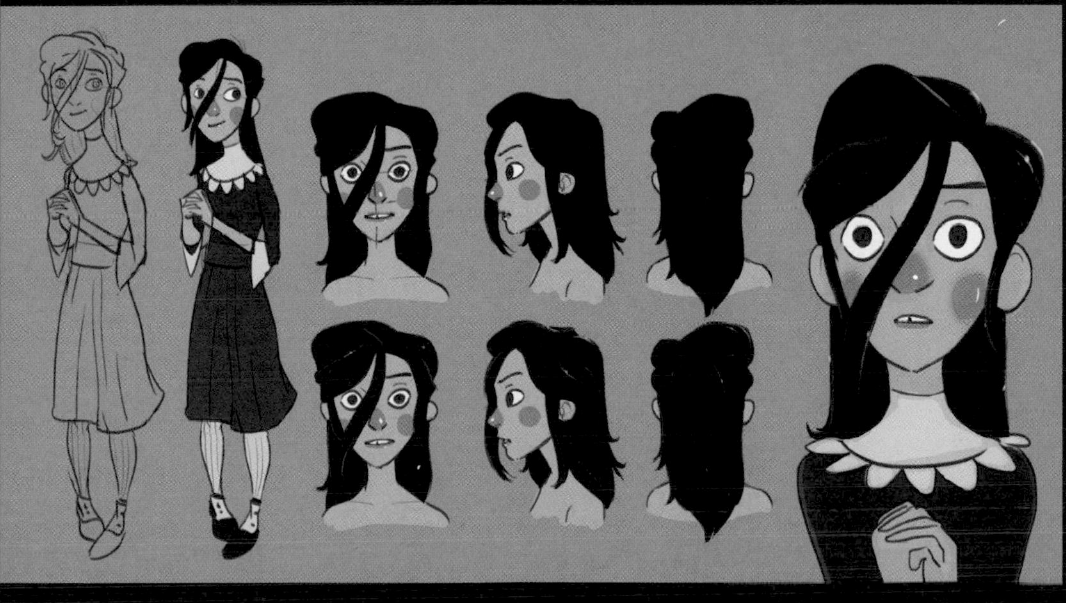

FLEMMING AND THE BANDITS

Originally, we wanted to base the look of our charming rogue on contemporary actors such as Owen Wilson and Brad Pitt. To our own surprise, the final design ended up looking more like the old Hollywood legend Errol Flynn.

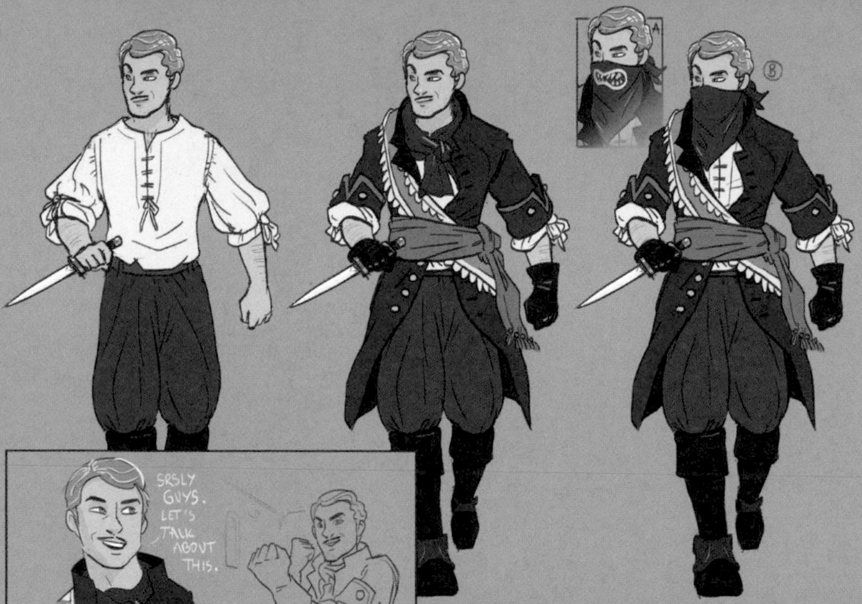

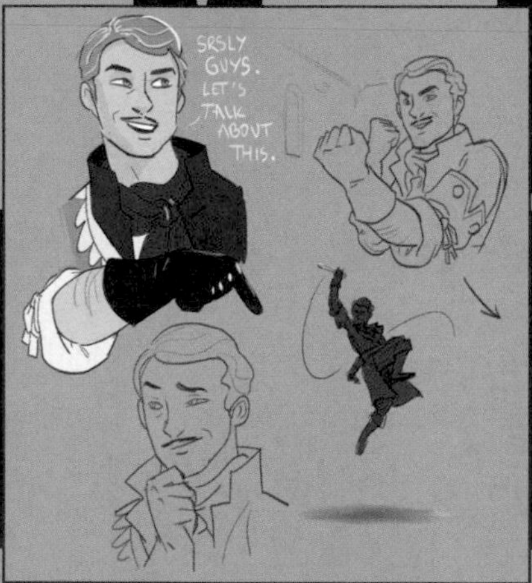
SRSLY GUYS. LET'S TALK ABOUT THIS.

The bandits are a colorful bunch of misfits. Although they are just supporting characters, it was really important that each of them had a very interesting look. Ideally, readers should want to know more about them and their past adventures.

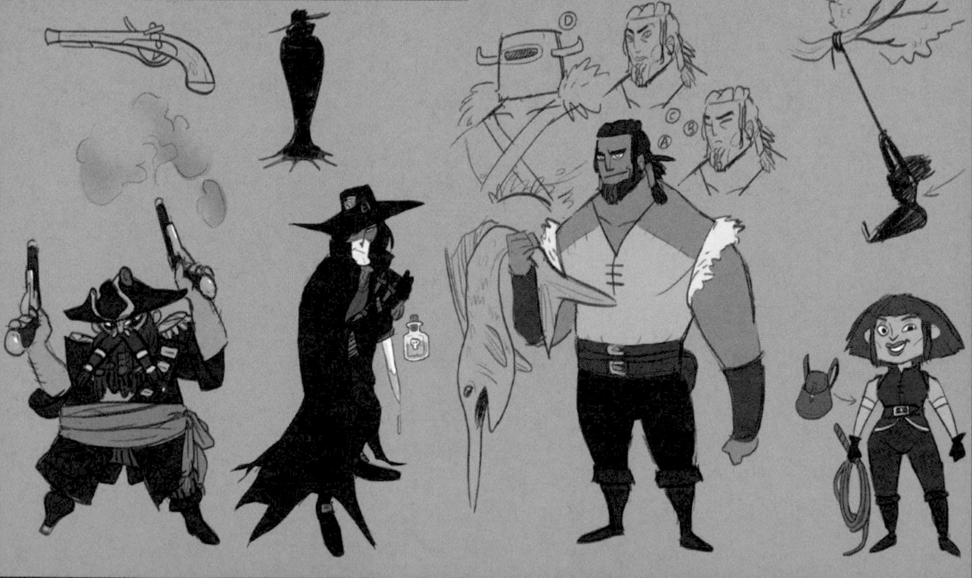

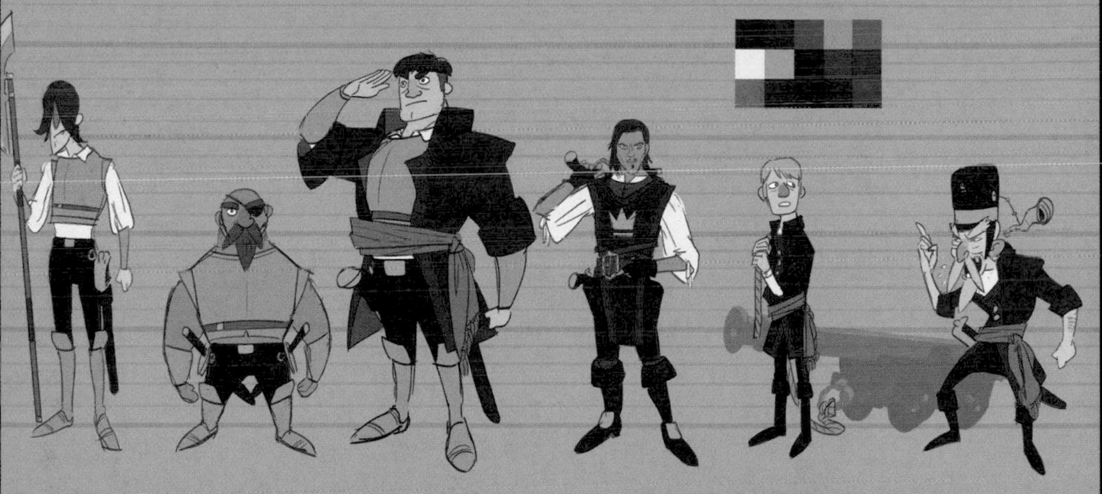

CAPTAIN BOONER

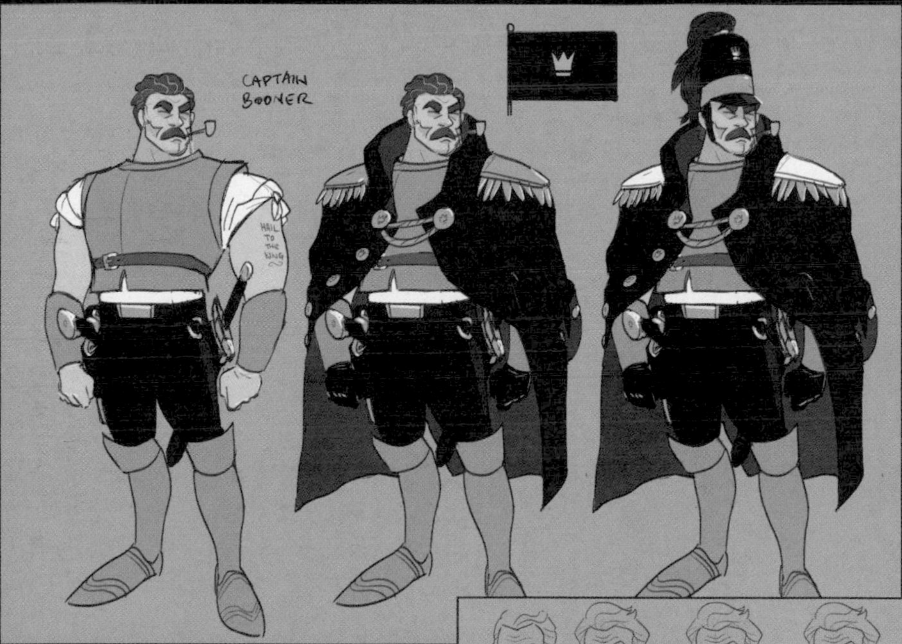
CAPTAIN BOONER
HAIL TO THE KING

Captain Booner is a stern leader, and his design reflects his no-nonsense attitude. For his magnificent moustache, we took some inspiration from actor Tom Selleck and his equally impressive facial hair.

When it came to designing his fearless soldiers, we tried to use a range of different silhouettes, so everyone would be easily identifiable from far away.

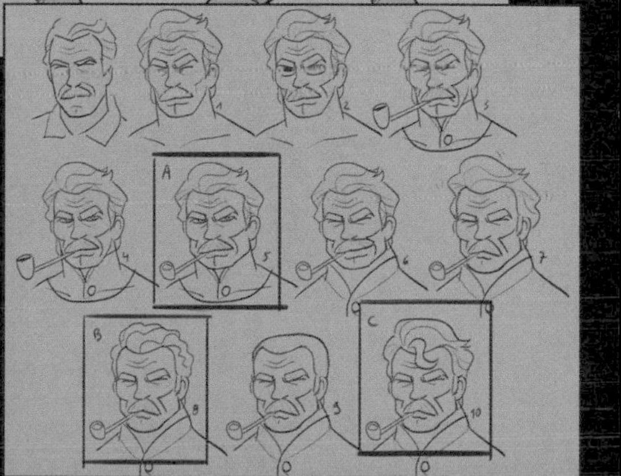

MOIRA KETTLEBREW

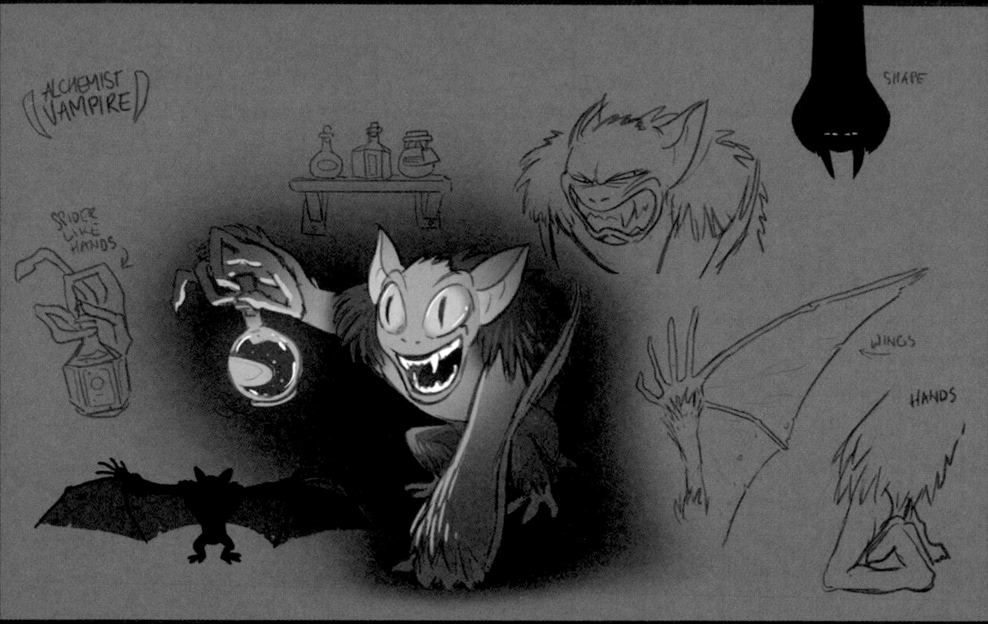
ALCHEMIST VAMPIRE
SPIDER LIKE HANDS
SHAPE
WINGS
HANDS

Although Moira is an ancient vampire, and a pretty scary-looking one at that, she doesn't really care about drinking blood or other related vampire habits. She'd rather spend her time brewing new magical potions, conducting alchemical experiments, or cuddling with her pet bugs. When it came to designing Moira's big grin, we took some inspiration from some of Hayao Miyazaki's classic designs.

THE THIRD SIMULACRUM

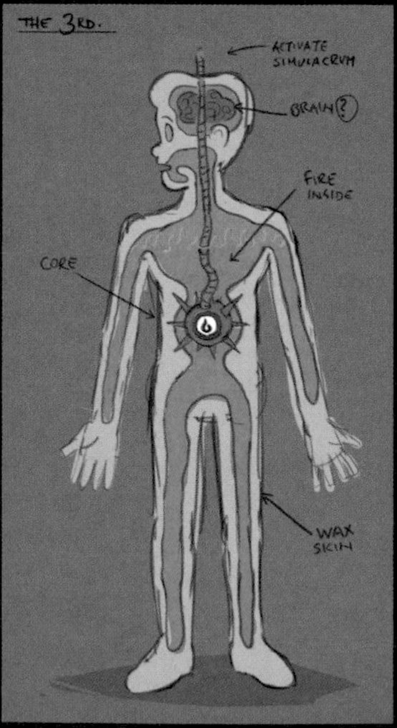
THE 3RD.
ACTIVATE SIMULACRUM
BRAIN(?)
FIRE INSIDE
CORE
WAX SKIN

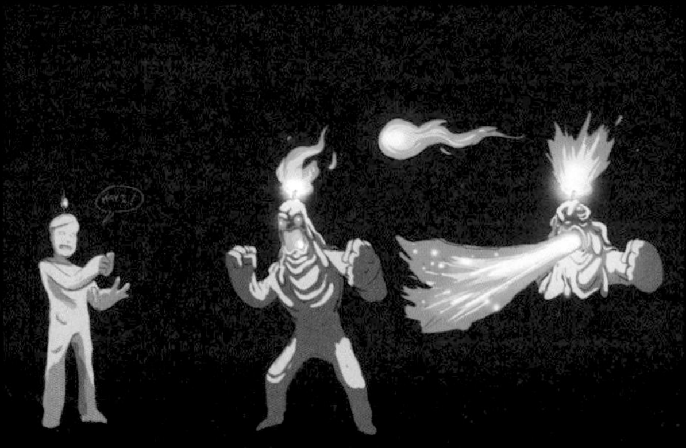

The Simulacra are mysterious magical creations of Ornun Zol. The candle boy might look harmless, but the angrier he gets, the hotter his flame burns, melting away the human facade.

ABOUT THE AUTHOR

Haiko Hörnig spent his childhood in his parents' comic book store, where he developed a love for sequential art at an early age. In middle school, he quickly became friends with Marius Pawlitza. The two of them first enjoyed role-playing games together and later started to make comics. Since 2013, Haiko has worked as a screenwriter for animated shows and feature films. A House Divided is his first published book series. He is based in Frankfurt, Germany. He's also active on Twitter (@DerGrafX) and Instagram (@ahousedividedcomic).

ABOUT THE ILLUSTRATOR

Marius Pawlitza was born in Poland in 1984 and grew up in Ludwigshafen, Germany. Years later, he studied communication design in the German city of Mainz. It was a good excuse to spend as much time as possible playing video games and making comics with Haiko Hornig. Since 2011, he has worked as an art director for different agencies and companies in Frankfurt, in addition to creating sequential art. On Twitter, he's @pengboom.

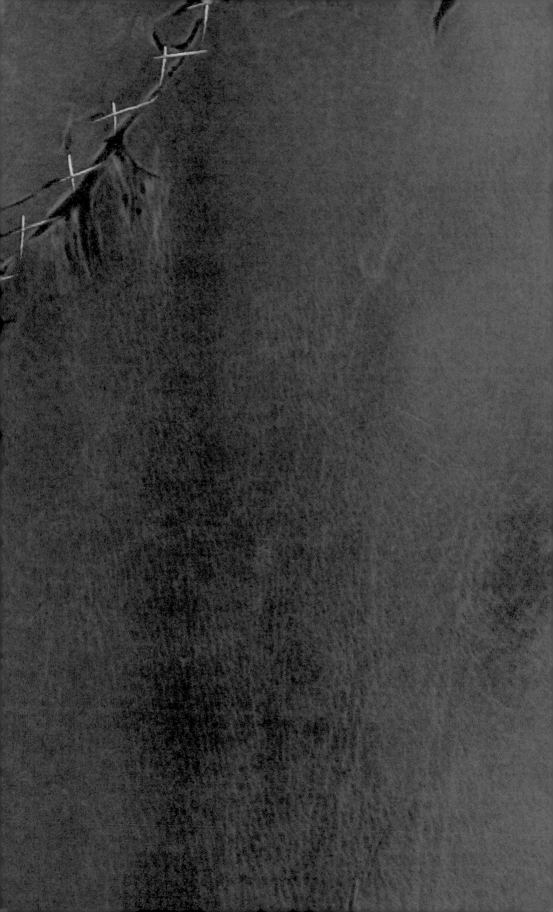

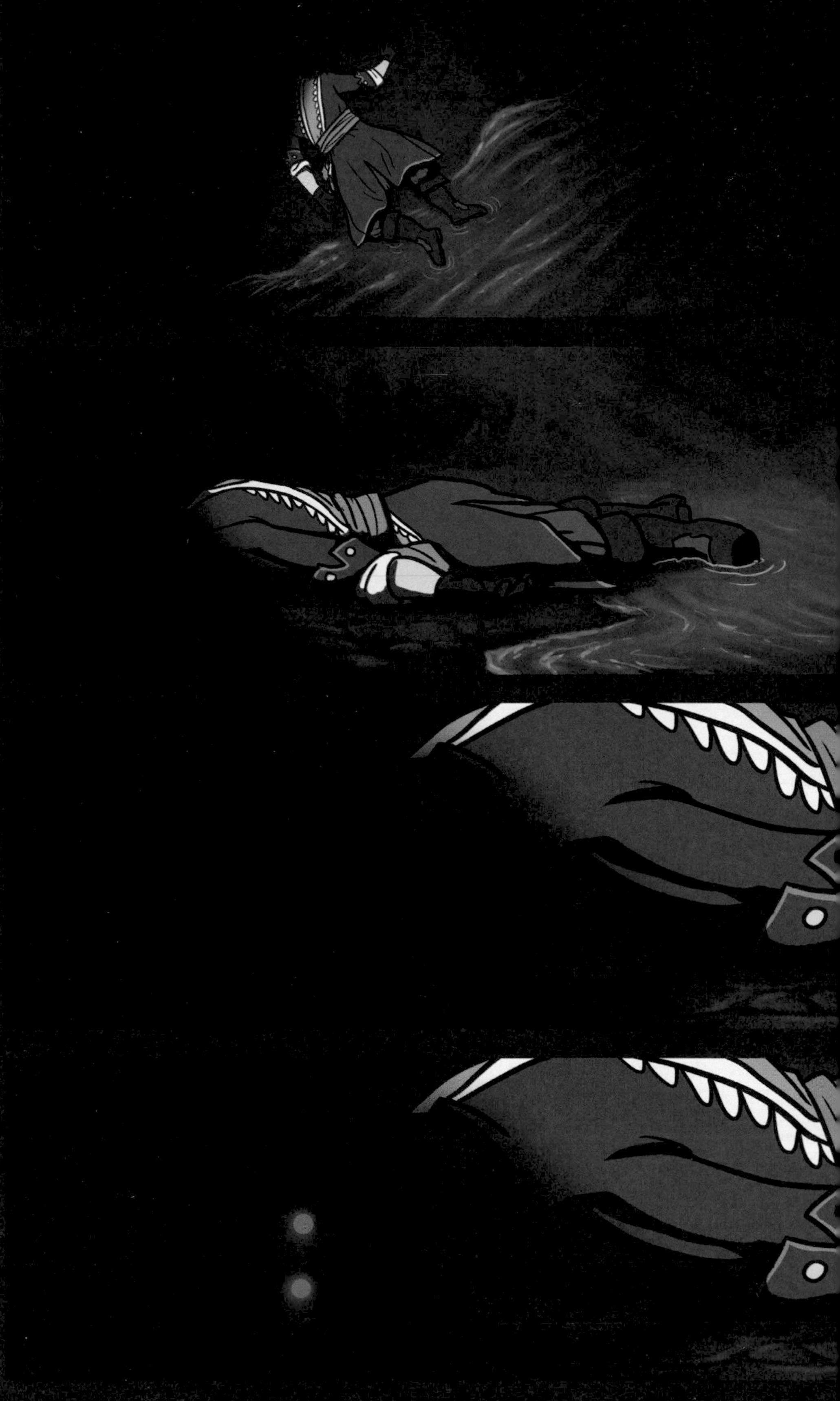